76c7...

MORTIMER

THE COLLECTION

CAROLE MORTIMER

THE COLLECTION

ONE CHANCE AT LOVE

TO LOVE AGAIN

THE LOVING GIFT

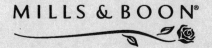

MILLS & BOON®

*All the characters in this book have no existence outside the imagination
of the author, and have no relation whatsoever to anyone bearing the same
name or names. They are not even distantly inspired by any individual
known or unknown to the author, and all the incidents are pure invention.*

Harlequin Mills & Boon Limited,
Eton House, 18-24 Paradise Road,
Richmond, Surrey, TW9 1SR

CAROLE MORTIMER THE COLLECTION
© 1998 by Harlequin Books SA

One Chance at Love, To Love Again and *The Loving Gift* were first
published in separate, single volumes by Mills & Boon Limited in 1988.

One Chance at Love © Carole Mortimer 1988
To Love Again © Carole Mortimer 1988
The Loving Gift © Carole Mortimer 1988

ISBN 0 263 81251 0
62-9807

*Printed and bound in Great Britain
by Caledonian Book Manufacturing Ltd, Glasgow*

Carole Mortimer says: 'I was born in England, the youngest of three children—I have two older brothers. I started writing in 1978, and have now written over ninety books for Mills & Boon®.

I have four sons, Matthew, Joshua, Timothy and Peter, and a bearded collie dog called Merlyn. I'm in a very happy relationship with Peter senior; we're best friends as well as lovers, which is probably the best recipe for a successful relationship. We live on the Isle of Man.'

Carole has currently sold more than 44 million copies of her books, which have been translated into more than 20 languages—including Hungarian, Polish, Japanese and Brazilian!

About Carole Mortimer

"Carole Mortimer delivers quality romance"
—*Romantic Times*

ONE CHANCE AT LOVE

For
Matthew and Joshua

CHAPTER ONE

'I'M GOING insane! If something doesn't soon happen to free me from here, they're going to have to lock me up in a real prison for killing my own uncle!'

Dizzy held the receiver away from her ear as her friend's voice rose in desperation. 'Do I take it, Christi, dear,' she drawled during a brief respite in the tirade—probably so that Christi could take air into her starved lungs, for she hadn't stopped bemoaning her fate since Dizzy answered her call five minutes earlier, 'that this visit with your uncle isn't working out?' She again held the receiver away from her poor abused ear, as Christi told her exactly what she thought of her visit to the Lake District. 'And I didn't even realise you knew words like that!' she mocked teasingly.

'I mean it, Dizzy,' Christi said frantically. 'I can't stand it here much longer without breaking out in some way that's going to totally destroy any chance of my uncle agreeing to my inheriting my money on my twenty-first birthday!'

Christi always had had a flair for the dramatic, which was perhaps as well, since she had chosen acting as a career, Dizzy acknowledged ruefully. But she very much doubted Christi really would do anything desperate, not when so much depended on her remaining her usually serene self. In fact, this Zachariah Bennett must be a bit of a monster to have ruffled Christi's feathers at all!

'You only have another month to go,' she reminded her friend gently.

'Three weeks and five days,' Christi corrected sharply. 'I've been counting! And I could have murdered him, disposed of the body, and disappeared without trace by then!'

Dizzy couldn't help but chuckle at this uncharacteristic violence from a woman who usually avoided stepping on an ant where possible!

For the last week Christi had been staying with her uncle in his Lake District home, intent on impressing the man who had the guardianship of her inheritance with her maturity and ability to handle the considerable amount of money her parents had left in trust for her on their deaths three years ago. Christi was all too aware that if her uncle decided otherwise she would have to wait until she was twenty-five, when the money would come to her automatically. Dizzy could quite see that murdering her uncle and burying him in an unmarked grave could jeopardise that good impression Christi was trying to make!

'What's wrong with him?' She frowned her puzzlement.

'He's fusty, dusty, spends all day working on history books that no one's going to read——'

'Oh I don't know about that,' Dizzy objected mildly. 'I found his book on the Romans very interesting——'

'I don't consider you any judge of literature when you can spend half an hour looking at a children's annual!' Christi dismissed disgustedly.

And enjoyed every minute of it, too, Dizzy thought with a mischievous grin. But she knew Christi wouldn't appreciate hearing about that in her present mood. 'I was just making sure it was a suitable present for a five-year-old,' she defended without rancour.

'One of your godchildren, I suppose,' her friend sighed acknowledgement. 'How many do you have now?'

'Six,' she related proudly. 'And, in case you're interested, Sarah loved the annual.'

'The only thing I'm interested in at the moment is getting away from here,' Christi groaned. 'When my uncle isn't working, he has his nose stuck in a research book. And Castle Haven is exactly that, Dizzy,' she added incredulously. 'A huge monstrosity of a castle, stuck in the middle of all this water and mountains. It's like being in a giant freezer!' She sounded distraught. 'I never thought I'd be able to sympathise with a joint of beef! I ask you, Dizzy, whoever heard of wearing a jumper in the house in June!'

'A castle, hm?' she repeated interestedly. 'Is it——'

'Dizzy, it's just a draughty old castle!' Christi cut in impatiently. 'It's stuck out in the middle of nowhere, and if my uncle has any friends in the neighbourhood then I haven't met them. Good grief, Dizzy, I actually went to bed at nine-thirty last night. Nine thirty!' she repeated, in case Dizzy hadn't been able to believe it the first time around— as Christi herself obviously hadn't!

And she could quite understand why: Christi was a night person, who didn't usually wake up until ten o'clock in the evening. Things must be more desperate than Dizzy had given Christi credit for!

'How am I going to convince my uncle I'm a responsible adult, perfectly mature enough to handle my own money, if I give in to this craving I have to put my hands around his throat and strangle the life out of him just to relieve the boredom?' Christi wailed emotionally.

This time Dizzy held back her chuckle, trying desperately to appreciate the seriousness of the situation. 'I can see how that might make him have second thoughts,' she finally said, wryly.

'He already thinks I'm irresponsible because I dropped out of college to go to drama school,' Christi told her worriedly.

Dizzy gave a snort of laughter. 'If he thinks you're irresponsible, I hate to think what he would make of me! Christi, why don't you——'

'Oh, damn, the gong just sounded for dinner,' her friend muttered frantically. 'I'll have to go, my uncle "deplores tardiness".' Her change of voice, to stern reproval, over the last two words indicated that it was a direct quote. 'Try and come up with a believable excuse for me to come back to London, Dizzy,' she urged desperately. 'Before I go completely *insane* . . .'

Dizzy rang off more slowly than her friend, her expression thoughtful as she finished preparing the pilchards on toast that was to be her own dinner. She adored the fish, ate them for breakfast, lunch, and dinner if she had the chance, and indulged the addiction to the full whenever she was alone, which wasn't very often. If having two cats and a dog constantly underfoot could be classed as being alone now! She jealously guarded her dinner as all three animals tried to steal it from her plate as she ate; she really would have to have a word with Christi about the deplorable manners of her pets.

She looked around the flat appreciatively, loving the mellow décor and comfortable furniture, mentally thanking Christi for inviting her to stay and care for her pets for her while she was away. If only Gladys would stop trying to steal her pilchards, she grumbled under her breath, even as she tapped a sneaking paw away from her plate.

Feeling grateful that she wasn't subjected to Christi's enforced early nights, she pulled a tattered and dog-eared book from her capacious shoulder-bag, opening it to the page she had marked half-way through the seven hundred pages, instantly losing herself in the page-turning historical adventure by one of her favourite authors. She had read the book many times before, but Claudia Laurence knew how to write a book so that it was possible to gain something new from it every time it was read. A reader's delight!

Two hundred pages—and five hours—later, Dizzy decided it was time to go to bed. She felt as if she had barely fallen asleep when the telephone beside the bed began to ring, and she shot upright in the bed, completely and suddenly awake. She felt half drunk with tiredness as she picked up the receiver.

'I've got it!' came the eagerly disorientated whisper of a voice.

An obscene telephone call, Dizzy acknowledged disgustedly. 'Well, now that you've got it, you know

what you can do with it, don't you?' She reached
out to replace the receiver.

'*Dizzy!*' came the distressed cry down the telephone line, halting her action. 'Dizzy, don't you
dare hang up on me!'

She blinked; obscene telephone callers didn't
usually know their victims' names, did they? Not
that she was an expert on the subject—heaven
forbid!—but she didn't think they did. And now
that the voice had been raised slightly from that
eerie whisper, it did sound vaguely familiar—in fact,
it sounded a little like *Christi*. But why on earth
would Christi be calling her at—a quarter past six
in the morning? she wondered, as she glanced at
the bedside clock. Christi hadn't been known to
surface before at least eight o'clock before—but
then, she had never been known to go to bed at
nine-thirty before, either!

Dizzy leant up on her elbow, pushing her long
hair back from her face. 'Christi, is that you?' she
yawned.

'Of course it's me,' her friend hissed. 'Who else
would be calling you at this time of the morning?'

The answer to that was so obvious that Dizzy
didn't even attempt to make it. 'Why are you whispering?' she asked curiously, still attempting to clear
the fog of sleep from her brain.

'So that no one can hear me!' came the explosive
reply.

Logical, she thought as she yawned again, very
logical. 'Why don't you want anyone to hear you?'
she asked uninterestedly.

'Because it's only six o'clock in the morning!'
Christi said exasperatedly, forgetting to whisper,

then muttering self-disgustedly as she realised what she had done.

Dizzy ignored the mutterings; she thought it was best to do so. 'Why are you telephoning at six o'clock in the morning if it's going to disturb people?' she urged sleepily, wishing *she* hadn't been one of the people disturbed.

'Because I've come up with a way of getting *me* out of this place!' Christi announced triumphantly.

'Congratulations,' drawled Dizzy drily. 'But couldn't you have waited until a decent hour to let me in on the secret?'

'No—because *you're* going to help get me out!' her friend said with satisfaction.

'You want me to bake you a cake with a metal file in it, and send it to you?' she derided.

Christi groaned at her levity. 'Can't you even be serious when you know what trouble I'm in?'

'Sorry.' Dizzy sobered. 'What do you want me to do that will help you escape from the fusty, dusty Zachariah? Sorry,' she grimaced, as she could sense Christi's rising anger at her teasing. 'Go ahead, you have my full attention,' she encouraged interestedly.

Christi gave a snort that clearly said she doubted that, but she launched into her explanation anyway. 'It was something you said that gave me the idea, actually,' she told Dizzy excitedly, hastily lowering her voice as she realised that, in her enthusiasm, she had once again forgotten to whisper. 'I mean, how can I be considered irresponsible when I'm training for a career, have lived in the same apartment for years, have pets that are well cared for, have——'

'I get the picture—you sober citizen, you,' Dizzy drawled. 'And, as it is now almost six-thirty in the morning, and I've barely had any sleep, do you think you could get to the point?'

'Oh, yes.' Christi gave a dismissive sigh as she realised she had been going on a bit. 'The answer isn't to show my uncle how responsible *I* am——'

'It isn't?' Dizzy frowned; she must have dozed off in the middle of this conversation somewhere, for she had thought Christi's proving to her uncle that she was more than capable of managing her own monetary affairs was exactly the point!

'No,' Christi confirmed impatiently. 'It's showing him how *irresponsible* I'm not!'

From her friend's triumphant tone as she made the announcement, Dizzy knew this was the place she was supposed to come in and tell her how clever she was being, but so far this still didn't make a lot of sense to her.

'Dizzy, you haven't fallen asleep on me, have you?' Christi snapped suspiciously at her pro-longed silence.

She roused herself wearily. 'Of course not. And don't shout, you'll wake up the household,' she reminded tiredly.

'It could *do* with waking up,' Christi muttered with feeling.

'We've been through all that,' Dizzy said drily. 'I don't mean to sound unsympathetic, love, but I really can't understand what's so terrible about staying with your uncle for a few weeks. And——'

'You soon will,' her friend said with satisfaction.

'—surely a few early nights aren't going to——

What do you mean, I soon will?' Suddenly, sleep didn't seem so important any more. 'Christi, what are you up to?' she prompted sharply, knowing that whatever it was, she probably wasn't going to like it!

'Who is letting you make free use of her apartment while she's out of town?' Christi prompted calmly.

'Who is baby-sitting your pets—at the cost of pilchards and solitude!—while you are out of town?' she instantly returned.

'Who got up in the middle of the night to open the school dormitory window so that you could climb in off the roof——'

'Who forgot to come down to unlock the door and fell asleep until I climbed up and *knocked* on the window?' she reminded pointedly.

'Oh, all right,' Christi acknowledged impatiently. 'Maybe that was my fault. But who helped get you out of spending the night in prison the time the police raided that illegal gambling——'

'You know very well that I had gone there with a reporter who was doing research for an article,' she protested.

'But who came to the police station and managed to convince the police of that? Who got you away from there before it became public knowledge, and your picture appeared on the front page of all the tabloids?' Christi pounced triumphantly.

'You did,' Dizzy conceded heavily. 'And now I owe you one, right?'

'Oh, no, Dizzy!' Her friend sounded genuinely shocked at the suggestion. 'It isn't a question of paying me back. I was just trying to point out that we're friends, and that friends try to help each other when they can.'

Dizzy gave an indulgent smile, easily able to visualise Christi's earnest expression: that faintly hurt look in enormous blue eyes that dominated the beauty of her face. Christi was tall and elegant, with a natural serenity and kindness; Zachariah Bennett had to be dense not to be able to see that.

Dizzy sighed, freely acknowledging that Christi was the best friend she had ever had. 'What do you want me to do?'

'Come up here and——'

'Not that, Christi,' she protested, visions of being sent to bed at nine-thirty by Christi's ancient uncle flashing through her mind. A truly free spirit, just the thought of it reminded her too much of her childhood.

'—show my uncle just what an irresponsible person is!' Christi finished triumphantly, totally deaf to Dizzy's protest.

'Thanks!' she grimaced ruefully.

'Don't go and act all wounded on me,' her friend chided lightly. 'You've deliberately cultivated your life-style, enjoy having no permanent home, no visible means of support, no real belongings except what you carry about in that cavernous sack you call a shoulder-bag, and the pack you throw on your back.'

'I admit I like to travel light——'

'*Travel* being the operative word,' Christi derided. 'I never knew of anyone wearing out their passport before!'

'I didn't wear it out,' she protested. 'It just got— a little full,' she excused dismissively.

'Exactly,' Christi said with satisfaction. 'You're *everything* that my uncle would consider irresponsible; drifting through life, staying with friends whenever you get the chance——'

'Christi——'

'And God knows *where* you live the rest of the time,' Christi concluded in a starchily disapproving voice—as if she were quoting verse and chapter from a too-familiar sermon.

As indeed she was! Dizzy had heard those very same words from her father too often not to know where they came from. After hearing the same thing for years, she had taken Christi home with her once as self-defence; but even her friend's presence hadn't prevented the usual lecture. Obviously Christi had never forgotten the humiliating experience, either!

'I thought you also called me friend,' Dizzy reminded her drily. 'Although I'm beginning to wonder about that!' she mocked.

'My uncle doesn't have to know that,' Christi dismissed. 'We can say you're just an old school acquaintance of mine who happens to be——'

'Drifting through,' Dizzy finished derisively.

'Exactly,' Christi said eagerly. 'And of course I'm your friend,' she defended indignantly. 'Goodness, *we* know that none of that drivel is true. And, even if it were, it wouldn't make any difference to those of us that love you. You're the most generous, giving, totally unselfish——'

'Enough, enough,' she drawled ruefully. 'When do you want this drifting wastrel of an *acquaintance* to arrive on the castle doorstep, expecting another hand-out?' she prompted drily.

'Today,' Christi pounced eagerly.

Dizzy had been expecting that, otherwise there would have been no need for this hasty call in what was, to her at least, still the middle of the night. 'And who will take care of your food-stealing pets if I leave?' she reminded lightly.

'Lucas will come in from next door and do that,' Christi dismissed. 'They all love him, and he usually does it for me if I go away. And if you hate looking after the cats and dog so much, how come they are always completely spoilt after one of your visits? Last time you came to stay, Gladys and Josephine spent the next week sniffing my food cupboard, looking for your tins of pilchards. And I just bet Henry is sharing your bed right this minute!' she announced disgustedly.

Dizzy looked down guiltily to the foot of the bed, where the Yorkshire terrier was curled up, asleep, on the quilt. 'He gets lonely in the kitchen at night,' she defended. 'And he has such soulful brown eyes that I don't have the heart to say no to him.'

'A pair of soulful brown eyes and loneliness are not reasons to take him into bed with you! He—Oh, damn, I think I heard someone coming.' Christi lapsed back into that desperate whispering. 'I'll see you later, OK?' she urged frantically, sounding more and more like a hounded animal.

The impression didn't in the least endear the idea of going up to the Lake District to Dizzy, to show herself off as some lost cause just so that Zachariah Bennett could say to Christi, 'Thank God you didn't turn out like *her*, here's your money and welcome to it'!

If it really were going to be as easy as that . . .

*   *   *

Dizzy had heard much about the beauty of the Lake District, and as her travels usually took her out of the country, rather than around it, this was the first time she had ever seen this lovely part of England.

But nothing she had heard about the Lake District had prepared her for the scenery before her now. No one had told her she could expect to see naked men, one naked man in particular, as he cavorted about in one of the smaller lakes!

As Christi had said, the man in the flat next door to hers had been only too happy to pet-sit Gladys, Josephine and Henry, and so the only hitch there could have been to her setting off for Castle Haven had neatly been removed.

In the clear light of day—after several more hours' sleep—Dizzy was less sure than ever that Christi's plan was a good one. It might work if Zachariah Bennett—the old curmudgeon!—could be made to believe she and Christi *were* just acquaintances, but the two of them had been friends since their first term together at boarding-school over twelve years ago. The familiarity of a friendship like that might be a little difficult to disguise. A telephone call to Christi to tell her just that had elicited the information that her friend had gone out for the morning with her uncle, and so, not knowing what else to do, Dizzy had set out for the castle. They would just have to hope for the best when she got there.

It had been a pleasant trip up on the train. She might be a free spirit, she thought, but she wasn't stupid—it was no longer safe to hitch-hike, if it ever had been! Enquiries at the station, when she got off the train, had told her that the castle was about eight miles away and, after the long train journey, stretching her legs for a few miles sounded like a good idea.

The first six miles of her walk had been really enjoyable—the view of this lake was even more so!

She sat on top of one of the hills that surrounded the lake on all sides, unashamedly watching the sleek-bodied man as he cavorted about in the water like a dolphin. Even water-slicked, his hair was discernible as dark blond, with blond highlights that any woman would envy, but which were obviously perfectly natural on this man. From the deep tan of his body, he swam naked like this often. Old Zachariah Bennett would probably have a seizure if he could see the guest, who was going to soon turn up unexpectedly on his doorstep, watching the antics of this naked man. And enjoying it, too!

He really was a very handsome specimen, she thought admiringly as he stepped out of the water to dry off in the sun. He was tall and lithe, and from the look of him he either cut down trees or built roads for a living, for his muscles had been rippling powerfully. Or else he was just a secret weight-lifter. Whatever he was, a fusty scholar like Zachariah Bennett would probably recoil in horror at such virility: the man's shoulders wide and strong, golden hair glinting on his bronzed chest, his stomach taut and flat, and his hips and thighs... Apollo himself couldn't have looked better!

Dizzy reluctantly drew herself away from the beauty of the scene as the man stretched out in the sun to dry some more. No doubt he wouldn't mind at all that she had been admiring him—he wouldn't have been swimming in a lake where anyone could come along and see him if he did—but she really did have to be getting along to the castle now. It was a pity to spoil the moment, but time was quickly passing, and Christi's thoughts were probably on the unmarked grave again by now!

But she didn't forget the man as she walked the last two miles, whistling happily to herself, the day suddenly seeming full of new possibilities. Maybe the man was a local, maybe Christi would know who he was... But, of course, her friend had said she hadn't met anyone else in the area. What a shame; it might have been interesting meeting the Greek god. It might have helped her irresponsible image along a little more, too, if she could have brought the local womaniser back to the castle to meet the professor.

Not that her image needed any help, she acknowledged ruefully as she glanced down at herself. Her denims were old and patched at the knees, the material faded in the usual places, her T-shirt just as old, but out of shape after numerous washes. She put a self-conscious hand up to the blonde bubbly curls that had escaped the long plait down her spine and that had helped give her her name, framing her small, heart-shaped face that was dominated by green, catlike eyes. Small, just over five feet, with breasts that were slightly too large for her body, and her fly-away blonde hair, she was the perfect 'dizzy blonde' image. No doubt she would be Zachariah Bennett's most unusual house—*castle*—guest, to date!

Castle Haven proved to be exactly what Christi had claimed it was, a huge turreted castle that seemed totally out of place among the placid lakes

and tree-covered hills and mountains that surrounded it on all sides.

Unlike Christi, however, Dizzy found the castle
fascinating, and longed to know its history. But she
supposed that would never do, not when she was
supposed to be showing Zachariah Bennett just how
wayward and uncaring the youth of today could
be, and, in the process, what a shining example of
responsibility his niece was. It would never do to
let old Zach know she was probably as interested
in history as he was!

The castle was a fitting home for him, as a historian of some repute—Dizzy knew him mainly
from his books—and as she drew nearer Dizzy
could see that on the outside, at least, it had been
maintained in beautiful condition. Writing history
books must pay very well! she thought.

The butler who opened the door several minutes
after she had pulled the bell—hoping it was ringing
somewhere in the depths of the castle—looked as
if he might have been here doing this very same
thing since the castle had originally been built!
Snowy-haired, with an aloofness that was felt rather
than physically visible in his thin body and blandly
expressionless face, his disapproval of the 'person'
standing at the huge heavy oak door he had swung
open was a tangible thing. Maybe he was old
Zachariah himself; probably what he earned as a
historian didn't run to a butler as well as a castle!

'Hi!' She gave him her brightest smile, easing her
backpack on to one shoulder. 'My name's Dizzy
James, and I——'

'The castle is not open to the public, Miss James,'
he informed her frostily.

She had been going to say 'I'm a friend of Christi's', but his condescending attitude brought out the devil in her. 'What a pity,' she drawled. 'I'm sure you would get thousands of people wanting to tramp all over the place if you decided to change your mind.' She looked up at him innocently as he stiffened in shock at the suggestion.

His raised eyebrows and pursed lips showed his distaste. 'Let me give you directions back to the main road,' he said coldly. 'You go back the way you just came, and then——'

'Oh, but I don't want to go back to the main road!' She smiled at him, her eyes gleaming like a cat's.

'This is private property, Miss James, and——'

'But I'm here to see Christi Bennett,' she informed him happily.

'Miss Christi?' This time his guard was completely down, due to severe shock and horrified disbelief that 'Miss Christi' could even know such a person!

Obviously, he was the family butler, after all, and as she had only come here to shock Zachariah Bennett, not upset the whole household, she gave the man in front of her her most engaging smile. It had been known to melt frostier hearts than his, although not always, and never when she really willed it to. This time she was partially successful, although only grudgingly, as the butler slowly opened the door for her to come inside.

He nodded to her to wait where she stood, just inside the huge reception area. 'I'll go and tell Miss Christi that you're here——'

'That won't be necessary, Fredericks.' Christi came bounding down the wide stairway like a whirlwind, her face flushed with excitement—the first she had known for some time, by the look of the shadows beneath her usually sparkling blue eyes. 'Dizzy!' she greeted thankfully, clasping her hands in hers before hugging her tightly.

She allowed Christi the indulgence for several seconds, realising her friend was under severe strain. But all the time she was aware of Fredericks as he watched them with distant curiosity, and so she finally whispered to Christi, 'Acquaintances, remember?'

Christi stiffened at the reminder, her arms falling back to her sides as she stepped back reluctantly, forcing indifference into her expression. 'That will be all, thank you, Fredericks,' she said, turning to the butler. 'Dizzy, how nice to see you again!' Her words were the insincerely polite ones of a host having an unwanted guest foisted upon them, although her eyes were dancing with mischief as she looked at Dizzy.

Easily one of the most beautiful women Dizzy had ever seen, with glorious ebony hair and huge blue eyes, and a model-girl figure, Christi wasn't in the least conceited about her looks, but felt them merely to be her stock-in-trade for the career she had chosen for herself. She had even been warned that being too beautiful could hinder her career, rather than help it, if she was serious about becoming an actress of any repute.

The two women stood grinning at each other once they were alone in the high-ceilinged entrance hall, their breathing echoing hollowly against the grey stone.

'I thought you weren't coming.' Christi finally sighed her relief that she had been proved wrong.

Dizzy's smile widened. 'I needed a little time to wake up,' she teased, reminding her friend of the earliness of her call. 'Besides, how could I let down the person who probably stopped me being put in jail—at least overnight?' she mocked, thinking of her friend's efforts of bribery and corruption.

Christi looked embarrassed. 'I only——'

'What's going on here?'

Dizzy didn't need the confirmation of her friend's suddenly guiltily apprehensive expression to guess that the man who had silently entered the hall through another door was fusty, dusty Zachariah Bennett. He spoke quietly, but nevertheless with a complete assurance that he was entitled to the explanation he demanded. If he had come in on the conversation soon enough to overhear her reference to almost being put in jail, then that wasn't so surprising!

'Uncle Zach.' Christi quickly regained control, crossing to the man as he stood slightly in the shadows beneath the stairway, the door he had used just behind him, probably belonging to the kitchen or cellar, Dizzy thought. 'I asked you if an old school acquaintance of mine could come to stay,' Christi reminded lightly.

Dizzy turned to look at her; she had *told* her uncle of her visit? What had happened to the 'old acquaintance' who had just happened to be 'drifting' through, had 'heard Christi was in the area and decided to pay her a call'?

Christi had changed the story without warning her! But she wasn't able to dwell on that, as Zachariah Bennett at last stepped out of the shadows.

Baggy, and definitely *untailored* corduroys, a cream shirt that looked more than a little creased beneath the too-large tweed jacket, were exactly the sort of attire she had expected the bookishly austere Professor Zachariah Bennett to wear. But, as her wincing gaze rose, and she saw the gold-streaked blond hair, she knew that the ill-fitting clothing covered the magnificent body of the Greek god she had watched as he had swum naked not half an hour ago!

CHAPTER TWO

COULD this man have a twin brother, a man who looked exactly as he did, but who was the type to go skinny-dipping? That could be the only possible explanation for Zachariah Bennett having the same curiously light brown hair beneath gold that her Greek god had possessed. But Christi had told her numerous times that her uncle Zachariah was her only living relative, so that couldn't be the answer to the similarity. And Dizzy refused to believe there was another man in the area with the same beautiful-coloured hair. Which only left the one possibility she had started with: Zachariah Bennett was her naked Greek god.

Who would have believed that such a magnificent body lay beneath those hopelessly shapeless clothes? Obviously not Christi, or she wouldn't have called her uncle 'fusty and dusty'. Or maybe she would. Somehow, Christi had given her the impression that her uncle was an elderly man, but the mid-thirties this man must be wasn't that, either. At least, it didn't seem so to Dizzy. Maybe, to Christi, he just seemed old because he was her uncle. Whatever the reason, Dizzy knew that no man with a body like this one had, powerfully muscled and so blatantly male, could ever be fusty or dusty!

To give Christi her due, she had never seen him like that, and the rest of his appearance—his clothed appearance, that was—didn't hint at anything other than the impression of a professor of history. Oh, his face was handsome enough, even if it was set in austere lines right now, his jaw square and determined, with a barest hint of a cleft in the chin, his mouth a tautly drawn line, although his lips looked as if they might be sensual if he ever relaxed them enough to let them be—and Dizzy knew from her view of him earlier that he could be *very* relaxed when he chose to be!

Black-rimmed glasses covered his eyes, but, even so, she could see they were a beautiful light brown, looking like golden warm honey. The lovely sun-streaked hair, that had been drying in attractive curls on his forehead earlier, was now brushed severely to the side and back. He only needed a pipe to complete the picture of the professor of history that he was!

Even as the amused thought crossed her mind, she saw that his right hand was patting absently at the bulging pocket of his tweed jacket, lean fingers pulling out a well-used pipe that he clasped between strong white teeth as he began a vague hunt for his matches.

The only thing wrong with the image was that Dizzy couldn't get the memory of the naked Greek god out of her mind!

Try as she might—and she had to admit she wasn't trying *too* hard—she couldn't forget the absolute vision of him as he stood in the sunlight, letting the warmth of the day dry him off after his swim. If she looked closely at him now she could even see a couple of damp tendrils of hair behind his ears, where the sun hadn't touched him. And she knew she would never be able to feel in awe of him the way Christi obviously was; she could feel *aware* of him, yes, but never in awe of him!

But right now she had to try and fill in the gaps to Christi's new story about her visit. Obviously she was no longer 'drifting through', but what was she doing here? Nothing to recommend her, if what Christi was saying was to be believed!

'Poor dear,' she was telling her uncle. 'When Dizzy told me she had nowhere else to go...' She shook her head sadly.

Dizzy winced at the obvious implication; surely Christi was laying it on a bit thick, even if it was to show 'Uncle Zach' how kind and *responsible* she was!

She felt Zachariah Bennett's disapproving gaze on her, inwardly cringing at the role she was having to play in the name of friendship. In any other circumstances, she would have enjoyed meeting this man, would have been full of questions. Playing what was now turning out to be little better than a parasite didn't sit well with her.

She gave Zachariah Bennett a bright, meaningless smile, not able to meet his penetrating gaze, which was probably convincing him she was shiftless, too! 'Christi can be so kind,' she said noncommittally, still floundering in the dark a little.

Eyes, that should have been as warm to look at as the honey they resembled, frosted over as Zachariah Bennett's gaze raked over her with disgust. 'Kindness is not always the wisest thing,' he bit out coldly. 'In fact, in some circumstances, it is better to be cruel.'

'Oh no, Uncle Zach,' Christi protested with wide-eyed innocence. 'I told you, I couldn't bear to think of Dizzy having to—well, perhaps sleep on a park bench somewhere.' She sounded distraught at the idea.

As well she might do! What amazed Dizzy was that the possibility had even been mentioned between Christi and her uncle. *She* had been doing Christi the favour by pet-sitting her flat in the first place; there were plenty of other places she could have been. She had thought then that she was helping out a friend, but from the contemptuous look on the professor's face he believed every sad word of woe which Christi was feeding him!

'I'm sure I would have been able to find—somewhere else to go, if you hadn't been able to take me in,' she grated, giving Christi a warning look. Her friend was going a little too far, she felt!

'I'm sure you would,' Zachariah Bennett acknowledged distantly. 'But my niece considers she should help out an old school acquaintance when she can.'

Christi was visibly preening at the praise, and Dizzy just wanted to shake her. Not only was she a drifter and a wastrel, she *was* supposed to be a parasite, too!

As soon as she got Christi on her own she was going to tell her exactly what she thought of this new plan of hers. She might have 'cultivated' her life-style, but she had never taken advantage of anyone's kindness. And she had to admit she didn't like Zachariah Bennett thinking that she had; even the dark-rimmed glasses didn't hide the contempt for her in his eyes. Usually she didn't give a damn what people thought of her, or the way she lived, but with this man she did. And she wasn't about to analyse *that* too deeply.

'And as, for the moment, this is my niece's home,' he continued, 'may I also extend an invitation for you to stay with us,' he added grudgingly. 'Now if you'll excuse me, Christi, Miss——'

'James,' she supplied, realising, as he hesitated, that Christi hadn't told him *everything* about her. Her expression was bland as she sensed her friend's sharp gaze upon her. 'Dizzy James,' she enlarged.

'Miss James,' he nodded dismissively, puffing distractedly on the pipe, now that he had finally managed to get it lit. 'I'll leave you two to get re-acquainted, while I go and change.' He nodded, as if satisfied with his decision.

'Uncle Zach has been out bird-watching,' Christi explained indulgently.

Something suddenly seemed to be stuck in Dizzy's throat. She coughed chokingly, tears streamed down her cheeks, for the air couldn't reach her lungs. *Bird-watching?* Any birds that had been in Zachariah Bennett's vicinity half an hour ago had been watching *him*, curious of the unusual antics of the human in their midst!

'It's all right. I'm all right,' she gasped when she could finally find the strength to speak, firmly discouraging Christi from administering any more of the hearty slaps to the back she had been giving her since she first began to choke. 'Really, Christi, I'm fine.' She held up her hands defensively as her friend still looked undecided about administering one more slap for luck.

'The mention of ornithology seemed to have a strange effect on you?' Zachariah Bennett raised dark blond brows questioningly, once Dizzy was calm.

She kept her expression deliberately bland as she looked up at him. 'Not at all, Professor Bennett. In fact, the reason I was slightly later in arriving than I had said I would be was because I became interested in watching a bird myself.' A golden eagle, she decided.

The honey-brown gaze sharpened. 'Really?' he prompted harshly.

Still he didn't invite her to use the familiarity of his first name but, as he now seemed to think she had only said she had been bird-watching as a means of insinuating herself into his good graces, perhaps that was understandable! The sooner she and Christi had a private word the better.

'Oh yes,' she nodded. 'Christi will tell you, I'm very much into bird-watching.'

Christi gave her a glaring look. 'I really don't know your likes and dislikes that well, Dizzy,' she said through gritted teeth. 'It must be—how many years, since we last met?'

Dizzy gave her friend a reproachful frown. For all his absently distracted ways, she knew the professor to be a very intelligent man, and she and Christi were going to need to be very much on their guard to keep up the pretence Christi was getting them into more and more by the minute.

'I really can't remember,' she muttered warningly. 'But I'm sure it can't be that long ago.'

Christi gave an affected laugh. 'Dizzy seems to have moved around so much since we left school that she's forgotten time altogether,' she confided lightly to her uncle. 'Come on, Dizzy.' Her smile lacked warmth as she turned to her, her expression purposeful. 'I'll show you up to the room you're to use during your stay.'

Her friend's grip on her arm was only just short of vicelike, and Dizzy winced slightly, while trying to give the professor a reassuring smile. 'I do appreciate your kind invitation.'

He gave her a look which clearly indicated that if it had been left to him she would have been looking for the park bench, nodding curtly before moving agilely up the wide stone stairway.

Dizzy instantly turned to Christi as she pulled her towards the stairs. 'What do you——'

'Ssh,' her friend warned, looking frantically about them to see if they could be overheard. 'We can talk when we get to your room,' she muttered.

'But——'

'Dizzy, I am not in the mood to be argued with!' Her voice rose shrilly.

She did sound more than a little strained—and she was probably going to be even more so once Dizzy told her she didn't think this plan of hers could possibly work.

If only she could have spoken to Christi when she'd called earlier, or at least before she'd had to meet the uncle! The way things stood at the moment, she had no choice but to continue with the plan Christi had started before she'd arrived. Unfortunately, it was a plan she felt was doomed to failure, although Christi didn't agree with her.

They had strolled up the stairway together, Dizzy having assured Fredericks, when he quietly appeared back in the entrance hall, that she could manage her own shoulder-bag and backpack. She smiled, as if she hadn't seen his scandalised look that that was *all* of her luggage.

Christi gave her a running commentary as they went. 'Only the east wing has been renovated for habitation so far,' she pointed out, then explained why the rest of the castle was closed off to them. 'Uncle Zach has the work done as he gets the money. He must get paid very well to have the work done at all,' she added in a whispered aside. 'But what he's had done so far is lovely,' she continued in her normal voice.

For her uncle's benefit, Dizzy acknowledged wryly. There wasn't an angle possible that Christi wasn't playing, and it was all so unnecessary, when just being herself would probably have made the best impression.

The renovation that had so far been done to the castle was very impressive, and looked very much as it must have when it was first built in the fifteenth century. Dizzy realised it also had some of the discomfort that must have gone with it at that time, as she gave an involuntary shiver from the cold. Obviously Zachariah Bennett had gone for complete authenticity, omitting the central heating that might have made the castle more appealing. She could only hope that authenticity hadn't gone as far as the plumbing; carrying buckets of water up the stairs for her bath didn't exactly appeal to her!

'I've given you the bedroom next to mine.' Christi threw open the heavy oak door.

Dizzy was mesmerised from the first, from the tapestry that was the height and breadth of one wall, to the four-poster bed that totally dominated the huge room.

As she walked dazedly into the room, she touched the brocade curtains on the bed wonderingly, knowing by their thickness that they would pull completely around the sides and bottom of the bed, affording its occupant complete privacy. Her eyes aglow with pleasure, she walked across the room to gaze out of one of the long, narrow windows that graced two walls of the room. The view was magnificent—lakes and mountains as far as the eye could see. Heat warmed her cheeks as she realised that the small lake Zachariah Bennett had swum in earlier was just behind the first hill to the east, that it might even be part of the land that obviously adjoined the castle.

She was never going to get tired of the scenery if every time she looked out of this window she remembered Zachariah Bennett's nakedness so vividly!

'—so far, don't you think?'

She turned back to Christi, realising she had missed half the conversation in her musing over Zachariah Bennett. From the sudden impatience in Christi's expression, *she* had realised it, too!

'I said,' her friend bit out with slow emphasis, 'I think everything is going well so far, don't you? Or, at least, it would be, if you would enter into the spirit of the thing a bit more,' she added critically.

'Christi, I don't think this is going to work.' Dizzy put all thoughts of Zachariah Bennett's nakedness from her mind, as she concentrated on convincing Christi that her plan wasn't such a good one, after all.

Thankfully, she noted, as she turned back into the room, that an adjoining door revealed a fully fitted bathroom. It wouldn't be as good as a naked swim in a lake, but a bath would certainly refresh her!

'It's obvious you're trying to convince your uncle I'm some sort of leech,' she sighed. 'But, personally, I think you've gone over the top. You're making me out to be little more than a parasite to everyone I've ever known. No wonder he disliked me on sight!' she grimaced.

'Oh, that didn't have anything to do with being a leech,' Christi shook her head with certainty.

Her expression became wary. 'Then what did it have to do with?'

Christi shrugged. 'Henry.'

'Henry?' she repeated in a puzzled voice. 'What does your dog have to do with this?'

'Nothing, really.' Christi began to smile, starting to relax, at last.

'Then—Christi, what is going on?' she demanded impatiently.

Her friend was really having trouble not openly laughing now. 'Oh, Dizzy, it couldn't have worked out better if I'd planned it that way!' she said excitedly. 'Of course I didn't,' she assured hastily.

'What are you talking about?' she prompted warily, sure that, whatever 'it' was, it didn't augur well for her!

Christi grimaced. 'You remember this morning that I told you I heard someone coming, and quickly ended our call?'

'Vaguely,' she dismissed with a sigh. 'I don't function too well at six o'clock in the morning!'

'Well, apparently my uncle does,' Christi said drily. 'He was the one I heard. It seems he likes to take long walks first thing in the morning, before starting work for the day. He asked who I was talking to on the telephone.' She pulled a face. 'And so I explained that you had got my number from *another* schoolfriend, and asked if you could come and stay.'

That part of things seemed to be clear enough; it certainly explained the change of plans about her supposed arrival at the castle. 'OK, I accept that you had no choice about that,' she said wearily. 'Although I think you might have warned me about it,' she added sternly.

'I haven't had a minute to myself since I called you at six o'clock!' Christi protested indignantly. 'Uncle Zach insisted I join him for his walk, and then, when we got back, he watched over me while I ate a nauseously enormous breakfast.' She shuddered at the memory and Dizzy remembered that she was ordinarily only a coffee drinker for her first meal of the day. 'He thinks I don't eat enough,' she grimaced. 'Then, of all things, he decided we hadn't spent enough time together during my stay, and dragged me off for a tour of the area. I have never been so bored in my entire life, Dizzy. He really——'

'Christi, this is all very interesting,' she cut in with a decided lack of sympathy. 'But we seem to have forgotten Henry,' she reminded.

'Henry?' Her friend frowned. 'What on earth— oh! Oh, yes.' Her expression cleared, and she bit her lip to once again stop herself from smiling. 'Uncle Zach was quite shocked at the idea of your taking a man into your bed just because he has soulful brown eyes and looks lonely!'

'*Taking a man*——' Dizzy stared at her in horrified disbelief. '*What* man?' She shook her head dazedly.

Christi was choking with laughter. 'Surely you remember what you said on the telephone about——'

'—about letting *your dog* sleep at the foot of my bed,' she finished explosively, as she *did* remember. 'Are you telling me your uncle actually thinks Henry is a man?' Her eyes narrowed.

'Isn't it hilarious?' Her friend chuckled.

'Oh, hysterical,' she scorned. 'I may start screaming at any moment!' she groaned.

'Oh, come on, Dizzy,' Christi chided lightly. 'It's very funny.'

'Not if you're me. Or Henry,' she added disgustedly. 'We'll just have to hope his girlfriend down the road doesn't get to hear about this!'

'Hey,' Christi's eyes lit up with mischief as she ignored Dizzy's nonsensical ramblings, 'maybe what's really worrying my uncle is that *he* has brown eyes and must get very lonely here in this mausoleum!'

'His eyes aren't brown, they're golden,' Dizzy told her absently, colour warming her cheeks as she realised what she had said.

Luckily, Christi didn't seem to have taken any undue interest in the comment. It was testament to how disturbed by this situation her friend was that she hadn't noticed Dizzy's very personal observation about her uncle. Usually, Christi never ceased trying to interest her in one man or another, chagrined that Dizzy seemed able to keep her life man-free, while she somehow managed to attract a cluster of them, more often than not at the same time!

Dizzy could only breathe a sigh of relief at Christi's lack of attention just now, although she recognised it was mainly because her friend couldn't see that her uncle was an attractive man. But then, Christi *hadn't* seen him the way she had!

She gave an impatient sigh. 'Couldn't you have just explained to your uncle that Henry is your dog?'

'Of course not.' Christi sounded irritated. 'If I had done that, he would have realised you were pet-sitting at my flat. We aren't supposed to have seen each other for years,' she reminded. 'And *you* were supposed to have called me this morning!'

'Oh, I realise that.' She shook her head. 'You really went over the top with that "park bench" story,' she said disgustedly. 'Especially as I'm sure your uncle must have heard my comment about your having kept me out of spending a night in jail!'

'This isn't *all* my fault,' Christi returned caustically. '*You* were the one who told him your name is Dizzy James!'

'It *is* my name,' she said firmly. 'Professionally, at least. Besides, do you really think your uncle would have believed your story of my destitution if he had realised who my father is?' she drawled derisively.

'You're right.' Christi chewed worriedly on her bottom lip, then she grimaced. 'I told him your family lost all their money shortly after you left school. That was very quick thinking on your part, Dizzy,' she said thankfully.

Dizzy raised her eyes heavenwards. She hadn't given her name as James to try and further Christi's ridiculous plan, and Christi would have realised that if she was thinking in the least bit straight. Unfortunately, she wasn't. But Dizzy had given up using her father's name years ago, as she preferred not to be connected to him.

'I'm glad you approve,' she derided drily. 'Now, what are we going to do about this mess you've got us into by telling your uncle these outrageous lies?' She quirked blonde brows.

Christi looked wounded, and then a little sheepish, as Dizzy continued to meet her gaze mockingly. 'OK, so I'll have to think a little more before I speak,' she accepted uncomfortably. 'But other than that, everything is working out perfectly,' she defended. 'Since I told him about you, and the circumstances behind my inviting you to stay, my uncle hasn't mentioned the fact that I'm going to Drama School, and that I don't have the same boyfriend for more than a month at a time, sometimes less than that!'

'I'm glad to have been of service!' Dizzy's sarcasm was barely veiled.

Christi, however, seemed to have missed it completely in her feeling of self-satisfaction. 'I knew you would be.' She hugged her. 'Oh, Dizzy, it's so good to have you here!' she told her enthusiastically.

Her expression softened at her friend's genuine pleasure. 'It's good to be here,' she said wryly.

'It's going to be so much more fun now.' Christi smiled her delight.

Poor pet, thought Dizzy, she really looked as if she had been having a miserable time of it, although the vivacity was fast returning to her enormous blue eyes. 'I thought there was nothing to do,' she teased.

'There isn't,' Christi grimaced. 'But I can never remember a dull moment in your company in the past.' She brightened.

'I'm getting too old to be the class clown,' Dizzy dismissed absently, her gaze drawn towards the window that faced in the direction of the lake she had seen Zachariah Bennett in earlier. 'But, talking of things to do,' she turned interestedly back to Christi, 'does your uncle go—bird-watching, often?' She arched blonde brows expectantly.

'Most afternoons,' Christi confirmed in a bored voice. 'He says it helps relax him after a morning of intensely draining work!'

Skinny-dipping should certainly blow away the cobwebs!

'I don't honestly know why he bothers,' Christi added disgustedly. 'He only comes back and buries himself in work for another couple of hours!'

After his nude swim, he probably felt completely invigorated! 'It must be expensive maintaining a castle,' she pointed out softly.

'I suppose so,' Christi conceded grudgingly. 'But if he would just release my money I would be willing to help him out.'

Dizzy gave her friend a reproving look. 'I have a feeling your uncle takes his guardianship role very seriously, so for goodness' sake don't even think about offering him any money. I'm sure he would consider it a bribe.' And if his disapproving eyebrows rose any higher they would disappear into his hairline!

'I know that,' Christi dismissed impatiently. 'Or else I would have done it an hour after my arrival!' she added mischievously.

'I'm sure it can't be that bad here.' Dizzy shook her head ruefully, sure that a man like Zachariah Bennett would have an extensive library. Her fingers itched to touch all those wonderful books.

'Give it a few days,' Christi assured her. 'Even school was fun compared to this—and you know how I loved school!' she grimaced.

The daughter of a very happily married couple who unfortunately travelled a great deal, because Christi's father had been an archaeologist, Christi had been completely miserable at being sent away to boarding-school at only eight. It had been their mutual unhappiness with the situation they had both been thrust into that had initially drawn Dizzy and Christi together that first term. Over the years, they had become as close as sisters, helping each other through those difficult years. Dizzy had been able to keep Christi's spirits up, not because she didn't dislike the school as much as her friend did, but because, to her, it was preferable to being at home. Anything had been preferable to that!

'Look, I'll give you a few minutes' peace from my chattering while you shower and change—into something equally as disreputable, please!' she encouraged gleefully. 'And then I'll show you around—what there is to see!' She made a face.

Dizzy nodded, her smile fading once her friend had left, her attention once again drawn to that window that faced east.

Just over that small tree-covered hill lay the lake where Zachariah Bennett had bathed naked. And, if Christi was right about the 'bird-watching', he did the same thing every afternoon...

CHAPTER THREE

WHY hadn't she told Christi about seeing her uncle bathing nude?

The two of them had been together for a couple of hours before they parted to change for dinner, and yet she had remained silent about what she had seen at the lake. And she knew that knowing something like that would certainly help to relax Christi. How could Zachariah Bennett preach to Christi about irresponsibility when only hours ago he had been bathing in a spot where anyone could come along and witness it? She had since learnt that the lake area was part of the castle estate, but, even so, the act hardly fitted in with the professor's 'fusty, dusty' image.

And that was partly what kept her silent.

Christi was right when she claimed Dizzy had deliberately cultivated her life-style of having no tangible ties, where, quite literally, she carried all that she owned on her back. And that also meant, quite contrary to what Zachariah Bennett had been led to believe, that there had been no men in her life. Somehow, admitting to Christi what she had seen that afternoon wouldn't make that true any more. Christi would want to know all the intimate details, and most prominent in her memory of that afternoon was her own response and attraction to a man she had labelled a 'Greek god'—Christi's uncle, a man who believed she went to bed with a man for

44

no better reason than he looked lonely and had soulful brown eyes!

She had spent years evading emotional entanglement, having a small circle of friends that she knew she could rely on completely, and who could rely on her, too. But, like Christi, most of those friends would have liked to see her happily in love, with perhaps a family of her own. Only her lightly dismissive attitude towards men had kept them from anyserious matchmaking on her behalf. And she felt far from lightly dismissive where Zachariah Bennett was concerned!

And so she hugged the memory of that afternoon to herself, wondering how long it would be before she gave in to the temptation to return to that lake one afternoon during her stay...

'Knollsley Hall in Cornwall,' remarked an abrupt voice from behind her.

Dizzy spun around as if she had been caught in the act of stealing the family silver, rather than merely gazing up at one of the paintings that adorned the stone walls in the room that had been made into quite a comfortable lounge.

Having showered shortly after she arrived, she had merely had a quick wash and changed her clothes when she had returned from the tour of the castle. Consequently Christi was still relaxing in the bath when she was ready to go down to dinner, and so she had come down without her, indulging in a more leisurely look around. Christi's whistle-stop—and obviously uninterested—tour had merely brushed the surface of it.

The first things to capture her attention in the lounge were the magnificent paintings on the walls, in particular, the one she now stood in front of, and which Zachariah Bennett had just supplied information about.

She had changed into one of the only two dresses she owned, the 'simple little black number' that was supposed to be suitable for any occasion, but which she dragged about with her merely because it didn't get creased in her backpack!

Unfortunately, Christi had been right about the 'freezer' temperatures in the castle, and so the sleeveless style of the dress wasn't 'suitable' at all! The only visible heating she had seen so far was the fire roaring away in the cavernous grate in this room, and for all its size it didn't even take the chill off the room. At least she had left her long hair loose tonight, so that her ears weren't actually freezing off! However, the wild tumble of blonde curls gave her the look of a wild wanton. No doubt Christi would be delighted with her appearance, although the professor looked far from pleased!

The black evening suit and white shirt were a definite improvement on his previous appearance. At least, they would have been, if the suit had been in the least tailored to the magnificence of his body, and the collar of his shirt wasn't sticking up on one side! The fact that his hair was newly washed, and once again brushed severely back from his face, didn't add to his attraction either, and his pipe seemed to have gone out long ago, although it was still clamped between his teeth to the side of his mouth.

To Dizzy, he just looked all the more endearing because of his lack of the sophisticated perfection that most of the men she had met in the past seemed to consider a must if they were to be successful with women. Maybe if she hadn't seen how beautiful he was beneath his ill-fitting clothing she might have accepted the face-value impression of the absent-minded professor, but her first sight of him had made that impossible.

'It's the house of the MP Martin Ellington-James,' he added, breaking her prolonged silence.

Her indulgent smile faded as she turned dutifully back to the painting of the gothic manor house, the artist having captured the cold ugliness of it perfectly. 'Quite impressive,' she said non-committally.

'Valerie Sherman is the artist,' he continued, as if even the polite conversation was a strain to him.

Dizzy turned back to him, transfixed, as she found his attention was riveted on the painting, those golden eyes aglow with admiration. Her breath caught in her throat at how breathtakingly handsome he was, and she couldn't help wondering what it must feel like if he looked at a woman in that way. She would like to see him without his glasses, and couldn't help wondering if he really needed to wear them when he wasn't working, or if they were some sort of shield to him. His eyesight had seemed perfectly all right this afternoon as he swam in the lake ... Colour heated her cheeks as, once again, her thoughts unconsciously returned to that time.

'She used to live there, I believe.' He spoke tersely now.

Dizzy blinked, giving a self-conscious grimace as she realised Zachariah Bennett had stopped looking at the painting and was now looking at her—and was obviously wondering what she found so fascinating about him. She doubted he would look quite so impatiently polite if he knew the truth about that!

'I believe you're right,' she confirmed drily.

Honey-gold eyes widened. 'You know something about paintings and their artists?'

'Something,' she nodded wryly.

He couldn't completely keep the surprise out of his expression. 'You like Miss Sherman's paintings?' He seemed relieved to have found a subject he could talk to her about while they waited for Christi to join them.

'I appreciate good paintings,' she evaded, not really wanting to get into a discussion about this particular one. 'I don't think there can be any doubt that Valerie Sherman is a talented artist,' she added abruptly. 'She's certainly captured the sheer ugliness of Knollsley Hall perfectly!'

His attention returned to the painting. 'Perhaps it is a little——'

'Grotesque,' Dizzy supplied abruptly.

'Possibly,' he nodded. 'Although it's haunting, too.'

The reason Dizzy hated the painting of Knollsley Hall was because it was too lifelike!

'I have other Shermans,' the professor told her lightly. 'Ones that perhaps aren't so—gothic. You must let me show them to you some time.'

It was the politely meaningless offer of a host to a guest in his house—even an unwanted one—and Dizzy accepted it as such. He had no real desire to show her the Valerie Sherman paintings, and she certainly had no interest in seeing them.

'I'd like that.' She turned away from the disturbing painting. 'I—oh, excuse me,' she said awkwardly, as an involuntary shiver racked her body. 'I—it's a little chilly in here,' she excused with a grimace.

A ghost of a smile lightened his austere features. 'Not at all what you're used to, I'm sure.'

Oooh, ouch! Dizzy acknowledged ruefully. Obviously, he believed that when she sponged off her friends she made sure it was only the ones who could give her all the creature comforts!

Her gaze was widely innocent. 'It's certainly an improvement on a park bench.'

His mouth twisted as he stepped back from her. 'Come and stand beside the fire,' he ordered curtly. 'Would you really have slept on a park bench tonight?' he probed softly, as she obediently joined him beside the fire.

She sent up a few silent words of reproach to Christi for the lies she had entangled them in. A park bench, indeed! 'I'm really not sure,' she dismissed non-committally.

Gold eyes raked over her speculatively. 'I'm sure it's never actually come to that,' he said coldly. 'Probably—Henry would have been able to help out again.'

Dizzy drew in a sharp breath. Where was the instigator of all these lies when she needed her? 'I don't think so.' She shook her head. 'I—he's sleeping with someone else tonight.' Good lord, she was doing it herself now!

'I see,' Zachariah Bennett bit out abruptly. 'Do you see much of Christi when you're both in London?'

Nothing like finding out straight away whether or not she was a constant bad influence on his niece! 'I believe she told you that we haven't seen each other for years,' she dismissed. 'I can't tell you what a piece of luck it was to find out Christi was staying up here.' At least that was true; she wouldn't have got to meet him or see his castle if Christi hadn't been staying here, and she wouldn't have wanted to miss either one of them!

'Exactly why are you in the area, Miss James?'

'Dizzy, please,' she invited for a second time—while she frantically tried to think of a reason she *could* be in the Lake District. Her expression cleared as the most obvious one occurred to her. 'I—er—needed to get out of London for a while,' she told him lightly, keeping her expression deliberately bland.

He frowned. 'Henry—has a wife?' he rasped.

And she had always thought a professor of history couldn't have an imagination! 'No, nothing like that,' she dismissed without rancour. 'I just—well, I wanted to get away for a while. I'm sure you know how it is.' She gave him a bright smile.

'No—no, I can't say that I do. Could I get you a drink?' he offered abruptly, looking as if *he* certainly needed one.

If a drink would help thaw her out, then she would have half a dozen of them! Although, if she asked for the whisky that would have warmed her, she was sure Zachariah Bennett would be convinced she was an alcoholic on top of everything else he seemed to think she was!

'Just a small sherry, please,' she accepted with another shiver.

'Perhaps you should go and get yourself a cardigan,' he suggested as he saw the shiver. 'I don't feel the cold myself, but Christi assures me the evenings can be chill. I'm sure Christi would be glad to let you borrow something of hers if you don't have a sweater with you,' he added at her hesitation.

Well, really, he was going too far, even for the parasite he thought her to be. 'Thank you, I have one of my own—it comes in handy for the nights on the park bench,' she said sharply.

His gaze narrowed as he handed her the glass of sherry. 'Don't your parents worry about—the life you lead?'

'Not at all,' she answered truthfully; the lectures from her father had stopped long ago—about the same time he had lost interest in her completely! 'They have problems of their own,' she shrugged.

'Of course,' he accepted, still believing Christi's story of the financial difficulty of Dizzy's parents.

'The castle doesn't have any heating other than individual fires?' she asked, in the hope of changing the subject.

'Not yet,' he replied distantly, the frown between his eyes seeming to indicate that the question irritated him.

'It's a wonderful place,' she enthused, her earlier antagonism gone as her eyes glowed with interest. 'Do you——'

'Sorry I'm late.' Christi burst smilingly into the room. 'Here, Dizzy, I brought you this to wear, in case you didn't have one.' She held out a cream cashmere cardigan.

Dizzy gave her friend a frowning look as she absently took the garment and pulled it on, noting that Christi's face was a little flushed and she was breathing heavily—almost as if she had *been running*!

She gave Christi a hard glare as she realised that that was exactly what she had been doing, that her friend must have been standing outside the lounge door when she and Zachariah Bennett had the conversation about cardigans, that Christi must have rushed back up to her room to get her one, just to add to the impression of Dizzy's destitution. Only this afternoon she had cautioned Christi to ease up a bit, and here she was making it look as if even the clothes on her back were borrowed!

'Thank you,' she accepted in a hard tone, uncaring of the fact that the cashmere cardigan was making her feel a lot warmer.

She had been going to ask Zachariah Bennett about the history of the castle, but now the moment was lost, and she felt sure that Christi had spoilt it deliberately. Christi seemed determined to let her uncle believe their school had produced an idiot, rather than let him realise she had an avid interest in his own subject. Obviously she and Christi were going to have to have another little chat—and soon!

'You're very welcome,' Christi dismissed, putting her arm through the crook of her uncle's. 'Have the two of you been getting acquainted?' she prompted brightly.

How could she become genuinely acquainted with a man who believed the things about her that Zachariah Bennett did! And that was a great pity, because she found him very interesting indeed.

'Yes,' he answered Christi curtly. 'Could I get you a drink before dinner?'

'Just my usual juice,' she accepted lightly.

The only time Dizzy could remember Christi drinking juice was when they were at school, and then it had only been because it was that or milk, and she couldn't stand milk! Christi was going to go home from this visit with a halo if she didn't take care.

'Dizzy?'

She gave a start at Zachariah's first use of her name, finding she liked the slightly husky tone to his voice as he said it. 'I'm fine with my sherry, thanks.' She refused another drink. She knew it would have pleased Christi immensely if she had said yes, but as she usually drank very little she wasn't about to change *that* for Christi's benefit.

Ordinarily, she wouldn't have minded this situation, would have been glad just to help Christi out, knowing her friend really was mature enough to handle her own affairs. But she found she intensely disliked this false impression of her that she and Christi were so determined to give Zachariah Bennett. She would probably never see him again after this brief visit, never have to worry *what* he believed about her, but she couldn't help disliking it all, none the less.

'Cut it out, Christi,' she muttered, once the professor had crossed the huge, high-ceilinged room to get Christi's juice.

Her friend looked at her with innocently wide blue eyes. 'What do you mean?'

'The cardigan,' she sighed.

'Don't you like it?'

'I love it,' she muttered. 'What I didn't like was your perfectly timed interruption with it!'

Blue eyes flashed. 'Well, what do you mean by talking to him about his precious castle?' Christi attacked. 'That isn't going to help your image at all.'

'As you obviously heard *all* of our conversation,' she muttered sarcastically, keeping a wary eye on the broad back of Zachariah Bennett as he stood in front of the drinks' cabinet, 'you must have realised that my reputation has already taken enough of a beating tonight. It's time to give it a rest, Christi.' She sighed again. 'Unless you *want* your uncle to become so worried by my presence here that he tells you to ask me to leave?'

Christi looked panic-stricken. 'You really think I'm going too far?'

'About three hours ago,' she said drily. 'And you could have warned me about the Shermans.'

'I——'

'Tell me,' Zachariah Bennett looked at Dizzy as he turned back to them, crossing the room to hand Christi her juice, 'how did you come by the unlikely name of Dizzy?'

She glared at her friend as she almost choked over her juice. 'Unlikely, Professor Bennett?' she returned coolly. 'Most people consider it suits me very well.' She deliberately ignored the mischief glowing in Christi's eyes.

'Surely it isn't your given name?' he frowned.

'I didn't say that,' she shrugged. 'Although it's the only one I'll answer to!'

She cringed every time she thought of the names her father had let her mother give her. At the time, he had been so disappointed she wasn't the son he had wanted, that there could be no more children, that he hadn't cared what the daughter he hadn't wanted was named. It had only been later, when the shock had worn off, that he had realised how totally unsuitable his only child's names were. Out of desperation he had begun to call her by her initials of DC, but with the mischievous humour of children, those initials had become Dizzy once she began school.

To her mother she was still—but she was in total agreement with her father about *those* two names, it was probably the only thing the two of them *had* ever agreed upon! To her father she was still DC—when he called her anything, which he probably didn't do any more! But to everyone else she had been Dizzy since she was eight years old. And she intended remaining that way!

Zachariah Bennett gave the ghost of a smile. 'And I usually answer to Zach, or Zachariah, if you prefer. Only my students ever called me Professor!'

At last! It was a little unnerving to think of a man who affected her as deeply as this one did by the formal title of 'Professor', or the equally unsuitable 'Zachariah Bennett'. 'Zach, I think.' She smiled warmly. 'Thank you.'

He nodded curtly, as if he already regretted the impulse. 'I'm sure dinner should be ready by now.' He strode out of the room to find out why it obviously wasn't.

'That must be a first,' Christi murmured a little dazedly.

Dizzy frowned at her, her thoughts miles away from the coldness of this room—well, at least *two* miles away! 'What must?' she prompted with slight impatience.

'Didn't you notice?' Christi mused. 'He actually seemed—self-conscious, not at all like his usual arrogant self.'

Arrogant? The professor? She didn't believe it! 'I think you've just got used to a lack of parental influence, love,' she teased. 'Besides the fact that your uncle obviously disapproves of me—as you've meant him to do—he's been perfectly polite.'

'*I've* got used to a lack of parental influence?' Christi returned indignantly. 'What about you and your——'

'Let's leave my parents out of this, shall we?' cut in Dizzy warningly.

'Sorry.' Her friend looked shame-faced. 'I think you're right, the strain of all this is getting to me. But, you know,' she frowned, 'it gave me a whole new perspective of my uncle when he asked you to call him Zach,' she admitted ruefully.

Dizzy gave her an indulgent smile. 'What did you expect me to call him, "Uncle Zach"?'

Christi smiled, shaking her head. 'I've just never thought of him as just Zach before,' she shrugged.

'Hm,' she conceded wryly. 'But he must obviously be your father's younger brother?'

Christi nodded. 'By ten years. I know he looks—and *acts*—years older, but he's only thirty-five,' she grimaced.

Maybe as Professor Bennett he did look older than that, but as her 'Greek god' he looked much younger! And as time was passing Dizzy was having more and more difficulty separating the two.

'—would have that effect on you,' Christi was saying sadly.

'Sorry?' she prompted, sure from Christi's expression that she had missed something important.

Christi gave her a reproving look for her lack of attention. 'I said, I suppose a love affair that ended unhappily would have that effect on you,' she repeated patiently. 'Although it happened so long ago, I'm sure he has to be over it by now,' she frowned.

'It?' Dizzy asked with casual uninterest.

'My uncle's fiancée died—oh, almost eleven years ago now,' her friend explained thoughtfully. 'It was such a shame, she was so nice. I remember she used to make clothes for my favourite doll of the time,' she murmured fondly.

'Mercenary little baggage, aren't you?' Dizzy teased drily, all the time her thoughts on Zachariah Bennett's tragic loss. Eleven years ago, and from what Christi had said there hadn't been another serious relationship since; he must have loved his fiancée very much. It just confirmed her belief that loving people hurt too much, took too much, while seeming to give nothing back.

'I didn't mean she was nice because of that,' Christi retorted indignantly, relaxing with a rueful smile as she saw Dizzy's teasing expression. 'I only used the example of the doll's clothes to show you how nice she was, how she even had time for the objectionable brat I was at the time... Some people might say I haven't changed all that much,' she added ruefully, as Dizzy looked even more amused.

'Really?' Dizzy returned innocently.

Christi grinned. 'I can't imagine how you've been able to stand me the last twelve years!'

'It hasn't been easy.' She gave a heavily affected sigh.

'But you've muddled through,' Christi derided.

'Someone had to take pity on you and be your friend.' Dizzy sounded as if she had the weight of responsibility on her shoulders.

Christi grimaced at her sacrificial expression. 'There hasn't been a day gone by during those years when I haven't been grateful that you were the one to do that,' she told her seriously. 'Sometimes I don't know what I would have done without you.'

Dizzy squeezed her shoulder, knowing the death of Christi's parents three years ago had been a terrible shock to her, that without the support and love of her friends at that time Christi might have broken down completely. Christi had gone to stay with her uncle for a few weeks after the accident, but the real shock hadn't seemed to set in until she had been back in London for several weeks. And then it had been up to her friends to rally round, Dizzy most of all, to make sure that she didn't fall apart. If anything, the tragedy had brought the two girls even closer together, Dizzy having looked up to Christi's parents more than she did her own.

'It was mutual,' Dizzy said huskily, thinking of all the times Christi had helped her when she had been upset or alone. 'Although,' she added briskly, 'I think you might have made some effort to warn me about the Shermans your uncle seems so proud of.' She looked reproving.

Christi blushed, grimacing. 'I was hoping you wouldn't notice them,' she said apologetically.

Dizzy gave her a chiding look. 'Not notice *that* monstrosity?' She nodded at the huge painting of Knollsley Hall across the room.

'It's awful, isn't it?' Christi winced. 'He has several others, too,' she admitted reluctantly.

'So he told me,' she acknowledged drily. 'Although I doubt any of them could be as ghastly as that one!'

'Well, actually...'

'Dinner is finally ready.' An impatient Zachariah Bennett returned to the lounge, effectively cutting off what Christi had been about to say. 'It appears there was some sort of panic in the kitchen,' he apologised abruptly.

'Anything serious?' Christi prompted concernedly.

'Fredericks assures me everything is under control now,' her uncle dismissed.

Obviously he was a man who didn't like his routine upset, and that included any delay in the serving of meals, Dizzy thought with some amusement, as they went through to the dining-room for their meal.

Everything new she learnt about this man made him all the more endearing to her. And it wasn't an emotion she particularly welcomed.

Possibly, at the moment, she should be more concerned with Christi's unfinished comment of, 'Well, actually...' concerning the Sherman paintings...

CHAPTER FOUR

'WHAT on earth are you doing?'

Dizzy froze, wincing as she slowly withdrew from within the huge larder she had been searching through so avidly seconds earlier.

She ran her hands nervously down her thighs as she reluctantly turned to face Zachariah Bennett. Talk about being caught in the act! Here she was, raiding the larder, and she had been caught at it by none other than her host.

The first thing she noticed, as she looked across the brightly lit kitchen at him, was that he bought his pyjamas from the same chain-store she did, for their blue and white striped pyjamas were matching pairs!

She laughed, she just couldn't help it. 'Snap!' she managed to murmur before laughing again.

Zach wore a blue woollen robe over his pyjamas, neatly tied at his waist, although the rest of his appearance wasn't quite as neat: his hair falling across his forehead in soft curls, his glasses missing altogether. Obviously he had left his bedroom in rather a hurry.

Probably hoping to catch a burglar, Dizzy acknowledged ruefully, sobering as she realised he didn't look too pleased about having had his sleep interrupted.

'I was—er—I fancied a midnight snack.' She lamely explained her presence in the kitchen.

He glanced at the clock on the wall. 'It's one-thirty in the morning,' he said drily.

Without his glasses, the full impact of those honey-coloured eyes was inescapable; Dizzy was completely lost in their depths at first glance.

'Dizzy?' He frowned at her lack of response to his comment.

She blinked, momentarily breaking the spell. 'I—I fancied a one-thirty-in-the-morning snack,' she said, giving a rueful shrug.

'Didn't you have enough to eat at dinner time?' He arched blond brows.

'Oh, yes,' she nodded. 'I just—I always get hungry this time of night,' she grimaced.

'I see,' he sighed, relaxing slightly. 'Well, what were you looking for? Perhaps I could help you,' he offered, in the way of a man who just wanted to get this over with so that he could go back to bed.

It wasn't very complimentary to her, Dizzy acknowledged ruefully. OK, so the striped pyjamas weren't the sexiest nightwear in the world, but they were *all* she was wearing; there should have at least been a spark of sexual awareness in those golden eyes. Instead, Zach was looking at her much the same as the teachers had at boarding-school when they caught the boarders having a tuck-party in their dormitory after lights-out!

'Pilchards,' she sighed, for the first time wishing to see those instant thoughts of bed that came into a man's eyes when they looked at her—and not with sleep in mind, either! She had been plagued by her 'bedroom' body all her adult life, and now, when she somehow *wanted* Zach to notice her, he couldn't see past the schoolgirl acquaintance of his niece!

His eyes widened. 'I beg your pardon?'

She smiled at his complete lack of comprehension. 'It's a fish,' she provided lightly. 'Belonging to the herring family. A bit like a large sardine,' she added as he still looked unimpressed. 'They come in tins, in either tomato sauce or oil,' she explained further.

He still didn't look impressed. 'Really?'

'Yes,' she nodded frantically.

Zach crossed his arms across his chest. 'And you expected to find some of them in my larder?' he prompted patiently.

'I—well—I thought everyone had pilchards in their kitchen store-cupboard,' she said lamely, guessing by his deadpan expression that the fish had never had a place in *his* store-cupboard! 'Maybe some sardines, then,' she suggested hopefully.

She wasn't sure if it was her imagination, or if she really did see a glimmer of amusement in the golden depths. And then it had disappeared completely, his expression even more fierce than before.

'You aren't pregnant, are you?' came the instant explanation for that fierceness.

Much as she loved Henry, and hated to see that soulful expression in his big brown eyes, she wished now that she had never let the little devil go to sleep on the bottom of her bed!

'No,' she answered irritably. 'I just happen to like pilchards.'

'Well, you won't find any in here,' Zach bit out. 'Why don't you try the fridge? There might be a drumstick or two in there.'

'Anything else but pilchards keeps me awake if I eat it this time of night.' She shook her head.

He looked as if just the *thought* of eating the revolting-sounding fish might keep him awake for the rest of the night! 'I'm afraid I can't help you.' He stepped pointedly away from the doorway.

Dizzy hung back, knowing she wasn't going to be able to sleep just yet. When she had finally managed to speak to Christi on her own she had been most disturbed by what her friend had to tell her. After reading for three hours—they had all gone to bed at ten-thirty—having finished the Claudia Laurence book she had been enjoying so much, she still hadn't felt tired enough to fall asleep as she usually did after a long read. Sitting down with a tin of pilchards and a mug of hot milk usually worked if all else failed.

'Could I—is it all right if I have some hot milk instead?' She looked at Zach hopefully.

'Of course,' he agreed with barely concealed impatience. 'Would you like me to get it for you?'

'No, I—sorry.' She gave an awkward grimace as an involuntary shiver racked her body. 'The kitchen seems to have cooled down since dinner was cooked in here.' She hastily set about pouring the milk into a saucepan to put on to heat.

'Here.'

She turned abruptly as she felt the warmth of the woollen garment about her shoulders, blinking dark lashes over wide green eyes as she realised that the suddenness of her movement had put her and Zach into a closeness that meant their pyjama-clad bodies were only inches apart.

Zach looked taken aback by the sudden tension of the situation, and stared down at her intently, neither of them seeming capable of movement.

Dizzy had never felt so aware of a man. The V of his pyjama jacket revealed the start of the golden hair she knew covered the whole of his chest, and lower. That chest moved up and down rapidly, and she knew in that moment that he was just as aware of her as she was him, that the fusty, dusty façade of Professor Bennett had a wide crack in it.

Quite what would have happened next Dizzy didn't like to guess, although she hoped, for the sake of her peace of mind, that they would have moved apart as they were doing now, she to snatch the saucepan of milk from the top of the cooker as it began to boil over, Zach to stand across the room from her.

Her hand shook slightly as she poured the hot milk into a mug, the robe about her shoulders slipping to the floor as she reached out to put water in the used saucepan. She tensed as she heard the pad of Zach's slipper-clad feet on the tiled floor; still facing the sink, she felt his presence behind her.

'Turn around,' he instructed gruffly.

She drew in a ragged breath as she reluctantly did as he asked, finding him standing in front of her, holding out the robe for her to put her arms into.

'You need it more than I do,' he prompted as she hesitated. 'There isn't too much of you to keep you warm,' he added derisively, as she slipped her arms into the too-big robe.

Obviously he considered her nomadic life-style didn't provide enough food for her to get fat. He probably thought she had been raiding his larder for the same reason! After an evening of feeling as if he must consider her a charity case, she wasn't in the mood for further reminding of the role she was supposed to be playing!

'I'm not small all over,' she pointed out with deliberate provocation.

Zach faltered only slightly in the act of turning up the too-long sleeves, looking up into her face reprovingly, although Dizzy noticed his gaze didn't return immediately to the sleeve he was working on after leaving her face, but lingered on the suddenly uneven rise and fall of her breasts.

'There.' He stepped back with some relief once he had completed the task. 'You look like a child trying to appear older by dressing up in an adult's clothes,' he murmured, this time the amusement in his eyes completely obvious.

Her eyes flashed at the condescension of unmistakable maturity. 'Does anything you've heard about me lead you to believe I'm still a child, in any way?' she challenged.

He stiffened, his expression suddenly harsh.

'Oh, look, I'm sorry.' Dizzy gave a weary sigh. 'It's been a long day, and I'm feeling a little disgruntled because I can't seem to get to sleep.'

'Possibly it's the unusual occurrence of sleeping alone that's causing the disturbance,' he told her frostily.

If he didn't so obviously mean every word he was saying, it might have been funny: she was the original virgin, hadn't even been kissed properly in her twenty-one years. Although she had a feeling she might have come close to it a few minutes ago!

It was because she knew how close she had come to being bent to the will of another person that her reply was made so caustically. 'You're probably right,' she snapped. 'Perhaps you would like to offer to rectify that?' Her chin rose challengingly.

His mouth twisted. 'I don't believe so, thank you,' he said with obvious distaste.

'Why not?' she taunted. 'Aren't I good enough for you?'

'I'm sure you're very good,' he drawled contemptuously. 'Fortunately,' he stressed the word, 'I'm not attracted to over-experienced children! Your milk is cooling,' he added coldly. 'I'm sure I can leave you alone to enjoy it.'

'Aren't you frightened I might steal the family silver, a painting or two, and just sneak off into the night?' she mocked hardly.

He drew in an angry breath. 'No.'

'Why not?' she derided.

He shrugged. 'The silver—what there is of it— is locked away, and the paintings are all wired to an alarm.'

Dizzy's mouth twisted. 'I might have known it wasn't a question of trusting me!'

Zach gave a weary sigh. 'How long have you had that chip on your shoulder?'

'I think I was probably born with it,' she said ruefully, knowing that she did have a defensive shield that usually kept the world out. Except that this man had been able to get under her guard. One moment she didn't mind that he had, even welcomed it, and the next moment she wanted her shield back in place again. She wasn't used to these feelings of insecurity, not any more.

He shook his head. 'I'm sure there's a wealth of conversation to be made from that comment, unfortunately it's too late—or early, depending on your point of view,' he said drily, 'to go into right now. Don't forget to turn the lights off before you go back to bed,' he advised briskly.

'Your robe.' Dizzy stopped him at the door.

'You can return it tomorrow,' he dismissed abruptly. 'Maybe you would also like to go into town and get in a store of—pilchards——' he named the fish as if he even found saying them difficult! '—as you seem to be addicted to them,' he added derisively.

She looked at him with innocently wide eyes. 'What will I do for money?'

He sighed, as if he had half been expecting that question. 'I have an account at one of the stores in town. Just tell them it's for the Castle Haven, and it will be OK.'

'You're so kind,' she mocked softly.

'As I told you earlier today,' he rasped coldly. 'It can sometimes be kinder to be cruel.'

Dizzy sat down shakily once he had abruptly left the room, knowing that this round had definitely gone to Zach. She had allowed temper and resentment to overrule good sense, her defences going into overdrive as she realised how close she had come to allowing an emotion other than friendship into her life. But at least she had managed to so disgust Zach that the closeness wasn't likely to happen again.

Zach was a man who had lost, to death, the woman he loved; he certainly didn't need the complication of someone like her in his life. And she, well, she made a point of keeping *all* complications out of her life!

Dizzy was up early the next morning, for the main reason that she hadn't been to sleep.

The milk had done little but fill her up so that she felt uncomfortable. So, instead of going to sleep as she had planned, she had dug to the bottom of her bag and pulled out yet another of her favourite books, and read her way through that until seven o'clock, mindful of the fact that Christi said her uncle usually left the castle at six-thirty to go for his morning walk.

Christi was still fast asleep when she glanced in on her, lying serenely back on the pillows, not a hair out of place. Even in sleep Christi was beautiful, Dizzy acknowledged ruefully.

Her own appearance wasn't quite as neat, her hair once again plaited down her spine, the usual wisps escaping about her face and neck. She wore a different T-shirt from yesterday, although it was just as baggy, and the same patched jeans from the day before. She had noted with rueful acceptance that there were even several freckles across her nose today from her walk in the sunshine yesterday. If Zach *had* found her childlike the night before, it wasn't so surprising!

She was looking for the library, knowing that it was there she would find what she sought. Christi had told her last night that it was there, and the sooner she got the confrontation over, the better it would be. Much better that she should do it alone, too. Maybe, then, she might even be able to start sleeping again.

Her hands were clammy, her heart beating wildly, as she looked for the book-lined room, even the thought of the books not able to detract from that other ugliness.

As she passed the corridor leading to the kitchen, she thought she heard a child crying, and felt a shiver down her spine, her memories so vividly disturbing that she knew that haunting unhappiness was once again with her, making her imagine things, that the child she could hear crying was herself, the child deep inside her which had had to die so that she might live.

But as she heard the cry again she realised it was a real cry, that there was a child in the kitchen, crying as if its heart would break!

She couldn't bear the pain behind that cry, and she hurried down the corridor to throw open the kitchen door.

Seated at the table, her arms about a little girl of perhaps four or five, was the cook, her stricken face evidence that she was greatly disturbed by the interruption.

Dizzy was too concerned by the little girl's distress to worry about the middle-aged woman's feelings. Going down on her haunches, she smiled gently into the most angelically beautiful face she had ever seen, dark hair framing that little face, deep blue eyes tear-wet, a tiny snub nose, and a tiny quivering mouth.

'Hello,' Dizzy said warmly. 'I'm very hungry for my breakfast, aren't you?' She sat down in the chair on the other side of the little girl, taking over the task of feeding her the toast the cook was having so much trouble with. 'Could I have some of this lovely toast too, please?' she requested of the cook, as the wide-eyed little girl took a bite of the toast she held out to her temptingly. Realising that the dumb-struck obedience wouldn't last once the little girl got over her shyness, she knew she had to distract her attention. 'My name's Dizzy, what's yours?' She held the little girl's gaze as the cook slowly got to her feet to prepare more toast.

'Dizzy?' the little girl echoed sceptically, revealing that she had a slight lisp from where her two front teeth were missing.

'That's right,' Dizzy grinned. 'And I bet your name is something pretty, like Annabel, or Melissa, or——'

'I want Melissa,' the little girl cried, her lips quivering again as tears flooded and overflowed her eyes. 'I want Melissa!' she sobbed in earnest.

Dizzy put down the toast, turning enquiringly to the distressed cook at the emotional outburst she had provoked.

'She woke up in the night asking for her,' the other woman said frantically. 'Her mother—that's my daughter, was rushed into hospital yesterday, and Kate's been with me ever since. Her father's away on business, although he's going to be back tomorrow. I've tried to explain to Kate that she'll be able to see all her friends again soon, but she still keeps asking for this Melissa.' She sounded completely frayed.

'Kate.' Dizzy turned back to the little girl as she buried her fists in her eyes, still sobbing noisily.

'Your Mummy isn't well just now, and so Nanny is taking care of you,' she explained gently. 'Nanny is very upset you can't be with your friends just now, but——'

'I want Melissa!' the little girl wailed.

Dizzy felt the constriction of her heart at the pained plea, watching impotently as the little girl jumped up and ran from the room.

'I just don't know what to do.' The cook sat down wearily in the chair opposite Dizzy's, looking completely frazzled. 'Maureen—Kate's mother, was rushed to hospital with appendicitis. It was all such a panic, but once we knew the operation had been a success I brought Kate back here with me.' She sighed. 'There are some children in the house next door to Kate's, maybe this Melissa is one of them.' She shook her head. 'But they live thirty miles away and, what with cooking for the professor and visiting Maureen, I just don't have the time to take Kate to see her friend.'

At a guess, Dizzy would have said the little girl's presence here had something to do with the 'panic' in the kitchen the previous evening.

Poor Kate. She knew herself exactly how traumatic it was to be suddenly separated from your parents, to be taken away from all that was familiar to you. She knew exactly how cruel it could feel, too.

'I could take her, if you like,' she offered decisively.

'Oh, I couldn't let you do a thing like that!' The cook looked shocked at the suggestion. 'You're a guest of the professor's, and——'

'Actually, I'm a guest of his niece,' Dizzy corrected drily, sure that Zach wouldn't like his staff to think *he* had invited her to stay. 'And I have to go into town today, anyway.' The thought of several more days without pilchards was too terrible to contemplate! 'So a few more miles on my journey isn't going to make that much difference. As long as you don't mind trusting Kate to my care, Mrs——' She looked at the older woman enquiringly.

'Mrs Scott,' the cook instantly supplied, looking embarrassed. 'I am sorry, I should have introduced myself sooner. It's just——'

'I understand,' she assured her gently. 'It can't have been easy for you, suddenly having a—five-year-old?—thrust upon you.'

Mrs Scott nodded at the age-guess. 'My job here doesn't leave me too much time for visiting my family. Don't get me wrong,' she added hastily. 'I'm not complaining. Work was what kept me going after my husband died, and Maureen had already had a home of her own for several years. But it means I perhaps haven't spent as much time with little Kate as I should have done, and she's finding it all a bit strange here now that her mother is poorly.'

'Of course she is.' Dizzy sympathised with the whole situation. 'How about if I suggest taking Kate out with me today? You never know, she might have forgotten all about Melissa after we've done some shopping together.'

The cook didn't looked convinced of that. 'It's worth a try, I suppose. As long as you're sure you don't mind?' she added anxiously. She was a small, plump lady with pepper-coloured curly hair, and eyes as blue as Kate's.

'I'm sure,' Dizzy smiled encouragingly, standing up. 'I'll go and talk to Kate while you finish preparing the professor's breakfast. That is his bacon you have out to cook, isn't it?' she prompted teasingly.

'Oh, my goodness, yes!' Mrs Scott gave a frantic glance at the kitchen clock. 'He'll be back any moment, and here's me, not even started cooking!' She hastily got up and moved to the cooker.

Dizzy could see that the other woman had enough to do without the extra worry about her granddaughter, and she went off in search of the little girl. It wasn't all that difficult to find her, the gentle sobs were easily discernible through the partially opened bedroom door.

The staff's quarters were at the back of the wing, and Kate seemed to be sharing a room with her grandmother, a cot-bed having been brought in and put next to the single bed for her.

She looked so small and defenceless as she lay curled up in a ball of misery on the cot-bed, her face wet with tears again.

'Kate,' Dizzy sat down next to her, gently smoothing back the dark tangle of her hair, 'would you like to go out with me today?'

Wide blue eyes were turned to her. 'To go and get Melissa?' she suggested hopefully, still sobbing gently.

'I have some shopping to do first—but afterwards we could go and see Melissa,' she quickly added, as the small face began to crumple.

Kate frowned, wiping away her tears with the back of her hand. 'Why can't she come back with us?'

There was a possibility that Kate would be going home with her father when he returned tomorrow, but there was also the possibility that, between his job and visiting his wife in hospital, Kate's father might think it best if she stayed on with her grandmother for the moment. If that were to happen, it wouldn't do to lead Kate to believe she could see her friend any time she wanted to.

'Don't you think she would miss her home if she did that?' Dizzy said softly. 'And her Mummy and Daddy would miss her if she came to stay with you.'

'But she doesn't have a Mummy and Daddy.' Kate's frown deepened.

Dizzy had to admit to feeling a little puzzled herself. Unless ... 'Kate,' she said slowly, 'who *is* Melissa?'

'I told you, she's my friend.' Kate was becoming agitated now.

'Is she a big friend or a little friend?' Dizzy persisted.

'A little friend, of course,' Kate dismissed impatiently, as if she found the question an extremely silly one.

'Does she have blonde hair or black?' Dizzy encouraged.

Kate looked at her consideringly. 'It's the same colour as yours,' she decided. 'Not as long, but Melissa is awful pretty,' she defended with that endearing lisp.

'And are her eyes blue or brown?' With each answer she received, Dizzy became more and more convinced she was right about Melissa.

'Blue, of course.' Kate was really tiring of all these questions now. 'All my dollies have blue eyes,' she reported in a grown-up voice, as if Dizzy ought to have already known that.

Dizzy hugged the little girl impulsively. A doll, of course Melissa had to be a doll. Children missed their friends when they were away from them, but they didn't wake up in the night calling for them! She should have realised sooner, should have known Kate's behaviour was much more serious than being away from a playmate; with her mother in hospital and her father away, the doll had become Kate's one security. It was obviously the doll the little girl usually took to bed with her. She had forgotten about it until she realised it wasn't there, and had woken from sleep when she realised that.

It was all so reminiscent of what had happened to Dizzy when she had been sent away to school, only in her case it had been a tattered, old, lop-eared, cuddly toy rabbit that she had had since she was a baby. When her things were unpacked at school, she found that the rabbit hadn't been included, and had written to her father, asking him to send it on to her. And written to him. And written to him. For a whole term she had dutifully written to him every Sunday, always adding the request about the rabbit at the end of the letter. It wasn't until she went home for Christmas that she managed to sneak Snuggles back to school in her suitcase. For fourteen long weeks she had cried herself to sleep every night, because her father ignored her request for her childhood friend.

Her arms tightened about Kate as she realised the suffering the little girl had gone through without the security of her doll, although she knew Kate's suffering hadn't been deliberate, as hers had, that Melissa had just genuinely been overlooked in the panic of yesterday.

'We'll go and get Melissa after breakfast,' she told the little girl emotionally.

'We will?' Kate pulled back slightly, her eyes wide.

'We will,' she nodded, feeling tearful herself at how easy it had been to allay Kate's suffering—and how easily her own father had found it to ignore her pain. When he had at last found out what she had done that Christmas, he had demanded the return of the rabbit, and told her she was too old for cuddly toys. Maybe she was, but Snuggles wasn't just a cuddly toy to her, he was so much more. For the first time in her life she had told her father a lie, had told him she had lost the rabbit. It had satisfied him, and she got to keep the one thing she truly loved at the time, but the guilt of that lie lay in the bottom of her backpack upstairs . . .

'Mummy was in too much pain to think of Melissa yesterday, pet,' she comforted the child in her arms. 'And Nanny didn't know about how important Melissa is to you. Now let's wash your face,' she smiled, gently touching the silken cheeks. 'And then you can go and eat some breakfast with Nanny before we go and get Melissa.'

Kate scrambled off the bed, hesitating as she reached the door. 'We really will go and get Melissa?'

Dizzy swallowed hard. 'We really will.'

'Oh, great!' Kate bounced out of the room, wriggling impatiently as her face was washed, eager to get the business of eating breakfast over so that they might leave. 'I can take Melissa with me this afternoon when we go to see Mummy,' she was telling Dizzy as they entered the kitchen a few minutes later.

The kitchen smelt of cooked breakfast, and was noticeably empty of food, so Dizzy could only assume that Zach was now in the dining-room, eating his breakfast. She hoped he didn't disappear into his office too quickly, for she wanted Christi to ask him for the use of a car so that they could go and get Kate's doll.

Mrs Scott looked relieved to see her grand-daughter obediently sit down and begin to eat the toast she had abandoned earlier, although she frowned a little at the mention of Melissa going to the hospital with them.

'A blue-eyed, blonde haired doll,' Dizzy explained in an aside.

'A doll!' the cook predictably gasped.

'Not just any doll,' Dizzy told her softly. 'A very special friend of Kate's.'

'I understand.' Mrs Scott looked thankful that *that* worry, at least, was over. 'I had no idea...'

'Of course you didn't.' Dizzy squeezed her arm understandingly. 'Kate and I plan to go and get her after breakfast,' she added.

'I don't know how to thank you,' the cook said warmly. 'You don't even know Kate and me, and yet you——' She broke off as a bell rang in the room. 'That will be the professor, wanting his second pot of coffee. I really ·am grateful, Miss James——'

'Dizzy,' she invited smoothly, laughing softly as the other woman frowned. 'It really is my name,' she said derisively. 'See you after breakfast, Kate.' She lightly touched the little girl's shoulder on her way to the door. 'Make sure you eat it all up.'

Kate nodded eagerly, her mouth stuffed full of the toast she had refused to eat earlier.

Dizzy was still smiling as she left the room, although she sobered as she remembered why she had been in this part of the house in the first place, and returned briefly to the kitchen doorway. 'The library?' she prompted, as Mrs Scott turned to her enquiringly.

'Down the corridor and turn right, you can't miss it,' she smiled, picking up the coffee-pot to take through to the professor.

Dizzy wished she *could* miss it, wished she didn't have to put herself through this. But it was inevitable.

It was a beautiful room, a deep red carpet adding a richness to the book-lined room, a fire lit invitingly in the hearth.

Over the fireplace hung the painting she had come here to see, and she reluctantly raised her gaze from the orange and yellow flames, gasping as raw pain ripped through her.

CHAPTER FIVE

THE background of the painting looked harmless enough. It was a children's playroom, with every conceivable toy you could think of or imagine either on the thickly carpeted floor or along the shelved walls. It was like an Aladdin's cave, paradise for any child.

But not for the child who stood to the right of the foreground as she gazed out of the window before her, the toys obviously meaning nothing to her, her expression one of cold uninterest.

She was a child of about seven, neat black patent shoes on her feet, her socks pristine white, not a fold of the pink dress and white over-pinafore out of place, her hair tamed into plaits that lay over each shoulder.

'Perhaps you find this Sherman more to your liking?'

Zach's habit of catching her unawares was becoming too disturbing by half. Especially now. How could she turn and face him when—— She *had* to turn and face him, she admonished herself, straightening her spine, clearing her face of all expression as she slowly turned.

He was wearing an equally comfortable and ill-fitting pair of corduroys as he had yesterday, black this time, coupled with a blue jumper that actually revealed the powerful muscles beneath. It was already warm outside, but inside there was still a chill in the air, although not enough for Zach to wear the baggy jacket that yesterday had so successfully concealed how masculine he was.

With her defences already down, his blatant masculinity was the last thing Dizzy needed just now!

She drew in a ragged breath. 'Is this a Sherman, too?' She pretended surprise, evading a direct answer concerning her feelings for the painting, as she had initially last night about the one of Knollsley Hall.

Zach nodded. 'I told you I had others of hers.' He came further into the room, looking up at the painting appreciatively. 'This is one of her best, I think.'

Dizzy's brows rose. 'A poor-little-rich-girl too bored to play with her toys?' she taunted.

He turned to her slowly, frowning slightly. 'Is that the way you see the painting?'

Defiant colour burnt her cheeks. 'Isn't that exactly what it is?' she challenged, her body held in a defensive stance.

He slowly shook his head. 'Not to me.'

Dizzy shrugged. 'I'm sure I read somewhere that the critics disliked this painting because it lacked emotion.'

'It's full of emotion,' he contradicted impatiently. 'Look at the eyes.' He moved to stand just below the painting. 'Can't you see the suggestion of tears in their depths? Look at the mouth,' he instructed again. 'There's vulnerability beneath the stubbornness. The title of it should tell you that it's a painting of emotion. "Lost Child",' he supplied, as she raised her brows questioningly.

She knew the title of the painting, had seen photographs of it, although never the original before. Zach was right, there *were* tears in the green eyes, and the mouth *did* look as if it trembled on the verge of tears.

But it was all a sham. Her mother had never seen her like that, had already been out of her life for three years by the time she was seven. Oh, the child was definitely her, but she had never had a playroom like this one, and the emotions were purely her mother's, a spoilt child of a woman who found herself in a marriage where she could have everything—like the child in the painting with her toys—except the freedom that lay beyond that window!

Knollsley Hall had become like a prison to Valerie Sherman for the five years she was married to Martin Ellington-James, and by the time Dizzy was four she hadn't been able to stand the restrictions being a politician's wife put on her any longer. She had gone out shopping one day, and just not come back.

Dizzy hadn't been able to believe her mother's desertion of her, had felt sure she was coming back one day. Her father told her he wouldn't take her mother back, even if she came crawling to him on her knees, but, even so, Dizzy had hoped. She had never seen her mother again after that day, just after her fourth birthday.

But she had seen photographs of this painting, had hated her mother anew for using her to depict her own emotions. Last night, Christi had told her that her uncle had the original of the painting, and although she hated the thought of it, Dizzy had always made a point of not running away from anything. But she couldn't run away from the pain of disillusionment this painting evoked even if she had wanted to, it was something that was always with her, had shaped her into the woman she was today. The fact that Zach saw the pain inside the child in the painting only made it worse, as if he had once again pierced the shield she had over her emotions.

'She doesn't look very lost to me,' Dizzy answered him in a hard voice. 'Unless it's among all those toys,' she dismissed coldly. 'Now, if you'll excuse me, I have to go and see Christi.' She couldn't get out of the room, away from Zach, fast enough!

'Dizzy?' He stopped her at the door.

She kept her gaze averted from the painting as she turned to look at him, knowing that although the books tempted her, she would probably never be able to return to this room during the rest of her stay here. 'Yes?' she prompted abruptly.

He looked puzzled by her behaviour, and Dizzy was easily able to guess why. All this emotionalism wasn't really in character with the woman who gave her body at a glance from soulful brown eyes! Well, damn him, she couldn't *be* the clown when she felt as if her soul had been stripped bare!

'If you still want to go into town today, I can have a car put at your disposal,' he offered gruffly.

She relaxed slightly. 'Assuming I can drive, of course,' she drawled.

'I'm sure Christi would be only too happy to accompany you,' he told her distantly.

'I would have thought you would have wanted to keep her away from me as much as possible,' she taunted.

'Dizzy——'

'Sorry.' She held up her hands defensively, knowing she was being unfair, that his reactions had all been to the type of woman he was supposed to believe her to be, although if that were so it made some of his behaviour the night before a little difficult to explain! 'I would appreciate the use of a car.' Especially as that was why she had been going in search of Christi! 'And I'll invite Christi to go with me, if that's all right with you.'

Golden eyes widened. 'Christi is an adult, completely capable of making her own decisions.'

'Yes, but——' She broke off awkwardly.

Zach looked at her consideringly. 'Yes?'

She shrugged, realising how close she had come to ruining everything for Christi with the casual remark that she was hardly likely to want to upset her uncle in the circumstances. No doubt, if Zach knew she was aware of the conditions of Christi's parents' will, he would think her visit here now more than timely!

'Christi and I were never that close,' she dismissed. 'And you've made it very clear you disapprove of me as a companion for her.'

He stiffened. 'As I said, Christi is an adult, capable of making her own decisions about people.'

'OK,' she shrugged. 'I'll ask her and see what she says.'

'You do that,' he invited tersely. 'And eat some breakfast before you leave.'

'Yes, sir,' she returned impishly.

He gave a rueful smile, looking years younger. 'Please,' he added drily. 'I'm sorry we can't accommodate you with pilchards, but...'

Dizzy chuckled. 'I think I'll go and find Christi.' She was still smiling as she left the room, Zach's humour a pleasant surprise. Obviously the sternly disapproving expression was as deceptive of his real character as the ill-fitting clothes were of the body that lay beneath them. And with that thought she couldn't help wondering if he would be skinny-dipping again this afternoon...

'Only you, Dizzy,' Christi said affectionately, glancing indulgently at the back of the car, where Kate sat cuddling Melissa as if she would never let her go again. 'Most people would have just bought her another doll, instead of driving out to get this one.'

Dizzy shook her head, her gaze on the road ahead as she drove the station-wagon. 'It wouldn't have been the same.'

'Obviously.' Christi smiled at the ecstatic Kate before settling back into her seat. 'But most people wouldn't have cared.'

'Don't make me out to be some sort of heroine, Christi,' she dismissed. 'It will simply be quieter, and your uncle will get his dinner on time in future, now that Kate has her doll.'

'This is Christi, Dizzy,' she reminded gently. 'And I know exactly how hard you aren't!'

She sighed, some of the tension leaving her body. 'I saw the painting, Christi. It's all right,' she ruefully assured, as Christi glanced anxiously into the back of the car. 'Kate's fallen asleep. Apparently she was awake most of the night, crying for her doll.' And, like the little angel she was, she had fallen into an exhausted sleep now that she had her beloved doll back.

'Little love,' Christi murmured indulgently before straightening in her seat, her face full of concern as she looked at Dizzy. 'I thought you probably would have seen the painting by now, but I didn't know how to bring the subject up,' she grimaced.

'You haven't heard the worst of it,' she frowned. 'Your uncle walked in while I was looking at it.'

'Oh, lord,' Christi groaned. 'Did he realise the little girl was you?' Her eyes were wide.

'She isn't me,' Dizzy grated with feeling. 'She's a figment of my mother's—Valerie Sherman's,' she amended tightly, 'imagination.'

Christi gave her a sideways glance. 'You've still made no effort to see her?'

'Why should I want to see her?' she dismissed coldly.

Christi shrugged. 'She is your mother.'

'You know,' Dizzy said thoughtfully, her eyes pained, 'I think your uncle may be right about it sometimes being kinder to be cruel. I know I would have found it easier to understand—and accept—if my father had told me my mother had died and wasn't coming back, rather than the truth, that she just couldn't stand living with either of us any more!' Even now, all these years later, she couldn't keep the bitterness out of her voice.

'I'm sure that can't be the way it happened, Dizzy——'

'What other explanation do you give for her walking out and leaving me with the monster I

called Father?' she attacked, her hands tensely
clutching the steering wheel, her gaze fixed firmly
ahead.

'None,' Christi sighed defeatedly.

'And to think the great British public go out at
election time and vote for him in their thousands.'
Dizzy shook her head. 'The wonder of it is, he's
actually *good* at being an MP; there's even talk of
him being successful when the leadership of the
party comes up again.'

'Maybe you should write one of those exposé
books like all the other kids of famous... Maybe
you shouldn't!' Christi backed down ruefully as
Dizzy looked at her with raised brows. 'As you say,
he's very capable when it comes to his job,' she
added hastily. 'It's just that at being a father he
falls flat on his face!'

Dizzy's attention returned to the road. 'Not every
parent can love their child,' she said flatly.

'How can a father help but love a child like that?'
Christi looked affectionately at the sleeping Kate
in the back of the car. 'And you were much cuter
as a little girl: lovely blonde curls, big green eyes,
and freckles,' she defended.

Dizzy self-consciously touched the golden
freckles that covered the bridge of her nose today.
'Suffice it to say, my father found it impossible to
love me,' she dismissed without emotion. She didn't
know how it was possible to feel that way about
your own child, either, especially when that child
loved you so unquestioningly, but she had come to
terms years ago with the fact that *her* father totally
rejected her love.

Christi leant her ebony head against the head-rest. 'I think that's partly why I'm so particular when it comes to the man I'm going to marry,' she remarked thoughtfully. 'You really have to care about the same things, want the same things, or you just end up hurting people besides yourselves.'

Dizzy gave her a smile of affection. 'Maybe you should get your dates to fill out a questionnaire before you even consider going out with them!'

'Or put an advertisement in a newspaper stating my own likes and dislikes, and the things I would like in the man I fall in love with,' Christi laughed, easily falling in with the teasing, relieved that the tension of the conversation had passed.

Dizzy's eyes widened. 'Can you do things like that? I thought it was only certain magazines that—well——'

'Not *those* sort of things!' Christi giggled. 'And I'm sure there must be some respectable publication that could deal with it. Although,' she frowned thoughtfully, 'I can't say I've ever seen one,' she admitted disappointedly.

Dizzy gave her friend a rueful smile. 'Wouldn't it be easier to go to one of those dating agencies, where they feed all the relevant information into a computer, and——'

'And come up with the man most compatible to you that they have on their files?' Christi finished disgustedly. 'Advertising in a magazine would be better,' she said, having shaken her head. 'It would reach a much wider audience. If you chose your publication wisely, of course.'

'*Playboy?*' Dizzy arched innocent brows.

'Certainly not,' her friend said indignantly. 'Can you imagine the sort of replies you would get from an advertisement in *there*?'

Laughter glowed in Dizzy's eyes. 'Might be interesting to find out,' she said mischievously.

'Wouldn't it just?' Christi agreed with anticipation. 'Seriously, though, Dizzy——'

'I've always had an aversion to conversations that begin, "seriously, Dizzy",' she winced.

Christi gave her a chiding look. 'You won't sidetrack me with your flippancy,' she warned. 'Your friends, all of us, are worried about you. I mean, talk about the sublime to the ridiculous!' she added ruefully. '*I* have too many boyfriends, and *you* steer clear of having any!'

Ordinarily, Dizzy would have been able to fence off this conversation with comments like she 'had yet to find a man that interested her to that extreme', or she 'was perfectly happy with her life the way that it was'. But since coming to Castle Haven she wasn't sure either of those comments was true any more. She found Zach Bennett not only interesting but exciting, physically and mentally, and with that awareness had come a certain dissatisfaction with the emptiness of her life. Because she wasn't comfortable with any of those emotions, she kept putting off thinking about them, which was a little difficult when she was seeing so much of Zach.

She smiled brightly as she saw Christi watching her curiously, hoping to divert her friend's attention, but knowing she had failed when Christi turned in her seat determinedly.

'Or are you still?' she pounced. 'Tell me, Dizzy, is there someone in London?'

'No,' she answered with some relief.

'New York?'

'No.'

'Toronto?' Christi persisted.

'No,' she laughed.

Her friend's mouth set stubbornly. *'Anywhere?'* she said desperately.

She hesitated only briefly over the fourth denial, but she could see by the speculative gleam in Christi's eyes that she had noticed it—and was relishing it! 'It's nothing serious, Christi——'

'Just having you admit to being *interested* in someone is serious,' Christi refuted. 'Who is he? What does he do? Are you——'

'Enough,' Dizzy cut in laughingly. 'It really isn't anything,' she dismissed lightly. 'I've only *noticed* him. It certainly hasn't been reciprocated, in that way, at least,' she added ruefully, remembering just how Zach was being led to think about her!

'Oh,' Christi looked disappointed. 'Although the fact that you *have* noticed him is something.' She brightened a little. 'It's all right having all these godchildren, Dizzy,' she reproved. 'But you need children of your own.'

'I've barely noticed the man, and you have me married off with children!' she spluttered indignantly. 'Remind me never to confide in you again,' she said disgustedly. 'When *you* manage to find Mr Right, maybe I'll start thinking about it. In the meantime, concentrate on your own lovelife,' she advised firmly.

'Spoilsport!' Christi pouted.

She couldn't help smiling. 'Remember, once you fall in love, I'll start thinking about it,' she teased softly.

'You make me sound so fickle,' Christi sulked. 'There's a man out there for me somewhere, I just have to go out and find him. Once this inheritance nonsense is out of the way, and my career is firmly established, I'm going to do just that!' she announced defiantly.

Dizzy grinned. 'That gives me at least a couple of years, then!'

'Very funny,' her friend derided with sarcasm. 'You never know, I could finish Drama School and walk straight out into a wonderful part that gives me instant stardom!'

'I hope you do, love,' Dizzy told her with quiet sincerity. 'I know how hard you've worked for it, how difficult it was to make the change into acting in the first place.'

'Mummy and Daddy would have been proud of me,' Christi said quietly.

They would have, too. Michael and Diana Bennett had believed that life was to be lived the way you wanted it to be, not the way society decided it should. Having spent more of her formative years with the happy couple than with her own father, she had quickly come to learn that their philosophy on life was a true one: be true to yourself and others. Michael and Diana would have been pleased that Christi was doing what she really felt was right for her.

'Let's not get maudlin,' Christi announced into the sudden silence that had fallen over the car, as they both indulged in affectionate memories of her parents. 'Kate has her doll back, you have a secret love——'

'He isn't secret——' She broke off her indignant denial as she saw the teasing in Christi's eyes. 'Remind me never to play poker with you,' she muttered ruefully.

'*I* don't happen to know any illegal gambling clubs,' Christi announced innocently.

'You introduced me to Jason in the first place,' Dizzy reminded her indignantly.

'He never took *me* to illegal gambling clubs. Come to think of it,' she frowned, '*why* didn't he?'

'Probably because he knows you can't keep a secret,' Dizzy teased.

'You would be surprised,' her friend announced haughtily.

She gave her an indulgent smile. 'I would?'

'Yes.' Christi turned to her eagerly. 'There's something about——' She broke off as she saw Dizzy's teasing expression. 'You tricked me!' she accused.

Dizzy laughed softly. 'Only a little.'

'Well, don't,' her friend complained. 'Uncle Zach would be furious if he realised that *I* know, let alone that I've told anyone else!'

Dizzy had tensed just at the mention of Zach's name, and now that she realised Christi had been about to confide something about him she wished she hadn't teased her about it. She had a burning curiosity to know all there was to know about Zachariah Bennett.

One thing she did know about him: it was almost two-thirty, the usual time Christi had said her uncle went off to do his bird-watching. It was hotter today than it had been yesterday, and she didn't doubt that Zach was once again at the lake, indulging in a naked swim . . .

CHAPTER SIX

'JUST what sort of unfeeling monster do the two of you think I am?'

Dizzy and Christi both looked up with a start as Zach strode furiously into the lounge where they were both waiting for him before dinner.

It was the first time Dizzy had seen him since their conversation in the library that morning, having used a walk with Christi this afternoon to keep herself from the magnetic pull going to the lake to watch Zach had for her.

As far as she knew, Christi hadn't seen her uncle since this morning, either, and from the puzzled look her friend was shooting her she had no more idea of the reason for Zach's anger than Dizzy did.

Her gaze returned to Zach, loving the springy softness of his hair as it dried in the loose waves even the shortness of the style wasn't able to deter. Once again he wore the black evening suit and a white shirt, and once again his magnificent virility shone above the ill-fitting clothes. She couldn't understand why Christi wasn't able to see just how attractive he was; he was becoming more and more so to her by the hour!

'What did you think I was going to do when I found out Mrs Scott's daughter had had an emergency operation and that her granddaughter was staying here with her?' he rasped at their puzzled expressions. 'Throw them both out into the street?'

Christi's face cleared, and she turned to give Dizzy a rueful grimace before answering her uncle. 'Of course not, Uncle Zach,' she soothed. 'Mrs Scott seemed to be handling the situation, and I— we, believed Fredericks would have told you about it if he believed it was important,' she added triumphantly as the thought obviously just occurred to her.

Zach didn't look impressed by the claim. 'Fredericks obviously *didn't* feel it was important,' he bit out abruptly. 'But Mrs Scott is full of the fact that my niece and Miss James have been taking care of her granddaughter for her today, that the two of you even drove thirty miles to Kate's home so that she could be reunited with her favourite doll!'

'That was——'

'—Christi's idea,' Dizzy put in softly, shooting her friend a silencing look as she gave a sudden frown. 'A very thoughtful and kind one, considering that Kate was so upset about not having the doll with her.' She smiled approvingly at Christi.

'Oh, but——'

'Don't you think so, Zach?' she prompted him, giving Christi another warning glance.

'Very,' he snapped. 'And I'm sure Mrs Scott appreciated it as much as the child did.' His expression softened as he looked at his niece. 'But,' he added in a controlled voice, 'if either of you had taken the trouble to tell me about the domestic difficulty Mrs Scott was having, I would have given *her* the time off to see to her granddaughter and go to the hospital to visit her daughter.'

And it was because they hadn't that he obviously considered they believed him to be 'some sort of monster'!

Since he was Mrs Scott's employer, someone probably should have told him about little Kate. Christi still seemed to be floundering under the surprise of hearing herself described as the 'Good Samaritan', so she wasn't going to be much help in explanations just yet!

'We all managed perfectly well, without having to worry you,' Dizzy placated. 'This way, Christi and I kept busy, Mrs Scott felt free to take care of your needs, knowing her granddaughter was in Christi's more than capable hands——' again Christi frowned at being given the praise for that deed '—and I don't think anyone can doubt Kate's happiness,' she rushed on.

'Probably not,' Zach acknowledged abruptly. 'Is it my imagination, or did "master of my own home" seem to get forgotten among all this organising?' He arched questioning brows.

Dizzy suddenly felt on safer ground, sure that over the years she had become an expert on trying to placate an indignant male. 'You're such a busy person, Zach,' she said warmly. 'None of us wanted to interrupt your work by bothering you with this trivial problem.'

His eyes were cold as he looked at her. 'I doubt Mrs Scott's daughter considered it trivial.'

'No—well——'

'Or Kate last night, as she cried at the strangeness of her surroundings. Or Mrs Scott, as she tried to comfort her,' he bit out with controlled violence.

This wasn't going at all as she had planned; usually she only had to simper and tell her father how important she realised his work was, and he would become so lost in his own self-importance he would forget what the lecture had been about. Obviously Zach was made of much sterner stuff. Or, more likely, he wasn't so full of himself that he didn't have time for other people's feelings. She was sure that both of those things were true about Zach; he wasn't about to be side-tracked by effusive compliments about his work, and he obviously cared for other people very much, as much angered by the misery he might have averted if he had known of Mrs Scott's predicament as he was by the fact that no one had chosen to tell him. She didn't doubt that, if he had known, he would have given Mrs Scott the time off to go and stay with Kate at her own home rather than having the little girl come here, where nothing was familiar to her. No doubt the cook herself would have realised that, if she hadn't been in such a panic after yesterday's emergency.

'It wasn't a deliberate omission on anyone's part, I'm sure,' Dizzy shrugged uncomfortably.

'It was just that no one thought I would be interested!' Zach rasped.

She grimaced. 'Yes. I mean—no. I mean——'

He drew in an impatient breath, turning to his niece. 'Is that what you thought, too?'

Christi frowned. 'I——'

'Of course it isn't,' Dizzy defended, aware that Christi was fast losing ground in her uncle's esteem. 'Christi——'

'—is perfectly able to answer for herself,' Zach finished firmly. 'Do you have anything to say, Christi?' His voice softened a little as he spoke to her.

Her head went back. 'Yes, I do.' She looked at Dizzy before turning back to her uncle. 'We didn't commit any crime, Uncle Zach, unless it was by omission,' she defended firmly. 'At the time, we were more concerned with Kate than your possible hurt feelings.'

Dizzy stared at her friend in amazement. She didn't need anyone to tell her what was happening, after all the years she had known Christi she knew that, although slow to anger, when Christi reached a saturation point she nevertheless bubbled over. And she was fast approaching that point when it came to impressing her uncle with her maturity and kindness. Dizzy was aware that taking the credit for collecting Kate's doll had probably contributed to it; although Christi didn't mind having a little fun at her uncle's expense, she found the subject of Kate's distress too serious to be played around with.

So did she! But thoughtfulness towards a child hardly fitted in with the selfish drifter she was supposed to be!

Zach looked slightly taken aback by the attack, gently made as it was, and then his expression softened. 'You're right,' he sighed. 'The important thing is that the situation has been resolved to everyone's satisfaction. And Kate was definitely looking bright enough when I saw her in the kitchen just now,' he added indulgently.

'I knew you would understand, Uncle Zach.' Christi gave him a spontaneous hug, grinning up at him affectionately as she pulled back.

Dizzy watched with longing as Christi did easily what she had longed to do since the moment she had first seen Zach, what she had also been fighting against in an agony of doubt and confusion.

Over the years she had chosen her friends well, felt able to relax and share affection with them, but falling in love with a man was a different matter altogether, involved a commitment she had sworn never to make to any man. These feelings she had, to lose herself in Zach's arms, were as frightening as they were unsettling.

'Speaking of kitchens,' he was telling Christi now, 'as I've given Mrs Scott the rest of the evening off so that she can spend it with Kate, we have the little problem of who is to serve up the supper she has left prepared for us. I thought the two of you could do it,' he told them blandly.

The two women burst out laughing at his totally innocent expression, Christi hugging him again.

'You're just a big softie, after all,' she chuckled indulgently.

Blond brows rose over honey-brown eyes. 'Did you have some reason to suppose I wasn't?'

'No, of course not,' Christi denied instantly. 'Come on, Dizzy,' she added briskly. 'Let's go and see to the food before it spoils.'

Mrs Scott might have been given the evening off by her employer, but she hadn't gone until the soup, chicken dinner and dessert had been prepared. There was little for Dizzy and Christi to do except put the food into the vegetable dishes, ready for Fredericks to bring into the dining-room for them.

'That was a close thing,' Dizzy remarked as she strained the vegetables over the sink. 'I thought you were going to lose your temper just now,' she explained at Christi's questioning look.

'So did I,' her friend grimaced. 'I know why you gave me the credit about Kate's doll.' She held up her hands defensively. 'But I wasn't comfortable with it; I suddenly wasn't comfortable with the whole situation,' she admitted ruefully. 'Uncle Zach's a strange one.' She shook her head. 'I just think I have him taped, and he shows me yet another side of his character.'

'He was certainly angry at not being told about Mrs Scott's daughter,' Dizzy replied non-committally, not willing to get into a discussion about how fascinating *she* found the different facets of Zach's nature!

Christi grinned. 'Not so angry he couldn't make a joke about giving us this work to do.' She placed the last of the serving bowls in the food warmer. 'I know one thing,' she announced with satisfaction as they left the kitchen together. 'I've certainly been proven correct about there never being a dull moment when you're about! So far we've spent the day chasing after a doll, taken over the castle kitchen for the evening, and you've had the *strangest* effect on——'

'Yes?' Dizzy prompted sharply as she broke off abruptly, Christi's eyes wide as she looked at her as if she had never seen her before. 'Christi!' she prompted with suspicion. 'What is it?'

Christi gave a start of surprise at having her train of thought interrupted, shaking her head as she gave a sudden, overly bright smile. 'Nothing,' she dismissed, a little too lightly for Dizzy's peace of mind. 'Shall we rejoin my uncle?'

Dizzy didn't like it when Christi became secretive; it usually meant she was up to something. 'Christi,' she began warningly, 'you——'

'Fredericks is ready to serve the soup,' her friend prompted, as the butler appeared in the corridor behind them with the tureen.

Dizzy gave her a look that promised this wasn't the end of the subject. Her uneasiness increased as Christi seemed to be watching her closely through dinner.

She deliberately kept her conversation light, although she noticed that Christi stayed pretty much out of that, too, leaving it up to Dizzy and Zach to keep the conversation flowing.

By the end of the meal, Dizzy was feeling decidedly uneasy by Christi's preoccupied expression. Her friend was plotting something, and this time she wanted to know what it was before she was thrown *into* the situation.

'I don't know what you're talking about,' Christi denied, after Dizzy had followed her to her bedroom and demanded to know what was going on.

'Christi——'

'It was pretty decent of Uncle Zach to help with the washing up like that,' Christi commented as she unzipped her dress.

It had been a little too cosy in the kitchen, with the three of them doing the washing up, for Dizzy's peace of mind, but she had to agree that it had been a pleasant surprise when Zach had offered to help them. If it had been *her* father in that situation, he wouldn't have given Mrs Scott the evening off in the first place, let alone helped do some of the work.

But she hadn't needed Zach's show of kindness to know he was nothing like her father, she had known that instinctively. It was the commitment of a relationship that she feared, rather than the man himself.

Her father hadn't remarried after his divorce from her mother, and when she was older Dizzy had secretly wondered if that weren't because the role of a wronged man who had never got over the loss of his wife was considered rather appealing to the electorate. Maybe she was being unfair to him because of her own feelings of resentment towards him, but she had known he hadn't felt her mother's betrayal enough not to have had a succession of quietly discreet affairs over the years. As for her mother, if newspaper reports of her life were to be believed, each successive lover was younger than the last. They would soon be younger than Dizzy herself!

Being brought up in a background like that didn't make for a trust in everlasting love. Even the happy marriages of several of her friends could not change years of mistrusting the sort of love that left one open to pain and disillusionment.

Knowing how close she was to feeling that sort of love for Zach Bennett, she should be running away from here as fast as her legs would carry her.

But instead she stayed, and it wasn't just for Christi's benefit, either.

'Very nice of him,' she answered Christi's comment. 'But stop changing the subject and tell me what you're plotting in that devious little mind of yours.'

Christi gave a pained frown. 'I think I take exception to the "little" part of that.'

'You're up to something.' Dizzy wasn't to be diverted. 'And I want to know what it is!'

She wasn't at all reassured by Christi's look of pained innocence at the accusation.

'All right.' She dropped the act as Dizzy simply continued to look at her. 'But I'm not up to anything, or planning anything. In fact, this development could completely ruin everything for me,' she added ruefully, but without too much real distress, as if the price she had to pay was worth it.

Dizzy tensed, looking at her friend warily. 'What do you mean?'

Christi's face was full of affection, her blue eyes softened with love. 'You and Uncle Zach are so aware of each other, the air simply crackled with it tonight at dinner,' she said softly.

Fiery colour burnt Dizzy's cheeks. 'What non- sense!' she finally managed to splutter. But it wasn't; as she and Zach had talked tonight she had been fully aware of him, and Christi had just con- firmed that she hadn't imagined Zach's response to her.

Christi squeezed her hand. 'We can't let him go on thinking those things about you, love——'

'You really are imagining things, Christi.' She deliberately made her voice lightly scoffing. 'The fusty, dusty professor and me!' She shook her head as if Christi had gone slightly insane.

Her friend looked unmoved by the act. 'How long did you continue to think of him as fusty and dusty?' she gently chided.

She never had; how could she when her first sight of him had been as he swam naked only feet away from her?

Her guilty blush gave her away. 'All right, so I don't think of him that way,' she admitted sharply. 'But I don't think of him in connection with husband and children, either! Leave things as they are, Christi, please,' she pleaded.

'Dizzy, would you recognise love if it came up and bit you on the nose?' Christi prompted softly.

'Would *you*?' she attacked, completely on the defensive.

Her friend didn't look in the least offended. 'I've had my moments,' she shrugged. 'Nothing like the electricity flowing between you and Uncle Zach, though,' she said with satisfaction.

'I think you've been reading too many happy-ever-after stories,' Dizzy dismissed. 'Real life just isn't like that.'

'It can be,' Christi told her quietly.

'Not for me!' She strode angrily to the door. 'So please keep your matchmaking efforts to yourself!'

'All right,' her friend shrugged.

'I mean it, Christi.' She was breathing raggedly in her agitation, not trusting Christi's ready agreement one little bit. 'If you try to get your uncle and me together, I'll leave here so fast, you'll have some difficult explanations to make.'

'I said all right,' Christi said irritably, picking up her nightgown and robe, in preparation of taking a shower. 'But the two of you could be good for each—— *All right,*' she snapped frustratedly at Dizzy's furious glare. 'But don't blame me if you're passing up your one chance at love.' She slammed into the adjoining bathroom.

Dizzy left the room slowly, deeply disturbed. The last thing she would have wished for was that Christi would realise her awareness of Zach. Or accuse him of being equally aware of her! Was that really true? There was an electricity between them, that couldn't be denied, but was Zach really aware of it, too? If he was, she was surprised *he* wasn't the one running away!

Once again she had trouble sleeping after her nightly read, getting up to move restlessly about the room. She had purchased the pilchards today, and a glass of milk and something to nibble on might have helped her to relax enough to sleep, but after her conversation with Christi, and what had happened last night, she was loath to venture downstairs. Her defences were a little dented tonight, and if Zach should come down again... She dared not risk it.

Instead, she sat in front of one of the windows and looked out at the mountains and lakes that were clearly visible in the bright moonlight, hoping to gain some relaxation from their soothing presence, but finding the memories of the lake she tried to keep her gaze averted from too disturbing.

How long she had been sitting there when the gentle knock sounded on the door she had no idea, but she knew it had to be very late—or very early, as Zach had pointed out the night before. Damn, he was in her thoughts so much now, she was even starting to refer to his comments and opinions.

She almost fell over with shock when she opened the door to find him standing there!

She had been expecting it to be Christi, believing her friend couldn't sleep either. Instead it was Zach, dressed just as he had been last night, and he was carrying a tray.

He smiled as her gaze rose shyly from the milk and biscuits on the tray to his face. 'I'm afraid I just couldn't bring myself to open the tin of pilchards,' he teased softly, as he carried the tray into the room and placed it on the side of the dressing-table Dizzy quickly cleared. Then he turned to face her, his hands thrust into the pockets of his robe.

'I didn't expect—you didn't have to bring me this.' She shook her head dazedly, even more disturbed by his presence in her bedroom than she had been at being caught in the kitchen last night.

He shrugged. 'I saw a light under your door and, remembering how you couldn't sleep last night . . .'

She couldn't take this. Her friends were kind, always considerate, but they understood that she needed to be alone sometimes, and they never intruded. No one had *ever* brought her milk and biscuits in bed because they knew she couldn't sleep.

The tears weren't welcome and she cursed them, but she couldn't stop them.

Zach's rueful smile faded as he saw the well of tears she wasn't quick enough to hide, and he looked suddenly alarmed. 'If you really want the pilchards, I could——'

'I don't want the pilchards,' she choked with a watery smile. 'I want—I want——' She looked up at him beseechingly.

He drew in a ragged breath, then took a step towards her, hesitating slightly before his arms came around her and drew her fiercely against him. 'Oh, God, how I've wanted this too!' he groaned into the softness of her fly-away hair. 'Dizzy!' he breathed softly, as if he couldn't believe this was happening.

Dizzy didn't believe it was happening either, their hearts thundering loudly together in the silence of the room, their arms about each other as not even a wisp of air could come between them.

Held against him like this she could feel the hardness of the rippling muscles she had witnessed that first day, knew the strength of him, knew what it felt like to feel cherished, as if she were a fragile butterfly he had to protect.

He captured her chin as she looked up at him, staring deeply into her eyes, flames flickering in the depths of honey-brown. And then his head lowered, and his lips claimed hers.

Dizzy had never been kissed before. Whenever she went out, it was always with a crowd of friends, and the men were always as much friends as the women, treating her like 'one of the boys'. For any of them to think of her in a romantic light would have been laughable. And so, in her twenty-one years, she had never been kissed.

But she was being kissed now, and by a man who knew exactly what he was doing, if the gentle way he pulled lightly on her chin, so that her lips were open to his, was anything to go by!

Pleasure rippled through her body at the gentle movement of his mouth against hers, and she clung to the broadness of his shoulders as the caress deepened.

The kiss went on and on, and she literally *felt* dizzy by the time Zach's mouth moved to her cheek and then down to her throat, nuzzling against the silky skin there as Dizzy quivered with response, her senses heightened to fever-pitch. She had never felt so alive, so—so sensitised, trembling as Zach's hands caressed her back and sides in rhythmic motions.

'Dizzy, I——' Whatever he had been about to say was cut off by the sound of an eerie scream echoing up the stairway and bouncing off the walls.

'Kate!' Dizzy tensed, her face flushed as she pulled out of Zach's arms, unable to meet his gaze as she moved away from him. 'She must have had a nightmare. I—I have to go to her.'

Zach straightened, the flames dying in his eyes, a frown to his brow as if he, too, were puzzled at what had just happened between him and the unwanted guest of his niece. His mouth tightened. 'Of course,' he nodded tersely. 'I'll come down with you.'

'No!' She swallowed hard at the scowl that settled on his brow. 'I—of course you must come down—if you want to.' She moved jerkily to the door, still shaking very badly.

He nodded again. 'I want to,' he bit out.

Dizzy preceded him out of the room, amazed that her legs could support her. She gave a rueful glance at Christi's closed bedroom door; her friend might like to go to bed late, but once she was asleep it would take the house falling down to wake her before she was ready!

She was very conscious of Zach just behind her all the way down the stairs and through to Kate's room. The little girl could be heard sobbing quietly now, and Mrs Scott looked grateful to see Dizzy when she entered after a brief knock, although the poor cook looked more than a little disconcerted when her employer entered the room directly behind Dizzy. Clasping her nightgown to her buxom figure, she put up a self-conscious hand to the rollers in her hair.

'Dizzy!' As soon as Kate saw her she pulled out of her grandmother's arms and launched herself at Dizzy. 'I want my mummy,' she sobbed, her arms tightly clasped about Dizzy's neck.

Dizzy spoke to her softly, reminding her that her mother was in the hospital, getting well again, but that her daddy would be here tomorrow to take care of her.

All the time she spoke to the distressed child she was aware of Zach as he stood across the room. He had come to an abrupt halt in the doorway, as if realising his presence here was more than a little unexpected. He frowned as he watched her holding and soothing Kate.

Mrs Scott had managed to pull on her robe, obviously still uncomfortable with the intimacy of the situation, but doing her best not to show it. 'I hope we didn't wake you both.' She sounded flustered. 'She just woke up screaming,' she apologised lamely.

'It's all very strange for her,' Zach excused softly, his hands thrust into the pockets of his robe, his hair falling rakishly over his forehead in golden waves.

Dizzy blushed as she remembered the way her hands had run through the softness of that hair only minutes earlier. She turned quickly away as she realised he had evaded answering Mrs Scott's query about having woken them, although she doubted it had crossed the other woman's mind that the two of them might have been awake *together*!

Dizzy was doing her best to pretend it had never happened, and she was sure Zach felt the same way about it—that the lateness of the hour and the intimacy of her bedroom had brought about the situation. In future, she would make sure the light didn't show under her door when she lay awake at night!

Kate's sobs quietened as she held her, and she was relieved to see tired lids drooping over the deep blue eyes.

Suddenly Kate jerked herself wide awake, her arms tightening about Dizzy once again. 'Stay with me,' she pleaded brokenly.

'Of course, darling,' she assured her unhesitatingly. 'Nanny and I will both be here.' She looked up as she saw a movement out of the corner of her eye, realising by the tension in Zach's body that he had taken the remark to be a dismissal. And he looked far from pleased about it! She hadn't actually meant it that way, had meant only to reassure Kate, but after what had happened between them a short time ago it would be a relief to have his presence removed. Her head went back defensively. 'I'm sure we can manage here, Professor,' she told him with quiet firmness. 'If you would like to get back to bed...'

He seemed about to say something, and then obviously changed his mind, nodding abruptly. 'But I'd like to see you in the morning, Dizzy.' He spoke softly but, nevertheless, the fact that he would brook no argument to his request was clearly apparent.

She swallowed hard. 'Yes. Of course.'

'In the library. At ten o'clock,' he added precisely.

'Not in the library!' She blushed at the unmistakable vehemence of her tone, although she was relieved to see she hadn't woken Kate. But Zach and Mrs Scott were giving her frowning looks, and she made a concerted effort to relax herself. 'I have a horror of all those books.' She was deliberately flippant. 'I'd prefer to talk over a cup of coffee in the lounge.'

Despite his incongruous appearance, Zach was every inch the professor at the moment, as remote and disapproving as he had been when Christi introduced the two of them the day before yesterday. God, was it really only then? So much seemed to have happened since then.

'Very well,' he agreed distantly. 'Goodnight, ladies,' he added with a slight softening of his expression as he looked at Mrs Scott.

'Oh, dear,' the cook groaned, once she and Dizzy were alone with the sleeping Kate, Dizzy settling the little girl back on the pillows before tucking the bedclothes in around her. 'I hope he isn't too angry about all this.' She looked worried.

Dizzy straightened. 'He isn't angry at all,' she assured with certainty, knowing Zach *wasn't* angry about Kate's having woken up in this way. His feelings concerning what had happened in her bedroom a short time ago were, however, a different matter altogether! No doubt he wanted to see her in the morning so that he could tell her succinctly that he would not appreciate her telling Christi what had taken place between them. He needn't worry about that; telling Christi was the last thing on her mind! 'Now you get some sleep,' she soothed the older woman gently. 'You need your rest after being awake most of last night. I'll just sit with Kate for a while, if you don't mind.'

Mrs Scott looked down lovingly at the angelic little girl, her dark hair splayed out across the pillow as she slept. 'I don't think there's any need now,' she spoke softly. 'I'm sure she'll sleep until morning.'

'I'd like to sit with her for a while, if I'm not intruding?'

'Of course not,' the cook smiled. 'Promises mean so much to children, don't they?' she said understandingly. 'But I think I will just try and snatch a few hours' sleep, if that's all right?'

'I'd rather you did,' she smiled encouragingly. 'I'll just sit beside Kate until I'm sure she's going to stay asleep.'

She knew by the even breathing several minutes later that the exhausted cook had gone back to sleep, relaxing slightly herself now that she didn't have to put on that cheerful act for anybody.

Mrs Scott was right, promises did mean so much to children, and she had had far too many of them broken when she was a child not to appreciate how hurtful it was when an adult let you down. And she had no intention of being guilty of that herself.

Besides, she had no wish to return to her bedroom just yet, for she was hoping that, by the time she did return, her time in Zach's arms would all seem like a dream.

But when she returned to her bedroom several hours later, she knew that it hadn't been. The cold milk and biscuits that stood on her dressing-table reminded her all too vividly that it had really happened.

And a few hours from now she was going to have to face Zach across the lounge and pretend she had been as unaffected by it as he was...

CHAPTER SEVEN

'BUT what does he want to talk to you about?' Christi persisted.

The two of them were eating a late breakfast together and, although Dizzy hadn't relished telling her friend about her appointment with Zach this morning, she had realised it had to be done.

She had told Christi about Kate waking up the night before, how both she and Zach had gone down to investigate, what she hadn't told her friend was that she and Zach had been together in her bedroom when they had heard Kate cry! Without that relevant piece of information, his asking to see her this morning seemed slightly out of context.

'Maybe he's thinking of asking me to take over full-time as cook, while Mrs Scott goes off to take care of her family?' she teased. 'At least I'd be earning my keep!'

'I hate it when you're flippant,' Christi reproved gently.

Dizzy shrugged unconcernedly. 'Well, then, maybe he wants to ask me to leave so that there's one less mouth to cater for.'

'I don't believe that.' Christi shook her head, looking very beautiful in the rich blue sun-dress that perfectly matched the colour of her eyes. Next to her, in her denims and green vest-top, Dizzy felt less attractive than she usually did!

She sipped her coffee. 'Then I'm as much in the dark as you are,' she dismissed, not quite truthfully, for she was sure that last night in her bedroom would enter into the conversation *somewhere*.

Christi chewed on her bottom lip, uncaring of the fact that the act removed her lipgloss. 'Maybe I should have a word with him——'

'No!' Dizzy drew in a steadying breath as Christi looked at her sharply for her outburst. She really would have to calm down, or Christi would have the truth out of her, and then there would be no stopping the other woman from her matchmaking! 'I'm sure it's nothing important,' she said brightly.

Christi gave her a suspicious frown, but she didn't pressure her any further. 'I shall expect a full report when you're through,' she warned, as Dizzy went off to keep her appointment.

She hesitated outside the lounge. She knew Zach was in there, because Mrs Scott had just performed her last duty before she and Kate went off to meet her son-in-law at the airport, the coffee just waiting in the lounge for Dizzy to go in and pour it.

She straightened her shoulders and took a deep breath, before firmly opening the door and entering the room, faltering only slightly as Zach looked up at her without the screen of his glasses to lessen the impact of those beautiful honey-brown eyes.

The baggy tweed jacket was back today, with an open-necked shirt that didn't look as if he had slept in it—something she knew he didn't do, anyway— and a pair of neatly pressed brown trousers. The clothes still didn't fit him that well, but they were an improvement on that first day.

Dizzy's heart skipped a beat as her gaze once more returned to his face, affected as she usually was by the male perfection she found there.

She tensed as he crossed the room towards her, watching him warily as he firmly removed her hand from the door and closed it behind her.

His mouth twisted as he looked down and saw her apprehension. 'Come and sit down, Dizzy,' he invited softly. 'I don't bite. Although perhaps you can't be too sure of that after last night.' His gaze shifted to the lobe of her ear before quickly moving away again.

Dizzy felt a quiver down her spine as she remembered the ecstasy of having him nibble on her earlobe. She hadn't known there could be such pleasure from such a simple act.

'Come and have some coffee,' Zach prompted as he saw her uncertainty, gently touching her arm.

At the first touch of his fingers against her bare flesh she moved into uncoordinated action, almost running across the room to sit on the sofa in front of the coffee tray.

Zach followed more slowly, a deep frown between his eyes. 'Dizzy——'

'Coffee?' she suggested sharply.

He sighed, thrusting his hands into his trouser pockets. 'Maybe it would help ease the tension a little,' he nodded slowly.

Tension? What did he have to feel tense about? Dizzy wondered dazedly. *She* had been the one to turn a simple gesture of friendship into something neither of them were comfortable with. She should have just accepted the tray of milk and biscuits and let Zach go back to his own room, not looked at him with such longing that he had felt compelled to take her into his arms!

'Thanks.' He accepted the cup of coffee she handed him, walking over to the window. He turned suddenly, as if he had just come to a decision. 'I realise I owe you an apology for last night,' he bit out abruptly. 'But, somehow, in the circumstances, an apology doesn't seem enough.' He looked grim.

Dizzy sat back in puzzled surprise. *He* owed *her* an apology?

Zach shook his head self-disgustedly. 'You're a guest in my home,' he rasped. 'I had no right to take advantage of your situation here.'

Take advantage? She had almost been begging him to make love to her last night!

'I'm not surprised that you don't feel you have anything to say to me.' He put his untouched coffee cup back on the tray with controlled violence. 'I'm pretty disgusted with myself right now,' he bit out grimly. 'I can only apologise again, and hope that you'll believe me when I say it won't happen again.'

Dizzy was still speechless; this was the last thing she had been expecting when she had kept this meeting with him this morning. She had thought it might be somewhere nearer what she had teasingly told Christi: that he wanted to ask her to leave. She just didn't know what to say.

'That's all I had to say,' Zach told her abruptly, moving awkwardly to the door. 'Please believe it won't happen again,' he said again before leaving the room, closing the door behind him, as if to give her a few moments' privacy.

She blinked dazedly, realising that during the whole conversation all she had said was 'Coffee?'.

Zach had apologised for kissing her. He wasn't angry with her, didn't believe she had deliberately encouraged him, as she had been afraid that he would. It was incredible, unbelievable, but he had taken full responsibility for those kisses.

For the first time, she allowed herself to remember what he had said just before he kissed her, how he had 'wanted it, too'. He really had wanted to kiss and caress her, long before last night in her bedroom?

As far as she knew, no man had ever wanted to kiss her before, let alone apologised afterwards for taking advantage of her.

Had Zach *really* wanted it as badly as she had? It put a whole new aspect on their relationship if he had. Zach had been hurt in the past, too, a different sort of hurt, but he had known the pain of losing someone he loved, and stayed away from involvement since that time. But last night he had taken a chance on her, had allowed her to see the emotions behind the man. It was going to be up to her to make the next move. If there was a next move...

'Well?' Christi burst unannounced into the room, her face alight with curiosity. 'Uncle Zach went to his study ages ago. I've been waiting for you to come and tell me what he said!' she complained as she threw herself into the chair opposite Dizzy.

She smiled. 'What were you doing, lurking about in the hallway, waiting for him to leave?'

'Nice. Very nice,' Christi drawled with sarcasm. 'Actually, I was "lurking about" in the dining-room,' she admitted ruefully.

Dizzy chuckled. 'At least you're honest about it.' And she wasn't about to be quite so honest, for if she told Christi the truth there would be no stopping her! 'Your uncle just wanted to check that everything went all right last night with Kate,' she invented lightly.

'Is that all?' Christi looked disappointed. 'I imagined him inviting you out to dinner, at least.'

Dizzy gave her a chiding look. 'Is that very likely?'

Christi grinned. 'Considering the state of our catering situation, yes! He could have offered to take us both out: I don't mind doing breakfast and lunch, but it would have been nice to go out for dinner.'

'For your information, Fredericks has arranged for an agency to send along a cook until Mrs Scott can come back here,' she told her drily.

'I still think Uncle Zach could have taken us both out for dinner,' Christi said wistfully. 'Do you suppose that when the two of you are married he'll let me just call him Zach?' she added with a sideways glance at Dizzy.

After her outrageous suggestions last night, Dizzy was ready for her, and answered calmly, 'When Zach and I are married the sky will be green!'

Christi was unperturbed. 'I mean, I have no intention of calling my best friend "Aunt"!'

Dizzy shook her head. 'You're incorrigible.'

Her friend smiled confidently. 'I'm determined.'

'Christi,' she sobered, 'don't interfere in this, hm?'

'Too important?' her friend prompted gently.

'Too delicate,' she corrected ruefully.

'I don't have to tell you that I wholeheartedly approve of the idea?' Christi told her softly.

'No.' She gave a grateful smile.

'I'll even give him away at the wedding,' Christi joked lightly, although the affection in her eyes belied the teasing.

'He doesn't have to be given away; I do.' She sighed. 'And my father would have done that years ago if he could!'

'I refuse to let you think about *him*,' Christi said firmly, standing up. 'Just remember that none of your friends would ever willingly lose your friendship. Especially me.'

'So you won't do anything to make things awkward for Zach and me?' she prompted beseechingly.

'I'll be the model of decorum,' Christi promised. 'Just don't wait too long, hm?' she grimaced, frustrated at the restraint being put on her impulsive nature.

The lake was even more of a temptation that afternoon, as it was, Dizzy spent most of that time looking out of the window, wishing she could magic away the hill that hid the lake from her view!

Was she really ready for a relationship with Zach? It was the question she had to answer before taking things any further. And she didn't know. She just *didn't know*.

She had never believed there could be anyone for her like Zach. That instant attraction had deepened into liking and respect, into a physical awareness that made her tremble. But her mother must have felt that way about her father once, and look what had happened to that relationship! She was frightened of taking a risk on her emotions, although she was very much afraid it was already too late for that!

'Isn't this nice?' Christi announced with satisfaction, looking at them expectantly.

Despite the fact that the replacement cook had arrived at the castle that afternoon, Christi had still got her way and persuaded her uncle to take them both out to dinner. Walking down the wide stairway to meet Zach had been a little difficult for Dizzy to do after their earlier conversation, but Christi's light chatter had easily covered the moment of awkwardness, the three of them talking lightly together as they drove to the restaurant.

Nevertheless, Dizzy was very aware of Zach as he sat across the table from her, and watched his hands, because heat flooded her cheeks every time she looked into his face and found him looking right back at her. His hands were strong and tapered, the backs covered with tiny golden hairs—and oh, so sensual to watch.

Christi was matchmaking in the nicest possible way, doing nothing to force them together, but making sure they just spent time together. It was what Dizzy most needed, so that she could be sure of her feelings, and she silently thanked her friend for her tact.

It was a pleasant restaurant, cosy little tables in alcoves, subdued lighting; the sort of place for lovers to gaze across the table at each other and let their eyes talk of their love. The three of them looked a little out of place, a man alone with two young women.

'This will do wonders for your reputation, Uncle Zach,' Christi teased, seeming to pick up on her amused thoughts, not at all perturbed that neither of them had chosen to answer her earlier statement. '*Two* beautiful women!'

Zach smiled at her mischievous grin. 'I wasn't aware that my reputation needed "wonders" doing for it,' he drawled, very handsome in a dark brown suit that fitted him better than anything else Dizzy had seen him in, and a tie which was knotted meticulously at his throat. His hair had been neatly brushed back from his face when they met him in the entrance hall at the castle but, because it was still damp from his shower, and a light breeze blew outside, his hair now lay in an endearing wave across his forehead. She found everything about this man attractive, Dizzy admitted to herself in panic!

'Every man likes to have his ego boosted now and then,' Christi said with certainty.

'Taking my niece and her friend out to dinner doesn't do a thing for mine!' he returned drily.

Christi's friend—but that wasn't the only way he thought of her, Dizzy was sure of it. Tonight she was wearing the only other evening dress she carried around with her, a soft green dress that emphasised the colour of her eyes, making them look almost luminous. Zach's eyes, as he watched her descent down the stairs earlier, had told her that she was completely a woman to him, a woman he was very much aware of. Her hair had been loosely swept up on top of her head, giving her a sophistication that was usually lacking, and Zach had noticed that, too.

'Being escorted by a handsome man does a lot for mine,' Christi reproved. 'Doesn't it yours, Dizzy?'

She looked at Zach beneath lowered lashes, knowing by his embarrassed expression that he was uncomfortable with being called handsome, maybe even thought Christi was teasing him. And that would never do, not when he was the most attractive man in the room.

'Very much so,' she answered with firm sincerity, holding Zach's gaze. 'You underestimate yourself, Zach, if you think otherwise,' she told him softly.

Warmth blazed in his eyes, his gaze was deeply searching, and it was suddenly as if they were the only two people in the room, those lovers that Dizzy had imagined a few minutes ago, as they told of their feelings with their eyes. Zach's were saying he wanted her, and she was very much afraid hers were saying the same thing! And she still wasn't ready for this.

She looked away. 'It is very pleasant here,' she finally answered Christi's statement of a few minutes ago. 'Do you come here often, Zach?' she added politely, the smile on her lips distantly enquiring.

He shrugged, his gaze still intent. 'Never before, I'm afraid.'

'Uncle Zach doesn't have much of a social life usually, do you?' Christi said brightly.

Dizzy shot her friend a warning look, guessing she was trying to get Zach to admit to not being involved with anyone. She didn't know him that well, but the little she did know about him told her that he wouldn't have kissed her the way he had last night if there were another woman in his life.

'My work keeps me very busy,' he dismissed abruptly. 'I'm just a dull old professor of history, I'm afraid,' he added harshly.

'Dizzy doesn't find the subject boring at all,' Christi assured him enthusiastically. 'She has a passion for history; it was her favourite subject at school.'

Dizzy shot her a reproving look. 'I'm surprised you remember my favourite subject at school, we were never that—close,' she reminded drily.

Christi blushed as her enthusiasm for match-making overshadowed her good sense, and made her briefly forget the tale she had told before and after Dizzy's arrival in the Lake District. 'I remember *that*,' she defended awkwardly, 'because it was *my* worst subject!'

'Does anyone want any more coffee?' Dizzy affected a yawn. 'I'm a little tired after my disturbed night last night.' She deliberately kept her gaze averted from Zach, as she recalled all too vividly just how responsible he had been for the unsettling feelings.

'Mrs Scott told me that you sat with Kate for some time after I'd gone to bed,' Zach frowned.

She shrugged. 'I'd told her I would sit with her.'

'But she was asleep.'

Dizzy looked up at him. 'She could have woken up, and then she would have known I'd broken my promise to her.' In fact, she had sat with Kate until Mrs Scott began to stir at seven o'clock, only snatching a couple of hours' sleep before joining

Christi for a late breakfast, her friend having slept through the whole thing.

Zach was giving her a searching look, as if she puzzled him more than anything else he had ever experienced. 'You must be extremely tired,' he finally conceded softly, signalling for the bill.

Actually, she knew that, as with every other night, once she got to bed, no matter how tired she was, she wouldn't be able to sleep for hours yet. She had finished reading the two books she brought with her, as she had expected to be able to indulge herself in Zachariah Bennett's library. With that painting in there that was now impossible.

She accompanied Christi to the Ladies' room while Zach paid the bill, securing a couple of loose tendrils of hair while her friend renewed her make-up. Not that Christi needed the aid of much artifice, her features already perfect, her colour naturally attractive.

'You were doing very well until the end,' she finally told her friend drily.

Christi blushed. 'I was only trying to give the two of you a push in the right direction,' she said uncomfortably. 'Really, Dizzy, the man eats you up with his eyes and talks to you like a polite stranger!'

So Christi hadn't missed that burning look that had passed between them! 'It's only been three days, Christi,' she teased. 'I know patience isn't one of your virtues, but neither Zach or I are the type to leap into a relationship until we're ready for it.'

'You could have left to become a nun and he could have entered a monastery before either of you realise that you actually glow when you look at each other!' Christi said disgustedly.

Dizzy smiled. 'I have no inclination to become a nun,' she chuckled. 'And I don't think Zach has the qualifications to become a monk!'

'Really?' Christi pounced interestedly.

She blushed as she realised the trap she had fallen into. But any man who kissed like Zach did, who made her feel the way he did, couldn't possibly spend the rest of his life denying himself the 'pleasures of the flesh'. It would be a crime to himself and the vocation.

'Really,' she acknowledged drily. 'And that's all you're getting from me tonight, young lady,' she added firmly as Christi's eyes glowed with satisfaction.

'It's enough,' Christi said with glee. 'Believe me, it's enough!'

She smiled indulgently at Christi's buoyant mood as they went out to join her uncle. Even though it would spoil all Christi's plans if Dizzy and Zach did fall in love, her friend was pleased for her, not worrying about what she stood to lose. It was typical of Christi's generosity.

She watched Zach surreptitiously beneath lowered lashes on the drive back to the castle, Christi having announced, when they reached the car, that she intended 'stretching out' on the back seat, giving Dizzy no choice but to take the seat next to Zach.

With Christi sitting so quietly in the back it was almost possible to believe she and Zach were returning after a date together, that the evening would end in a lingering goodnight kiss once they reached the castle. She gave a disappointed sigh that it wasn't to be so, for she had a burning curiosity to be back in Zach's arms.

'That was a big sigh.' He turned to her briefly, smiling gently.

She glanced at Christi in the back. Her friend was giving a good impression of being asleep even if she wasn't, her eyes firmly closed as she leant back against the seat.

She turned back to Zach. 'I was thinking of last night,' she told him honestly, her voice low.

He frowned. 'Kate——'

'No—not Kate,' she said firmly.

Zach looked at her sharply, swerving the car suddenly as the movement of a rabbit in the road caught his eyes. He drew in a controlling breath after straightening the car, keeping his gaze firmly ahead. 'Not Kate?' he repeated with forced lightness.

'No,' she confirmed.

He breathed raggedly. 'Dizzy——'

'It's all right.' She put a hand on his arm. 'You don't have to say anything. They were my thoughts,' she dismissed with a shrug.

'And if mine have been the same all evening?' he bit out raspingly. 'Despite my assurances to you this morning?'

Her eyes were wide in the darkness. 'Zach?'

'Yes—Zach,' he echoed disgustedly. 'I'm too old to be having the thoughts I've been having about you! So much for my apology this morning——'

'Christi,' she reminded him softly, sure that her friend was no more asleep that she was, but she did have a ringside seat to a very personal conversation!

'Yes,' he conceded impatiently, his strong hands tightly gripping the wheel.

They lapsed into a silence that lasted until they reached the castle, Dizzy giving her friend a rueful smile as she made a show of supposedly waking up when the car came to a halt. She and Zach had been talking softly, and Christi may not have heard all of their conversation, but Dizzy didn't doubt she had heard enough!

Christi kept her expression bland as they all went into the lounge for the nightcap Zach had suggested; Dizzy couldn't get her to meet her gaze at all. And as Zach handed her the small brandy she had asked for she found out why!

'Not for me thanks, Uncle Zach,' Christi refused the nightcap. 'I think I'll just get straight up to bed. I'll see you both in the morning,' she added lightly before leaving the room.

Her friend had left so abruptly that she left an awkward silence behind her. Dizzy had felt brave enough in the darkness of the car on the drive home, but being left alone here in the lounge with Zach was a different matter altogether. It wasn't that she was a tease, never that, but she was sure neither of them had any idea where they went from here, and Christi's leaving them alone like this had just precipitated the moment of truth.

'I *have* been thinking about you, Dizzy.' Zach suddenly spoke, staring down into his glass of whisky. 'I haven't come to any conclusions, but— damn it!' He slammed his glass down, taking hers out of her unresisting fingers and placing it beside his own. 'I know I said this wouldn't happen again, but——' He didn't finish the sentence, his mouth forcefully claiming hers instead.

It was more, so much more than she even re-membered, and her memories were already so vividly disturbing!

Her body curved instinctively against Zach's, her arms moving impulsively about his neck, her lips parting beneath his as he had taught her last night.

He was every inch the Greek god; demanding, possessive, claiming her response as his right.

And it was his. There was no denying it any longer; she wanted this man, in every way it was possible to want a man. She wanted him to love, to care for, to be made love to by. Morning might bring back the uncertainties but she didn't think so. She was in love with Zach, completely, irrevo-cably, and she knew he was the type of man who would never hurt her intentionally.

Her joyous realisation of her love, a love she had thought never to feel for any man, made her re-sponse all the more intense, deepening the kiss as she knew she wanted to belong to this man completely.

There was no gentleness in Zach tonight, only fierce demand, a need to show them both this was what they wanted, what they needed to make them sane again.

And then it all changed, his lips nibbling at hers, his teeth gently biting, the pleasure-pain sending quivers of delight through her whole body. She trembled uncontrollably as his tongue moved slowly around her parted lips before plunging deeply inside.

Her legs gave way beneath her, and the strength she had seen that first day, and which she knew the tailoring of the brown suit hid, enabled Zach to swing her up into his arms before carrying her over to the sofa.

He sat down with her still in his arms, their mouths still fused, tasting her, taking her, again and again.

Dizzy felt weak with longing, with a burning that she couldn't control, her arms about Zach's neck as she clung to him.

While his lips and teeth nibbled at her exposed throat, his hands caressed the length of her body. Dizzy's breathing was erratic as he lightly grazed the sides of her breasts, and she gasped as she felt the light caress of his thumb-tip, her nipple hard and pulsating.

Her breasts were always the one part of her body she felt self-conscious about, having developed them long before most of her friends, but as Zach deftly unzipped her dress to expose the uptilted peaks to his heated gaze she knew only pride that she had been able to put that glow of pleasure in his golden eyes.

He pulled the dress lower, freeing her completely, his hand trembling slightly as he cupped one upward sweep, gazing his fill of the pink-tipped loveliness. And then he wasn't content to just look; his gaze briefly met hers, finding no resistance there as he slowly lowered his mouth to her breast.

It was like an electric shock, tiny pinpricks of pleasure that made her arch up into him, wanting more, receiving it as he nibbled and sucked, nibbled and sucked.

Her head moved back of its own volition, and she was sent into a frenzy of longing as Zach laved first one nipple then the other, her whole body a throbbing ache that needed to be assuaged.

She fell back on to the sofa, taking Zach with her, welcoming his weight against her, their thighs melded together as they moved restlessly against each other, needing to——

'My God, what the hell am I doing?' Zach's groan of self-condemnation halted the madness. Dizzy looked up at him with unfocusing eyes as he pulled himself up off the sofa; his suit jacket was still on, but his shirt had been partly unbuttoned down his chest by her eager fingers, seconds earlier. His hair fell rakishly across his forehead, his mouth looked as swollen from their kisses as hers felt; he looked exactly what he was, a man who had drawn back on the brink of making love!

Dizzy sat up shakily, doing her best to straighten her dress. 'It's all right, Zach——'

'It is *not* all right.' He impatiently pushed her shaking hands aside, to pull up her dress and rezip it, pausing to look into her too-wide eyes, the swollen vulnerability of her lips. He straightened abruptly, drawing in a deep breath. 'I will not take advantage of a guest under my own roof!' he rasped.

Dizzy swayed uncertainly, her hair in disarray about her shoulders. 'I——'

'I won't!' Zach said again firmly, bending down to kiss her hard on the lips before striding out of the room.

What if the guest *wanted* to be taken advantage of?

CHAPTER EIGHT

DIZZY was still mulling over the problem the next day as Christi berated her for not confiding in her what had happened after she'd gone to bed the evening before.

She was in love with Zach, admitted it, accepted it *and* the pain she knew could come along with the acceptance. But Zach was determined not to repeat last night while she was still his guest and, short of moving out to a hotel, she didn't see how they were going to go on from here. And they had to move on, had to discover exactly how they felt about each other.

'—don't you think?'

She blinked, looking up at Christi as she realised her friend had asked her a question. 'What did you say?'

Christi looked ready to explode. 'Will you please get your mind on this conversation?' she snapped. 'It's very rude of you to be lost in thoughts of last night when you refuse to tell me *what* those thoughts are!'

She smiled at her friend's frustration with her preoccupation. 'Sorry,' she grimaced ruefully.

Christi gave a disgusted sigh. 'I was saying that I think it's a little unfair of you not to confide in me, when I was the one who made it possible for you to be alone with Uncle Zach last night.'

Her smile deepened; she was completely at ease with her emotions now, knowing they had been inevitable from the moment she had first gazed at her 'Greek god'. And she was convinced that Zach was nothing like her parents, that he would never let her down the way they had. Admitting to loving him made her feel vulnerable, but at the same time she had never felt so alive and happy in her life. Figuring out what to do about this love, now that she cherished it, was what filled her thoughts at the moment.

'Don't think we didn't appreciate it,' she teased her friend.

Christi perked up interestedly. 'How much?'

She shrugged. 'Your uncle and I haven't spoken at all today, so what do you think?'

Zach had kept to his usual routine of an early walk, early breakfast, working in his study until lunch time, a quick lunch in there, and then disappearing for the afternoon. It had given her no opportunity to see him, let alone attempt a private conversation with him.

'I think the two of you are just being stubborn,' Christi said disgustedly. 'You're so right for each other.'

Her eyes widened. 'We are?'

'Of course you are,' Christi nodded impatiently, pacing the room, the two of them having just had coffee in the lounge after a late lunch.

Perhaps they were, although from what Zach had been led to believe about her it probably wasn't as apparent to him. He probably thought he was having a nervous breakdown, being attracted to a drifter and a sponger, a woman who shared a man's bed just because he was 'lonely and had soulful brown eyes'!

He would have to be told the truth about that before things went any further, and that could make things awkward for all of them. Even if Zach were still attracted to her, she had no reason to suppose he would want to be involved with a twenty-one-year-old virgin with as many hang-ups as she had. No man welcomed complications like that into his life!

'Maybe,' she said non-committally. 'But don't go making any plans for calling him Zach,' she warned ruefully. 'Even supposing your uncle does admit to being attracted to me—*supposing* he does——' she repeated firmly at Christi's sceptical snort '—I would say one night in his bed is all he would be interested in with a drifter like me who shares anyone's bed for the night just for somewhere to stay.'

'We'll see about that!' Christi said indignantly. 'He'll answer to me if he dares... Oh, God, what a mess I've made of things!' she groaned.

'You weren't to know this would happen.' Dizzy shook her head. 'None of us were.'

Christi straightened determinedly. 'Well, I'm going to go and tell him the truth right now, and be damned with the consequences.'

'Let me tell him.'

Christi halted at the door, her expression uncertain. 'I should really be the one——'

'Let me,' Dizzy repeated softly. 'I—there are some other things to discuss, too,' she reminded gently. 'Like my relationship to the artist of

Knollsley Hall and the portrait in the library,'
she explained flatly as Christi looked puzzled.

'None of that was your fault,' Christi defended
instantly. 'We don't get to choose who our parents
are.'

'No,' she conceded dully. 'And they usually don't
get to choose us, either.'

'Most parents would be proud to have you as
their daughter,' her friend said indignantly.

She gave a bitter laugh. 'My parents aren't like
"most parents".'

'Oh, I know that,' Christi said fiercely. 'Sometimes I could——'

'Don't waste your energy being angry at them,'
Dizzy advised softly. 'I wasted too many years doing
that. It just makes you bitter and twisted, and in
the end achieves nothing.'

'Maybe you're right,' Christi accepted with a
sigh. 'But Uncle Zach isn't going to be concerned
because your father is Martin Ellington-James, and
your mother is Valerie Sherman,' she said with
certainty.

Her mouth twisted. 'But does it make me more
acceptable, looking at the way I am and the way I
live, to admit that they're my parents, or is it easier
for him to believe I'm just an old school acquaintance whose parents lost their money several years
ago?' She gave a rueful smile.

'We both know that neither of those versions are
true,' Christi defended. 'Besides, we all have a secret
or two it's difficult to admit to.'

'Including Zach?' she said disbelievingly.

'Including him,' Christi nodded. 'And your
secrets aren't so deep and dark that they should

matter. Good gracious, you can't really believe he *wants* to go on thinking you're a sponging drifter!'

She shrugged. 'The daughter of Martin Ellington-James, MP, isn't going to be quite so easy to dismiss as penniless Dizzy James.'

'Uncle Zach isn't like that,' her friend said with certainty. 'And he does care for you, I'm sure of it.'

She was sure he felt something for her, too, otherwise he wouldn't have drawn back last night, no matter what code of ethics he had been brought up with. But he had loved his fiancée, been devastated when she died, and second best in the life of the man she loved just wouldn't be enough for her.

'We'll see.' She gave Christi a reassuring smile.

'When?'

She blinked at the abruptness of Christi's question. 'When what?'

'When are you going to tell him?' her friend prompted determinedly.

'Well—I—the next time I see him, I suppose,' she shrugged.

'Why not now?' Christi pressured. 'He can't have gone far.'

If only Christi knew! Zach hadn't gone very far at all. But offering her the temptation of going in search of Zach, when she knew he was off bathing nude in a lake only two miles from here, was something she wasn't sure she could resist any longer. Maybe finding him at a disadvantage like that wouldn't make her feel quite so nervous about what she had to tell him.

'Go on,' Christi urged as she saw her hesitation. 'He always goes off towards the lakes,' she supplied eagerly. 'I suppose there are more birds to watch around there,' she shrugged.

Poor Christi didn't know her uncle at all if she still believed that bird-watching tale, although, if *she* hadn't seen Zach's nude bathing for herself that first day, perhaps she would have found it difficult to believe, too!

'OK.' She firmly made her decision. 'But if I'm not with him when he comes back send out a search party,' she attempted to tease.

Christi hugged her impulsively. 'Good luck.'

Dizzy gave a rueful smile. 'Just don't expect too much, hmm?'

'Are you kidding?' her friend grinned. 'I already have my bridesmaid's dress of sackcloth and ashes all picked out! Uncle Zach's sure to make me do some sort of penance for the lies I've told him about you,' she grimaced.

'Half-truths,' Dizzy comforted.

'Lies,' Christi insisted. 'Although maybe he'll be so relieved to know the truth he'll forget all about being angry with me,' she added hopefully.

Dizzy felt the same way herself. She had been a party to Christi's deception, even if she hadn't altogether approved of the idea.

She didn't exactly rush to the lake, for she was in no hurry to make her confessions.

She looked much as she had that first day, her hair confined in the thick braid down her spine, although, as usual, curling wisps insisted on framing her face. The baggy T-shirt was clean, even if it did nothing for her figure, the same with the faded and patched denims. She wasn't exactly dressed in a way guaranteed to convince Zach she was the daughter of very wealthy parents!

She could hear the splash of the water even before she came down the last hill that sided the lake, although it took her a few minutes to spot Zach's sleek head as he swam effortlessly about a hundred yards from the shore.

When he spotted her, was he going to walk unconcernedly out of the water, unselfconscious of his nakedness, or would he stay in the water that must still be a little chill, despite the warmth of summer?

She tensed nervously as she realised she was about to find out. Zach's gaze narrowed on her as he swam lazily back to the shore, where his clothes lay in a neat pile at her feet. After the intimacies they had shared the night before, she was self-conscious about facing him again, all the more so because she knew he was naked beneath the water.

She was unprepared for his opening comment as he trod water several feet away from her!

'I wondered if you would ever come back here.' He met her gaze steadily.

Dizzy gave a start of surprise, swallowing hard. 'Back?' she repeated in a voice that sounded slightly higher than normal.

He shrugged broad shoulders. 'From the time you must have arrived the other day, and the way you looked at me when we met, I suspected you might have seen me here on your way to the castle.'

Deep colour brightened her cheeks, and she thrust her hands into her denims pockets. 'Was it so obvious I was attracted to you?' she snapped.

'Hardly,' he drawled lightly. 'You looked more surprised than anything. But when you began to choke, as soon as Christi mentioned I had been bird-watching all afternoon, I was certain you must have seen what I was really doing.' He became suddenly still. 'Did you like what you saw, Dizzy?' he prompted huskily.

'I—yes,' she answered in a rush. 'I—I liked it very much.' Her cheeks felt as if they were on fire, her wide-eyed gaze fixed on him as she wondered if he intended walking out of the water to dry in the sun today.

Her eyes widened even more as he began to walk towards her, her breath catching in her throat, only to be released in an unsteady groan as black swimming trunks were revealed as he left the water behind him.

He shot her an amused glance as he picked up the towel from beneath his clothes, to begin drying his hair. 'What did you expect, Dizzy?' he teased softly. 'I haven't swum in the nude since I realised you must have seen me that day, and that you could do so again any time you felt like taking a walk down here.' He took pity on her, and explained, 'I've been waiting for some comment from Christi about my afternoon activities,' he added with a questioning look.

Dizzy shrugged, still slightly shaken by the expectancy she had felt as Zach waded out of the water towards her. Not that he was any less devastating in this minute pair of bathing trunks, with water glistening on the golden beauty of his body, and his true masculine power revealed.

'I didn't think it was right to tell Christi,' she sighed. 'It would have been almost like breaking a confidence.' Besides, it would have put her in the awkward position of trying to pretend Zach's nakedness that day had meant nothing to her!

He hung the towel around his neck, the impact of his honey-coloured eyes all the more apparent without his glasses, his hair falling untidily across his forehead. 'I'm glad you didn't say you didn't think Christi would be interested,' he drawled.

'Zach——'

'Dizzy,' he derided.

She frowned. He seemed different today somehow, almost as if—as if he were *flirting* with her! And why shouldn't he? After last night he must think she was more than willing to fall into his arms any time he asked her to.

Zach watched her curiously. 'What's Christi up to, Dizzy?' he finally asked. 'And why have you let her get away with it?'

She blinked, dragging her gaze away from the flatness of his chest and stomach, and up to meet his golden gaze. She instantly felt as if she were drowning in a sea of sensuous honey.

'Dizzy.' He took the step that separated them, clasping her arms. 'I've known from the first time I kissed you that your experience with men must have been limited to the platonic rather than the sensual,' he told her gently.

She shook her head. 'How could you know that?' she defended. 'I haven't——'

'I know because of this, Dizzy.' Even as he spoke huskily, his head was lowering to hers, his thumb on her chin, parting her lips to receive his, gently savouring the taste of her before deepening the kiss.

Her hands were drawn instinctively to touch him, to feel the silky texture of his skin, to know the strength of the muscles that rippled beneath that skin. He was steel and velvet at the same time, and her fingertips tingled as she touched him, her hands moving up and down the strength of his back, halting uncertainly as she encountered the material of his bathing trunks.

His lips left hers to travel across her cheek. 'Yes,' he encouraged gruffly. 'Touch me, Dizzy!' he urged at her self-conscious hesitation.

He was like satin to touch, a flesh sculpture, perfect in every way. And from the reaction of his body, her inexperienced caresses pleased him immensely.

Finally he put her away from him, gazing down at her with warm eyes. 'We have to talk,' he said apologetically.

Dizzy's senses were so fevered that it took her a few moments to realise he didn't intend making love to her. 'But we aren't in your home now,' she pointed out disappointedly.

He smiled gently. 'We're still on my land. And we have several things to talk out before we do anything else. Shall we make ourselves comfortable first?' he suggested softly.

She was very much afraid that making themselves 'comfortable' included Zach putting his clothes on, and as Zach began to do just that she bit back her regretful sigh and sat down on the grass to wait for him to join her.

Dressed in the professor's clothes, his hair neatly brushed, he made it seem as if the moment of closeness a few minutes earlier had not happened.

Zach carefully filled and lit his pipe before joining her on the grass, sitting a polite distance away, as if he, too, felt the chasm yawning between them.

'Tell me,' he leant back against a tree, the smoke from his pipe filling the air, 'who is Henry?'

It had been the last question she had expected, and for a few seconds she just stared at him. 'Henry?' she finally managed to repeat.

'Yes,' he nodded. 'Whoever he was, he certainly wasn't your lover,' he added with certainty.

'Did I ever say he was?' she defended indignantly.

'Stop delaying the inevitable, Dizzy,' he said wearily, the glasses back as a screen between her and his emotions. 'Is Henry a boyfriend of Christi's she doesn't want me to know about?'

'Certainly not,' she frowned.

Zach sighed. 'Well, my dear niece is definitely hiding something.'

Dizzy blushed. 'Then why don't you ask her these questions?' She pulled up a blade of grass beside her, ripping it to shreds in her agitation.

He watched her steadily. 'Because you're as involved in this as she is,' he stated calmly. 'The two of you are so familiar and at ease with each other that it speaks of a long and loyal friendship, not the old school acquaintances who can barely stand each other, but feel a certain loyalty because of a girlish equivalent of the "old school tie", that you would have me believe.'

She had *told* Christi that wouldn't work, knew they had given themselves away numerous times over the last few days. And Zach was far from the unobservant man buried in his books that Christi seemed to believe him to be!

'If you weren't so judgemental, Christi wouldn't have had to try to convince you of her maturity to handle her own money by showing you just how irresponsible she could be but isn't!' Dizzy attacked, breathing hard in her anger. Zach had lulled her into a false sense of security with his kisses and caresses, leaving her defences wide open, she realised now, when it was too late to do anything about them. Christi knew she was going to tell Zach the truth, but she doubted her friend expected it to be in quite this way, she thought in dismay!

Zach's eyes narrowed behind the glasses. 'Is that what the two of you have been doing?'

She shrugged resentfully. 'Well, you have to admit that I'm a perfect example of irresponsibility!'

'Not quite,' he drawled, his gaze considering. 'Who are you?'

Her head went back. 'Dizzy James.'

'Who are you really?' he repeated in a hard voice.

She drew in a ragged breath. 'A friend of Christi's.'

'That's obvious,' he bit out raspingly. 'But it doesn't answer my question.'

He was angry, angrier than her, and she couldn't really blame him after the stupid, *stupid* game she and Christi had been playing at his expense.

She swallowed hard. 'If I tell you my father's name is—is Martin Ellington-James,' she completed almost defiantly at his compelling glance, 'maybe that will help you,' she snapped.

Zach gave a puzzled frown. 'I didn't know he had remarried.'

'He hasn't,' she scorned. 'And no, I'm not illegitimate, either,' she derided at the surprised rise of his eyebrows, her mouth twisting mockingly as she saw the truth dawn in those expressive eyes.

'Your mother is Valerie Sherman?' He spoke slowly, as if still uncertain of his facts.

'That's right, Professor.' As usual, she was on the defensive when discussing either of her parents, the shield over her emotions, which she had allowed to slip while she searched her feelings for this man, firmly back in place. She had been a fool to believe they could ever care for each other!

'Then Knollsley Hall was your home?' he enunciated carefully, as if he still couldn't believe what he was being told.

Knollsley Hall hadn't been her home, it had been her prison! Oh, until her mother had left when she was four it had had the semblance of a home, but after that it had become somewhere to escape from. But very few people knew or understood that, and she wasn't about to confide in Zach, now that they were suddenly so distant from each other. She should have known better than to allow her emotions to take over, even briefly!

'It was my father's home.' She gave a cool inclination of her head.

'Then you went to live with your mother after the divorce?' Zach sounded puzzled.

Dizzy gave an impatient sigh. 'I don't think where I spent my childhood has any relevance to this conversation,' she bit out dismissively.

'Now that we've established that, far from having fallen on ill-fortune, and so leaving you to make your way in the world as best you can, your father is one of the richest MPs in the country—and that's saying a lot!—and your mother is a very wealthy artist,' Zach acknowledged disgustedly, 'I don't think your privileged background has any more relevance to the conversation, either!' he bit out grimly.

Privileged background! Was it privileged to be ignored by her father until she was four and her mother ran away from him, when she then became the only thing he could vent his anger and frustration on without fear of retribution? Was it privileged when she was sent away to school at eight so that he didn't have to see her marked resemblance to her mother as she got older? Was it privileged when he wouldn't even have her back in the house for the holidays after that first year, because each time he saw her she reminded him of the woman who had walked out on both of them, so that she either had to remain at the school during holiday times or accept the open invitation she always had from Christi's parents to stay with them? If that was privilege then she didn't know what abuse was!

Tears glistened in her pained green eyes, tears she quickly blinked away as she met Zach's gaze steadily. 'I'm twenty-one now, my parents are no longer responsible for me, and as you can see I live my life the way I want to,' she told him defiantly. 'Who my parents are doesn't change the fact that I live out of a backpack, stay with friends whenever I can. Whereas Christi——'

'Christi has some explaining of her own to do,' Zach cut in harshly, standing up. 'Now that I know the truth, your presence here is no longer necessary, to give a false impression, or try to convince a rather staid professor of history that he's the best thing you've seen since sliced bread——'

'I *hate* sliced bread,' Dizzy put in defensively. 'And all of my responses to you have been real!'

His mouth twisted as he looked down at her. 'A sham,' he corrected bitterly. 'But you have no further need to sacrifice yourself in the name of friendship——'

'It was no sacrifice!' Dizzy derided.

His mouth firmed angrily. 'I'm sure Henry is just longing for you to return to his bed. Possibly he finds your act of innocence more to his liking than I did!'

They were hitting out at each other in angry defiance, each blow more cutting than the last, until in the end they would rip each other apart. Zach believed she was responsible for playing with his emotions because she was trying to help Christi, and he wasn't about to forgive her for that.

Looking at this from his point of view, what choice did he have? She had lied to him; why shouldn't he think her innocence was all a lie, too?

'Possibly,' she said heavily, standing up to brush the grass from her hands and denims. 'I take it you want me to move out of the castle as soon as possible?' All her anger had gone now, leaving her aching inside like never before.

'If not sooner,' Zach confirmed harshly.

She drew in a ragged breath. 'I'll make sure you don't have to see me again before I leave.'

He nodded abruptly. 'I would appreciate that,' he bit out.

Dizzy bowed her head. 'I thought you might.'

'Now I have to go and find your partner in crime,' he said grimly, a steely quality in his voice that she had never heard before. 'But I'd like you to know you could have both saved yourselves all this trouble.'

Dizzy looked up at him dazedly. What did he mean by that?

He gave a bitter smile. 'I invited Christi up here so that we could get to know each other a little better, perhaps cement a friendship, before I released my guardianship of her and we perhaps drifted apart. Which would have been a pity when we're the only family each of us have.' He returned Dizzy's stunned gaze contemptuously. 'I never had any intention of not releasing Christi's inheritance once she's twenty-one!'

CHAPTER NINE

'COULD you put your hand a little to the left of Jim's chest, please, Heather?' Dizzy instructed distractedly, gazing in dissatisfaction at the couple across the room. 'That's perfect,' she nodded, as the other woman complied.

A bitter smile curved Dizzy's lips as she wondered what interpretation Zach would put on this situation if he were to walk in now.

Not that there was much chance of that. She had been back in London since yesterday, and she hadn't heard a word from Zach *or* Christi.

Christi and Zach had already been in his study by the time she had followed him back to the castle, and so she had quietly packed her bags and left, knowing that Christi was in enough trouble without her adding to it by hanging around when she had bluntly been told to leave. She had no doubt that Christi would contact her once she got back to London herself.

But it hadn't made the waiting any easier, and, after a night of lying awake thinking of Zach and the misunderstandings between them, she had decided that indulging in her other love in life was what she needed to take her mind off him. Heather and Jim had been only too pleased to come over when she called them.

Her father had never considered the artistic talent that she had inherited from her mother to be a

147

foundation for a career, but had called the accurate drawings she would present to him as a child's 'scribblings', until in the end she stopped sharing them with him.

The boarding-school had been even less thrilled by her talent, more interested in the academic than the arts. The teachers had not been at all impressed with the caricatures she often did of them to amuse her classmates, and more than once her drawing equipment had been confiscated.

But her talent for sketching and painting had been the one thing she *was* grateful to accept from her mother, and she knew by the time she was eighteen that, whatever career she chose, it had to involve sketching of some kind. With her mother already established as an accomplished artist, it had narrowed her field down somewhat unless she wanted to be constantly referred to as 'Valerie Sherman's daughter'. As that was the last thing she had ever wanted to be known as, she had steered very clear of that area of art.

Once again, it had been Christi who set her on the right track, introducing her to a family friend who also happened to own a publishing house, and who was always on the look-out for illustrators for the covers of his books. With her avid interest in history, and her artistic talent, Dizzy had been a natural at producing the glossy evocative covers that enticed a reader to pick up a book to read the back cover and see what the story was about.

Her year of working for Astro Publishing had been an experience she would always be grateful for, bringing her worldwide recognition for the DC James illustrations that firmly established her at the

top of her field. The last two years on her own had
been filled with hundreds of offers of work, both
here and in North America, and she hadn't refused
any of them that looked interesting, enjoying the
travelling almost as much as she did the work. There
was just one professional dream she had left to
fulfil, a dream that didn't seem to stand much
chance of becoming reality when Claudia Laurence,
the one author she longed to illustrate for, didn't
seem to have heard of her *or* the provocative covers
she had given to dozens of historical romances!

Her studio, and the place where she occasionally
stayed for a few days between assignments, was at
the top of an old warehouse that had later been
converted to flats: a huge barn of a place that gave
her the space and light she needed to work. It
couldn't exactly be called her home, but it was the
closest she came to calling anywhere that.

She was working on a Regency cover right now,
Heather wearing a delicate pink dress that was cut
in the alarmingly low fashion of the day, Jim every
inch the aristocratic duke as he looked down his
haughty nose at the saucy young woman of spirit
he would eventually marry. For some illustrators
this could just have been another one of 'those'
covers, but each piece of work Dizzy produced was
special to her, and to the people who constantly
wrote, praising her work. She never ceased to be
thrilled herself when she knew she had done a good
job.

Unfortunately, today wasn't going to be one of
those days! Try as she might to put all thought of
Zach out of her mind, seeing how close the couple
were she was supposed to be photographing only

reminded her that hours ago *she* had been in Zach's arms. That was before everything had all blown up in her face.

If Christi didn't call her soon and tell her what was going on she was going to wring her friend's neck when she *did* see her again!

Christi had to know how worried she was. Or perhaps her friend was so devastated by the obvious retribution her uncle could give for her scheme that she didn't feel like talking to anyone just now!

Zach *had* been very angry yesterday, everything Dizzy had told him seeming only to convince him she had gone further than trying to help convince him of Christi's maturity, that she had tried to use a relationship between the two of *them* to try and persuade him to release Christi's money.

Money had never been important to her on an everyday basis; as long as she had enough to live on, she wasn't interested in 'putting money aside for a rainy day'. Life was too short and precarious for that. But she had been lucky, she was paid well for doing something that she loved, and so, despite all her feelings to the contrary, she had managed to amass a small fortune. Her father would be stunned if he knew how much his daughter was worth! She had decided from the first not to confide in him about her career, had deliberately chosen to illustrate under the name DC James because of that. No doubt knowing that she earned her living legitimately, after all, would give him a certain amount of relief, but knowing what that work was was sure to bring down his scorn on her. He had been scandalised that his wife could choose to be an artist, so God knew what he would make of the provocatively lovely covers she chose to illustrate to whet people's appetite for the story between those covers! She certainly wasn't in any hurry to find out!

Possibly Zach would view it the same way; it certainly wasn't the type of thing a professor of history would like the woman in his life to be involved in!

Not that she *was* the woman in his life. They may have come close—Zach's gentle lovemaking before he learnt the truth about her and Christi had certainly given her hope—but she had watched as that was slowly destroyed with each new thing she revealed about herself. Far from believing in the innocence he had guessed at as he made love to her, he now believed she was a better actress than Christi could ever be!

'Dizzy, are you all right?'

She looked up at the couple across the room as Heather spoke concernedly, realising as she did so that she had been staring fixedly at the floor for the last five minutes. She gave a rueful smile, realising that the photographs she had intended taking, so that she could later do her preliminary sketching from them, weren't even half done.

She straightened. 'I'm afraid I'm not really in the mood for this today,' she said apologetically. 'Do you mind if we stop now?'

'Not at all,' Jim replied for both of them. The couple instantly relaxed their pose, both he and Heather were actors who modelled when they weren't doing other work. 'Are you sure you're feeling all right? You don't seem like yourself today.'

If only she *were* someone else! If only she could have listened to Zach's accusations and then neatly turned around and told him she hadn't been in his arms for any other reason than that she loved him. But love was too new to her, the feeling of vulnerability leaving her too raw to pain, for her to do anything else but back away from it. She was very much afraid she had had her one chance at love, and lost it.

'I don't think my short holiday did me any good.' She gave a forced smile. 'Could you both come back tomorrow?' she said hopefully, very much aware that time was passing and that she had done little or nothing towards this cover.

'Morning?' Heather suggested with a frown. 'I have a cover to do for Carla in the afternoon.'

Carla Fortune was an illustrator who worked mainly on mysteries, but both Heather and Jim were very much in demand by most illustrators, both of them having that elusive quality that allowed them to express the exact emotions required. It didn't surprise Dizzy in the least that she was going to have to wait in line for them, in fact, she had been thrilled earlier when they had been able to come over for a few hours this morning. Probably Carla had Heather booked for this afternoon, too!

'That's fine,' she nodded. 'I——' She broke off as the doorbell rang, her heart starting to pound as she hoped it was Christi. 'Why don't the two of you get changed while I answer the door?' she suggested nervously. 'I—you—I'll see you both tomorrow,' she added in a rush, before hurrying to the door.

Christi looked just the same as she usually did, beautiful and calm, striding past Dizzy into the studio, turning back to her chidingly after taking in the photographic equipment.

'I should have known you would get straight back to work,' she drawled, throwing off the linen jacket, that matched the blue sheath of a dress she wore, before dropping down tiredly on to one of the over-stuffed cushions that served as Dizzy's chairs. 'I feel as if I haven't stopped running the last twenty-four hours.' She rested massaging fingertips against her aching temples.

Dizzy swallowed nervously, standing across the room from her friend. 'From your uncle?' she prompted, in a voice too casual to be genuine.

Christi looked up at her with accusing eyes. 'Well, didn't *you*?'

She sighed, moving to switch off the bright lights that had spotlighted Heather and Jim minutes earlier. 'He told me to go,' she muttered.

'Well, of course he told you to go,' Christi said disgustedly. 'You gave him the impression you were some sort of trap we both wanted him to walk into, so that it made it easier asking him to release my money!'

Dizzy turned sharply, her eyes blazing. 'I did no such thing!' she snapped fiercely. 'That was the conclusion that he *enjoyed* jumping to,' she scorned hardily.

'And that you were too proud to refute,' Christi rebuked.

'That I didn't get the *chance* to refute,' she corrected firmly, her hands clenched at her sides. 'He wasn't prepared to listen to anything I had to say once he knew my parents were Martin Ellington-James and Valerie Sherman. He seemed to find my ''privileged'' background totally suited to the teasing little vamp who tried to make a fool out of him!'

'Oh, Dizzy,' Christi groaned apologetically.

'For God's sake, don't pity me,' she warned fiercely, holding on to her emotions with tremendous effort. 'I'll fall apart into a million pieces if you do that!' she explained shakily.

Christi flinched, her eyes pained. 'You're in love with him.'

It wasn't a question, just a statement of fact, a fact that had to be all too obvious to this woman who knew her so well. 'A lot of good it's done me,' she dismissed brittly. 'I always said love was a very overrated emotion.' She tried to sound lightly unconcerned, but unfortunately her voice broke emotionally, and she only sounded as devastated as she was.

'Oh, love, it isn't——' Christi broke off awkwardly as Heather and Jim came out of the room they had been using to change in. 'Hi,' she greeted brightly to cover Dizzy's obvious distress if anyone looked at her too closely. 'What were you today, Jim?' she said familiarly. 'A reformed outlaw or a rampaging Viking?'

He grinned, straightening his jacket. 'A cynical duke,' he drawled.

'Oh, one of those!' Christi nodded ruefully. 'In that case, you must have been the Simpering Miss, Heather,' she teased lightly.

Heather shook down her long red hair, obviously relieved to have it loose about her shoulders once more. 'None of Dizzy's heroines ever look *simpering*,' she said, scandalised, her eyes glowing with laughter. 'Even though the hero and heroine have all their clothes on—usually—Dizzy still manages to imply the sensuality boiling beneath the surface.'

'You've got the job, Heather.' Dizzy was in control again now, at least, on the surface. 'No need to overdo it,' she chided self-derisively.

Their laughter served to ease the awkwardness when Jim and Heather had come into the room, the other couple taking their leave a few minutes later.

'Just tell me,' Dizzy turned back to Christi once they were alone, 'did Zach get really angry and tell you you would have to wait for your money, or did he keep to his initial decision to let you have it when you're twenty-one?' She held her breath as she waited for the answer, knowing there was no chance of Zach ever forgiving her for her part in this if he had decided to make Christi wait until she was twenty-five.

'He *was* angry, wasn't he?' Christi grimaced expressively. 'When he came back to the castle after talking to you, I thought he was going to——'

'Christi!'

'Sorry,' her friend sighed at her unmistakable tension. 'Well, he——' She broke off as the telephone began to ring.

Dizzy scowled at the interruption. 'It's like Picccadilly Circus in here this morning!' She glared, grabbing the receiver and barking a response into the mouth-piece.

Whatever she had been expecting—if she had been expecting anything—it wasn't what her friend and agent, Dick Crosby, was telling her!

'Claudia Laurence has asked for you to do her next cover,' Dick announced triumphantly.

Was this the way it worked: fate took away one dream and replaced it with another? She had lost Zach, but she could have the Claudia Laurence cover instead? Given a free choice, there was no way she would have chosen to have it that way around.

'Dizzy, I said you've got it.' Dick sounded puzzled at her silence. 'The new Claudia Laurence cover is yours!'

She had heard him the first time, and she had thought that if this day ever came it would be the happiest time of her life, illustrating for her favourite author having been what she had always considered the pinnacle of her career. Now it didn't seem important at all, nothing did.

'Dizzy——'

She heard no more as the receiver was gently taken out of her hand and Christi took control of her end of the conversation, after identifying herself.

However, Christi seemed as stunned by the news as Dizzy was! 'What did you say?' she demanded sharply, her hand tightly gripping the receiver. 'Sorry,' she muttered as Dick obviously made it clear he didn't welcome that sort of reaction from her, too! 'They did? She did?' Her eyes lit up excitedly as Dick related the details.

Dizzy turned away. This was what she had always wanted, what she had dreamt of, but loving Zach, losing him, had taken away her pleasure in anything, even something that had once been as important to her as this.

Was this what her life was going to be like from now on, this flat, nothingness existence, where nothing really mattered any more? How could she stand it? She didn't have any other choice *but* to stand it, unless she went to Zach and begged him to listen to her, to believe her.

Was she really that desperate? Yes, she was! Could she do something like that? Not yet, she recognised sadly. Maybe in a few days, when the initial heartache had eased to a dull throb instead of this tearing ache inside her, maybe then she would be able to accept it if Zach still rejected her, even after she had convinced him she really did love him.

While she had been asking herself questions, and then answering them, Christi had been involved in an excited conversation with Dick. 'She'll be there,' she concluded firmly before ringing off.

Dizzy frowned. 'I take it that was me you were talking about?' she derided wryly.

'It most certainly was,' Christi nodded, her air of suppressed excitement unmistakable.

'And just where will I be?' she mocked drily.

'Empire Publishing,' her friend supplied economically. 'This afternoon. Two o'clock.'

'Don't you think you should have consulted me before—— This afternoon?' she echoed disbelievingly. 'At *two* o'clock?' she repeated, with even more disbelief. 'But that's only just over an hour away,' she protested after glancing at the wall-clock.

Christi nodded. 'Which is why you have to get ready and go now. You can't wear jeans, of course, so——'

'Christi, I'm not in the mood to go and see a publisher this afternoon!' she groaned emotionally.

'Not the publisher.' Christi had already walked through to Dizzy's bedroom and was sorting through the meagre contents of her wardrobe, obviously finding nothing there that suited her. 'Although I suppose he'll be there,' she dismissed vaguely, holding up a green suit against Dizzy for inspection, then shaking her head with a horrified groan, both of them recognising the suit as the one Dizzy had left school in three years earlier. 'You're going to meet the author herself, Dizzy.' She resumed looking in the wardrobe, sighing as the only thing left that she hadn't already rejected was a pale green sun-dress that wasn't really suitable for visiting a publisher and his famous author in either. 'It will have to do, I suppose.' She pulled it out resignedly. 'It probably makes you look about sixteen, but . . .' She didn't need to finish the sentence, her disgust was obvious. 'I'd lend you this dress and jacket, but it would probably reach down to your ankles——'

'Besides having to be split in the bodice to accommodate another part of my anatomy,' Dizzy drawled.

'Hmm.' Christi looked at the part of Dizzy's anatomy in question as she obediently buttoned on the sun-dress after stripping off her denims and T-shirt. 'Maybe you don't look sixteen, after all!' she admired, as the dress left no doubt as to the full curve of Dizzy's breasts.

'Christi.' She halted her friend in the act of un-plaiting her hair so that she could brush it loose about her shoulders. 'Much as I appreciate your help,' she mocked lightly, 'I'm really not in the mood to see an author this afternoon, either.'

'It's not just "an author", Dizzy,' her friend reproved in a shocked voice. 'It's Claudia Laurence!'

She sighed. 'I'm not in the mood to meet her, either.'

Christi stared at her as if she had gone insane, giving a sudden shake of her head. 'Of course you are,' she decided briskly. 'Do you have any sandals to go with this dress——'

'Christi, I really don't want to go,' she said wearily.

'Well, you're going,' her friend decided stubbornly. 'Claudia Laurence asked for you personally.'

'And it's very nice,' Dizzy nodded. 'But not this afternoon, hmm?'

'Most definitely this afternoon,' Christi told her firmly. 'Apparently, your Miss Laurence is something of a recluse, and she's only up to town this afternoon before going back to her home.'

'I never knew that,' Dizzy frowned. 'I knew she didn't like publicity, but I never realised she actively avoided it.'

'According to Dick, you're very privileged,' her friend confirmed. 'Oh, come on, Dizzy,' she encouraged as she still hesitated. 'You're not doing any good just sitting around here, moping!'

Was that was she was doing? Yes, it was. She was also asking herself a lot of questions she didn't like the answers to!

'All right.' She gave in with a deep sigh. 'And the sandals are at the back of the wardrobe,' she added in answer to Christi's earlier question to avoid having Christi tell her she was doing the right thing by getting on with her life. She knew she was doing the right thing, but that didn't make it any easier!

Christi looked down at the darkness at the bottom of the cupboard, pulling out the pair of black sandals that stood next to a pair of disreputable sneakers. 'I'm not surprised I missed seeing them among all your other shoes,' she derided disgustedly.

Dizzy couldn't help laughing at her friend's horrified expression; Christi possessed suitable shoes, in almost every available colour there was. It felt good to laugh, even if it was about something as silly as her own lack of shoes. What did she need dozens of pairs of shoes for? She could only wear one pair at a time!

Christi didn't quite seem to have forgiven her as she accompanied her in the taxi to Empire Publishing, although she was somewhat mollified by the fact that Dizzy had let her loosen her hair after all. Not that she thought David Kendrick would be that impressed by her appearance; the previous half-dozen times she had met the dynamic young publisher she had been wearing her customary jeans and T-shirt! However, she didn't tell Christi that; in her place, her friend would have lost no opportunity to try and romantically interest the multi-millionaire, and would be horrified that Dizzy had so blatantly thrown away the chance. She hadn't seen it that way herself at the time, but had merely seen it as being herself.

But owning up to being herself didn't seem to have got her very far with the man she *did* love, so she doubted this transformation would interest David in the least, either. Still, it had kept Christi happy, and as her friend was having to come back to the studio this evening, so that they could finish their earlier conversation, that wasn't a bad thing. An uncooperative Christi could be very uncomfortable indeed.

'I'll come back to the studio about eight,' Christi confirmed as she stayed in the taxi after Dizzy had got out at the Empire Publishing building. 'Good luck,' she called out as Dizzy entered the building.

She turned to give her a vaguely reassuring smile, giving herself a pep-talk as she was shown up to David's office. This was the opportunity she had been waiting for, she mustn't ruin it all now just because her heart was breaking. *Just* because? Good God, she had never known such unbearable pain before.

'Go right in,' David's secretary told her smilingly as soon as she entered the outer office. 'He's expecting you.'

Empire Publishing had been started by David only ten years ago, but in that time it had grown to challenge all the more established publishing houses, mainly, Dizzy knew, because of the unshakable enthusiasm and instincts of its creator, David Kendrick. He was that unusual thing today, a youthful entrepreneur who seemed to make a success of everything he did. And he fired those around him with the same enthusiasm. Dizzy wasn't at all surprised when Claudia Laurence had begun to be published by him five years ago, the partnership launching both parties into the higher echelon of their professions.

This was her own opportunity to be touched by their magic and, for this brief time at least, she had to put Zach out of her mind.

Which wasn't all that easy to do, when the first person she saw as she opened the office door was Zachariah Bennett, standing in front of the window, the sunshine turning his hair to gold!

She blinked, sure that when she opened her eyes it would be David standing there, dark-haired David with the deep blue eyes, not the golden-haired Greek god who haunted her every moment.

Zach was still standing there when she opened her eyes, the same Zach who made her body quiver and her heart beat erratically, and yet not the same Zach at all. Gone was the absent-minded professor with his ill-fitting clothes and endearing ways, and in his place was a man who wore the expensively tailored brown suit and cream shirt with an elegance that left no doubt as to his virility. His hair was shorter, too, and had been styled so that it fell enchantingly across his forehead, drawing attention to the golden eyes that she had always guessed had no necessity of the heavy-rimmed glasses he had so easily discarded today.

She wasn't sure she was at all comfortable with this new Zach!

But what was he doing here at all? She had come here to see David Kendrick, this was his office, and yet she and Zach were alone. She didn't understand this at all. And there was nothing to be gained from looking at Zach, for his expression was enigmatic in the extreme.

She shifted uncomfortably. 'I think there must have been some sort of mistake——'

'No mistake, Dizzy,' he spoke huskily, crossing the room to close the door behind her, stepping back to look down at her.

There was complete silence in the room, and the office was so high up the building that all Dizzy could see out of the window was sky; it was as if she and Zach were suddenly completely alone in the world, not a sound penetrating the room.

'I came to see David Kendrick,' she began awkwardly, wondering if, somewhere between getting out of the taxi downstairs and arriving up here, she could have gone insane. What other explanation could there be for Zach being in David Kendrick's office?

'He told me you were coming to see Claudia Laurence.' Zach gazed down at her intently.

Dizzy avoided direct contact with that glance, knowing she *would* go insane if she should actually lose herself in that honey-brown. 'What are *you* doing here, Zach?' she asked flatly.

'I wanted to talk to you——'

Her eyes blazed as she looked up at him. 'Wouldn't it have been easier coming to my studio— which I'm sure Christi must have told you about— than setting up this elaborate charade?' She drew in a steadying breath as her voice rose emotionally. 'Isn't it enough that I know how contemptuous you are of me?' she spoke levelly. 'Are you so angry about what Christi and I did to you that you want to discredit me in the only world I'm comfortable in?' She looked at him with pained disbelief.

The fact that there was no Claudia Laurence cover after all didn't bother her, but that Zach disliked her enough to go to this extreme did!

'David Kendrick is a friend of mine,' Zach told her gently. 'This "charade", as you call it, will go no further than this room. And I'm not angry with you, Dizzy. I'm not sure anger was ever the way to describe how I felt when you told me the truth about yourself yesterday,' he added heavily.

'Then maybe it was what Christi told you about me after I left,' she dismissed contemptuously, hardly able to believe he was capable of such vindictiveness. And yet he was here, wasn't he?

'Christi told me nothing——'

'I can't believe that,' she derided scornfully.

Zach gave a heavy sigh. 'No, perhaps that isn't true,' he conceded. 'She did tell me one thing about you. That you have your own reasons for keeping your relationship with Martin Ellington-James and Valerie Sherman secret,' he supplied at her sceptical look. 'And that those reasons had nothing whatsoever to do with the subterfuge she persuaded you to enter into with her.'

'I can't believe that's all she told you about me.' Dizzy shook her head.

'Christi is completely loyal to you, Dizzy,' Zach assured her gently. 'And she assured me your numerous friends, and six godchildren, felt the same way,' he said drily. 'I think at the time I must have still been giving the impression that I would like to put you over my knee and administer the sound beating you obviously missed out on as a child.'

Tears instantly filled her eyes. 'There are other ways to punish a child besides physical violence.'

He frowned, his breath harsh. 'And I want you to tell me all of them,' he urged softly. 'But not before I've told you a few things about myself that might make you feel more like confiding in me,' he added ruefully as she tensed.

Dizzy faced him defensively. 'I doubt there is anything you have to say that would make me feel like that.'

His mouth twisted. 'I know I deserve that, that I should have had more faith in you. But, if it's any consolation, I knew before I had finished sorting things out with Christi that I had been wrong to flare up at you the way I did.'

'Because Christi had explained all the misunderstandings to you——'

'I told you, she told me nothing,' he cut in firmly. 'She reminded me that we all have secrets we find it difficult to confide in other people,' he said flatly.

'Not you.' Dizzy shook her head with certainty.

He gave a deep sigh. 'Especially me,' he grimaced.

Her expression softened. 'If you're talking about your fiancée, and the fact that she died eleven years ago, Christi has already told me about that.' She gave an apologetic shrug.

'Obviously,' Zach drawled. 'But I don't find it difficult to talk about Julie at all.' He shook his head. 'As you said, it was eleven years ago, and although I loved her very much I can't bring her back. My life has gone on, Dizzy,' he spoke softly. 'Progressed. Julie and I perhaps wouldn't have anything in common if we were to meet again now.

Not like you and I do,' he added huskily, his gaze gently caressing.

They had *nothing* in common! Her childhood had emotionally scarred her; the way she lived, her deliberate lack of a place to call home, were a direct result of those scars. Zach had his life all mapped out for him, had a castle for a home, that he obviously loved very much. He was a staid and settled professor—although she had to admit he looked a little less so today, looked younger, too—while she lived like a bohemian. How on earth could he claim they had *anything* in common!

'Dizzy.' Zach's voice was compelling, demanding she look up at him, his expression softly caressing when she finally did so. 'Dizzy, *I'm* Claudia Laurence.'

CHAPTER TEN

DIZZY blinked, and blinked again, but he still stood there, looking down at her with rueful apology.

She swallowed hard. 'You—you're——'

'Claudia Laurence,' he repeated heavily. 'Come and sit down,' he took hold of her arm and led her docilely over to the sofa, 'before you fall down!' he added drily, as she still gazed up at him disbelievingly.

She did sit down, heavily, staring up at him. 'Won't——' She cleared her throat as her voice came out a croaky squeak. 'Won't David be wanting his office back?' she finally managed to ask.

Zach shook his head, sitting down beside her, taking her hand in his. 'He told me to take as long as I like to try and sort out the mess I've made of things between us,' he encouraged gently.

'Us?' Dizzy echoed, half fearfully—but oh, so hopefully!

His other hand moved up to caress one of her cheeks in gentle wonder. 'I love you, Dizzy James——'

'Ellington-James,' she corrected harshly, her eyes suddenly full of all the unhappy memories.

Zach settled back on the sofa, pulling her against him, so that her head rested on his shoulder as he caressed her silky hair. 'I have a solution to that, if you would like to hear it?'

She could feel his tension beneath her cheek, knowing he wasn't as relaxed as he would like to appear. She nodded wordlessly, not in the least relaxed herself.

He let out a shaky breath. 'How does Dizzy Bennett sound to you?'

She sat up abruptly, staring down at him, finding only pleading sincerity in his face. She moistened her lips dazedly. Was Zach asking her to *marry* him? Well, he wasn't offering to adopt her, she admonished herself! But marriage? Oh, Christi had joked about it during their stay at Castle Haven, but Dizzy had never actually thought it might happen.

Zach swallowed hard. 'If you find that idea so distasteful that it leaves you speechless, perhaps you would prefer——'

'I don't find the idea of being your wife in the least distasteful!' she burst out in desperate denial. 'I just—you took me by surprise,' she admitted in understatement. 'You don't know anything about me.' She shook her head, sure he couldn't be serious.

'I know that you're completely loyal to those you care about, that you have compassion and love for a child you didn't even know——'

'Kate?' she frowned.

'Kate,' he nodded. 'Mrs Scott was most distressed that you had left before she had had time to thank you properly for all the help you gave her with Kate.'

'Oh,' she grimaced.

'Hmm!' He gave her a reproving look. 'So much for Christi the Good Samaritan!'

'She would have done the same thing if she had found out about Kate first,' Dizzy defended.

'You see,' Zach said with satisfaction, 'completely loyal. Maybe she would,' he conceded as Dizzy still continued to look indignant. 'But she didn't know about Kate first, you did, and you did the only thing someone as loving and lovely as you could do: you did everything within your power to make Kate happy again.'

'Anyone would have done the same,' she said uncomfortably.

'Anyone didn't, you did.' He tapped her reprovingly on the nose for her modesty. 'It's just part of your nature that you didn't want any thanks for what you did.'

'Is that *all* you know about me?' she frowned.

He smiled. 'Isn't it enough?' he teased.

'It doesn't seem an awful lot to base a marriage proposal on.' She still frowned. 'Unless you're just trying to get a Dizzy James illustration free for your next book?' she added lightly, the fact that everything might, just *might*, be going to work out after all, beginning to penetrate the misery she had known the last twenty-four hours.

'I never thought of that,' he said ruefully. 'Will I? As your husband?'

'No,' she mocked.

'As your lover?'

'No.' She began to smile, more and more sure with each passing second that Zach *did* love her, and began to be filled with a rosy glow of love reciprocated.

'As your husband *and* your lover?' he amended hopefully.

'Well...' She began to weaken. 'But you don't *have* to marry me if you would prefer—well, prefer——'

'I know I don't *have* to marry you,' he chided teasingly. 'Even I'm not so old and fusty and dusty that I don't realise you have to indulge in a little more lovemaking than we have so far to produce offspring.'

Colour heightened Dizzy's face at his easy use of the way she and Christi had used to describe him before Dizzy had actually met him. 'Christi told you about those names?' she grimaced.

He nodded, his eyes filled with laughter. 'They were among the few choice ones she chose to call me when she realised I had asked you to leave. And believe me, they were the more polite names she used!'

Dizzy bit her lip, but she couldn't completely stop the smile that formed on her lips. 'Christi is slow to lose her temper, but when she does, watch out!'

'So I discovered,' he grimaced ruefully. 'I concluded that any woman capable of language like that was more than able to take care of herself, and her money!'

Dizzy's eyes lit up with excitement. 'You decided to let her have her inheritance, after all?'

'There was never any doubt about it, Dizzy,' he said gently. 'I told you that yesterday. I had no idea of the interpretation Christi had put on my invitation to come and stay for a few weeks. If I had, I would have disabused her of that conclusion right away. Michael and Diana merely wanted Christi and me to remain close, not to have me test her, like some Victorian uncle.'

'I bet Christi is pleased.' Dizzy settled back against his shoulder.

'Not so that you would notice the last time we spoke,' he admitted ruefully. 'She made it perfectly clear that, if I was too stupid to do anything about my love for you, then she washed her hands of me until I did something about getting you back. This "charade" was supposed to do that, at the same time as showing you I was hiding something, too.'

It thrilled her to hear him talking so naturally about loving her. She wished she could admit the emotion as easily.

'That's sounds a bit strong for Christi,' she frowned at her friend's vehemence.

He gave a rueful sigh. 'I had just told her that I thought I was too old for you, too fusty and dusty, and that maybe you saw me as a father figure, as you didn't seem to be all that close to your own father,' he admitted reluctantly.

'You *what*?' Dizzy moved to glare down at him. 'How dare you——'

'Please,' he held up his hands defensively, wincing dramatically, 'Christi has already made it plain what you would think of that conclusion.'

'I should hope so,' she said indignantly. 'Did I kiss you as if I considered you a father figure, did I *want* you as if I felt that way? Honestly, Zach— is that why you've had your hair styled differently and been out and bought a new suit?' she frowned suspiciously.

He gave a rueful smile. 'I didn't think it would do any harm to smarten myself up a bit. I haven't bothered——'

'Of course it's done some harm,' she scolded. 'I'm probably going to have to beat all the other women off you now that the tailoring of that suit reveals the obvious masculinity of my Greek god! That was my name for you after I saw you swimming naked in the lake that day,' she revealed awkwardly.

'I'm flattered,' Zach grinned, sobering abruptly as he realised what else she had said. 'Does that mean you're going to marry me?' he prompted eagerly.

She swallowed hard. 'I may not be very good at being a wife——'

'You'll be perfect for me,' he said with certainty. 'And just think of the fact that you'll have exclusive rights to all the Claudia Laurence covers from now on,' he tempted.

'Are you really Claudia Laurence?' She looked at him quizzically, unable to envisage him writing those steamy historicals that were so famous worldwide.

Zach gave her a gently reproving look. 'Are you really avoiding giving me an answer?'

Dizzy drew in a ragged breath, her hand moving shakily to the hardness of his cheek. 'Only for the moment,' she admitted. 'Until I've had a chance to get used to the idea of your loving me.' She gave him a pleading look.

Love blazed out of his eyes before he bent his head to kiss the palm of her hand. 'I'll always love you, Dizzy,' he told her gruffly. 'You're the sort of woman a man meets only once in a lifetime, utterly unique. I knew it the moment I first looked at you.'

Just as she had experienced attraction for the first time when she looked at him, had known instinctively that Zach was her one chance at love. She had no doubts that her love for him would ever change, or that she would always want him in a way she had never even dreamt of wanting any other man. It was having him love her in the same way that was so hard to become accustomed to. There were still so many misunderstandings between Zach and herself, and yet now that he was over his own pained humiliation of yesterday she didn't doubt that he loved her unquestioningly. No one had ever loved her like this before; the love of Christi and her other friends was a different sort of love altogether.

'I'm in no rush,' Zach comforted as he saw her bewilderment. 'As long as you don't move further away from me than you are right now while you make your decision,' he added ruefully.

Dizzy gave a shaky laugh. 'I promise!' She snuggled down against him.

'Then, to answer your question,' he said briskly, 'yes, I really am Claudia Laurence.' He sounded a little embarrassed at having to make the admission.

Dizzy frowned, remembering what he had said about Christi reminding him that everyone had secrets they would rather weren't made public. Could this be the answer to the obscure statement Christi had once made about 'knowing' something about her uncle that he wouldn't be too pleased about if he realised she knew? She had a feeling it was.

'Does Christi know?' she asked lightly.

'Oh, yes,' Zach grimaced. 'Apparently she came looking for me in my study one day, and saw some papers I had left lying about on my desk. Also, there was the evidence of my parents' names. Claudia, and Laurence,' he supplied as Dizzy looked at him questioningly. 'Well, how else was I supposed to come up with a pseudonym for a writer of "hot historicals"?' he defended at Dizzy's grin.

'It sounds perfectly logical to me,' she teased.

He sighed. 'I started out writing them because I needed the money—you may have noticed that buying and keeping up a castle doesn't come cheap,' he added self-derisively.

She nodded. 'Christi and I wondered about it several times.'

'No doubt, with the sort of opinion you two young ladies had of me, you decided I'd robbed a bank or something!' he said disgustedly.

'Nothing as shocking as that,' she teased.

'No,' he drawled heavily. 'That would probably have been a little too exciting for the fusty, dusty professor.'

Dizzy put a silencing finger over his lips. 'I only thought of you in that way until I had met you; then I found you *very* exciting!'

His eyes gleamed. 'Have you had long enough to think yet?' he leered.

They were both making a game out of it now, both knowing that she had already made her decision, that she wouldn't be talking to him this way if she hadn't.

'Not quite,' she dismissed haughtily. She shook her head. 'No wonder Christi was so eager to help me get ready earlier to come over here; she knew exactly who she was sending me off to meet when she arranged the appointment and dropped me off in a taxi downstairs.' She chuckled indulgently. 'She was at my studio when my agent rang,' she explained at Zach's puzzlement. 'She took over the conversation with him once it became obvious I was still too upset about yesterday to even attempt to talk to him.'

'Oh, darling——'

'It's already forgotten,' she quickly reassured at his anguished groan, not meaning to remind him of that unhappy time.

'It isn't,' he said grimly. 'But I swear I'll never mistrust you again.'

Dizzy chuckled to ease the tension. 'Some of the answers to the questions you're going to ask are going to take some believing,' she warned.

'I believe them already,' he promised instantly.

She laughed softly. 'Don't be too hasty! As Christi is always reminding me, the illegal gambling one is a little difficult to accept—and she was the one who persuaded the police not to charge me!'

'Illegal——'

'I warned you,' she teased at his astounded expression.

'Yes, but——' He drew in a deeply controlling breath. 'If you say there's a perfectly logical explanation for it, then I believe you.'

'Oh, I didn't say it was logical.' Dizzy shook her head, her eyes shining like twin emeralds. 'Only that I had an explanation.'

Zach closed his eyes, and he was under control again when he reopened them. 'Just tell me one thing,' he said calmly. 'Is that the only occasion Christi stopped you being locked up in prison?'

The laughter deepened in her eyes. 'Yes, that is the only time,' she confirmed, bursting into unrestrained laughter as Zach obviously had difficulty restraining himself from asking any more questions. 'At the time, I had it in mind to forget about a career where I could use my artistic talent, and Christi knew this reporter——'

'—who just happened to be covering a story about illegal gambling,' Zach finished drily.

'There, now that wasn't so difficult, was it?' She had difficulty holding her laughter in check.

Zach muttered under his breath for several seconds, before looking at her reprovingly. 'I won't bother to point out how serious it could have been.'

She sobered. 'No. Are you ready to hear about Henry yet? Or has Christi already told you about him?' It was highly likely that she had, during her own explanations.

'I told you,' he grimaced. 'All Christi did was tell me what an idiot I was for having let you go out of my life.'

'She didn't explain away any of the half-truths and lies she told you?' Dizzy gasped.

He shrugged. 'I already knew you were closer than sisters, that you couldn't be destitute, considering who your parents are. Besides, Christi refused to explain herself, claiming that if I was stupid enough to let you go then I was also stupid enough to hang on to her money no matter what she said to vindicate herself.'

'And you're still going to let her have her money?' Dizzy gasped with incredulous laughter.

He grinned. 'It was almost like being back twenty years ago with my brother. He was very slow to boil, too, but when he did he let you have it with both barrels! Besides, it's Christi's money, not mine, and besides trying to put one over on her not-so-fusty uncle she seems a very sensible person. She has you for a best friend, doesn't she?' he said, as if that settled the whole matter.

'Oh, Zach!' Dizzy threw her arms around his neck, tears streaming down her face as she kissed him with all the love she had inside her.

Zach returned the kiss with a hunger of his own, tasting her again and again, both of them lost in the wonder of their love, oblivious to the gentle knock on the door.

The man who opened the door stared un-abashedly at Dizzy James in the arms of his star author. 'I know I said you could have my office for as long as you like,' David Kendrick drawled, when it seemed they weren't even going to come up for air. 'But I do have a publishing company to run,' he mocked as they both turned to him in as-tonishment, as if they had both completely for-gotten they were in *his* office on a sunny afternoon in summer.

As indeed they had. Dizzy looked shyly at Zach's ruffled appearance, his tie slightly off-centre from where her hands had been inside his unbuttoned shirt, and knew that her own face must be flushed, and her hair in wild disarray.

'Thanks, David.' Zach was the one to collect himself first, deftly rebuttoning his shirt. 'But I haven't had an answer to my proposal yet,' he added ruefully.

The other man grinned at him. 'Of course you have.'

Zach turned to her with eyes full of tenderness. 'I have?'

Her smile couldn't have been any wider if she had tried, dazzling both the men in the room. 'You have,' she glowed.

'I'd like to be best man,' David drawled as he moved to sit behind his desk.

'And Christi wants to be our bridesmaid,' Dizzy told Zach with a breathless laugh, hardly able to believe this was really happening.

'Then that seems to be settled, then.' His arm about her shoulders held her tightly to his side, and his face was full of pride as he looked down at her.

'Not quite,' she grimaced. 'I still haven't told you who Henry is.'

'You can tell me on the way to your studio,' he decided firmly. 'Maybe I can also be one of the privileged few who know what DC stands for,' he added teasingly.

'Oh, that's easy——' David broke off as they both turned to him, Dizzy with a silencing frown, Zach with open curiosity. 'It's on her contracts,' he shrugged lamely.

'Talking of contracts, David——' Zach spoke authoritatively, effectively ending the subject of Dizzy's names, knowing she would rather they were alone when they were revealed.

'I know.' David put up defensive hands. 'You want your money as soon as possible so that you can put heating into your castle. I suppose that's only reasonable when you intend taking your bride back there,' he teased. 'Or do you intend generating your own heat?'

Zach's gaze was frankly sensual as he gazed down at Dizzy. 'Oh, I think we'll get by for a while,' he murmured throatily.

Dizzy put her arm through the crook of his. 'More than a while,' she breathed huskily.

'Get out of here, before you set fire to my office!' David complained, grinning widely as they left the room, having eyes only for each other.

Dizzy went with Zach unhesitantly, knowing she could trust him implicitly with her future—and her past.

Zach held her tightly against his side as they walked to the lift. 'I've just remembered something else I learnt about you in the few days I've known you,' he murmured against her ear as the lift doors opened smoothly in front of them.

Dizzy looked up at him with glowing eyes. 'Oh, yes?'

'Yes.' He turned her into his arms, moulding her body against his, a move perfectly in keeping with her Greek god. 'I learnt——' His lips moved against her earlobe. 'I learnt,' he began again, 'that you excite me beyond thinking. There hasn't been a moment go by when I haven't wanted to make love to you. And I know I'm going to feel that way for the rest of my life,' he told her deeply, his gaze holding hers as he told her of his love.

Dizzy flung her arms about his neck. 'I love you!' she groaned emotionally as the lift doors closed behind them to quietly whisk them down to the ground floor.

Her ecstatic statement was followed by a very satisfactory silence, and then the soft murmur of voices, and then Zach's, 'Henry's a *what*?', followed by Dizzy's giggles of pure happiness.

'That young lady needs to be taught a lesson,' Zach stormed as they stepped out of the building to hail a taxi.

Dizzy gave a secretive smile. 'That's just what I've been thinking.'

Zach looked down at her suspiciously. 'What are you up to?' He voiced his reservation.

'Nothing,' she dismissed innocently. 'Yet,' she added softly.

'That's what I was afraid of.' He frowned with the look of a man who had suddenly realised he had his very own 'tiger by the tail'. But the satisfied smile that instantly followed the frown negated any idea that he was dissatisfied with the arrangement; rather, he looked as if he were going to enjoy every moment of the rest of his life. 'Do you think we might have a few months' grace before you start teaching Christi this lesson?' he grimaced.

'Of course!' She looked at him with widely innocent eyes. 'I have the new Claudia Laurence cover to keep me occupied for—— '

'You have *me* to keep you occupied,' Zach growled with mock ferocity.

This laughing together was a side of a man and woman together that Dizzy had never experienced. From her memories of them together, her parents had either been arguing or not talking at all, so that the closest she had come to this warm satisfaction of teasing each other had been with her friends. And being like this with Zach was nothing like that.

But all the laughter stopped once they reached her studio. Zach took her in his arms and made such exquisite love to her that tears streamed down her cheeks as they reached total fulfilment together, the moment so poignantly beautiful she never wanted it to end.

Even when that aching pleasure did end, the closeness didn't, and she knew a oneness with Zach that totally engulfed and protected her.

Talking about her parents, her childhood, didn't seem so difficult to do any more, although, as Zach tensed beside her in the narrow bed, she knew he was furiously angry at the suffering her parents had caused her.

She didn't look at him as she told him how her father had never wanted her, how her mother had walked out on them both when she couldn't take any more. She trembled slightly as she remembered how she had been bewildered by her mother's disappearance, pleading with her father to tell her where she had gone. His answer had been to send her to her bedroom without company or food for the rest of the day, the dark shadows of Knollsley Hall taking on frightening proportions to the lonely little girl who cried alone for the mother who hadn't wanted her and the father who couldn't love her.

'The bastard!' Zach rasped fiercely. 'My God, no wonder that painting of Knollsley Hall gave you the shudders! And that little girl in "Lost Child" is you, isn't she?' he realised with a pained groan.

Dizzy shook her head. 'I think that would be crediting my mother with feelings she doesn't have. I've always believed the painting was a self-portrait, her way of expressing her own unhappiness with my father, the indulged prison she felt he had locked her into. She has the same colouring as me, you see, even down to this fly-away hair,' she said, attempting to lighten the tension, while Zach's arms gripped her tightly to him.

He stroked her hair tenderly. 'I love your hair.' He kissed the silky softness.

She gave a shaky smile. 'My mother couldn't have cared anything about me, because she never even attempted to see me after she ran away from my father, didn't care that she had left me with the monster she couldn't stand being married to,' she added bitterly.

Zach breathed unevenly beneath her cheek. 'Tell me what else he did to you,' he encouraged tautly.

She did, vividly remembering how she had met the same terrifying fate every time she asked when her mother was coming home, so that in the end she stopped even mentioning her mother, for fear of being sent to the loneliness of the room that was fast becoming her own prison, the dark rooms and corridors of Knollsley Hall becoming a nightmare to her.

Zach held her close as the tears fell softly against her cheeks, and she told him of the fear she still had of darkness, how most nights she read with the light on until she either fell into an exhausted sleep or the dawn began to break.

'You'll never be alone in the darkness again,' he assured her raggedly, kissing the tears from her cheeks. 'And you'll never have to even think of your parents again. Two people like that don't deserve the beauty of a daughter like you!'

She gave a shaky smile, relieved the truth was all told. 'You could be a little biased,' she gently teased him.

He frowned. 'I'm a lot biased,' he agreed firmly. 'I loved you the minute I saw you, and I'll go on loving you until the day I die.'

Dizzy responded with all the warmth there was in her, their lovemaking even more fiery than the first time, all the shadows forgotten as they once again lay replete in each other's arms.

Zach absently played with the wildness of her hair, he was flushed and younger looking, his face softened by love. 'You still haven't told me what DC stands for,' he realised lazily.

All the secrets *hadn't* been revealed! She had completely forgotten the mystery that still surrounded her names.

She leant up on one elbow, bending to whisper softly in Zach's ear.

'Really?' he gasped as she straightened. 'Good lord,' he added dazedly.

Dizzy laughed softly at his reaction, confident she would know nothing but the complete happiness of being loved by Zach for the rest of her life.

Dizzy sat on the grassy slope, watching her husband as he cavorted about in the water, smiling brightly as he saw her there and swam to the shore, gasping breathlessly as he stepped naked from the water.

Almost three months of marriage had given him a relaxed and confident appearance; he moved with a feline grace that never ceased to make Dizzy's heart spin.

He was beautiful, and in that moment she wanted him with a need that bordered on desperation, standing up to slowly begin removing her clothes.

Zach grinned as he helped her with the buttons to her blouse. 'I thought you would never join me,' he murmured appreciatively as he bared her breasts for his enjoyment.

Dizzy's back arched as he drew one sensitised peak into his mouth.

The seclusion of this lake had become their own little paradise, Zach having confided in her that he had discovered the delights of nude bathing while researching the practicality of it for one of his books. Dizzy was more than willing to aid him with all his research now!

It was some time later before she was able to think clearly again. She was nestled snugly on top of Zach's body, their breathing slowly steadying.

She kissed the golden skin of his chest. 'I have some news for you,' she muttered between kisses.

'Hm?' Zach groaned his sleepy satisfaction.

'We're going to have a baby.'

She had known he wouldn't remain sleepy for long after she had made this announcement, and suddenly found herself lying on the blanket at his side as he stared down at her incredulously.

'Don't look so shocked, Zach,' she teased him as he remained speechless. 'It's perfectly natural, after what we've been doing constantly for the last three months,' she told him indulgently.

His stunned gaze moved slowly over the slenderness of her body, lingering on the flatness of her stomach before moving sharply to her face. 'Are you sure?' he breathed raggedly.

She knew the reason for his dazed disbelief: the two of them had made a conscious decision two months ago to try for a baby, but neither of them had expected to be so immediately successful.

'Oh, I'm sure, Zach.' She stretched lazily. 'They taught us in biology at school that——'

'I didn't mean are you sure about *that*,' he reproved impatiently at her teasing smile. 'I meant, are you sure about——' His hand came to rest possessively on the flatness of her stomach.

She made a concerted effort not to laugh with sheer happiness. 'I opened a tin of pilchards for my lunch just now and they made me feel nauseous,' she told him in a deadpan voice.

'You *are* pregnant!' He gave a joyous cry, sweeping her up into his arms, then becoming suddenly still as he looked down at her anxiously. 'Are you all right? Is the baby all right? You shouldn't be lying on this damp grass in your condition!' He hastily began to bundle her back into her clothes.

'I'm fine.' She helped him as best she could, pushing her arms into her blouse, as he seemed intent on strangling her with it. 'The baby is fine. And the grass isn't damp,' she teased indulgently. 'It may be September, but it hasn't rained for weeks.'

'I don't want you catching a chill.' Zach didn't seem to have heard her reassurances, he was so intent on dressing her. 'I'm going to be with you the whole time, you know,' he told her as he zipped her back into her denims. 'No one is going to push me out of the delivery-room just as my daughter is about to be born!' he added firmly.

'We have months to go yet,' she laughed happily. 'And it could be a son,' she warned.

He shook his head. 'A daughter, as beautiful as her mother.'

'But not with such awful names!' Dizzy wrinkled her nose self-disgustedly.

Zach grinned. 'I think one Delilah Cleopatra is enough in any family!'

'Ssh!' She looked about them anxiously.

He laughed at her hunted expression. 'I'll never forget the look on the vicar's face when you asked him if he *had* to read out your full names!'

Dizzy gave him a reproving glance. 'It almost stopped me marrying you!'

'No chance,' he said confidently, taking her into his arms. 'Look at it this way, Dizzy,' he taunted at her outraged expression. 'By marrying me, only a few guests heard your "skeleton in the cupboard". If you had refused to go through with it, the whole world would have known about Delilah Cleopatra when I gave the information to the media!'

'You wouldn't have dared!' Her eyes were wide with indignation.

'Of course I would,' he said without remorse. 'Then you would have had no reason not to marry me.'

'Except that you would have been in hospital in traction,' she frowned fiercely.

He chuckled softly. 'I love it when you get aggressive.'

'Zachariah Bennett——'

'Yes—Dizzy Bennett?' he prompted gently.

She became suddenly still in his arms, her expression softening. 'I *love* you,' she told him breathlessly.

His own laughter faded. 'I love you, too. But then, that's as it should be between two people who are going to spend the rest of their lives living and loving together.'

The rest of their lives...

Yes, she didn't doubt it would be that way between her and Zach.

How lucky she was that the one man she had known she could love was in love with her, too. That 'one chance at love' had been all she needed!

TO LOVE AGAIN

For
Matthew and Joshua

CHAPTER ONE

CHRISTI stared in horror at the man who took up most of the open doorway to her flat, holding her hands up defensively. 'Whatever you do, don't come in here!' she warned fiercely.

To her chagrin he smiled, although he made no effort to come further into the room. 'What are you doing on the floor?' he drawled unconcernedly.

Christi came up off her hands and leant back on her knees. 'I—oh, no!' she groaned as a brown and grey bullet entered the room, finding herself almost knocked over as the tiny creature leapt up and down in front of her face, trying to lick her nose. 'No, Henry.' She desperately tried to still the movements of her excited Yorkshire terrier. 'Henry—— Oh, damn!' She gave in with a resigned groan, taking the dog into her arms to receive the ecstatic greeting.

'He's missed you.' Lucas made the understatement mockingly, grinning his amusement as Christi gave him a censorious frown.

'I've only been gone a couple of days,' she dismissed distractedly, her attention once again on the carpet in front of her now that Henry had calmed down enough to sit relatively still in her arms. 'Take him, will you?' She reached out to hold the dog up to Lucas. 'But don't come any closer,' she warned as Lucas strode forcefully into the room, having let

7

himself into the apartment with the key she had given him.

He gave a weary sigh, coming to an abrupt halt. 'Make up your mind, Christi,' he said drily. 'Either I can come in, or I can't. Is there a man in your bedroom? Is that it?' He quirked dark brows interestedly.

Christi shot him a look that clearly told him the question was beneath contempt. 'I happen to have lost a contact lens——'

'Not again,' Lucas groaned impatiently. 'Last time you lost one of them it was down your——'

'I know where it was,' she put in hastily, blushing.

'Well, have you looked down there this time?' He looked speculatively at the creamy perfection of her cleavage, which was visible above the open neckline of her blouse. 'I could always help you if you haven't,' he flirted easily.

That was the trouble with Lucas; he flirted with lazy ease, having a constant stream of women in his life, who seemed to remain his friend even after the relationship had ended. He and Christi seemed to have skipped the first part and gone straight on to the friendship, Lucas's teasing of her just that. It was rather depressing to be thought of as just a 'pal' by a man like Lucas!

Everyone she had ever introduced him to had envied the fact that she actually had him living in the flat next door to her own. And that wasn't so surprising, for Lucas was devastating to look at; tall and dark, with piercing grey eyes that could be dark with laughter or glittering silver with anger, his body of the type that looked beautifully elegant in the superbly tailored suits he wore, or obviously masculine in the shorts he wore when he played tennis. He possessed a sense of humour that enchanted, a honeyed charm that enthralled, and a raw sexuality that acted like a magnet to any woman in the vicinity.

But he was also thirty-seven to her almost twenty-two, and had taken her under his protective wing since she had moved into this flat almost four years ago, acting more like her uncle than her real uncle did! He had also helped her find her missing contact lenses more times than she cared to think about, had taken care of her pets when she'd been away, and had fed her lemon juice when she had been flat out in bed with a cold, doing a good impersonation of Rudolf! No wonder he had never looked on her as anything more than 'the kid next door'—she *was* the kid next door!

'Just take Henry, will you?' She sighed her irritation. 'I haven't had the best of weekends, and if I can't find my lens I won't be able to go for that audition this afternoon.'

Lucas held the dog lightly in his arms as Christi resumed her search, her two Siamese cats entwining themselves about his long legs. He reached down to absently stroke Josephine and Gladys, straightening as Christi gave a triumphant cry, holding the truant lens as she scrambled to her feet to put it in before it did another disappearing act.

He frowned as she turned to face him. 'I thought you were looking forward to spending the weekend with Dizzy and your uncle.' He spoke slowly. 'There's nothing wrong with the baby, is there?' he added, concern in his voice.

Christi's expression instantly softened. 'Laura is the most beautiful, contented——'

'The baby is fine,' Lucas drawled drily.

'—little love I have ever seen,' Christi finished proudly. 'She has lovely golden curls—which is only to be expected when Dizzy and Uncle Zach—just Zach,' she amended with a grimace. 'He finally got around to telling me I can call him that, now that he's been married to my best friend for almost a year,' she derided. 'But, with both of them being so fair, Laura was sure to be blonde herself,' she completed her earlier statement.

Lucas looked pointedly at her ebony hair. 'They can't all be blondes in your family.'

'The Bennetts are,' she nodded. 'You know I got my colouring from my mother.' She experienced the usual sadness she felt whenever she thought of the wonderful parents she had lost four years ago, the two of them on an archaeological dig when it had capsized and buried them beneath tons of earth.

She hadn't been quite eighteen at the time, and remembered that the birthday she had spent with her Uncle Zach had been a miserable time, both of them numbed by the accident that had left them the only two remaining members of their family. Her uncle had been distant from her then, a remote professor of history who seemed to live among his books. Falling in love with impetuous madcap

Dizzy had changed all that, and when he wasn't amused by his young wife's antics he was *bemused*!

But, four years ago, Dizzy had been a long way from entering his life, and the two of them had found little to say to each other to ease the pain of their loss. Lucas had helped to ease her pain more than her uncle had, had held her as she'd cried bitter tears, had sat with her as she'd brooded in silence, had taken her out on picnics and walks when it seemed she would finally come out of the dark tunnel of depression her parents' deaths had caused.

Their friendship had grown from those months of anger and pain shortly after she had moved in here; it was a friendship Christi knew she would find it hard to live without now, and she dreaded the day one of those women in his life became more than lover and then friend, sure that another woman wouldn't welcome Lucas's friendship with her into their married life.

She wasn't conceited; as an actress she had been taught to evaluate her looks, to know her advantages and her limitations, and shoulder-length ebony hair, enormous sparkling blue eyes, straight nose, and widely curving mouth, tall and curving body, added up to quite a few advantages. No other woman was ever going to believe there was just friendship between herself and Lucas! She wasn't sure she believed it herself, considering how sexually attractive he was, having had more than her own share of men in her life. But friends they were, and it was a relationship they were both comfortable with. Certainly neither of them was willing to risk what they had for what would probably amount to a few days or weeks of being lovers.

'So what was wrong with your weekend?'

She frowned, concentrating with effort, her frown turning to a scowl as she thought over Lucas's question. 'Dizzy,' she began in a barely controlled voice, 'in her role as aunt and new mother, has decided that it's time I settled down myself——'

'What?' Lucas said incredulously.

'Oh, yes,' Christi confirmed disgustedly. 'Last year, Dizzy and Zach were worried because I didn't go out with anyone for more than a month, and *now* they're worried because I haven't seen anyone for six months!' She shook her head.

'Hm, I wondered about that myself——'

'Don't you start,' she warned, moving automatically to the kitchen to get her pets some breakfast as they all milled about her legs, Lucas having put Henry down long ago. 'I've been concentrating on my career the last six months,' she firmly informed Lucas as he came to lounge in the kitchen doorway.

He nodded. 'Nevertheless, it's been pretty quiet around here lately,' he mocked.

Christi gave him a look that clearly told him she didn't appreciate his humour. 'It's a pity the same can't be said for next door,' she returned waspishly, referring to the party he had held on the eve of her departure to the Lake District to visit her uncle and Dizzy.

'Ouch!' His eyes laughed at her. 'I did ask you to join us,' he reminded, not in the least perturbed by her complaint, knowing it wasn't justified, for his parties were never of the 'loud' variety.

Her bad humour faded as quickly as it had come; she hadn't really been angry. People who really knew her, and Lucas was one of them, knew that she was slow to anger. But when she did lose her temper it was best to take cover as soon as possible!

'It sounded like fun,' she conceded ruefully. 'But I had an early start Friday morning and I didn't want to be overtired.' She gave a heavy sigh. 'I wish now that I'd never gone! Oh, it was lovely seeing Laura for the first time, and I'm always pleased to spend time with Dizzy and Zach——'

'But?' Lucas prompted softly, taking out the cups to pour them both a cup of coffee from the pot, with the ease of familiarity.

'Thanks,' Christi accepted absently. She drew in a deep breath. 'But,' she sighed again, 'Dizzy had invited three of what she called ''eligible'' men for the weekend, too, for me to look over!' she concluded disgustedly.

Lucas just stared at her, his coffee-cup held unwaveringly in one slenderly masculine hand; for once, the articulate businessman, who could make a success of any company he chose to take over, was completely struck dumb.

Christi couldn't blame him; she had been more than a little speechless herself when Dizzy had calmly introduced the three men as their other weekend guests!

If she had met those men under any other circumstances, she probably would have found each of them as interesting as Dizzy assured her they were, but as the only female guest among three attractive men it had been instantly obvious what Dizzy was up to. Much as she loved her best friend from childhood, she could cheerfully have strangled her when they had all sat down to lunch and she'd found her attention demanded by each man in turn. Dizzy's intent was about as subtle as a sledgehammer, and Christi had spent a very embarrassing three days trying to fend off three fascinatingly attractive men. Some would have said she was mad to even try. Most would have known she had failed miserably when she had returned from the traumatic weekend with separate dates to see each man again!

Dizzy had been completely unconcerned by Christi's embarrassed protests about what she was up to, reminding Christi of a conversation they had once had about Christi advertising in a magazine for her ideal partner, sure she had as much chance of finding him that way as she did with any of the men she had dated so far. It had been a light-hearted conversation, made completely in fun on Christi's side, but Dizzy had obviously taken it seriously. While her marriage to Zach, and his obvious disapproval of such a ridiculous idea as advertising in a magazine, had been a foregone conclusion, Dizzy had done the next best thing as far as she was concerned, picking three men out of her close acquaintance that she was sure Christi would like, inviting them all together for the weekend, and sitting back to watch the results. The result had been that, after months of not dating anyone, Christi now had three different men to see in the next week!

She grimaced as she saw Lucas was still staring at her. 'You can close your mouth now,' she taunted, feeling the first stirrings of amusement over a weekend which at best had been awkward, at worst downright uncomfortable!

He did so slowly, sitting on the side of one of the bar stools that sided her breakfast bar. 'Dizzy seemed like a sane woman the one and only time I met her, when she married your uncle.' He spoke dazedly.

Christi grinned. 'You saw her on a good day, on her best behaviour.'

He shook his head. 'Has no one ever told her that the custom of choosing a husband for a female relative went out of style years ago?'

Her smile widened. 'Something as trivial as that isn't likely to stop Dizzy once she makes her mind up to an idea,' she dismissed ruefully, having years of experience to base her claim upon.

Lucas whistled softly through his teeth. 'So, what are you going to do?'

Embarrassed colour darkened her magnolia cheeks. 'I'm seeing Dick on Tuesday, Barry on Thursday, and David on Saturday,' she revealed reluctantly.

His mouth twisted. 'That's certainly showing Dizzy that she can't push you around!'

'I was in an awkward position,' Christi defended. 'I'd like to have seen you come out of it any differently.'

'My dear Christi,' he drawled derisively, 'no one pressures me into going out with someone I'd rather not.'

Her irritation increased, for she knew full well that a man like Lucas, who had remained single since his divorce several years ago, wouldn't be forced into doing *anything* he didn't want to do. But he was different from her, had a way of getting what he wanted, and away from what he didn't want, without anyone challenging his right to do so. That arrogance seemed to be a part of his nature he, and other people, took for granted; she just didn't have the same determination.

'I actually liked Dick, Barry and David,' she told him defensively.

He pulled a face, perfectly relaxed now that he was over his first surprise. 'Dick, Barry, and David who?' he drawled.

'Dick Crosby—Dizzy's agent,' she supplied a little resentfully. 'I've met him before, of course, since Dizzy began working as a freelance illustrator. Barry is Barry Robbins, a friend of my uncle's from his university days, who apparently put his studies to use in directing films in Hollywood,' she added challengingly as Lucas looked unimpressed.

'I've heard of him,' Lucas nodded dismissively.

'Hm,' she acknowledged irritably; the tall, blond-haired director was handsome enough to have appeared in his films rather than remaining behind the camera.

'I think I met Dick Crosby, at least, at the wedding,' Lucas remarked thoughtfully.

'Possibly,' she dismissed. 'I believe Barry was unable to get here in time.'

Because it hadn't seemed suitable to take a man to her uncle and Dizzy's wedding that she probably wouldn't see again a couple of weeks later, she had asked Lucas if he would accompany her instead. She had been thrilled when he'd accepted, proud to have had such an attractive man as her partner for the day.

'Just think yourself lucky you weren't one of the men chosen by Dizzy as suitable for me,' she told him disgustedly.

Lucas's mouth quirked. 'I wasn't "chosen" by her because I'm not suitable as far as you're concerned.' He tapped her playfully on the nose. 'I'm far too old for you, even if I'm not quite old enough to be your father. I think I certainly qualify for the role of a much older brother,' he added drily.

'My uncle is fourteen years older than Dizzy,' she defended.

'And they're obviously deliriously happy together,' he nodded. 'It's always the ones who are happy who are trying to pair everyone else off,' he explained at Christi's questioning look. 'But it isn't very often these spring and autumn relationships work out.'

'I think of Zach and Dizzy more as early summer and late spring,' she protested. 'I do know they're

the best thing that ever happened to each other,'
she added indulgently, never having seen Dizzy quite
so confident of herself, nor her uncle quite so light-
hearted, as they had been since they had fallen in
love with each other.

'You haven't told me who the third man is yet,'
Lucas reminded softly.

Because she had been saving the best until last!
'David Kendrick,' she revealed a little triumphantly, knowing he *had* to be impressed by the
last man. 'Zach's publisher.'

Dark brows rose appreciatively. 'I know him quite
well,' he nodded slowly.

It didn't surprise her in the least that David and
Lucas should know each other; in fact, she remembered them talking briefly at the wedding last year,
David acting as Zach's best man. As businessmen,
Lucas and David had a lot in common, both
seeming to have the Midas touch, their interests di-
versified but, without exception, successful.

'I have to agree with Dizzy about him,' she said
softly.

'Why not Barry Robbins?' Lucas shrugged. 'You
said he's a film director, and you're an actress, so
maybe he'll be able to help your career.'

Her mouth tightened. 'I don't believe it's done
that way any more!'

Lucas looked at her frowningly, then his mouth
twitched with amusement as her meaning became
clear, and finally he grinned openly. 'I meant if you
were his wife, of course,' he said innocently.

'Of course,' she said sharply. 'But isn't that leaping into the future just a little?' she derided. 'I only have one date with the man. I certainly don't need you matchmaking, too!'

'Sorry,' he grimaced. 'I must try and remember that big brothers are for protecting you from big bad wolves like those three.'

Christi sighed, not appreciating his humour at her expense at all. She didn't find *anything* about the situation funny. 'Enough about my weekend,' she dismissed briskly. 'How did yours go?' she asked interestedly.

His humour instantly faded, a brooding look in his silver-grey eyes. 'Marsha didn't bring the children over until Saturday morning,' he revealed bitterly. 'Claimed Daisy had a temperature the day before.'

Christi gave him a sympathetic grimace. Lucas and his ex-wife didn't get on, and after she had met the brittly shallow woman a couple of times it wasn't too difficult to understand why a man as warm and charming as Lucas should find his ex-wife's grasping and manipulative nature highly distasteful.

Oh, Marsha hadn't always been that way, he had assured Christi. In fact, the two of them had been quite happy together when they had first married and produced first Robin and then Daisy. But, with the progression of their marriage, so had Lucas's success increased, and also Marsha's wants and ambitions. For the sake of their children, Lucas had given Marsha everything she asked for; he could afford it, so why not? Their marriage seemed to have survived only by Lucas giving and Marsha taking during the years. Until the day Marsha realised she could go on taking without having to remain married to Lucas.

Lucas had skimmed over the rocky years of his marriage to Marsha, playing down the difficult parts, enthusing over what a joy the children had been to him and Marsha both. It had been Marsha who had told Christi, in her brittle way, just how 'hellish' she had considered her marriage to Lucas to be, initially completely misunderstanding the friendship that existed between Christi and Lucas, warning her sharply of the dull life she could expect to lead if she became seriously involved with Lucas. Marsha's life as Lucas's wife had sounded far from dull to Christi, and her words more the fretful complaints of a spoilt woman.

As far as Christi could tell, Lucas's real regret at the breakdown five years ago of his four-year marriage was that his children had been left in Marsha's care, that he was only able to have seven-year-old Robin and six-year-old Daisy on the weekends and holidays Marsha agreed to let him have them.

It didn't seem right to Christi that such a woman should have the care of Lucas's children but, as he himself admitted, he had never been able to criticise Marsha's ability to be a mother to their two children.

But that caring didn't extend to the inclusions of bothering herself unduly about the feelings of the man she had dismissed so easily from her life once his wealth made it possible for her to still live lavishly without the restrictions of a husband, and so she didn't hesitate to callously let him down when he was expecting to see the children, always having a perfectly valid excuse for doing so, of course, so that there should be no legal repercussions.

Christie's heart ached for how much Lucas missed having his children with him all the time, how each time he saw them they seemed to have grown up a little more, achieved new things he had no sharing in. It was only the fact that Robin and Daisy seemed so well adjusted to the situation that prevented him being more bitter about things than he was.

But by the sound of it Marsha had been up to her usual tricks this weekend, seeming to take a fiendish delight in upsetting Lucas's plans for spending time with his children. Christi felt like shaking the other woman but, knowing the beautiful redhead, she would only laugh at accusations that she was being cruel to Lucas. She had claimed he didn't have a heart to be hurt on the one occasion Christi had tentatively mentioned how upsetting it must be for him to be parted from his children in this way.

Needless to say, there was no love lost between her and the other woman, although none of that showed as she smiled at Lucas. 'How did Daisy seem over the weekend?' she prompted lightly.

His expression softened. 'They were both fine. Having the cats and dog about the place helped,' he added soberly, unconsciously revealing the strain of only being allowed to be a part-time parent.

'I'm glad.' Christi gave a bright smile. 'Did Daisy lose her other front tooth? You said it was a bit wobbly the last time she stayed.'

The harshness of his face was completely softened with love for the two mischievous imps that looked so much like him, with their thick dark hair and silver-grey eyes. 'Lost it and started to grow the replacement,' he answered ruefully.

'And did Robin like the Transformer you sent for his birthday?' she smiled.

Lucas's mouth tightened, his eyes a fierce silver. 'His mother decided it wasn't suitable for him and exchanged it for something else,' he rasped.

Christi gave a pained frown, sure that the toy had been perfectly suitable for Robin. She had gone with Lucas to shop for the sturdy toy, Lucas having taken care not to buy anything with guns, respecting, and agreeing with, Marsha's decision that Robin had plenty of time before he needed to be introduced to the violence in life. The Transformer they had finally chosen did no more than change from a robust truck into a robot. What possible harm could Marsha have found in that? The obvious thing seemed to be that his father had bought it for him. The other woman wasn't averse to taking what she could from Lucas—the monthly allowance she received from him was enough to keep most families for a year!—but she wasn't about to let Lucas take the praise for anything. Christi didn't know how Lucas managed to control the anger he must feel towards his ex-wife!

'I'm sure he liked what he had instead,' she bit out tautly.

'He didn't say,' Lucas said grimly, glancing at his wristwatch as he stood up. 'I have an appointment at ten, so I have to go now,' he told her lightly, bringing back the smiling Lucas with effort. 'Good luck with the audition this afternoon.' He nudged her gently under the chin with his fist. 'Break a leg,' he teased.

She returned his smile. 'Thanks for looking after the pets for me.' She walked him to the door.

'My pleasure.' He moved with leashed vitality, grinning at her as they reached the door. 'And I shall expect a full report on your dates this week,' he derided. 'And remember, as an honorary brother, I expect an invitation to the wedding,' came his parting shot.

Christi watched him stride off down the corridor to the lift, returning his brief salute before the doors closed behind him.

Oh, she would honour the dates she had made with the three men while they were in the Lake District, but she knew with certainty that a wedding wouldn't result from seeing any of them again.

How could she marry anyone when it was Lucas she loved, that she had always loved?

CHAPTER TWO

PERHAPS always was putting it a little strongly, but Christi had certainly loved Lucas from the time he had first introduced himself as her neighbour almost four years ago.

Her parents had only recently died, the full impact of that not hitting her until weeks later, and her move from her parents' house to a smaller, more manageable apartment had been made with something like detachment. Certainly, it hadn't been until some of the suitable furniture from her parents' home was being moved into the apartment that she suddenly realised her mother would never be coming back to sit behind the delicate writing-table as she answered all her overdue correspondence, that her father—her dear, absent-minded father—wouldn't ever again have a need for the display cabinet that had housed his most precious objects, those artefacts now given to museums, as he had requested they should be in his will.

But seeing all that furniture moved into these strange surroundings had been the end for her. She had run from the apartment with a choked cry, coming to an abrupt halt as she crashed into a hard, but somehow soft, wall. Lucas's chest . . .

She had been eighteen years old, sheltered and cosseted all her life by over-indulgent parents, the men she had so far had in her life only a passing amusement at best. But, as she looked up into the harshly beautiful face of the man that held her so tightly against his chest, she had felt her heart leave her body and join with his. Not even a word had passed between them, but Christi knew she was looking into the face of the man she loved.

And when he had spoken it had been with gentle kindness, introducing himself as Lucas Kingsley, her new neighbour, insisting she join him in his apartment for a drink of some kind while the removal men finished bringing up her furniture.

Christi had felt wrapped in a protective glow, huskily explaining her recent loss, held tightly in his arms as she cried on his broad shoulder, her senses wallowing in the clean smell of him that was mingled with another smell that was all Lucas, a completely masculine aura that seduced and tempted, drawing her more fully into his spell.

He had left her only briefly, and that was to tip the removal men when they knocked on the door to say they had finished, returning instantly to take her in his arms once again.

But, during that time, or the many times afterwards when he had offered her the same comfort, it had never been the sort of embrace she wanted from him. He treated her more like the little sister he had never had, taking her firmly under his wing until she felt able to stand on her own two shaky feet, even then continuing to be the shoulder she could always cry on if she felt the need.

She had watched with dismay as first one woman entered his life, and then another, none of them lasting very long, all of them maintaining a friendship even once the relationship was over. With each new woman that entered his life, Christi lived in dread of this one being the one he decided to settle down with.

After two years of loving him that hopelessly, when it seemed he would never see her as more than the 'little girl next door,' she had decided something would have to be done to make him see she was all grown up now, a woman in every sense of the word. If she couldn't have Lucas, she was going to make sure he saw her with enough men to be convinced of her maturity.

The next year had been full of those men, but, instead of Lucas accepting she was no longer a child, he had merely offered her his shoulder to cry on whenever one of those friendships broke up!

After more careful thought, she had decided that it had to be the fact that she still had a guardian, in the shape of her uncle Zach, that prevented Lucas seeing her maturity, and consequently her love for him. That decision had provoked an elaborate—and, she accepted now a ridiculous—plan, that would show her uncle just how adept she was at taking responsibility for her own life. The result of that had been her uncle and Dizzy—who she had somehow managed to persuade to enter into the madcap scheme to hoodwink her uncle—falling in love with each other, her uncle releasing his guardianship of her and her inheritance into her own control at twenty-one, instead of the twenty-five it could have been—and with Lucas's attitude not changing towards her in the least!

She had been at a loss to know *what* to do after that, had drifted along for another six months, lost in a sea of self-pity. Then, as a last desperate plea for Lucas's love, she had stopped dating other men altogether, concentrating on her career, hoping that would finally make him sit up and take notice of her. Months later, she had to admit it hadn't affected him in the slightest.

And neither had the idea of her possibly becoming involved with Dick Crosby, Barry Robbins, or David Kendrick! He had even invited himself to the wedding!

She would just have to accept it, she didn't have anything to interest a man of thirty-seven who had been married and had a couple of children.

She couldn't accept that! She loved Lucas, had loved him for four long years, would go on loving him until the day she died. And she wouldn't give up trying to get him to return that love until that day came!

The last thing she felt like doing at the end of another exhausting—and disappointing—day, was getting dressed up to go out on a date with Dick Crosby.

She freely admitted that she had got out of the habit of going out on dates the last six months. Not that it had been too difficult; until last week she had had a one-line part in a long-running play, which had taken up most of her evenings. But last week the play had come to an end, and so she was back looking for work, or 'resting', as most people knew it. She knew she was one of the lucky ones; her allowance, and then her full inheritance, meant that she was never going to be one of the 'starving' actors who had to find work to survive. But she wanted to make a success of her career, and loved to act, going for any of the auditions her agent managed to set up for her. It was a bit much to expect success after only two days of looking, but the fact that she hadn't didn't add to the mood of wanting to go out for the evening.

It didn't help that she hadn't seen Lucas since he had so blithely invited himself to her non-existent wedding, either!

He had been out on a date last night himself, with a beautiful lawyer who possessed brains as well as all that blonde beauty; Christi had learnt this when Lucas introduced the two of them last week. He and Michelle had been seeing each other for a couple of weeks now, and Christi could tell by the way Michelle looked at Lucas that she was more than fond of him. It was like twisting a knife in her chest to see him with other women, to imagine him making love to those women. One thing she was grateful for, Lucas never brought those women home to spend the night with him, any lovemaking he did obviously taking place at the woman's home.

He had come home alone last night, late, because Christi had heard him letting himself into his apartment just after twelve.

He had already left for the office in town, from which he ran his considerable empire, by the time she'd got up this morning; and as she wasn't likely to see him tonight, either, now that she was going out herself, the evening looked bleak.

Poor Dick Crosby! She wasn't being fair to him at all, she realised ruefully. He couldn't help it if he wasn't the man she really wanted to be with, nor that she was in love with a man who was far out of her reach.

Because she felt so guilty about her reluctance to go on this date at all, she made an extra special effort to look nice for Dick, aware that the flaming red dress, that reached just below her shapely knees, made her hair appear more ebony than usual, and added colour to her pale cheeks.

Nevertheless, her heart gave a weary lurch when the doorbell rang promptly at eight o'clock, and there was no way she could force a sparkle into haunted blue eyes as she hurried to answer the door.

Dick Crosby was in his early thirties, with thick sandy-coloured hair that fell endearingly across his forehead, and brown eyes that warmed appreciatively as they took in her appearance. Not quite six feet tall, he nevertheless possessed a natural grace of movement that made him appear taller than he actually was.

'I must remember to thank Dizzy for finally introducing us properly,' he murmured softly.

Dizzy. Her best friend—and aunt—had rung her shortly after she had got in this evening, assuring her what a lovely person Dick was, and telling her to 'give him a chance'.

Mentioning Dizzy was the worst thing Dick could have done, if he had but known it, the evening losing what little glow it had had with the remembrance that Dizzy had been the one to set them up in this way. She meant well, but ...

'Shall we go?' Christi suggested sharply, sighing inwardly as Dick gave her a hurt look. 'Sorry,' she grimaced. 'Bad day,' she excused, picking up her jacket to follow him out into the corridor.

He relaxed again. 'Oh, I know what they are,' he said knowingly. 'Only too well, lately.'

'Oh?' she prompted with polite interest. Maybe if she got him chatting she wouldn't have to add too much to the conversation.

'Yes, I——' Dick broke off abruptly as he saw the stricken look on her face as the lift doors opened in front of them.

Christi stared disbelievingly at Lucas and Marsha as they stood side by side in the lift. Lucas was grim-faced, Marsha as kittenishly beautiful as usual as her ex-husband ushered her out into the corridor.

The two couples stared at each other as the lift doors closed, and the lift descended again without Christi having made a move to go inside it.

Marsha and Lucas made an arresting couple—Lucas so tall and handsome, Marsha so delicately lovely as her hand rested on the crook of his arm.

But what were they doing together like this? the question screamed in Christi's mind. How could Lucas *fail* to appreciate the beauty of the woman who had once been his wife, her hair curving alluringly about her beautiful heart-shaped face, the black dress she wore showing off her curves to perfection. Next to her, Christi felt like an ungainly giraffe!

And then reality righted itself, and with it came the realisation that Lucas and Marsha were divorced because they didn't love each other, that they had been more like enemies the last five years, that the only interest they shared was their children.

The children... Of course! Marsha would be here to discuss something with Lucas concerning the children. She could only hope, for Lucas's sake, that it was nothing too traumatic; Marsha had already made him suffer enough where they were concerned.

'You seem to have missed the lift,' Marsha purred mockingly, hazel-coloured eyes gleaming with catlike malice as she looked Christi over scornfully.

Christi's head went back challengingly. 'It must be the surprise of seeing you again,' she derided. 'It must be—almost a year since we last met?'

'Something like that,' the other woman dismissed in a bored voice. 'You haven't changed at all,' she scorned. 'Although the men in your life seem to have matured somewhat.' She looked Dick over appreciatively, giving him her most seductive smile.

Christi stiffened at Marsha's open derision for her lack of years, glancing uncomfortably at Lucas. He looked so grim, his eyes glittering silver with suppressed anger, that Christi just wanted to put her arms around him and tell him everything would be all right, that Marsha wouldn't be able to torment him with the upbringing of his children any longer. But it would be a hollow promise; while Marsha had Lucas's children, she took great delight in making him dance to her tune any time she wished. For a man as forceful and dynamic as Lucas, it was an impossible situation.

She woodenly made the introductions. Lucas's greeting was terse, to say the least, Marsha's a sensuous purr, and Dick's after his initial surprise at hearing that Marsha and Lucas, the flirtatious woman and the grim-faced man, were husband and wife, was cautiously warm; he kept a wary eye on the other man's face with its stony expression and hooded grey eyes. He obviously didn't know what to make of the oddly matched pair, and Christi took pity on him and suggested they had better leave now or they would be late for dinner.

She cast one last anxious glance at Lucas as the lift doors closed behind her and Dick, her heart twisting at how bleak he looked.

'What a strange couple,' Dick remarked dazedly at her side.

Christi's mouth tightened. 'They're divorced,' she snapped.

'Oh!' he said with some relief. 'Oh,' he repeated again in soft speculation.

'And yes, Marsha is very available, in case you're interested,' she told him sharply, marching out of the building to come to a halt on the edge of the pavement. She was shaking with anger, and drew in a deep, steadying breath to calm herself.

Dick caught up with her in a couple of strides; he seemed surprised by her outburst, and looked at her enquiringly.

'I'm sorry.' She gave a rueful grimace. 'Marsha doesn't bring out the best in me, and—well, I did warn you it had been a bad day.' And it was getting worse by the moment! Dick couldn't be blamed for finding Marsha attractive, especially after the woman had come on to him as strongly as she had. At the time, it had just seemed to her that Marsha was to blame for the fact that Lucas wasn't able to fall in love again, and that the man Christi did have interested in her was also succumbing to the other woman's undoubted sensual attraction. In that moment, it had just seemed too much! 'Although that's no reason to behave like a shrew,' she apologised again.

This time, instead of feeling annoyance when Dick mentioned Dizzy, Christi felt relieved to be on neutral ground, relaxing slowly on the drive to the restaurant as they discussed the success of Dizzy's illustrations. The most recent publication to come out with one of her illustrations was a Claudia Laurence book, one of the most successful ever.

Not many people realised it, but Christi's uncle Zach was, in fact, Claudia Laurence, the author of those 'hot' historicals that always had the public clamouring for more. Christi herself had found out quite by accident, shocked to learn that the man

she had once termed 'fusty and dusty' wrote those
enjoyable adventurous romps. As Dizzy's agent,
Dick was also in on the secret, and they both relaxed as they discussed the books.

Her uncle's secret was one she hadn't even told
Lucas, knowing how sensitive her uncle was about
the subject, for his career as a professor of history
was just as important to him. It wasn't that she
thought Lucas would tell anyone else, it was just
that—well, it wasn't her secret to tell. Maybe if he
had been able to love her...

'Is there anyone there?' Dick spoke in a ghostly
voice.

Christi blinked at him in surprise, having been
completely unaware of her surroundings; the exclusive restaurant, and Dick, had faded from her
mind as her thoughts had once again dwelled on
Lucas.

'I'm so sorry,' she apologised again. 'I'm afraid
I'm not very good company tonight,' she added
with embarrassment.

'That's all right,' he accepted ruefully. 'I guess
my conversation must have been boring for you.'

She had no idea what the conversation had been
about! But Dick didn't seem about to go over it
again, suggesting they order their meal instead.

Christi felt terrible about her inattentiveness,
putting Lucas—and what Marsha could possibly
want to see him about—firmly from her mind, and
concentrating on being charming to Dick.

Nevertheless, it wasn't the most successful
evening she had ever had, and as Dick kissed her

briefly at her door, obviously waiting for an invitation to come in, she knew it would be kinder not to encourage him any further. He was a nice enough man, but he certainly wasn't going to be the one to supplant Lucas in her heart!

'No?' he realised gently.

Christi gave a shaky smile. 'I am sorry——' She was silenced by his fingertips over her lips.

'It was a nice evening,' he smiled. 'I enjoyed your company—I'm not so sure you were actually with me most of the evening,' he teased without rancour, 'but it was a pleasant time.'

Pleasant. It wasn't much of a eulogy. She had to face it: as a return to the dating scene, it had been a disaster!

She was shaking her head as she walked aimlessly around her apartment, filled with a restlessness that wouldn't be satisfied until she had spoken to Lucas again. But she couldn't go knocking on his door at eleven-thirty at night!

Damn it, *why* couldn't she? They were friends, at least, and friends cared about each other, and he had looked awful when she saw him earlier with Marsha. He could even be ill. Or...

Why bother to search for excuses? She *had* to talk to him, and that was all there was to it!

Christi was encouraged by the fact that she could hear music playing softly inside the apartment next to hers, and hesitated only briefly outside the door as the possibility that he wasn't alone passed through her mind. She would take that risk; he could only ask her to wait until tomorrow before talking to him.

She knew she had been right to come when she saw how haggard he looked when he opened the door to her ring, his dark hair looking as if he had been running agitated fingers through it for most of the evening, his face pale, his pale grey shirt partly unbuttoned down his chest to reveal the start of the dark hair that grew there, a glass of whisky held in his hand. It was the latter that told her how disturbed he was; Lucas never drank alcohol, and only ever kept a supply in for guests.

She shifted uncomfortably on his doorstep as he looked at her with narrowed eyes. 'I—er—I thought I would come and tell you how my evening went.' It was positively the last thing she had meant to say, but suddenly she had felt as if she were intruding on something he didn't want to talk about just now. 'You did say you would like a report on each of my dates,' she added lamely as he continued to look at her.

To her relief, he relaxed slightly, a faint glimmer of amusement darkening his eyes as he held the door wider for her to enter.

The lounge was in shadows, with only a small table-lamp for illumination, the Kenny Rogers cassette she had bought him last Christmas playing softly in the background. Christi turned awkwardly to face Lucas, feeling as if she had walked in on something very private. What *had* Marsha wanted to talk to him about tonight?

'No Michelle tonight?' she enquired lightly as she sat down in one of the comfortable brown leather armchairs, the room completely masculine, the décor brown and cream, the furniture heavy and attractive.

'No,' he drawled, his voice gruff, as if the unaccustomed raw alcohol had burned his throat on its way down. 'I didn't think it fair to inflict my company on anyone tonight,' he added ruefully, taking another drink of the whisky as he dropped down on to the sofa, his long legs stretched out in front of him.

Maybe she should have had the same forethought, and not ruined Dick Crosby's evening for him! Dizzy was sure to telephone for a full report tomorrow, and she wasn't going to be too happy with what she was told.

Strange, she and Dizzy were closer than sisters, and yet she had never told her friend of her love for Lucas, had never told anyone. God knew *what* Dizzy would do if she knew it was Lucas she loved! Christi thought disgustedly.

But, right now, dealing with Lucas's depressed mood, a mood she had never seen him in before in all the years she had known him, was what was important to her. Lucas's happiness would always be important to her.

'So,' he spoke briskly, 'was he the one?' He looked at her interestedly, amusement darkening his eyes.

Christi relaxed slightly at his teasing. 'No,' she answered without hesitation.

'Oh!' Lucas looked surprised. 'He seemed a nice enough chap to me.'

'He was,' she nodded. 'But he wasn't for me.' You're the man for me, she cried inside, wishing— oh, God, *wishing* he could see her as more than a young sister, or, even worse, someone he treated as being on the same age level as his two children! Much as she liked Robin and Daisy, her feelings towards them weren't sibling, but more maternal. She longed to be their stepmother, to perhaps give Lucas other children. 'Crying for the moon,' her mother would probably have told her gently, her face softened with love.

Lucas sipped his whisky again. 'How could you tell after just one date? Love doesn't always hit you between the eyes like a fist, you know. Sometimes it takes time to develop and grow.' He relaxed back against the sofa, watching her beneath heavy lids.

But sometimes it did hit you like that fist, and when it did it was the hardest thing in the world to live without! 'Love doesn't,' she acknowledged with a nod.

He frowned. 'Meaning something else does?'

'Oh, yes,' she smiled.

'What—ah!' He gave a knowing sigh, his mouth twisted into a smile. 'That little monster lust rearing its head again,' he derided.

The bleakness was starting to fade from his eyes, and he had put down the half-finished glass of whisky on the coffee-table beside him. 'I don't think of it as lust,' she chided reprovingly. 'Merely a case of physical attraction,' she corrected with mock indignation, rewarded with a gleam of laughter in dark grey eyes.

'Lust,' he repeated drily. 'But there was none of this—physical attraction,' he teased her mockingly, 'between you and Dick Crosby?'

Another few moments of this nonsense and she would have the old Lucas back again, and not the man whose barely leashed savagery distressed her so much.

'Hm—maybe a little,' she conceded with exaggerated thought.

'On his part, at least,' Lucas taunted knowingly. 'Weren't you attracted to him, too?' he asked interestedly.

'He was very handsome, fun to be with,' she conceded with a shrug.

'And?'

'And nothing,' she dismissed lightly.

'You liked him, he was fun to be with, you found him handsome, and yet—nothing?' Lucas said disbelievingly.

'Hm,' she nodded, mischief gleaming in her eyes. 'I had my doubts throughout the evening, but it was the kiss that finally convinced me,' she said sadly, laughter lighting up her eyes beneath demurely lowered lashes.

Lucas sat forward, his elbows resting on his knees, a frown between his eyes. 'The man has got to the age of—thirty-one, thirty-two——'

'Thirty-one,' she confirmed.

'To the age of thirty-one, and is still a lousy kisser?' he said incredulously.

'On the contrary,' she drawled, 'he was a very experienced and accomplished kisser.'

'But——'

'There are kisses. And then there are kisses, Lucas,' she explained meaningfully, knowing they wouldn't be having this conversation at all if Lucas hadn't drunk the unaccustomed whisky. In the past, he had always shown a cursory interest in her dates, but they had certainly never discussed these sort of intimacies!

'There are?' he mocked.

'Platonic kisses, polite kisses, meaningless kisses——'

'I thought there was only *one* way for a man to kiss a woman he found attractive,' Lucas drawled. 'So that he leaves her in no doubt that he wants her.'

Christi felt her heart leap in her chest, knowing she could lose what she already had with Lucas, but also knowing she would perhaps never have another opportunity like this one. 'Then maybe Dick did do something wrong,' she accepted thoughtfully. 'Maybe you could show me how it should be done? Oh, I realise you would have to pretend to find me attractive, but at least this way I know what to look for in a man,' she concluded innocently, her hands clasped tightly together so that Lucas shouldn't see their trembling, her heart beating so loudly, she felt sure he must be able to hear it. She *could* lose everything with him, but oh, how she longed to know the touch of his lips on hers just once!

His expression darkened. 'I don't think——'

She quickly got up from her chair and joined him on the sofa, her legs folded beneath her as she faced him. 'How else am I to know what to want from a man if someone doesn't show me?' She looked at him imploringly.

He swallowed hard, a nerve pulsing at his jaw. 'The men you dated last year——'

'Did nothing for me, either,' she dismissed, telling him clearly that she had never found any man attractive enough to let him do more than kiss her.

How could she let any other man but Lucas touch her? She had loved him long before she had taken any other man seriously, and loving Lucas as she did meant she couldn't bear the thought of any other man making love to her.

Her heart pounded more loudly than ever as she waited for his answer, knowing she was perhaps taking advantage of the fogging the whisky had caused to his brain, but wanting—*so much*—to be taken in his arms. Regrets could come later. And she didn't doubt that there would be many.

Lucas sighed, shaking his head, obviously not as affected by the whisky as she had thought—hoped!—he was. 'I don't think that would be a good idea.'

She sat back with a shaky sigh, his rejection a bitter blow. 'Maybe Barry will be more co-operative,' she challenged angrily, blinking back her tears of disappointment. 'After mixing with all those Hollywood starlets, he's sure to be very experienced!'

Lucas clasped her arms, turning her to face him, his expression fierce. 'Don't go playing games with a man like Barry Robbins,' he warned grimly.

'Why not?' she said defiantly, so hurt she just had to hit out at him. She had taken the chance, and lost, but in a way that humiliated as much as it hurt. 'He's attracted to me, I can tell, and—oomph!' She was abruptly silenced as Lucas's mouth descended on hers, stealing her breath away.

He was kissing her out of anger, not passion, but to Christi it didn't matter; she melted into his arms as he bent her back against the sofa, her arms moving up about his neck as she clung to him, gladly returning his kiss.

And then his mouth gentled on hers, controlling the fiery passion that had instantly blazed between them, nibbling on her lips with slow enjoyment, tracing the outline of lips with the tip of his tongue, moving it temptingly against them, but making no attempt to probe within, promising but not giving.

Christi's body ached, her nipples hard pebbles against his chest as the kiss once again became fierce, no longer promising but giving fully, plunging again and again until her whole body shook and quivered with need, a need which was slightly assuaged when his hands began to move restlessly over her aching flesh.

She was floating, she was soaring, she was held totally captive, she was aching, she was hurting, she was more complete than she had ever felt before. She was Lucas's...

Suddenly he thrust her away from him, staring down at her as if he couldn't believe his eyes, moving forcefully up off the sofa to move as far away from her as possible, his back rigidly unyielding as he kept himself firmly turned away from her.

Christi knew how she must look to him, her eyes drugged with wantonness, her mouth a swollen pout, her hair wild about her shoulders, her breasts still thrusting against the soft material of her dress, that same dress having ridden up to show off the long expanse of her thighs.

And the wanton Lucas had produced obviously disgusted him.

She got up from the sofa with a choked sob, running from the room, from the apartment. She didn't stop running until she was safely hidden away in her bedroom.

CHAPTER THREE

IF CHRISTI had expected Lucas to follow her, to try to make things right between them again, she had been disappointed. He didn't come to her that night, and she saw nothing of him the next day, either, whether by his design or by coincidence she didn't know. She did know that he wasn't at his apartment all day and that he didn't even return to change before going out for the evening, although she had heard his return at three o'clock this morning.

She had ruined things between them, had pushed their friendship through a barrier Lucas had no wish for it to cross.

She curled up into an even tighter ball of misery as she lay in her bed at nine o'clock in the morning, trying to force herself to get out and get herself moving.

She had wanted Lucas as a lover, yes, but she didn't have that, and she certainly didn't have his friendship any more, either. At the time, she had wanted him so badly it hadn't seemed to matter, but after just one day of knowing she disgusted him she was finding it hard to live with herself.

What if she never saw him again? What if he decided to move out of his apartment because of the uncomfortable situation she had forced upon

44

them? Until these last two days, it had never oc-curred to her that Lucas would ever move away from living next door to her. But she had to admit that now it was more than a possibility. She tried to tell herself that she was too good a friend to Lucas for this upset to cause him to do that, but at the same time she knew she had made it imposs-ible for him to feel comfortable in his own home.

Then she would have to be the one to move out! Why should Lucas be forced out for something that had all been her fault, because her curiosity and good sense had got the better of her?

She didn't want to move, hated the thought of moving away from here, from possibly never seeing Lucas again. But if one of them had to go it would have to be her; she had no choice.

That decision made, she got wearily out of bed, the day stretching in front of her. She had no aud-itions to go to, no one to see until Barry Robbins tonight. 'Resting' was all well and good, but it gave you too much time to think and brood. About what might have been. How different things might have been if Lucas had known the same passion and desire she had the other night, she mused dreamily. They would have made love together all night, spent the day together, probably been together again last night, too. Instead of that, they weren't even talking to each other.

Whoever would have thought she and Lucas would come to this? What had possessed *her* to force that situation of the other night?

Tears that had fallen all too readily over the last
two days began to roll down her cheeks again. Oh,
Lucas! she cried inside as she dropped down on
one of the bar stools in her kitchen, the homely
sound of the coffee percolating not piercing her
misery. How often she and Lucas had sat down and
had coffee together before he left to go to work,
and how she had daydreamed, during those times,
that they were a happily married couple sharing
breakfast together. Reality had intruded when
Lucas had stood up to kiss her paternally on the
forehead, or, worse than that, had ruffled her hair
affectionately before picking up his briefcase and
leaving.

Christi gave a startled jump as her doorbell rang,
hastily brushing away her tears as she went to greet
the doorman with her mail.

But it was Lucas who stood on the doorstep, and
she gazed up at him apprehensively. Not that she
was in the least self-conscious about having him see
her in her short pink silk nightshirt; she had break-
fasted with him hundreds of times in the past
wearing similar night attire. It was having him treat
her as a stranger that was going to be so unbearable.

'Good morning, lazybones,' he greeted with an
indulgent grin, ruffling her hair affectionately as
he strode inside her apartment.

Christi followed him dazedly after closing the
door behind him; this was no stranger, this was the
Lucas she had always known!

'I was in my apartment working when I heard
you moving about—at last!' he rebuked teasingly,

grey eyes dark with affection. 'I knew you would
be putting coffee on, so I thought I'd come over
and share a cup with you.' He strode into the
kitchen with the ease of familiarity, getting down
the cups for their coffee. 'I must say, you look a
little hung-over this morning, Christi.' He handed
her a cup of steaming coffee.

She looked hung-over? *He* was the one who had
come home at three o'clock this morning! Not that
he looked any the worse for it; he was exuding good
health and vitality, while she—— Obviously what
had happened between them the other evening certainly hadn't kept *him* awake at nights!

Instead of feeling guilty about what had happened, Christi began to feel anger at Lucas's indifference. Didn't the passion they had shared mean
anything to him? Obviously not, she decided
indignantly.

Unless he just didn't remember it? He had been
drinking that evening, something he rarely did, and
maybe, just maybe—— But wasn't that the classic
excuse people used when something had happened
they would rather just forget, and didn't know how
else to achieve it?

She looked at Lucas suspiciously. Was that why
he was behaving like his usual cheerful self this
morning, because he wanted her to *think* he didn't
even remember what had happened between them
the other night, because he wanted to forget the
whole embarrassing incident *had* happened? Or—
and this seemed more like the Lucas she loved—
was he trying to save face for both of them, hoping

that, if he behaved as if nothing had happened between them, they would eventually both feel that nothing *had* happened?

Christi would give anything not to live through the mortification of the last two days again, and readily accepted that Lucas thought the whole thing was best forgotten, grasping at the friendship he offered with both hands.

At least, she took the coffee he held out to her with both hands, giving him a relieved smile!

He settled himself on one of her bar stools, facing out towards the kitchen, breathtakingly attractive in the dark navy suit and snowy white shirt, his striped tie meticulously knotted at his throat, his dark hair falling endearingly across his forehead.

'So,' he said lightly. 'Did you go out last night?' he asked interestedly.

'No.' She would have liked to ask him where he had been until three o'clock this morning but, considering Michelle's obvious beauty, and his continuing relationship with the other woman, the answer to that was all too obvious. And painful. 'I had a few chores to do,' she dismissed shruggingly. 'Did you have a pleasant evening?' She looked at him enquiringly.

'Fine,' he nodded. 'How are the auditions going?'

She gave a rueful smile. 'They aren't.' She sighed. 'There are too many actresses and not enough parts.'

'Hm, it's a pity the play had to close,' he nodded thoughtfully.

They were talking as they usually did, and yet to Christi there was something missing. At first, it was difficult to pinpoint, and then she knew it was the ease with which they were usually together. Unless it was just her, because Lucas seemed just as relaxed as ever. Maybe he really *didn't* remember the other night? Wouldn't he have mentioned it if he did remember, tried to clear the air?

She didn't know any more, all she did know was that Lucas was her friend again. She wasn't about to risk that friendship a second time, even if being kissed by him had been the most beautiful experience of her life!

'—something to offer you,' Lucas was saying as her thoughts came back to their conversation.

'Sorry?' She gave a grimace of apology for her inattentiveness.

He gave a rueful smile. 'I said, maybe Barry Robbins will have something he can offer you,' he suggested lightly.

Christi frowned. The other evening, Lucas had more or less warned her off the film director, now he seemed to find nothing wrong in again suggesting she use the man's connections to get herself work. But if he didn't remember what he had said the other night... It was becoming more and more obvious that he really didn't.

Her mouth twisted. 'I'm not sure I'm the type of material for Hollywood,' she derided.

'You're certainly more beautiful than most of those so-called stars over there,' Lucas encouraged.

What was the good of being beautiful if that beauty didn't appeal to the one man she wanted it to? 'Thank you, kind sir!' She curtseyed in the above-knee-length nightshirt. 'I'll be sure to tell Barry you said so,' she teased, feeling more relaxed by the minute, knowing now wasn't the time to introduce the subject of Marsha's visit the other night, and rekindle the discord.

Lucas stood up, glancing at his watch. 'If the man can't see that for himself, then maybe he ought to give up film directing,' he taunted. 'I have an appointment in half an hour, so I have to go now. Have a good time this evening,' he called as he let himself out. 'I'll be in later if you want to come and tell me all about your date.'

Christi rushed into the hallway just as the door closed firmly behind him. What had he meant by *that*? Had it been the casual remark it had seemed— or something more?

God, her whole world seemed to have turned upside-down since Tuesday night, so that she didn't know her right from her left any more. She had thought she knew Lucas so well, now she wasn't sure she knew him at all.

If Dizzy had hoped to introduce her to the man she could fall in love with last weekend, all she had done was cause more confusion!

Barry Robbins was undoubtedly one of the most handsome men Christi had ever met; slightly overlong blond hair that curled attractively at his nape and ears, sexy blue eyes that left her in no doubt as to his appreciation of her own looks, a tall, lithe body that could look as good in the casual clothes he had worn last weekend as he did in the biscuit-coloured suit and pale cream shirt he wore tonight, the plain brown tie a perfect complement to the more flamboyant suit.

And Englishman by birth, his years in America had given him a slight, and wholly appealing, drawl to his accent, and Christi enjoyed just hearing him talk. Which was perhaps as well, when she couldn't find a lot to say herself!

Barry had arrived exactly on time, refusing to come in for a drink, taking her to dinner before going on to the stage musical she had been meaning to go and see for months but which she hadn't found the time to do when the play she was in was showing at the same times.

They went to a quiet bar after the show, the first few minutes taken up with discussing the merits of the performance. Usually vivacious, Christi found it heavy going after that; she couldn't help glancing at her watch, wondering if it would be too late to take Lucas up on his invitation if she left now.

'I thought you weren't working at the moment,' Barry finally remarked.

Christi blushed guiltily. 'I'm not. I—I'm just a bit of a clock-watcher,' she excused lamely. 'It comes from months of making sure I was always on time for a performance, I expect.' She gave a bright smile.

'Yes,' he chuckled knowingly. 'I know I come to startled wakefulness for weeks after I've finished making a film, wondering why no one has woken me up at the crack of dawn! The stringent time-keeping is part of the business,' he said understandingly.

Christi relaxed once again; the two of them had so much in common, after all. 'You aren't working at the moment?' she prompted interestedly.

'I start filming late next week,' he dismissed. 'But I'm working on another project at the moment.'

'Sounds mysterious,' she teased, sipping her wine, having decided she had better stick with the one drink all evening.

'Not really,' Barry smiled. 'You know this business as well as I do; one minute you have a feasible idea, the next it's back to the proverbial drawing-board.'

'Like the play I was in,' she acknowledged heavily.

Barry looked at her consideringly. 'With your looks, I'm sure you would do well in Hollywood.'

So much for having to tell this man Lucas's totally biased opinion, she thought moodily. She didn't want to go to Hollywood, away from everything she held dear, away from Lucas!

'Just say the word and I'll——'

'Thanks, but I'm really not interested,' she cut in firmly.

'Bastardising your talent, hm?' he said ruefully.

'Not at all!' Christi was genuinely shocked. 'America has some really talented people. I'm not one of those actors who think the ''British theatre'',' she affected a haughtily English accent, 'is everything.' She shook her head. 'I just feel . . . This is my home,' she shrugged. 'My family—what little there is—is here.'

'But I thought Dizzy and Zach were your only family?' Barry frowned. 'And little Laura, of course.'

Christi gave a puzzled frown. 'They are.'

'Then when they go to the States———'

'What?' She faced him tensely. 'But they aren't going to the States,' she denied confidently, unnerved by Barry's guilty expression. 'Are they?' she voiced uncertainly.

'Nothing has been decided yet,' he answered awkwardly. 'But I've made your uncle an offer for the film rights to one of his books, with the inclusion that he will write the screenplay,' he explained slowly. 'He's still thinking about it.'

No mention of this had been made over the weekend, not in front of her, anyway. Was she the reason Zach and Dizzy were hesitating? She knew her uncle and Dizzy took their responsibility towards her very seriously, and they wouldn't lightly view leaving her alone in England for six months or so. She *would* miss them all, very much, but this was too good an opportunity for Zach to pass up, and she would tell him so when she made her weekly call to them on Sunday evening; to telephone earlier would be to make too much of their hesitation. She would just casually mention what a good idea she thought it was, and leave them to make their decision from there.

'It sounds marvellous!' She gave a brightly encouraging smile. 'Tell me more about it.'

Barry was only too happy to do so, for this was the other 'project' he was working on at the moment. It sounded wonderful, filming beginning early next year if her uncle was agreeable, the deal he was being offered probably enough to renovate the rest of Castle Haven, which was her uncle's lifetime ambition, only having been able to afford the work on the east wing of the rundown castle so far. The thought of leaving her alone in England for all those months *had* to be the reason he was hesitating.

'I'm sure we could find a part for you in the film if it would help Zach to—well——' Barry broke off uncomfortably as she looked at him with raised brows. 'It was only an idea,' he dismissed ruefully.

'I'm as much against nepotism as I am the casting couch,' Christi told him drily.

'That really was dumb of me,' he said with a groan, his adopted American accent more pronounced in his self-disgust. 'I really am sorry,' he grimaced. 'Although the part of the heroine's sister would be perfect—no,' he accepted drily as Christi slowly shook her head. 'Nepotism is a dirty word, right?' he dismissed.

'Right,' she agreed drily.

'But if it were someone else's script—but it isn't,' he sighed as Christi just continued to look at him patiently. 'I've said far too much, probably ruined what has so far been a perfect evening——'

'You haven't ruined it at all,' she assured him lightly, picking up her clutch-bag. 'After all, I asked you to tell me more about it. But it is late now,' she smiled. 'I really should be getting home.'

Barry sighed. 'I *did* ruin the evening——'

'Really—you didn't,' she insisted without rancour. 'I'm grateful that you told me about it.'

'If you're sure...?' He still didn't look convinced, his handsome face set in self-reproachful lines.

'I'm sure.' Christi stood up in one fluid movement, the soft wool of the pale blue dress she wore falling gently against her knees.

It was almost twelve by the time Christi searched for her door-key in her bag. Surely it was far too late to be calling on Lucas. Wasn't it?

'Here, let me.' Barry took the key from her unresisting fingers, deftly unlocking the door for her.

He had certainly had plenty of practice at that, Christi acknowledged warily. Still unmarried, at thirty-six, so perhaps that wasn't so surprising! *Whatever* his experience, he made her nervous.

She turned to face him in the doorway, effectively blocking his entrance. 'Thank you for a lovely evening. The dinner was superb and the show was excellent.' She gave him a glowing smile.

He looked chagrined at the obvious dismissal. And then he relaxed, chuckling softly. 'I guess I've lived in the glitz and glamour of Hollywood too long, where the usual thank you for an enjoyable evening is an equally enjoyable night in bed!'

'I guess you have,' Christi drily mocked him.

Barry shook his head, grinning widely, looking years younger. 'Dizzy told me I was going to like you.'

Christi gave an inclination of her head. 'She told me the same thing about you.'

He looked at her admiringly. 'She wasn't wrong as far as I'm concerned,' he told her huskily.

'Nor me,' she assured softly.

She was ready for his kiss, waiting, her face raised invitingly to his, his mouth firm and warm as it claimed hers.

His mouth moved against hers with expertise, eliciting a response; it was only when his hands began a slow exploration of her body that Christi froze, his caresses an intrusion, an act of theft against the man she really wanted.

Barry drew back ruefully, releasing her slowly. 'Can I see you again?' he prompted gruffly, blue eyes dark with passion. 'Saturday?'

'I—have a date for Saturday.' She couldn't quite meet his gaze.

'Oh, yes,' his voice hardened, 'with David Kendrick, right?'

'Right,' she confirmed uncomfortably. If she'd had Dizzy by her side right now, she would cheerfully have wrung her neck for her, new mother or not! Her friend had put her in such a compromising situation with these three men, that by the time the week was ended probably none of them would even want to talk to her again, let alone have their thoughts on matrimony!

'Then, how about next week?' Barry suggested lightly.

'Er—can I call you?' she prevaricated. 'I'm hoping to have found work by next week, and I'm not sure when or where I'll be working.'

He nodded acceptance. 'You have the number of my hotel. I'll look forward to hearing from you.'

Christi wondered ruefully how long it had been since an evening had ended so tamely for Barry Robbins, as she moved about her kitchen making herself a cup of coffee, having decided it *was* too late to bother Lucas now. The poor man probably hadn't been sent meekly on his way at the end of an evening for years. Oh well, at least he wasn't likely to forget the evening he had spent with her!

She had changed into her nightshirt and was sitting on the sofa, drinking her coffee, when she heard the soft knock on her apartment door.

Barry had seemed to take her refusal good-naturedly, but if he had come back for another try he couldn't have been quite as amiable about it as she had thought he was!

She gaped at Lucas as she peered up at him from around the edge of the door, straightening as she opened it wider.

'Don't look so surprised,' he derided, bending down to pat Henry as the dog yapped about his ankles, demanding attention. 'I think we had better go inside before he wakes our neighbours up,' he suggested ruefully.

Christi stepped back dazedly, following him through to the lounge, drinking her fill of him as,

Henry's feelings appeased, the two cats stretched and purred in the armchair for his attention.

Lucas certainly hadn't been drinking this evening; his hair was neatly combed, his eyes intelligently alert, no lines of bitterness were etched into his face. He had obviously spent the evening relaxing at home; the short-sleeved brown shirt was partly un-buttoned at his throat, faded denims rested low down on lean hips and thighs. It made Christi's breath catch and her palms grow damp just to look at him!

The cats lay on their backs in ecstasy as one leanly muscular hand caressed their silky tummies, and Christi quivered with jealousy as she longed to know the caress of those hands against *her* skin.

At last he straightened, but Christi's fascinated gaze still followed the strength of his hands as he thrust them into his denims' pockets, pulling the material even tighter across his thighs.

'I was waiting for you to come over.' Lucas's quizzical gaze met hers as she at last raised her eyes. He was smiling at her encouragingly. 'When you didn't come, even after you had made yourself a cup of coffee, I decided maybe you thought it was a little late to be making social calls.'

Their kitchens were the only two walls that met in this expensive apartment building and, while they couldn't hear every movement in each other's kitchens, it was possible to tell when an electrical plug had been pushed in. It had disconcerted Christi a little at first, but now she sometimes just sat in her kitchen, listening to the comforting sounds of Lucas moving about next door.

'It *is* after twelve,' she nodded ruefully.

'And we both know you're a nightbird.' Lucas sat down on the sofa, stretching his long legs out in front of him, his hands once again visible as he rested them on the cushions beside him. He relaxed back against the cushions. 'The times we've sat here drinking coffee together when you've returned from the theatre in the evening,' he murmured fondly.

'We went to the theatre tonight,' she rushed into speech, feeling uncomfortable at him having seen her in her nightshirt twice today. It was a dark blue one this time, that made her hair midnight-black and deepened her eyes to almost the same colour. 'To see *Phantom of the Opera*.'

He raised dark brows, stretching up to put his hands behind his head, the power of his chest and shoulders thrown into prominence. 'Good?'

'Very,' she nodded. 'I sometimes wish I could sing; there are so many good musicals about nowadays,' she said wistfully.

'I've heard you in the shower,' Lucas teased. 'I don't think you should inflict your voice on the general public!'

It was incredible how intimately their lives were intertwined; she had heard him singing in the shower once, too, while she'd waited for him to drive her to the theatre one night when her car had broken down. He had a fine baritone which was very pleasing to the ear, whereas she sounded more like Gladys or Josephine in one of their not-so-pleasant moods!

'Probably not,' she agreed lightly.

'Definitely not,' Lucas grinned.

She swallowed hard, somehow feeling at a disadvantage as she stood across the room from him—which was absurd; the person sitting down was usually the one to feel intimidated! 'Did you do anything interesting this evening?' Her lightness of tone didn't reveal her intense interest.

'Oh, no, you don't!' Lucas dismissed laughingly. 'It's your evening we're interested in. The fact that I've been doing paperwork all evening isn't even worth mentioning.'

She shrugged, relieved that his relationship with Michelle seemed to be coming to an end; he had only seen the other woman once this week that she knew of. But once this affair ended there would just be another one, she reminded herself, and one of these times the woman was going to be the right one for Lucas.

'Then we won't mention it.' Christi smiled to hide the nagging pain that thinking of Lucas, finally falling in love, always caused in her heart. 'And I've already told you that my evening went well.'

'No,' he corrected with a shake of his head. 'You said the musical was good. The next relevant question is, was Barry Robbins as good?' he drawled.

'Lucas!' She stared at him with wide eyes.

His mouth twisted. 'As in well behaved,' he explained drily.

'Oh,' she blushed. 'Yes, he was very—well, most of the time—until he brought me home——' She broke off, feeling uncomfortable at the speculative gleam in silver eyes.

'Well, you didn't invite him in, so—— My God, the man didn't try something on the doorstep?' he said disgustedly.

'No, he didn't,' she glared at him indignantly, finding his curiosity about her dates deeply embarrassing. 'He kissed me, that's all,' she told him defensively.

'And?' Lucas looked at her interestedly.

Christi gave a pained frown. 'Lucas, I don't think——'

'Tuesday night, you claimed the kiss was the way you knew Dick Crosby wasn't the right man for you. I merely wondered if you had discovered the same thing about Barry Robbins when *he* kissed you,' Lucas shrugged.

Christi stared at him as if she had never seen him before. He *did* remember the other night! It wasn't that he didn't remember what had happened, it wasn't that he was saving her blushes by not mentioning it, he just hadn't mentioned it earlier because what they had shared hadn't been important to him!

Her family and friends, Lucas among them, all knew that she was usually slow to anger, that it took a great deal to make her angry, but, for possibly the first time in her life, red-hot anger coursed through her like a tidal wave.

How dared Lucas feel nothing after those impassioned kisses they had shared! How *dared* he!

'No,' she replied tautly. 'Barry's kisses were very sensual, very enjoyable,' she told him challengingly.

Lucas's arms slowly lowered to his sides. 'Then, he is the man for you?' he said softly.

Her head was back in proud defiance. 'I didn't say that,' she bit out waspishly. How *dared* he!

Lucas looked puzzled. 'But you said——'

'His kisses were very sensual.' She nodded acknowledgment. 'It was when he began to touch me that I froze,' she shrugged dismissively, her expression deliberately bland.

Lucas sat forward. 'When he—touched, you?' His eyes were narrowed. 'Are you telling me that he tried to make love to you while the two of you were standing in the hallway?' he rasped.

Christi was glad he no longer found this amusing; she had ceased finding it funny a long time ago! 'Hardly,' she derided mockingly. 'He just touched me, that's all. Ran his hands over my body,' she enlarged as Lucas still looked puzzled.

His mouth thinned into a taut line. 'And?'

She shrugged again. 'I didn't like it.'

Lucas frowned darkly. 'What exactly did he do to you?'

Christi looked thoughtful. 'Well, he put his hand here,' she placed her own hand just under her left breast, 'and here,' she placed her other hand on her hip, 'and here,' she moved her right hand slightly higher against her breast. 'And then he—it's a bit

awkward for me to show you like this.' She shook
her head.

Lucas stood up and came to stand just in front
of her, holding out his own hands. 'Show me now,'
he invited gruffly.

She didn't hesitate, she was so angry with him
for putting her through the torment of the last two
days that, at that moment, she didn't *care* if he
never spoke to her again after tonight!

She took his left hand and placed it on the curve
of her bottom, placing his right hand exactly where
hers had been seconds earlier. And the sensation
was nothing like the aversion she had felt when
Barry had attempted to touch her so intimately. Her
whole body started to tingle, Lucas's hands burning
her through the silky material of her nightshirt.

'Now what?' Lucas prompted harshly.

Christi looked up at him; she was tall herself, but
Lucas easily towered over her. 'It's difficult to remember, really,' she said breathlessly, her nipples
already taut against silk. 'He was kissing me, you
see,' she shrugged. 'And his hands just sort of—
roamed at will.'

'At will,' Lucas echoed tightly, pulling her hard
against him, bending his head to claim her mouth
in a searing kiss.

At first, she was so lost in the power of that kiss
that she wasn't aware of his hands against her body,
but as his fingertips caressed the length of her spine
she became very aware of that touch, gasping out
loud as one of his hands moved to fully cup her
breast. Being tall as she was, it would have been

nice to be blessed with big breasts, but she hadn't been, and as her breast perfectly fitted into the palm of Lucas's hand she knew why she hadn't: her body had been perfectly fashioned to match and fit his.

All the time he caressed her, that punishing kiss went on, and on, and on...

Christi felt weak, clinging to the width of his shoulders, trembling anew as Lucas pulled her thighs tightly against his, at the same time as his lightly caressing tongue stopped playing with her lips and plunged into the waiting warmth beneath.

She felt claimed, possessed, giving a little whimper from too much pleasure all at once, as expert fingers parted her nightshirt all the way down the front, a thumb-tip moving erotically against the hardened tip of her breast.

His denims and shirt were another erotic abrasion against her naked flesh, and she felt herself filled with a moist ache as her body prepared to fully accept him, her limbs trembling expectantly.

She desperately drew air into her ragged lungs as Lucas's mouth left hers to travel the length of her throat, knowing another kind of desperation as that moist mouth claimed the aching tip of her other breast, one hand moving up automatically to thread her fingers through the darkness of his hair as she held him against her, the suckling pressure against her breast deepening the ache between her thighs.

Lucas had gone way beyond any caresses Barry Robbins might have attempted, but Christi didn't want to stop him; she wanted it all, wanted this ache taken away, replaced by the fulfilment she had always known only one man could give her. This man.

The gentle curve of her breast thrust forward moistly as Lucas's mouth left the creamy peak to travel slowly across the silky flesh.

It wasn't until she felt Lucas's fingers deftly re-buttoning her nightshirt that Christi realised his kiss was no longer passionate but soothing, lacking the fire that seconds ago had pulled them both towards the edge of oblivion.

Her body once again covered by blue silk, Lucas raised tender hands to smooth back the dark swathe of her hair from her flushed face. 'And you knew from the way Robbins touched you that he wasn't the man for you?' he prompted huskily.

'Yes,' she breathed shakily, waiting for his obvious conclusion after her response to *him*. Waiting. And waiting.

She was still waiting, minutes later, when Lucas had wished her a gentle goodnight and quietly left to return to his own apartment!

CHAPTER FOUR

CHRISTI had a job. Possibly not the sort of job she would have chosen for herself, given a choice. But the screen test she had had at the beginning of the week had paid off—she was now the glamour in an advertisement for a new liqueur the company intended televising in time for Christmas.

It was a job for a model, of course, although some people said she had the height and looks of a model, anyway, and there was some acting involved, according to the director. And it would mean her face would be seen by millions all over the country, possibly the world, if they chose to syndicate it, as they were doing with so many advertisements nowadays.

They were going to film four different adverts, starting next month, which was only a couple of weeks away, after all. Apparently the company had been searching for just the right girl for months now; it had just been a lucky chance that her agent had sent her along to them. A lucky chance for all of them. At least now she could encourage Dizzy and Zach to take up the opportunity in America, while being able to assure them that she was working and would be fine during their absence.

Ordinarily, she would have shared something like this with Lucas, would have gone over to his apartment as soon as he had got in from work and taken him out for a celebratory dinner.

But nothing was ordinary between herself and Lucas any more. For one thing, she no longer understood him, let alone what was going on between them.

They had lived next door to each other for four years—*four years*—and not once had Lucas shown more than a brotherly interest in her life. In the last four days, she had been in his arms twice, and both times he could have made love to her with no argument from her. And his response to her certainly hadn't been anything but that of a lover.

But the first time he had kissed her Lucas had been demonstrating how a man *should* kiss a woman he desired, and last night he had been pretending he was *another man* making love to her. Where things stood between herself and *Lucas* she had no idea!

However, if the last four days hadn't happened, Lucas was the person she would have wanted to celebrate with, and if he could face her as if the other night hadn't happened she, supposedly the trained actress of the two of them, could surely face him as if last night hadn't happened! Even if she, and her body, could remember every kiss, every caress...

Knowing that Fridays were always especially busy for Lucas, working later than usual before the office closed down for the weekend, Christi was aware that he rarely, if ever, made a date for that evening, so he should be free later on to help her celebrate.

Booking a table at their favourite restaurant should be an easy matter; in the past, she had always just had to mention Lucas's name and the table was arranged as if by magic. The management must wonder at her appearance every few months or so, after the beauties who usually accompanied him for a few weeks, before disappearing, never to be seen with him again!

She spoke to Simon, the *maître d'*, when she got through to the restaurant, mentioning that the table would be for Lucas Kingsley.

'But Mr Kingsley already has a reservation for nine-thirty,' he assured her.

Christi frowned. 'Are you sure?' What a silly question! If Simon said Lucas had a reservation, then that was exactly what he had; Simon was so good at his job, the restaurant ran like a well-oiled machine.

'Very sure, madam.' There was only a slight frosting to the confirmation.

Lucas already had a date for tonight, after all. 'How silly of me,' she said in a hollow voice. 'There must have been some confusion over who was to book the table,' she excused lamely, hoping this man didn't choose to mention the supposed 'mix-up' to Lucas, or his partner for the evening, when they arrived there later!

'Yes, madam,' Simon returned politely.

Christi replaced the receiver slowly, a dejected droop to her shoulders. Lucas must be seeing Michelle tonight, after all. So much for the relationship coming to an end! It was only on special occasions, and for special women, that Lucas broke his rule about keeping Friday evenings free to relax.

She looked down at the petrol-blue dress she wore, a silky shimmer of material that clung alluringly to her curved body, a perfect foil for her dark hair. She felt like Cinderella in reverse; all dressed up and nowhere to go!

She was still debating whether to change and spend the evening quietly at home—if it could be called quiet when the cats and Henry seemed to be going through one of their squabbling nights!—or whether to call up a couple of friends and do her celebrating with them, when she heard Lucas outside in the corridor.

It wouldn't hurt just to pop over for a few minutes to tell him about the job, now would it? Why was she trying to talk herself into it when she knew it was what she really wanted to do?

Her bright smile of greeting died on her lips as the door to Lucas's apartment was opened by none other than—*Marsha Kingsley*!

Christi stared at her in some disbelief. Visiting Lucas once in a week to talk about the welfare of their children seemed perfectly natural to her, but for the other woman to be here *twice* . . .

A slow smile spread over Marsha's mocking features, her eyes appearing catlike in their pleasure. 'Well, well!' She looked Christi up and down speculatively. 'Little girl going out to play, is she?'

If this woman had been anyone other than Lucas's ex-wife, Christi would have been able to handle the sarcasm, but it was because Marsha *had* once been married to Lucas, had known him more intimately for four years than any other person, that Christi at once felt at a disadvantage whenever she met her. And, of course, she *was* at a disadvantage; Lucas had once loved this woman enough to marry her.

'I'm going out later, yes,' she answered abruptly. 'Is——'

'With the man from the other evening?' Marsha drawled. 'Dick something-or-other?'

'Crosby,' she supplied tersely. 'And no, it isn't. Is Lucas—'

'At home?' the other woman finished softly. 'But, of course. He's just taking a shower,' she murmured throatily. 'Your men may have matured slightly, but *you* obviously haven't—not enough to keep them interested, anyway,' she added tauntingly.

Christi drew in an angry breath, hating this woman's derision, *furiously angry* at Lucas's easy familiarity of taking a shower with his ex-wife in his apartment. Just what was going on? 'Experience may count for something,' she snapped. 'But experience is something I'll attain. Youth is something *you'll* never see again!'

She hadn't meant to say that, bitchiness had never been one of her weaknesses. But from the furious glitter in Marsha's suddenly venomous eyes she knew she had surpassed herself at her first attempt!

She gave a weary sigh. 'I didn't come here to fight with you——'

'Then why did you come?' Marsha challenged harshly. 'To try and convince Lucas you're all grown up at last?' she scorned. 'Don't look so stricken,' she taunted as Christi paled. 'I guessed from the beginning that you imagined yourself in love with Lucas. But you're a child to him, you always will be.' She gave a derisive laugh. 'You could dance naked on a table-top and he would probably just offer you his jacket so that you didn't catch cold!'

It wasn't true... yet, wasn't it the same thing, but put in a different way, that she had been telling herself for years?

Even after Tuesday and Thursday nights? But she already knew that she had provoked him on both those occasions. And that afterwards Lucas had acted as if nothing unusual had happened. He probably just put it down as a further step in her education on his part!

'I don't know what Lucas ever saw in you!' she choked, her nails digging into her palms.

Marsha's mouth twisted. 'Give yourself another ten years or so and you'll know,' she mocked.

'Sex isn't everything!' Christi denied in a pained voice.

Marsha gave a derisive shrug. 'With a man like Lucas, it isn't nothing, either.'

Christi swallowed the nausea that rose up in her throat at the thought of Lucas with this woman. 'How fortunate for him that he's become more discriminating over the years!' she bit out with distaste.

Marsha was completely in control again now, her brief show of anger masked behind mockery. 'Has he?' she challenged softly.

She could feel the colour drain completely out of her cheeks. Marsha couldn't be saying—Lucas wouldn't—he *couldn't*——

But Lucas had cared for this woman once, had children with her, and it had never been his decision to end their marriage. Despite his bitterness about the way things had ended between them, Lucas had never once claimed to hate his ex-wife for what she had done.

Lucas and Marsha...

Christi readily admitted that during this last week, the man she had thought she had known for the last four years had seemed like a stranger to her at times, a man who looked like Lucas but who certainly didn't act like him. Would his having an affair with Marsha be any more difficult to comprehend than the occasions he had taken *her* into his arms the last week?

Lucas and Marsha...

Oh, God, she didn't want to believe that! This woman entwining her body around his like a sensuous cat——

'We always were pretty explosive in bed together,' Marsha taunted softly at Christi's obvious growing horror. 'Why don't you ask him? No, I don't suppose you'll do that, will you?' she derided with mockery. 'If it's any consolation, Christi, you could *never* hope to keep a man like Lucas satisfied.'

Christi wanted to wipe the knowing smile off the other woman's red-painted lips, wanted to deny the hurtful claim. But Lucas *hadn't* wanted her enough, on either of the occasions she had been in his arms, to lose his icy control and make love to her.

Oh, God, a week ago her life had been tranquil and secure, even if the man she was in love with had never been able to return those feelings. Now she wasn't sure what she and Lucas had any more, and he seemed to be involved with this—this——

'You really are so transparent.' Marsha gave a husky laugh. 'Maybe Lucas should have done you both a favour and put you out of your misery years ago; a brief affair would certainly have been kinder than fending off your adolescent devotion with brotherly affection all these years,' she dismissed in a bored voice.

Lucas didn't know how she felt about him, he couldn't know! *Why* couldn't he? a voice murmured inside her; this woman seemed to have had no trouble guessing at her love for him! Oh God!

'Marsha, I thought I heard——' Lucas broke off frowningly as he saw the two of them standing together in the doorway. He finished tying the belt to his robe as he straightened questioningly. 'Christi,' he greeted lightly.

Christi felt as if he had struck her a blow. Lucas was obviously naked beneath the bathrobe, and he had walked into the room to be with his ex-wife dressed that way, his hair still damp from the shower he had just taken.

Marsha had been telling the truth about that. And Christi had a sinking feeling that the other woman had been telling the truth about a lot of other things, too.

Her head went back defensively. 'I was just on my way out.' Amazingly, her voice didn't tremble and shake as she had feared it would! 'And I just thought I would let you know I've found a job.'

'That's great,' he said with genuine pleasure.

'Yes,' she agreed tersely, keeping her gaze averted from his dark masculinity. 'I didn't realise at the time that I would be interrupting anything——'

'But——'

'I really do have to go now, Lucas,' she continued brittly as he would have interrupted. 'I hope you both have a nice evening,' she added tautly, turning away.

'But, Christi——'

'Leave her alone, Lucas,' Marsha chided throatily. 'Can't you see the poor girl has more on her mind than talking to us?'

Christi heard the door close softly behind her, and she didn't need to turn to know that both Marsha and Lucas were still on the other side of it. She couldn't allow herself to think what they would be doing in a couple of minutes from now!

Marsha was wrong, very wrong; the *only* thing Christi had on her mind was Lucas and her. Together.

She closed her eyes, tears squeezing out between the lids.

She would have to keep to that decision she had made on Wednesday about moving. She couldn't go on living here now that Lucas was seeing Marsha, now that she knew he had realised all the time that she was in love with him.

She felt so humiliated. So hurt. So betrayed.

She hadn't been able to help loving Lucas. But he was so much older than her, so much wiser, couldn't he have found some way over the years to let her know, gently, that he realised how she felt but that there could be no future for them?

Maybe she was being unfair, the onus hadn't been on Lucas to deal with the problem at all, but on her. She had always known there could never be anything between them, she had just refused to accept it.

Well, now she accepted it! She loved Lucas, but her feelings were an embarrassment to him. She couldn't change the way she felt about him, she doubted she would ever be able to do that, but she could remove the embarrassment, herself, from his life.

Christi had wanted so badly to get out of her date for this evening, she had telephoned Dizzy to ask for David Kendrick's telephone number, only to find, when she called his home, that David wasn't at home to answer her repeated calls, but seemingly out for the day.

She looked terrible, and she felt even worse. She had crept quietly back into her apartment last night, so that neither Lucas nor Marsha should realise she

was hiding away like a wounded animal rather than
going out as they had expected her to do.

She had heard the other couple leaving just after
nine o'clock. Finally, she'd been able to move about
freely, yet she'd still been sitting dazedly in an armchair when she had heard Lucas's return. She'd
given a nervous start when his gentle knock had
sounded on the door, instantly silencing Henry with
a raised warning finger, as he would have barked
excitedly at the familiar knock.

She had trembled when Lucas had called to her
softly through the closed door, knocking again, a
little louder this time, almost as if he'd sensed her
watchfulness behind the wooden barrier. Again
she'd silenced Henry, waiting tensely for the sound
of Lucas going to his own apartment, her breath
leaving her body in a shaky sigh when he had finally done so.

Christi hadn't dreamt such misery existed; not
even her regrets after Tuesday evening had been as
bad as this raw pain. The last thing she wanted was
to move away from Lucas, but what if his relationship with Marsha deepened, became serious?
What if they decided to remarry?

Lucas had left his apartment shortly before David
called for her, and she could only guess that his
companion for the evening was Marsha. Oh, God,
just the thought of them together...

Her deep sigh of despair didn't go unnoticed by
her companion. David smiled enquiringly. He was
a tall, dark-haired man with laughing blue eyes and
a lithe attraction which must have set many female

hearts fluttering over the years. And which left Christi unmoved.

'Penny for them?' he encouraged at her silence.

She gave a wan smile. 'I'm afraid they aren't even worth that,' she dismissed wearily. 'I'm sorry I'm not better company. I did try to call you today to cancel our dinner date, but——'

'I've been out of town,' he nodded comprehendingly. 'I spent the day with Dizzy and Zach.'

'What?' That shook her out of her despondency. If David had been in the Lake District with Dizzy and Zach when she'd called, then Dizzy had deliberately not told her so! And she didn't need two guesses why; Dizzy had obviously guessed that the reason she wanted David's number had been because she wanted to cancel their date. And she had effectively balked her plans.

Damn Dizzy and her matchmaking! But for her friend's interference, she needn't have put David or herself through the unnecessary awkwardness of tonight. Although, she had to admit, David didn't seem too disturbed by her lack of enthusiasm for the evening. And she didn't for one moment believe it was a reaction he usually got from his dates. He was the sort of man to have women flocking around him, not the sort who had to try and cajole one insipidly reluctant woman into having a good time!

She readily admitted she wasn't looking her best tonight; the strain of the last week was beginning to tell on her, obvious by the dark shadows in and below her eyes, and the fact that her expression was lacking its usual sparkle. If things deteriorated any further, she was going to lose that advertising job before they even began filming!

'Did Dizzy forget to mention that?' David looked amused at her chagrin. He relaxed back in his chair, their meal over, Christi's barely touched. 'I suppose she thought it only fair that I should at least be given a chance to talk you around.'

'Around to what?' Christi gave him a curious frown; if he was trying to talk her into going to bed with him, it was the most direct approach she had heard yet!

'Into talking to Zach about writing the screenplay for his book so that Barry could make it into a film,' David told her shruggingly.

Christi stared at him as if she had never seen him before, going to speak twice before changing her mind, then finally swallowing hard. 'Is that what—— Were Dick and Barry——'

'Not very subtly trying to do that?' he finished amiably. 'Yes,' he confirmed drily.

She remembered now how Dick had changed the conversation at her lack of attention, claiming he must be boring her, how Barry had even offered her a part in the film as an inducement to persuading Zach into working on the script.

Her mouth tightened. 'Then why aren't you going to try, too,' she snapped with distaste.

He shrugged again. 'Dick doesn't know Zach very well, his main interest is in promoting Dizzy's work through the film. Barry may have known Zach years ago, but he doesn't know him too well now,' he said ruefully. 'On the other hand, I know Zach well enough to realise that only Zach will make his mind up about the filming of one of his books. And that's where the problem comes in; Zach isn't too thrilled at the idea of his identity as Claudia Laurence becoming public.'

She could imagine that her very private uncle wouldn't! 'Am I to take it by your admissions that *your* interest in me is the real thing?' Christi's voice dripped sarcasm.

David smiled at her obvious anger. 'The last woman I tried to deceive punched me in the eye— and then a week later she married me,' he recalled with obvious pleasure.

Christi gaped at him. 'You're *married*?' She was sure Dizzy couldn't have known *that* when she encouraged Christi to go out with him!

'Not any more,' he said regretfully. 'Sara died.'

'I'm so sorry,' Christi gasped, knowing David's simply made statement in no way reflected the pain that suddenly clouded his eyes.

'I'm sorry she died,' he nodded, looking older than his thirty-three years now that there was no laughter in his face. 'But I'm not sorry that I knew her, that I loved her, even if it was only for a very brief time,' he announced with feeling. 'The tabloids are always speculating as to why I haven't married again.' He pulled a face. 'I don't think any of them would understand if I said I've had my love and she's irreplaceable.'

Christi felt like crying, ashamed of her own self-pity tonight. Lucas might be out of her reach, but at least he was alive, at least she was able to *look* at him and know that she loved him!

'Irreplaceable, yes,' she clasped David's hand across the table, 'but, as that old saying goes, "when one door closes another one opens". The door on your love for Sara has closed, David,' she said softly. 'But there is room in your heart for someone else, I'm sure of it.'

He turned his hand over, taking her hand into his, gently smoothing the delicate skin there. 'You?' he prompted huskily.

'No,' she said regretfully.

He gave a rueful smile, releasing her hand. 'I didn't think so,' he accepted without rancour. 'Does Dizzy know about this man in your life?'

She didn't question how he knew she was in love with someone else; she had greatly underestimated this man, believed him to be something of a playboy, when he was really gentle and kind, with a perception beyond words. 'No,' she sighed.

'I didn't think so,' he smiled, the sadness fading from his eyes. 'If she did, Dick, Barry and I wouldn't have been the ones invited for last weekend,' he mocked.

'And Dizzy would be making my life more miserable than it already is!' she grimaced.

David gave her a searching look. 'You mean,' he said slowly, 'this man doesn't return your feelings?' He looked disbelieving.

'Doesn't return them. Doesn't *want* them,' she added, bitter at the way Lucas had let her continue to make a fool of herself all these years. She felt so *angry* at the way he must have been humouring her all this time. Just like the child he still believed her to be...

A *child*? My God, she was almost twenty-two years old, and a lot of women were married with children by this age. The majority of her friends were, for a start, including Dizzy. Damn Lucas and his patronising gentleness; it was the last thing she wanted from him!

'The man's a fool,' David murmured across the table from her.

'Yes,' she said firmly. 'Yes, he is,' she dismissed.

David grinned appreciatively. 'Do I detect a spark of rebellion in those amazing blue eyes?' he teased.

'You most certainly do,' she acknowledged with satisfaction.

'Going to give him hell, hmm?' he said ruefully.

Christi gave a rueful shake of her head. 'I'm going to give him nothing, David,' she stated flatly. 'I thought he was my friend, but——' She shrugged dismissively. 'Now I just feel a fool for loving him all this time.' She sighed.

David's expression gentled. 'I'm afraid that making a fool of yourself is part of being in love,' he told her softly. 'Take the word of the man who was still sporting the black eye at his wedding that his bride had given him at their very first meeting!'

Christi's mouth quirked. 'I'd really like to hear about this courtship some time.' She smiled her amusement at the idea of any woman punching this man in the eye, let alone marrying him a week later!

He chuckled. 'And I'd enjoy telling it to you. But there's no rush,' he said confidently. 'I have the feeling you and I are going to be good friends.'

She did too, and this would be a genuine friendship, with no deeper love hidden on either side. She couldn't help but admire David's frankness in explaining to her how much he had loved his wife, how much he still loved her. If nothing else, she should thank Dizzy for introducing her to a new friend.

'Let's go and have a brandy at my apartment,' she suggested impulsively as they were asked if they wanted a liqueur after their coffee.

David nodded dismissively to the waiter. 'Sounds like a good idea,' he told Christi warmly, holding her arm lightly as they stood up to leave.

David kept up a light conversation as he drove them both to her apartment, Christi as relaxed in his company as she used to be in Lucas's—before things had changed so drastically between them.

Thinking of Lucas sobered her, and she was very quiet as they went up to her apartment. She couldn't help wondering if Lucas had bothered to keep to his unspoken rule of not bringing women back to his apartment for the night. Did the same rule still apply when the woman was your ex-wife? she wondered bitterly.

'If you've had second thoughts about the brandy——'

'Certainly not!' Christi roused herself, smiling brightly, realising what rotten company she had been the last few minutes. She put her arm companionably through the crook of David's. 'I'm hoping to persuade you to tell me all about what sounds like an explosive courtship,' she confided with relish, unlocking her door.

David grinned. 'I——'

'Christi, I want—oh!' A stony-faced Lucas came to an abrupt halt in the doorway of his apartment as he saw she wasn't alone. 'Kendrick,' he greeted icily.

'Hello, Lucas,' David returned speculatively. 'I had no idea you lived in this apartment building, too.' He eyed the other man questioningly.

'There's no reason why you should have known,' Lucas rasped, his expression cold.

Christi had been struck dumb as soon as Lucas had put in his unexpected appearance. His bow-tie had been removed, his snowy-white shirt was partly unbuttoned at the neck, black evening trousers tailored to his lean waist and thighs. Was Marsha waiting in his apartment even now for him to rejoin her? What could be so important to say to her that he had interrupted his evening with the other woman, anyway?

'No,' David accepted lightly, lean fingers covering Christi's as her hand had tightened convulsively on his arm at her first sight of Lucas. 'Nice to have seen you again. If you'll excuse us?' he effectively dismissed the other man.

Lucas's mouth thinned, his eyes narrowed to icy slits. 'Christi, I want to talk to you,' he told her tightly.

She had regained much of the composure she had lost when he'd appeared so suddenly, her gaze direct and unblinking. 'Can't it wait until morning?' she dismissed coolly. 'David and I were just about to have a—nightcap.' She was deliberately provocative in her claim, sensing David's amusement at her side. He really was the *nicest* man.

Lucas's expression became thunderous as he drew in a controlling breath. 'I really think it would be better if we talked right now,' he bit out with abrupt precision.

'You——'

'Why don't I go and wait in your apartment for you, Christi?' David suggested lightly, patting her hand encouragingly. 'After all,' he added mockingly, 'we have all night; I'm sure we can spare Lucas a few minutes of your time.'

Christi shot him a grateful look, her smile fading and her eyes hardening as she turned back to Lucas. 'I'll just be a few moments,' she told him coldly. 'If you would like to wait in your own apartment?' she added pointedly, as he stood watching them.

He turned abruptly on his heel and slammed the door behind him.

'So much for consideration for our neighbours,' Christi muttered as she followed David into the apartment, her gaze averted in embarrassed awkwardness as she introduced him to Henry, Gladys and Josephine, her hands trembling as she poured him the promised brandy.

David moved to stand behind her, his hands coming down to rest comfortingly on her shoulders.

'We can talk about him or not, Christi,' he assured her gently. 'Whatever you're comfortable with, OK?' He looked down at her encouragingly as he turned her to face him.

She closed her eyes, biting her bottom lip to stop it trembling, tears shimmering in her eyes as she raised her lids. 'Maybe later,' she offered ruefully.

He squeezed her shoulders reassuringly. 'Whatever,' he repeated softly.

She drew in a ragged breath. 'I'd better go and see what he wants.'

David grinned, releasing her. 'From the smoke coming out of his ears when he saw me with you, I would say the first thing he'll do is warn you what a bad boy I am,' he said self-derisively.

'Whereas you're really just a nice man who has offered to be my friend,' she reminded defensively.

'Don't tell Lucas that!' he warned, scandalised. 'My reputation will be in shreds if it gets around I've been offering nothing but friendship to a beautiful woman!'

Christi chuckled at his nonsense. 'I promise not to tell him,' she said drily.

He laughed softly. 'I didn't think you would!'

They shared a smile of complete understanding; she no more wanted Lucas to know that yet *another* handsomely devastating man had been unable to offer her more than friendship, than David wanted it to be public knowledge that no woman had meant anything to him since Sara, his wife.

David settled down in an armchair, the two cats instantly vying for position on his lap, David watching them bemusedly. 'If you need any help next door just shout,' he offered absently.

Her mouth set determinedly. 'I may not be the one shouting for help!'

He grinned appreciatively. 'Lucas is big enough to take care of himself,' he dismissed, sipping his brandy unconcernedly.

Christi didn't even bother to knock on the door of the apartment next door; if Lucas had Marsha in there with him, that was his fault!

He was alone in the lounge, his face looking as if it were carved from granite, watching her approach with narrowed silver eyes.

Christi stopped several feet away, facing him defiantly. 'I have someone waiting for me,' she finally reminded harshly as he made no attempt to speak.

A nerve pulsed in Lucas's jaw. 'Waiting for what?' he rasped. 'Christi,' his voice softened as she gave an outraged gasp, 'I respect and admire David Kendrick immensely as a businessman, but as a man——'

'As a man, you think he's nothing but a user of women,' she finished furiously. 'I suppose *you* would know all about men like that.'

Lucas's face darkened ominously. 'What the hell is that supposed to mean?'

Christi eyed him contemptuously. 'Where is Marsha—waiting for you in the bedroom?'

'Marsha?' he frowned. 'But——'

'Don't tell me.' She held up silencing hands. 'I'm not interested in whether you intend making love to your ex-wife here or back at her home. What I do object to is your thinking you have some right to make judgements about the people in *my* life!' Her eyes glittered angrily.

'David Kendrick in particular?' he said, his voice dangerously soft.

'Yes,' she challenged, her head back proudly. 'I've only been out with him one evening, but I already know he's a man I can admire and respect—in every way!'

Lucas drew in a harshly furious breath. 'Enough to go to bed with him?'

'That's my business.' Her voice had risen angrily, for she was more furious than she could ever remember before, with an anger that had been building since yesterday, ever since she had found Marsha in Lucas's apartment for the second time in a week. 'You stay out of my life, Lucas,' she snapped. 'And I'll stay out of yours!'

'But Kendrick is a——'

'Stay out of my life, Lucas,' she warned, her eyes flashing.

'He passed the kissing and caressing test with honours, did he?' Lucas grated harshly.

'Oh, definitely,' she bit out challengingly.

A spasm moved in his throat. 'Then that leaves only one last test left,' he muttered grimly.

'Exactly,' she acknowledged brittly. 'Now if this conversation is over——'

'Christi!' Lucas grasped her arm as she would have turned away. 'Don't do this!' he compelled.

'Don't you think he'll be an experienced enough teacher for me?' she scorned.

He breathed raggedly. 'Don't make your first time with a man an act of defiance against me,' he pleaded softly. 'If I've interfered too much in your life, then I'm sorry, but please don't——'

'You arrogant b——!' She broke off disgustedly, flinching out of his grasp. 'My being with David will have *nothing* to do with you,' she bit out between clenched teeth. 'Now this conversation is definitely over!'

'Christi——'

She turned at the door, her eyes dull with pain. 'It's over, Lucas,' she told him bitterly. 'Whatever it was between us—friendship, tolerance?' She shrugged dismissively. 'It's over.'

She closed the door softly behind her, remembering what she had told David earlier this evening about doors opening and closing. The door in her life behind which Lucas stood was definitely closed. For ever.

CHAPTER FIVE

'FEELING better today?'

Christi gave a shaky smile at David's gentle query. She had remained completely calm on Saturday night until she had reached the sanctuary of her apartment, and then the enormity of what she'd done had washed over her and she had buried her face in David's shoulder as she'd sobbed out every angry tear. And they had become the cleansing tears to ease her pain. Except the pain hadn't gone away, a dull ache still in her chest.

David had been wonderful that night, holding her until the tears had stopped, gently washing her face, asking no questions, but helping her slip off her dress before putting her in her bed, kissing her lightly on the brow before inviting her out to lunch on Monday.

She had fallen into an exhausted sleep once he'd left, completely drained emotionally. She had barely moved from her bed on Sunday, although she had heard Lucas moving about in the apartment next door. Knowing he was so close, and yet unreachable to her, had made her feel even worse, and she'd resolved to start looking for somewhere else to live on Monday.

But at least she had managed to set Dizzy and Zach's minds at rest about her immediate future when she had made her customary call to them last night, managing to instil enthusiasm into her voice as she'd told them of the advertising campaign she was involved in and of her friendship with David, sure that it would help Zach in his decision about the film rights to his book, no matter what David thought to the contrary.

David. He really was the nicest man she had ever met. Except Lucas. Oh, damn Lucas, and the hold he had over her heart and her life! If it weren't for her love for him, she *might* have been the one to open that other door in David's heart. She was sure she would at least have wanted to try.

Her smile was wan. 'Not really,' she sighed heavily.

David shook his head. 'I didn't think you would be. You've loved him for a very long time, haven't you?'

'That shows too, does it?' she grimaced.

'No.' He clasped her hand across the table. 'I just remembered after I left you on Saturday night that Lucas was with you at Dizzy and Zach's wedding last year. I remembered thinking at the time that if Lucas weren't careful *he* would be the one standing before an altar before too long. With you at his side,' he explained gently.

'As you see,' Christi's voice was brittle, 'he was very careful!' She gave a self-derisive laugh. 'I never even had a chance with him. Never!' she repeated disgustedly.

'He's a lot older than you——'

'Not another one obsessed with age!' she scorned impatiently.

He quirked dark brows. 'Lucas has mentioned that too, has he?' he said slowly.

She sighed irritably. 'He never ceases reminding me that he's thirty-seven, and, if not actually old enough to be my father, at least old enough to be an uncle or much older brother. I already have an uncle, and I've never wanted a brother!'

David's mouth twisted. 'I doubt if Lucas particularly wanted a niece or a sister, either!'

'Then why relegate me to those roles?' she derided.

He shrugged. 'Protection?'

'From me?' She nodded dully. 'Yes,' she sighed. 'It was certainly one way of avoiding any embarrassing declarations of love from me.'

'That wasn't quite what I meant——'

'Oh, believe me, David,' she said wearily. 'I know what I'm talking about.' She clearly remembered every humiliating detail of that conversation with Marsha on Friday night.

David whistled through his teeth. 'That was certainly some argument you and Lucas had on Saturday night! I gather you haven't spoken to each other since—no,' he answered his own question at her derisive expression. 'From the shouting I heard through the walls, I would say the two of you had said enough. What can I say?' He held up defensive hands as she raised questioning brows. 'I was wandering around your kitchen when I realised that, although I couldn't hear what was being said, I could definitely hear your raised voices.'

Christi sighed. 'You're lucky that's all you heard,' she derided. 'For a brief moment, after I had told Lucas I intended going to bed with you, I thought he was going to hit me.' She could still clearly remember that convulsive spasm in Lucas's throat, the tightening of his hands into fists.

David gave a choked laugh. 'I'm not surprised. What I want to know is, what changed your mind between his apartment and yours?' he leered.

His teasing eased her tension, and she found herself returning his smile. 'I hope you don't mind my using you in that way,' she said apologetically. 'I was just so angry...'

'What man could possibly mind being thought worthy of taking a beautiful woman like you to bed?' He squeezed her hand reassuringly.

'Lucas, to name but one,' she returned drily. 'Oh, why does he have to enter into the conversation all the time?' she said exasperatedly. 'I'm sure you didn't meet me today to talk about him!' she added self-disgustedly.

'Well, actually...'

Christi looked sharply at David, frowning at his rueful expression. 'But I told you on Saturday that Lucas doesn't care for me the way I care for him. There's nothing else to say.'

He gave a gentle smile. 'I told you then, and I'll tell you again now, you don't have to tell me a thing about you and Lucas——'

'Because there's nothing to tell!' she bit out dully.

'I wanted to talk to you about Lucas,' he reproved softly.

Christi's frown deepened. 'I thought the two of your were merely acquaintances?'

David shrugged. 'I think we can actually be classed as casual friends. Our business dealings mean we often meet up, and we seem to go to a lot of the same parties.'

'Probably know a lot of the same women,' she sighed.

His mouth quirked. 'Probably. Although not in the same way,' he added softly.

Christi blushed, giving a self-disgusted sigh. 'I'm sorry.' She shook her head. 'I'm not normally like this,' she excused lamely. 'I'm just so angry with Lucas still that—— But you wanted to tell me something about Lucas,' she encouraged briskly.

David instantly sobered. 'Well, as I said, we go to a lot of the same parties, know a lot of the same people. One of those people is Marsha, his ex-wife,' he added softly.

Christi tensed, drawing a sharp breath into her lungs. 'Oh, yes?' she returned casually, so casually it was obviously a forced reaction.

He grinned. 'And when I say "know", I don't mean biblically,' he derided.

She put her hand on his in silent apology for her earlier remark. 'I realise that,' she said softly.

'Not that Marsha isn't a beautiful woman——'

'I realise that, too,' she interrupted sharply.

David eyed her speculatively. 'Did you also know that the ex-Mrs Kingsley is thinking of marrying again?'

All the colour drained from Christi's cheeks, her eyes wide and haunted. 'Who?' she managed to ask in a hushed voice.

But she didn't really need to ask, *Lucas* was the man Marsha had been seeing all week. God, did Lucas know of the other woman's plans for him? Did he know, and just not care what the other woman had done to him in the past, considered forgiving and forgetting worth having his children back once more? Or—more painful yet—was it possible Lucas did still love the woman who had once been his wife?

'His name is Julian Holland,' David put in softly.

Christi blinked at him dazedly, still lost in thoughts of Lucas remarried to the sensually kittenish Marsha; it made her feel ill!

'The man Marsha is contemplating marrying,' David told her more clearly, 'his name is Julian Holland. He's something important in the diplomatic service,' he added drily. 'Marsha obviously fancies herself as a diplomat's wife.'

Christi stared at him in bewilderment. But it was *Lucas* Marsha had been seeing all week, Lucas she had claimed was her lover. Claimed ... Oh, God, she hadn't fallen for the oldest trick in the book, had she, her own insecurity where Lucas was concerned making her a prime target for his ex-wife?

'What is it?' David prompted anxiously at her pained groan. 'Do you know him?' he frowned.

'No—but I'm suddenly knowing Marsha a lot better than I would ever have wished to,' she choked disgustedly. 'Oh, my God,' she breathed slowly, a look of horror on her face. 'If Marsha marries this man, that means he will effectively become Daisy and Robin's father.'

'Not legally,' David sighed. 'But in every other way that matters, their day-to-day lives, yes,' he acknowledged heavily.

No wonder Lucas had been drinking on Tuesday night, if Marsha had just told him she intended giving their children a stepfather in the near future! God knew, the woman made it as awkward as possible for Lucas to see his children now, but once she was remarried . . .

'This must be killing Lucas,' Christi choked, tears in her eyes. 'Eating him up alive!'

David nodded slowly. 'It must be hell for any man put in that position.'

Lucas must be going through hell already, and all she had done the last week was make life even more difficult for him, forcing herself on him, unwittingly taking advantage of his disturbed state, and then telling him to stay out of her life.

Her own hurt feelings no longer seemed important, just as it no longer mattered that Lucas had always known of her love for him. What *was* important was Lucas himself. And at the moment he was very much in need of a friend, of the friendship he had never once denied her.

She looked at David with tear-wet eyes. 'I've been very stupid and selfish, haven't I?' she said self-disgustedly. 'Acting just like that child I keep claiming not to be.' She shook her head dejectedly. 'And now I'm doing it again,' she said self-reproachfully, straightening determinedly. 'Lucas has been my strength over the last four years; now it's my turn to offer him my support.'

David grinned at her. 'If it's any consolation, *I'm* sure you aren't a child.'

She gave him a grateful look. 'Thank you for telling me about Marsha.' Her voice hardened as she spoke of the other woman. 'It explains so many things that have been puzzling me.'

'I thought it might,' he drawled. 'Marsha always reminds me of an octopus, maintaining one tentacle around all the parts of her life, past and present. She and Lucas have been divorced for years, and yet she's never quite let him go.' He shook his head disgustedly.

And obviously the other woman had taken great pleasure in putting him through hell during the last week!

'Would you mind if I didn't stay for dessert?' she told David apologetically. 'I'm really not hungry, and I—I——'

'Have a friend to go and see,' he nodded understandingly. 'I'll give you a call later in the week, maybe we can try for lunch again.'

'I really am sorry, David——'

'Don't be,' he reassured her lightly. 'I envy Lucas like hell,' he said ruefully.

Christi gave a shaky smile, moving to kiss him warmly on the cheek before hurrying from the restaurant. She had to see Lucas, apologise for her behaviour, tell him that she knew all about Marsha's plans to remarry. All she wanted was for them to be friends again, for him to be able to talk to her, the way he used to.

Lucas rented a floor on one of the buildings in the middle of town, having a couple of assistants and their secretaries, as well as his own private secretary, working for him. The outer room was empty when she entered his office, the secretary's desk clear of papers, evidence that she must have gone out for lunch.

How silly of her! It stood to reason that if she had been out to lunch then so were a lot of other people. Lucas included?

She knocked timidly on his office door, opening it to peer inside, expecting the opulence that met her gaze—the luxurious brown and cream décor, the imposing mahogany desk. She was a little unnerved by the man who stood so silently in front of the window that had views over London, the sunshine behind him making it impossible for her to see his expression.

'Lucas?' she said tentatively.

He straightened, stepping away from the sunlight into the room, his strain instantly obvious as the lines about his mouth and eyes could clearly be seen, his mouth set in weary lines. He looked all of his thirty-seven years at that moment, his expression harshly unapproachable.

Nevertheless, Christi knew she had to approach him, that after the other night he wasn't likely to

come to her again. And why should he? She was
the one who had told him to get out of her life and
stay out!

He frowned wearily. 'What can I do for you?'

She wanted so badly to take the pain and despair
out of his eyes, and felt violent towards Marsha for
doing this to him. How badly everyone suffered
after a divorce: the children bewildered because
their parents were no longer together, one of those
parents sad because they were suddenly deprived of
the children they loved. Lucas was the type of man
who wouldn't allow his pain to make him so bitter
he couldn't function without dwelling on the past,
but this last blow seemed to have been one too
many, and Christi felt tears in her own eyes as she
thought of Robin and Daisy being brought up by
any other man but Lucas, possibly learning to call
that man 'Daddy' in time. It wasn't fair, Lucas had
done nothing wrong, he didn't deserve this pain.

But he looked as if her sympathy would be the
'straw that broke the camel's back', as if he would
crack under the strain if she said one word about
Robin and Daisy, and Marsha's remarriage.

She forced a bright smile to her lips. 'I was
shopping—I didn't see anything I liked,' she excused as his brows rose questioningly at her empty
hands. Damn, she may be an actress, but her lies
could certainly do with improving! 'And so I
thought, why don't I go and see if Lucas is free for
lunch?' She looked at him enquiringly, acting as if
she couldn't see his strain. As if she didn't know

every mood change this man made! 'Are you?' she prompted lightly, knowing she wouldn't be able to eat a thing, but from the look of Lucas he hadn't eaten much at all the last few days; his skin had an unhealthy pallor, adding to his look of strain.

His expression softened slightly. 'I'm not really hungry, Christi, although I do appreciate the thought,' he bit out curtly.

He certainly wasn't going to make this easy for her. And why should he? She had behaved like a shrew on Saturday night, and Lucas hadn't even realised what she was so angry about!

'Oh, come on, Lucas,' she cajoled softly. 'I know I was a bitch on Saturday night, but you know how emotional women get.' She hated it when men put women's emotionalism down to 'that certain time of the month', but, without introducing the subject of Marsha's visits to his apartment, something that was sure to deepen the pain in his already shadowed eyes, she didn't know what else to do! 'And it did seem as if you were treating me a little too much like a child,' she teased.

He held up defensive hands, lithe and attractive in the dark blue suit, although even that seemed a little looser on him than the last time he had worn that particular suit; he *wasn't* eating properly. 'I realised immediately afterwards that I had overstepped the boundaries of our friendship——'

'We don't have boundaries to our friendship, Lucas,' she cut in sharply.

He sighed, running a hand through the thickness of his hair. 'Every friendship has boundaries,

Christi,' he said heavily. 'And just lately I've been going way too far over ours,' he grated harshly.

The kissing and caressing... But she wouldn't change a moment of those times she had been in his arms, she knew they were possibly the only memories she would ever have. 'Did it seem as if I minded?' she prompted softly.

Lucas drew in a harsh breath. 'That isn't the point,' he rasped. 'I had no right—— Are you and David Kendrick still seeing each other?' He looked at her with narrowed eyes.

After the earlier lie she had told him, she couldn't say she had just had lunch with the other man, but neither could she let him think she had carried out her threat of Saturday night with that 'one final test'!

She gave an exaggerated sigh. 'I think there must be something wrong with me,' she bemoaned. 'Every sexually attractive man I meet offers me friendship, rather than——'

'Kendrick didn't make love to you Saturday night?' Lucas demanded tautly.

She knew David would forgive her for telling the truth, that he was the type of man who really didn't give a damn what people thought about him, or the fact that he had 'offered a beautiful woman only friendship'. 'I told you, he wants to be my friend,' she grimaced. 'You'll have to tell me what my secret is, Lucas—so that I can do something to change it!' she said disgustedly.

He relaxed slightly. 'I'm not sure I want you to do anything to change it,' he told her ruefully. 'I don't think I'm ready to lose my friend just yet,' he shrugged apologetically.

Her expression softened. 'You'll never lose my friendship, Lucas,' she assured him gruffly. 'There may be times when you wish you could, but I'm afraid you're stuck with me for life.'

A nerve pulsed in his jaw. 'Promise?'

Christi flinched inwardly at the loneliness and despair in that question. Strange, she had never thought of Lucas as being lonely before, but after knowing the companionship of a family for those years it must have been difficult for him to adjust to being on his own again. No wonder he had taken such pleasure in being so protective of her the last few years! While the women in his life changed, with regularity, *she* had become the constant in his life; she wasn't about to let him down again!

'I promise.' She put her arm through the crook of his. 'Now, are you going to take me out to lunch or do I have to kidnap you?' she teased to ease his tension.

He gave a rueful smile. 'I'd like to see you try! But I really can't spare the time for lunch today,' he told her regretfully. 'I have an appointment in— ten minutes,' he said, glancing at his wristwatch.

Which meant he wouldn't be bothering to eat lunch at all today, she thought. 'Then I insist you come over for dinner tonight,' she decided firmly. 'Unless—you have a date?' She frowned her sudden uncertainty.

His mouth twisted. 'No date. I'll bring the wine, shall I?'

She smiled her relief at his acceptance. 'Make it champagne,' she encouraged, her eyes alight with mischief. 'We haven't celebrated my new job yet,' she explained at his raised eyebrows.

'So we haven't,' Lucas gave an indulgent smile. 'Champagne it is,' he promised lightly.

Christi reached up the couple of inches it took to put her on the same level as his cheek, allowing herself the indulgence of her lips against the firmness of his skin. 'I'll see you tonight.' She stepped back, her expression deliberately casual. 'About eight o'clock.'

'It's a date,' he nodded as he walked with her to the door.

If only it were! But she had Lucas's friendship back, and that was all that was important.

CHAPTER SIX

AFTER another week of watching Lucas suffer in silence, Christi wasn't so sure of that.

Oh, their friendship seemed to have returned to its previous familiarity, and yet not once had Lucas mentioned to her Marsha's plans to remarry.

He couldn't have forgiven her for her uncharacteristic behaviour last week if he didn't feel he could talk to her about his problems, she decided. And yet he discussed business with her as he usually did, spent a couple of evenings of the next week at her apartment just chatting the way they used to. But there was no mention of Marsha.

Christi didn't know what to do. She was sure the problem was just festering and growing inside him, tearing him apart, but until he spoke to her about it she didn't feel able to offer her sympathy.

She felt sure he would mention something about it when he told her he was having the children on Saturday, a move from the normal weekend he was allowed every month. But, other than inviting her to join them at the coast for the day, he said nothing.

Christi enjoyed Robin and Daisy's company; she couldn't fault the polite, fun-loving children Marsha had brought them up to be, and was easily able to understand Lucas's dilemma when it had come to custody of them and he had realised they would be happier with their mother.

But he couldn't still feel that way, Christi thought as she watched Lucas building sandcastles with the two children. Their relationship was unmistakable—Robin, a seven-year-old version of his father, Daisy, a feminine version of Lucas, too, obviously going to be a beauty in the years to come. She was sure Lucas couldn't bear the idea of giving their upbringing into another man's care. They were such adorable children, so spontaneously affectionate, that she just wanted to take them home so that Lucas could have them with him always. And she knew he had to feel the same way; she hadn't missed the sadness in his eyes, when he thought no one was looking, as he gazed at his children.

'Will you come and help me, Christi?' Daisy asked in her shy little voice, standing in front of Christi with her bucket and spade, a little frill around the bottom of her flowered bathing costume. 'Daddy and Robin have challenged us to a sandcastle contest.'

'Of course I'll help you.' She reached up to hug the little girl, her breath catching in her throat as she saw Lucas watching them steadily, pain etched into his face. Christi gazed back at him over the top of Daisy's silky head, wanting to reach out and hug him too, hating that deep-down sadness about him that not even spending an unexpected day with his children could erase. Because he wanted them for much more than a day!

But she was sure neither of the children noted their father's distracted mood, they were simply loving their day at the beach. The only note of discord came on the drive back to their mother's house.

'Will Mummy and Uncle Julian be home yet?' Robin asked sleepily from the back seat.

Christi's breath was drawn sharply into her lungs, and she glanced anxiously at Lucas, her heart aching at the naked pain in his eyes. She longed to reach out to him, to reassure him with her touch, but if she did that she would be letting him know she had been aware all along of Marsha's plans to remarry. And that would probably hurt him more than telling her about it himself!

So she remained quiet, unmoving, her hands clenched tightly in her lap.

'I should think so, Robin,' his father answered lightly. 'They just had some—arrangements to see to today,' he excused, his grim expression in no way reflected in his casual tone.

'Do you like Uncle Julian, Daddy?' Daisy asked with the innocence of youth, having no idea that the idly put question had caused her father's hands to tighten fiercely on the steering wheel.

'Daisy!' Robin hissed beside his sister.

'Well, I only asked,' Daisy told him defensively, a telltale quiver to her voice at this rebuke from her secretly admired older brother.

'Well, you shouldn't have done,' Robin continued to chastise. 'Don't you know——'

'Hey, come on, kids,' Lucas chided lightly. 'Let's not have an argument about this, all right? I don't really know Uncle Julian, Daisy,' he gently answered her question. 'So I don't know whether or not I like him. I think the important thing is, do you and Robin like him?'

Christi turned away to look out of the side windows, blinking back the tears that threatened to fall. This was only the start for Lucas; it could only get worse as the other man became a permanent fixture in his children's lives.

'He's all right,' Robin dismissed moodily. 'At least he doesn't talk to me as if I'm a baby.'

'And he sometimes reads me my bedtime story,' Daisy added with satisfaction.

This time Christi couldn't prevent it, the action was purely instinctive; she reached blindly for Lucas's hand, the tears falling unashamedly down her cheeks now.

But her vision cleared just as Lucas's hand clasped hers, naked agony in Lucas's eyes as he briefly met her gaze.

Daisy had only been just over a year old when her parents' marriage had broken up, had grown up with the knowledge that as far as she was concerned her mummy and daddy had always lived apart; she would have the least trouble adapting to another man in her mother's life. Whereas Robin had been a little older, two and a half, and still remembered the joy of being a real family, which made him slightly resent the intrusion of another man in his father's place. But he wasn't openly antagonistic towards Julian Holland as a stepfather, which meant he, too, would adapt, in time.

Lucas was the one who would never be able to accept the other man's usurpation of his place in his children's lives.

'That's nice,' Lucas answered his daughter gruffly.

'Although he doesn't do it as well as you do, Daddy,' Daisy assured him guilelessly.

Lucas briefly squeezed Christi's hand, as if thanking her for her support, before returning his own hand back to the steering wheel. 'Give him a chance, poppet,' he told his daughter lightly. 'Uncle Julian isn't quite used to being around little children yet; he'll learn.'

'That's what I said—ouch!' Daisy let out a yell as her brother obviously meted out retribution for her thoughtlessness. 'That hurt,' she said tearfully.

'Robin!' Lucas reproved sternly.

'Sorry,' his son muttered moodily. 'But sometimes Daisy can be such a——'

'That will be enough, Robin,' his father told him firmly. 'I—Uncle Julian is going to be in your lives from now on, so you might as well accept that.'

'But don't you care that—that——'

'Of course I care, Robin.' Lucas's voice was harsher than he would have wished, Christi knew, for the subject was one that had to be handled with extreme delicacy. 'But we have no choice but to accept that your mother loves Uncle Julian, that she wants him in her life. And consequently that means he's in your lives, too.' His tone had gentled.

'I'll always be your daddy, you'll always be able to come to me if you have a problem.'

'Couldn't we come and live with you?' Robin asked petulantly.

Christi stopped breathing altogether. This was far from the perfect place for a father and his children to be having this conversation, but unfortunately Lucas hadn't been able to choose the time and place, but had to answer his children's uncertainties as they came up. Nevertheless, Christi felt as if she were intruding on something that was just too private to be witnessed by what amounted to an outsider. She wished she could just disappear into the night, trying to make herself as inconspicuous as possible.

A nerve pulsed in Lucas's cheek. 'And what would Mummy do then?' he pointed out gently. 'She loves you very much, you know.'

'I know,' Robin accepted carelessly. 'But she has Uncle Julian now, and you don't have anyone.'

There was no arguing with logic like that, and Christi wondered what Lucas's answer would be.

'I have my friends, Robin,' he told his son softly.

'Like Aunty Christi?' Daisy put in brightly.

'Like Aunty Christi,' Lucas nodded abruptly.

'But she doesn't live with you ... Does she ...?' Robin frowned his uncertainty.

'You know she doesn't,' his father reproved.

'But she's at your apartment a lot,' Daisy chimed in pertly.

'That's the way friends are, Daisy,' Lucas told her gently.

'Uncle Julian is going to live with us,' Daisy frowned.

'That's because he and your mother love each other,' Lucas said harshly.

'Don't you love Aunty Christi?' His daughter looked puzzled.

'Of course I love Aunty Christi,' Lucas replied patiently. 'I told you, we're friends, and friends care about each other.'

'But——'

'Stop being silly, Daisy,' her brother rebuked scoffingly. 'Heather is my friend, but I'm not going to *marry* her!' His tone left no doubt as to what he thought of *that* idea concerning his schoolfriend!

'I'm *not* silly,' Daisy protested rebelliously. 'You're the one that's silly. You——'

'I said no arguments, children,' Lucas put in softly. 'We're almost home, and we don't want your mother to think you haven't enjoyed your day at the beach, do we?' he lightly chided.

Christi had no doubt that the idea would please Marsha immensely! The other woman made her so angry, having no compunction in changing Lucas's plans to be with his children whenever it suited her, but quite willing to use him as the willing babysitter he obviously was whenever it fell in with *her* plans.

It was now obvious that Marsha had only let him have the children today so that she could spend time with Julian Holland. It was also obvious that, although the other man was still something of an unknown quantity to Daisy and Robin, they already liked him. Lucas was having to walk a very thin line between his dislike of the idea of the children having a stepfather and not letting the children know of his feelings. And it obviously wasn't easy for him to do.

Marsha Kingsley's house was ablaze with lights as the car turned into the driveway, the children jumping up and down on their seat at the thought of telling their mother all about the lovely day they had had, their earlier disquiet forgotten for the moment.

Lucas had come to the house alone to pick up the children this morning, returning for Christi, and it hadn't occurred to her until this moment that she might actually have to see Marsha and her fiancé when they took the children home.

She hesitated in her seat as Lucas helped the children out of the back.

Lucas bent down to talk to her. 'Coming inside?'

She grimaced. 'I think I'll just wait out here.' She shook her head, not at all eager for another encounter with Marsha Kingsley.

Lucas nodded, the children having already run up to the house to ring the doorbell. 'I can't say I'm exactly looking forward to this myself,' he acknowledged grimly.

There was a pale green BMW parked in the driveway next to Marsha's grey Mercedes, and it didn't take much intelligence to realise the second car must belong to Julian Holland.

Christi made her decision quickly and unhesitantly, opening her car door to step out on to the gravel driveway. 'I think I will come in, after all,' she told Lucas lightly.

He gave her a derisive look as she walked around the car to his side. 'I'm not looking forward to it,' he drawled. 'But I *can* handle it.'

Christi gave a careless shrug. 'I don't really feel like sitting out here in the car.'

Lucas squeezed her arm as he took hold of her elbow to walk beside her up to the door that now stood open, Marsha reflected in the light. 'Thanks,' he murmured before they came into earshot of the other woman.

'Lucas,' Marsha drawled, her sharp hazel gaze turning to Christi. 'And little Christi,' she greeted mockingly. 'Did you enjoy your day at the beach, dear?' she taunted as she held the door open wider for them to enter.

She felt Lucas's fingers tighten on her arm at the deliberate challenge, but her own expression remained impassively calm. 'Of course, you're a little old to enjoy such pleasant pastimes, aren't you?' she returned sweetly.

Marsha's mouth twisted. 'Let's just say I prefer my—amusements, to be a little more mature than days at the beach,' she drawled.

Christi smiled confidently, her arm possessively through the crook of Lucas's; this woman had made her turn tail and run once, she wouldn't succeed in doing it again. 'Oh, I enjoy those sort of amusements, too, at the right time,' she taunted huskily.

Marsha's gaze narrowed on the way Christi and Lucas stood so close together. 'I hope you kept this—relationship from the children?' she snapped.

'Oh, you needn't worry, Marsha dear,' Christi answered before Lucas could, patting the other woman's arm reassuringly. 'Robin and Daisy are still as innocent as I—fortunately!—am not.' The statement was a double-edged sword, telling this woman of her confidence in her own femininity, but also warning her that she was completely wise to the deceit she had practised a week ago, and that she wouldn't fall for it a second time.

She could tell by the way Marsha's lips thinned that neither meaning had been lost on her, and her gaze was angry as it once again swept over the two of them. 'I suppose if you *want* to make a fool of yourself, Lucas——'

'I don't believe *Lucas* is the one making a fool of himself,' Christi cut in bravely, her eyes as hard as the sapphires they resembled.

Marsha flushed. 'What the hell do you mean by that?' Her eyes flashed fire.

Christi met her gaze unflinchingly. 'You must admit, it is a little odd for you to be behaving so possessively towards your ex-husband when, as I understand it, you're thinking of being married again quite soon—to someone else!'

The other woman's mouth tightened even more. 'You——'

'Darling, surely you aren't going to keep Lucas— and his friend,' added the short, slightly overweight man, with receding blond hair, who had joined them from the lounge, as he saw Christi standing at Lucas's side, 'standing out here all evening?'

This was Julian Holland? He wasn't at all what Christi had been expecting, and she stared at him in open astonishment.

He wasn't much taller than Marsha's five foot five in her three-inch-heel sandals, for one thing, and was certainly a couple of inches shorter than Christi herself. And, although his looks were quite pleasant—warm brown eyes and a round, friendly face—he wasn't what Christi could call in the least sexy or heart-stoppingly attractive the way Lucas was. Although his suit was obviously an expensive one, it didn't look half as good on him as Lucas did in jeans and a casual shirt, for Julian's stocky build was only slightly concealed by the excellent tailoring.

But he obviously *was* Julian Holland, his arm moving lightly about Marsha's waist as he reached her side, his bulkier appearance making Marsha look tinier than ever.

Lucas was the first to recover. 'Holland.' He held out his hand politely.

Something in Lucas's tone put the other man on his guard, Julian Holland eyeing him warily. 'Kingsley,' he returned slowly.

Lucas nodded tersely. 'If I could just say goodbye to the children?' He turned to Marsha.

Marsha's gaze swept challengingly over Christi before settling on Lucas. 'Don't you want to help me put them to bed, the way you usually do when you bring them home?' she suggested huskily.

His gaze unconsciously turned to Christi before he shook his head. 'I don't think——'

'Please go ahead and help put the children to bed, Lucas,' Christi cut in sharply, knowing he must be longing to spend even that little more time with the children he saw all too infrequently. 'I'm sure Mr Holland and I can amuse ourselves while we wait in the lounge for the two of you.' She gave the other man a brief smile, having chosen her wording carefully, knowing Marsha hadn't missed the implication. She looked outraged by the challenge.

Lucas hesitated. 'If you're sure you don't mind . . . ?'

'Of course I don't,' her smile was warm with feeling as she turned to him, 'and I'm sure the children will love it,' she added indulgently.

While Lucas rounded up the children for their baths, Julian Holland moved to pour Christi a drink, Christi and Marsha eyeing each other speculatively.

A grudging respect slowly entered the other woman's eyes. 'You really did grow up, didn't you?' she mused.

Christi gave an abrupt inclination of her head. 'I really did.'

Marsha glanced at Lucas as he laughingly threw Daisy over his shoulder to carry her out of the room. 'But I wonder if you grew up enough?' she murmured without a second glance, following the man who had once been her husband, and her children, from the room.

Christi let out a shaky breath, sitting down in the nearest chair before she fell down. Marsha might be going to marry the pleasant-faced man who was now handing her the sherry she had requested, but she certainly had no intention of relinquishing her claim on Lucas at the same time!

'Cheers!' Julian Holland held up his glass before taking an obviously welcome swallow of the whisky inside it. 'Have you known—er—Lucas, long?' he enquired casually as he sat down opposite her, obviously awkward with the familiarity after Lucas's terse formality.

'Several years,' she nodded abruptly, feeling a little sorry for him, but also very much aware that he was the reason for Lucas's present unhappiness.

His eyes widened. 'Really? I wouldn't have thought—you don't look old enough—well, isn't that nice!' He gave a bright, meaningless smile.

For a diplomat, this man certainly wasn't very diplomatic! 'Isn't it?' she agreed drily. 'Have you known Marsha very long?' He couldn't have done if he were contemplating marrying her!

He smiled as he thought of the woman he loved. 'A few months.'

'How nice.' She turned away uninterestedly, pretending interest in one of the paintings that hung on the wall. It wasn't this man's fault, and under any other circumstances she would probably have liked him, but she couldn't help but feel angry at what this man's marriage to Marsha would do to Lucas.

'Do you like that?' He squinted up at the abstract painting Christi was staring at so fixedly.

How could anyone like green and pink lines on a canvas? 'No,' she answered with blunt honesty, sighing as the man opposite her looked uncomfortable. 'Look, I'm sorry, this—this awkward situation isn't your fault, but I don't think either of us really feels like making polite conversation.'

'No,' he conceded with a weary sigh, relaxing back in his chair slightly. 'It is a little awkward, isn't it?'

A little? It was impossible! But if she *had* been the woman in Lucas's life, as this man believed her to be, it would have been even more uncomfortable.

God, if she'd really had the right to tell Marsha what she thought of her, she certainly wouldn't have hit out at the other woman with veiled innuendoes about Lucas and herself, she would have left Marsha in no doubt as to her claim to him and would have shown Marsha that she could have a fight on her hands for custody of the children. Instead, she had to stand by and watch Marsha destroy Lucas that little bit more. No wonder Lucas was incapable of loving another woman after Marsha! She had taken all he had to give, was *still* taking what little peace of mind he managed to attain for himself.

The silence in the room as they waited for the return of Lucas and Marsha was very uncomfortable, and Christi passed the time by looking at each

of the abstract paintings in turn and trying to visualise what had sparked off the monstrosities in the
artist's mind in the first place. She had just decided
the one on the far wall was a bloated fish when
Lucas and Marsha came into the room.

Under any other circumstances, their flushed and
dishevelled appearance would have looked highly
suspect, but the damp patches on their clothing told
their own story, although the indulgent smiles they
shared about their children's antics in the bath
caused a painful lurch in Christi's chest.

She stood up jerkily. 'Finished?' Her voice was
unnaturally high, her cheeks flushed.

'I——'

'Cook is just about to serve dinner,' Marsha
lightly interrupted Lucas. 'I'm sure there's enough
for four—if you would care to stay?'

If you would *dare* to stay! Christi read the challenge clearly in her words. The last thing she wanted
was to sit down to dinner with this woman in the
name of civilised behaviour, and yet she knew that
if Lucas chose to accept she would be at his side.

She deliberately kept her expression bland, her
gaze averted, not wanting to influence his decision.

'Thanks for the invitation, Marsha,' Lucas's
hand came to rest lightly against Christi's back, 'but
I'm afraid we've made other arrangements.'

Christi's breath left her in a relieved sigh, and as
she looked up at Lucas she could see the amusement
in his eyes, evidence that she had given herself away
seconds ago. She returned his smile ruefully.

'In that case, don't let us keep you,' Marsha's caustic voice interrupted the moment of shared humour.

Lucas nodded abruptly to Julian Holland as he stood up, his gaze then flickering to Marsha. 'If you need somewhere to park the children again soon, let me know,' he rasped.

'I think all the arrangements for the wedding next month are completed now, thank you,' Marsha returned scornfully. 'You'll receive your invitation in due time, of course,' she added bitchily. 'And you must bring dear Christi.'

Her eyes narrowed on the other woman. 'I wouldn't miss it for anything!'

Marsha gave a mocking smile. '"Always the bridesmaid, never the bride",' she taunted.

Although the barb hit its mark, it wasn't obvious from Christi's relaxed pose at Lucas's side. 'Is that an invitation?' she derided.

'What do you think?' Marsha snapped.

Christi gave her a mocking smile before turning to Julian Holland; the poor man was starting to look a little dazed by this whole encounter now. 'Nice to have met you, Mr Holland. I'm sorry the next time we meet can't be under better circumstances,' she added with sweet sarcasm.

How Lucas managed to get her out of the house without Marsha physically attacking her she couldn't say, but minutes later they were in his car, driving away from the house, and she didn't have a scratch mark on her!

Lucas chuckled at her side. 'I never thought I would see the day that Marsha would be left speechless,' he explained at her frowning look.

'Was that what it was?' she sighed, some of the tension starting to leave her. 'I thought she was just trying to prevent Julian Holland from seeing her true nature!'

Lucas instantly sobered, and Christi could have kicked herself for her lack of tact. 'You'll have gathered by now that the two of them are getting married,' he bit out abruptly.

How could she help but know? 'Yes,' she sighed.

'He wasn't quite what I was expecting—hell, I don't know what I was expecting!' Lucas shook his head. 'The kids seem to like him, don't you think?' He glanced at her before his attention returned to the road in front of them.

'They like you better,' Christi rasped.

'And the thought of any other man but me in their life breaks me up, but——' He broke off abruptly, sighing heavily. 'We all had a good day together today, didn't we?' he lightly changed the subject.

'Very good,' she agreed huskily. 'Robin and Daisy are lovely children.'

'Yes,' he said heavily. 'Yes, they are.'

There didn't seem to be anything else to say on the subject; Lucas was lost in his own thoughts as they drove back towards town, and Christi didn't want to intrude on those thoughts, knowing he needed this time to himself.

Finally he gave a deep sigh, shaking off his oppressive mood. 'Shall we go home and change first before going out to dinner, or do you want to find somewhere that will accept us dressed like this?' He looked down ruefully at the denims they both wore, he with an open-necked shirt, Christi with a pale blue blouse.

She was surprised to learn that he had meant it about the two of them having dinner together, had thought it had just been a way to get away from Marsha's invitation. After all, it was a Saturday night, and Lucas usually had a date on a Saturday night.

'No Michelle tonight?' she enquired lightly.

He smiled teasingly. 'I would hardly be asking you to go out to dinner with me if there were.'

Now, there was a logic she couldn't argue with—and didn't want to! She was glad the other woman at last seemed to have faded from his life. 'I could always get us something at my apartment,' she offered. 'I feel a little too salty and sandy still to go straight out,' she explained as he hesitated. 'And it will be a little late to go anywhere by the time we've both showered and changed.'

'Asking you to cook dinner doesn't seem very fair after you've helped me entertain the children all day,' he frowned.

She should have known the dinner invitation was a thank you for going out with them today! 'I really don't mind,' she said a little flatly.

'What if I cook dinner, instead?' he suggested lightly, giving her a brief grin. 'You seem just as sleepy from your day by the sea as the children were!'

Just what she needed, to be classed with a six- and seven-year-old! 'I'm fine,' she reassured him sharply. 'More than capable of cooking us some dinner.'

'OK,' Lucas accepted shruggingly.

Christi hurried into her own apartment once they got back, anxious to wash the salt and sand from her body now, absently acknowledging Lucas's comment of 'see you soon'.

If nothing else, she needed these few minutes alone to put the meeting with Marsha from her mind. The other woman was a possessive bitch who kept Lucas tied to her by using their children, and who had made it obvious she didn't intend relinquishing that hold even once she had remarried, by reminding him all too forcefully of his relationship with her through his children if he should ever start to think of a life of his own, separate from theirs. Lucas would *never* give up his relationship with his children, but surely he didn't have to pay for the rest of his life for the mistake of his marriage to their mother, a marriage that Marsha herself had chosen to end? It just didn't seem fair!

She must have spent longer under the shower than she had realised, just letting the steaming hot water beat down on her as *she* inwardly steamed at the injustice of the emotional blackmail Marsha felt no hesitation in using to keep Lucas running to her side, because she could hear the doorbell ringing now. Realising it must be Lucas, arriving for the dinner she had promised to cook him, she hastily switched off the shower tap, opening the door to wrap the towel around her wet hair in the process of stepping from the shower when a movement near the door caught her eye.

She froze in the action of picking up the second towel she had laid out to dry herself with, her startled gaze fixed on Lucas's suddenly pale face as he stood in the bathroom doorway.

'I used my key to get in.' He explained his presence gruffly. 'I thought you might have fallen and hurt yourself, or—God...' he breathed shakily, his dark gaze held mesmerised by her nakedness.

Christi knew she should pick up the towel from the side of the bath, that she should wrap it around herself, should laugh off this awkward situation. But she didn't want to do any of those things; she wanted to lose herself in the heated admiration she could see in Lucas's eyes, unconsciously standing more proudly, her breasts thrusting pertly forward, her waist slender and flat, her thighs silkily inviting.

Lucas swallowed hard, breathing raggedly. 'I think I should wait for you in the lounge,' he murmured huskily, although he made no effort to leave the confines of the steamily hot room.

Christi moved slowly forward, her breathing shallow. 'Lucas,' she said softly, holding his gaze with hers.

He stood rigidly still. 'I should go...'

But he didn't. He swayed slightly as she came to stand in front of him, but it was his only movement.

Christi put her arms up about his neck, absently noting how white her skin looked against the black shirt he wore with a clean pair of denims, her breath catching in her throat as the soft material of his shirt became a caress against her breasts.

Lucas moved as if in a daze, his arms slowly encircling her, reaching up to pull the towel from her hair.

Until that moment Christi had forgotten the towel wrapped about her wet hair, and shivered slightly as the cold tendrils fell on her heated shoulders. And then Lucas was threading his fingers through the silky dampness to cup her head for the descent of his lips, and fire was the only thing she was aware of.

There was no gentleness, only fierce demand, his mouth moving expertly against hers, tasting her like a man who had been starving in a desert.

She entwined her arms more tightly about his neck, glad of her height as their thighs met in abrasive demand, Lucas hard against her.

He wanted her! If she had ever doubted it before, she knew it for certain now, his body's involuntary reaction something he couldn't hide.

His hands were like fire against her, and she shuddered with emotions too long suppressed as one of those hands closed over the tautness of her breast, easing some of the aching heat there as his thumb-pad stroked the hardened tip.

'I want you,' he groaned against the silky length of her throat. 'Dear God, I want you so badly!'

Nerves pulsed and leapt as his mouth caressed her shoulders, his tongue searching out the creamy hollows of her throat.

Her whole body tingled with need, her back arching as his mouth finally took her breast, suckling against the fiery nub in a slow rhythm that made her legs tremble and quake.

Christi held him to her, wanting more, groaning her satisfaction as his teeth nibbled against her with pleasure-pain.

Liquid fire met him between her thighs as he caressed her there, groaning low in his throat at this evidence of her readiness for him.

She wouldn't have cared if Lucas had lain her down on the bathroom floor and taken her there, so great was her need for him, but Lucas had other ideas. He swung her up into his arms to carry her into her bedroom, laying her down gently on the bed, before standing over her.

Christi groaned at the indecision in his face. 'Don't go, Lucas.' She held out her arms to him, her expression pleading. 'Stay, and make love to me.' She almost sobbed with her need.

As he still hesitated, his face racked by indecision, Christi came up on her knees on the bed, holding his gaze as she began to unbutton his shirt, running shaking hands over the hardness of his flesh before slipping the shirt from his body completely.

His chest was covered with fine dark hair that disappeared in a V beneath the material of his jeans, and Christi's questing lips followed the path of that silky hair, gazing up at him with pleading eyes as her fingers moved to the fastening of his denims.

Lucas swallowed convulsively, one of his hands moving to cover both of hers. 'Christi, we can't——'

'We can,' she insisted firmly. 'Let me, Lucas,' she groaned, looking at him with dark blue eyes.

He gave a low moan, his eyes slowly closing as his hand fell away from hers, although both his hands moved into clenched fists as Christi slid the denims from his body.

She had seen him only that afternoon in bathing trunks, had thought then he was the most beautiful man she had ever seen. But naked he was even more so, like a gold and bronze sculpture come to life, every part of him beautifully smooth and firmly muscled.

He stood perfectly still as her searching hands and lips learned every inch of him, his increased ragged breathing and his tensed muscles the only outward evidence that he was fast losing control.

Suddenly he couldn't stand any more; his hands gripped her arms tightly as he stopped her caresses, pushing her down on the bed before covering her body with his, his mouth fiercely possessing hers as his tongue fought a silent duel with hers.

Christi felt like sobbing with the sheer beauty of the moment, giving herself up completely to the wild sensations coursing through her body as Lucas caressed her as intimately as she had him only seconds earlier, gasping as he sought her out in a way she hadn't dared to with him, writhing on the bed with heated abandon as that liquid fire flooded her whole body.

'Now, Lucas,' she choked her desperation. 'Lucas, it has to be now!'

The soft lamp-glow made his eyes look almost blue as he looked down at her searchingly. 'Did you really mean it—about those other men?' His voice was gruff.

'Mean it?' she echoed wildly, not understanding what he meant. And then, as his gaze roamed regretfully over her body, she knew. 'It isn't going to make any difference, Lucas?' she cried brokenly. 'You aren't going to be noble, are you?' She shook her head in silent denial.

He gave a self-derisive snort. 'I stopped being noble with you the moment I walked into your bathroom and found you naked. But I have to know, Christi.' His fingertips ran caressingly down one cheek. 'I don't want to hurt you.''

She swallowed hard. 'I've never wanted anyone else but you, Lucas. Does that answer your question?' She was completely vulnerable as she gazed up at him.

'Yes,' he breathed softly. 'Dear God, Christi,' he groaned suddenly. 'I wish I *could* stop this.' He grimaced as if in pain. 'But it's too late for that, far too late!' He shook his head weakly.

'I love you, Lucas.' She smoothed the frown from between his eyes. 'I've always loved you.'

'It doesn't help—I have no right—but I need— I *can't* fight that need any more!' He shook his head self-disgustedly, his mouth savagely claiming hers even as his thighs surged against her, seeking entrance, surging into her as he found his way blocked by that gossamer barrier, her cry of pain lost, and then forgotten, as she moved with him instinctively.

Christi felt complete for the first time in her life, and as that aching fire grew and grew in her body she knew there was even more, feeling herself rising higher and higher, seeking, searching——

'Marry me, Christi,' Lucas groaned heatedly, his body a silky caress against hers. 'Marry me!'

'Yes! Oh God, yes!' Sensations unlike any she had ever known racked her body, taking it in wave after wave of blissful pleasure, aware of the deep surge of Lucas's body as he too reached the peak of fulfilment, sobbing quietly in his arms as the beauty of their shared passion washed over her.

Long after Lucas had fallen into a deep sleep, neither of them interested in the dinner that had once seemed so appealing, Christi lay awake, her heart once again feeling as if it were breaking.

She had wanted Lucas's loving, had begged for it, but he hadn't spoken of loving her, had only allowed his body to do that, while his thoughts had remained detached from what he was doing.

She had watched him with the children today, knew the torment he was going through at the thought of some other man bringing them up, knew that he had been driven by desperation tonight, had been fighting for the right to have custody to his children in the only way that now seemed open to him: if he were married himself, he would have more to offer his children than ever before.

And what better choice for a wife than the young woman he had always known was in love with him? He had said he 'had no right', but that he 'needed', and in that moment Christi had known *why* he needed her.

But it hadn't mattered. Not then, and not now. Her heart was breaking at the way Lucas had finally become hers, but she knew he had no other choice, that at least they could be friends and lovers even if Lucas couldn't offer her any more than that. He *had* to have a wife if he were to stand any chance of getting custody of Robin and Daisy, and with Marsha's wedding next month he didn't have any time to waste.

Christi looked down at him with loving eyes as he lay against her breast. Long dark lashes fanned out across his cheeks, giving him a boyish appeal, leaving him completely vulnerable.

Her arms tightened about him. She didn't care how or why he was hers, only that he was.

And she was going to marry him.

CHAPTER SEVEN

'WHAT do you mean, you're getting married next week?' Dizzy blustered down the telephone line.

Christi smiled as she envisaged her friend's surprise: the green eyes wide with shock, her mouth open with disbelief.

These Sunday evening telephone calls between the two friends had been a ritual for as long as Christi could remember, carried on even after Dizzy's marriage to Christi's uncle, and although Christi didn't usually have anything too dramatic to report, today was different. Today she had to tell Dizzy and Zach that she intended marrying Lucas, very soon.

'Exactly what I said,' she mused. 'I hope you and Zach can make it before you have to leave for the States.'

'Zach's doing the work here for the moment,' Dizzy dismissed vaguely. 'You know how cautious he can be.'

'Except when he married you,' Christi chuckled. 'A three-day courtship had to take him a little by surprise!'

'No more than yours is going to!' Dizzy sounded as if she were frowning. 'I don't understand it, last week you said they were all nice, but none of them were special. Last week you were so angry with Dick

and Barry—and me!—because you found out they
were trying to use you to get to your uncle...
David!' she pounced. 'It has to be David,' she said
wonderingly.

Christi couldn't blame her friend for jumping to
that conclusion. She herself was still a little dazed
that *Lucas* was to be her husband next week!

Not that he hadn't given her the chance to change
her mind about accepting his proposal. His desperation of Saturday night seemed to have worn
off by this morning; he'd assured her that the
chances of her being pregnant from that one night
were unlikely, and that if she would like to recon-
sider her decision he would understand. Considering all that he had to lose if she should decide not
to marry him, she had only loved him all the more
for his unselfishness. But she loved him, even if his
only reason for wanting to marry her was his
children, and to be his wife this way was better than
not being his wife at all.

'No, it isn't David,' she told her friend drily.

'Not David? But—Lucas,' Dizzy said with satisfaction. 'He finally realised that he loves you!'

'What?' Now it was Christi's turn to be amazed.
How in the world had Dizzy guessed that Christi
was in love with Lucas?

'It is him, isn't it?' her friend persisted eagerly.

'Well, yes... But——'

'How did I know?' Dizzy finished excitedly.
'How did you know I was in love with your uncle
when I was still fighting the idea myself?' she dismissed. 'We've always been so close, Christi, how

could I not know? I took one look at the two of you together at my wedding and knew he was the reason no other man has ever meant anything serious to you. All those years he had been your next-door neighbour and I'd never guessed a thing, but as soon as I saw you together, I knew.'

'OK, Sherlock,' Christi drawled, 'what gave me away?'

'The love in your eyes every time you looked at him,' her friend said softly.

She swallowed hard. 'Oh—that,' she mumbled.

'And now the two of you are finally going to be married,' Dizzy cried gleefully. 'My effort at long-distance matchmaking paid off, then?'

'What do you——? Dick, Barry and David were supposed to make Lucas jealous?' she realised slowly.

'It worked, didn't it?' her friend gloated. 'Although, what Zach's going to say about the wedding being next week, I don't know,' she added worriedly.

Christi was still dazed by Dizzy's instinctive knowledge of the love for Lucas she had tried for so long to hide from everyone. 'What if your plan had gone wrong?' she protested weakly.

'And you had actually fallen in love with Dick, Barry, or David?' Dizzy said cheerfully. 'Well, that wouldn't have been so bad, would it? They're all very nice men, although I have to admit David is my favourite,' she added fondly.

'Mine, too,' Christi acknowledged softly. 'But, Dizzy——'

'Oh, love, you had tried everything else to get Lucas to see you as a woman,' Dizzy dismissed. 'I just had this feeling you were getting to the "it's now or never" stage.'

She should have realised Dizzy knew her too well! 'If you think back, I had also tried the jealousy bit before,' she said drily.

'Not with men of Lucas's own age and experience,' her friend returned confidently. 'That was sure to get him to sit up and take notice. Oh, love, I'm so glad for you,' she sighed happily.

'And *I* should be angry with you.' Christi tried to sound indignant.

'But you aren't, are you?' Dizzy chuckled.

How could she be, when possibly Dizzy's matchmaking *had* helped to show Lucas she was a grown woman, to prove to him that *other* men considered her mature enough to take on the responsibility of a relationship? He was marrying her, wasn't he? So he must finally see her as all grown up. At least, grown up enough to become stepmother to the two children he wanted back with him so desperately.

'No,' she admitted drily. 'I'm not angry with you at all.'

'I'll get Zach so that you can discuss the wedding with him,' Dizzy told her briskly.

'Coward!' Christi softly taunted.

'Guilty as charged,' Dizzy laughed before going off in search of her husband.

Knowing how Dizzy could twist her husband around her little finger, Christi knew her friend would have done her best to persuade Zach around to the idea of her marriage to Lucas before he even came on the telephone, especially as it now turned out to have been Dizzy's idea in the first place!

However, her best friend couldn't possibly have guessed at the impossible position Lucas found himself in that necessitated him having a wife.

She was proved right about Dizzy's influence with Zach, for her uncle gave his approval unhesitantly. Apparently, he had liked Lucas when he'd met him at the wedding last year and, as Zach wryly claimed, 'We older men make the best husbands.' A second later, he muttered, 'Ouch!' as Dizzy obviously hit him for his facetiousness.

Christi was chuckling softly to herself as she came off the telephone, her smile fading as the doorbell rang and Henry set up the excited yapping that told her it was Lucas at the door.

She hadn't seen him since they had had breakfast together earlier, Lucas claiming he had some work to do. Christi was sure the work had just been an excuse, that Lucas himself needed time to come to terms with the idea of becoming a husband again. Although surely the pill must be sweeter to swallow when it also meant he stood a chance of becoming full-time father to Robin and Daisy again!

Oh God, bitterness wasn't going to make a success of this relationship that was already a fact because of all the wrong reasons; she had made her decision with her eyes wide open, she didn't have room for doubts now.

'Lucas,' she greeted him warmly as she threw open the door, the shadows dispelled from all but the depths of her eyes.

He hesitated only fractionally before kissing her lightly on the mouth, but it was enough to be noticeable when Christi was already feeling so sensitive.

'I thought we would go out for dinner,' he suggested abruptly.

She could see that, his appearance in the dark evening suit taking her breath away. She didn't want to go out anywhere, she just wanted Lucas to take her in his arms and reassure her, in the only way in which they seemed to be close now, that everything would be all right, that he did care for her.

But the distant expression in his eyes, and the grim set to his mouth, didn't encourage such intimacies. The erotically beautiful man of the night before was far removed from this harsh-faced stranger.

'Just give me a few minutes to change,' she nodded lightly.

'Fine.' He sat down in an armchair, opening up the newspaper that had been delivered that day, immediately lost behind the voluminous pages.

Christi watched him woefully for several seconds before hastily leaving the room. Lucas didn't seem able to even look at her now!

She was shaking badly by the time she reached her bedroom, burying her face in Josephine's fur as the cat stood on her dressing-table to rub against her concernedly. 'I think he actually hates me,

Josie,' she wailed brokenly, the haughty animal not in the least offended by this shortened version of her name, butting her gently with her regal head.

No, he didn't hate *her*, she reasoned as the pain lessened, Lucas just hated the situation Marsha's remarriage had put them both in. But Christi loved him, would always love him, and it didn't really matter *why* he was marrying her, as long as he did.

All trace of tears had been deftly removed when she rejoined Lucas in the lounge a few minutes later, the off-the-shoulder white dress having a gypsy style to it, her hair secured to one side to fall in loose curls over one of those bare shoulders, her make-up suitably dramatic, hiding evidence of her earlier distress. She felt good, and she knew she looked good.

Lucas put the newspaper down slowly, the darkening of his eyes the only outward sign of his approval of her appearance as he stood up to briskly drape her jacket over her shoulders.

But that involuntary reaction was enough for Christi, and she shot him a provocative smile over one shoulder as his hands lingered caressingly against her.

His hands were abruptly removed as he turned away. 'With you dressed like this, I feel we should do more than just go out to dinner,' he rasped.

If their engagement were a normal one, she would have moved into his arms and told him she didn't want to go out at all, that she would much rather stay here, in his arms, making love as passionately as they had last night.

But they weren't like any normally engaged couple, and so she just smiled brightly. 'Dinner sounds just fine,' she assured him.

He nodded distantly, his hand politely on her elbow as they left her apartment to go down to his waiting car.

This wasn't the Lucas she was used to, the Lucas she could tell anything to, and know he would either sympathise or offer advice that wasn't intrusive.

She could have wept for the friendship they had sacrificed, but Lucas had to think it was worth it to have his children back with him. She pushed from her mind thoughts of what would happen to her and Lucas if he should lose the battle for custody of his children...

She smiled a little wanly at Simon as he saw them to their table, hoping he wouldn't connect her with the woman who had telephoned that night to arrange a table for Mr Kingsley, only to find Lucas was already taking Marsha out to dinner! She knew Simon to be a man of quick intelligence, his watchful gaze not missing a movement in 'his' restaurant, and if he had recognised her voice that night he remained silent now.

Lucas's tension didn't relent as the meal progressed, and conversation was an uphill battle Christi felt she was fast losing. Ordinarily, silence between them would have been companionable, but now Christi was afraid that if she left a lull in the conversation Lucas might take it to voice the doubts he seemed to be having about them, and seemed to be having more with each passing minute.

She couldn't even remember the meal she ate, and considering the exquisiteness of the menu served there that was evidence of her disturbed peace of mind!

'—Dizzy and Zach about the wedding...' Her voice trailed off lamely as she realised exactly what she had been babbling, her stricken gaze raised to Lucas's sudden stillness. She hadn't meant to mention that telephone call, hadn't meant to talk of their marriage *at all*!

Lucas sat back, his hands resting lightly on the table's edge. 'Oh?'

She swallowed hard. 'I wanted to make sure they didn't go off to America before I'd had a chance to tell them,' she explained with a grimace, having told Lucas over breakfast that morning of Zach's dual careers. He had been a little surprised, but obviously had other things on his mind. Now he was all too intent on what she was saying.

'I intended going up to see your uncle tomorrow,' Lucas bit out abruptly.

Her eyes widened. 'You never said...'

He shrugged. 'I haven't seen you all day to tell you anything.'

'No, but—I'm sorry if I ruined your plans,' she frowned. 'I thought I was just getting one obstacle out of the way,' she grimaced.

His eyes narrowed. 'And is it?' he drawled slowly.

She longed to tell him of the teasing comment her uncle had made about 'older men', but Lucas just wasn't approachable enough just now. 'Zach intends staying in England to write the screenplay,' she answered hollowly. 'So he and Dizzy will be in England for several more months yet.'

'How about next week?' Lucas grated.

She moved her shoulders shruggingly. 'Next week, too.'

'I meant,' he bit out slowly, 'how did your uncle feel about us being married next week?'

She gave a wan smile. 'He seemed to think that after knowing each other for four years it was about time!'

Lucas gave an impatient sigh. 'It seems to me he could show a little more concern for your welfare!' He looked angry.

'Why?' Christi looked at him curiously. 'Are you going to beat me? Keep me barefoot and pregnant for the next ten years?' Her eyes gleamed mischievously.

There was no answering smile in Lucas's expression. 'Of course not,' he rasped harshly. 'But I hope I would show a little bit more interest in the man Daisy chose to marry.'

Daisy. And Robin. The reason he was marrying her in the first place.

She gave a deep sigh. 'I think I've spoken of you enough over the years for my uncle to realise you're a kind and wonderful man, that you'll be good to me, c-care for me,' she completed briskly, not knowing if that last were true any more. 'And your business reputation is something he doesn't need to be told about,' she dismissed abruptly. 'What else does he need to know about the man I'm going to marry?' *That he loved her,* but that was something she couldn't assure Zach!

'So he's agreeable to the wedding being next week?' Lucas snapped.

'Of course,' she nodded.

Lucas lapsed into silence again, nodding for the bill, frowning darkly as he waited for it to be brought to the table.

'I was invited to a party tonight.' He spoke harshly once they had left the restaurant. 'I wasn't going to go, but—well, we might as well put in an appearance,' he shrugged.

Was he testing her? Had he decided that not just any wife would do, that she would have to fit in with his friends and life-style, too? She couldn't think of any other reason why he should suddenly decide the party seemed like a good idea, after all; he hadn't even mentioned it to her until now.

Accepting that he didn't return her love was one thing, understanding his need to have Daisy and Robin with him was another, but she wouldn't be put on trial as to her abilities to be a suitable wife for him!

'I'm not sure I——'

'Have a little patience, Christi!' Lucas gave a rueful grimace. 'I'm a little out of practice with considering another person's wishes. Would you *like* to go on to a party with me?'

Even this slight softening in his harshly remote mood was enough to make her feel like crying! 'I'd love to go to a party with you.' She gave a shaky smile.

She had been to dozens of other parties just like this one turned out to be, and even knew several of the people there, although she could tell she and Lucas were the centre of some attention for attending this party together.

'I know actresses like to "make an entrance", but this is ridiculous!' murmured a conspiratorial voice at her side.

Christi turned eagerly to greet David Kendrick, kissing his cheek warmly, having felt a little conspicuous standing on her own while Lucas went to the bar to get them both another drink.

'Do that again,' David invited wolfishly, his eyes gleaming with laughter.

She gave a husky laugh as she saw several people were looking their way. 'I don't think I'd better,' she said ruefully.

David glanced about them too, grimacing. 'Maybe not,' he drawled, suddenly very serious. 'Am I allowed to ask what you're doing here with Lucas?' He frowned his puzzlement.

'Enjoying the party?' she shrugged.

'Besides that,' he dismissed thoughtfully. 'As far as I know, you've never been to one of these parties with him before.'

Lucas was standing across the room, engaged in conversation with another man now, although she knew he was aware of her own conversation with David, having seen him glance in their direction a few seconds ago, only to turn away again uninterestedly.

She turned to give David a bright smile. 'That's right, I haven't.'

'Christi——'

'Would you like to be among the first to congratulate us—me?' she continued lightly. 'Lucas and I are to be married next week.'

Instead of answering her, David looked at her searchingly, concern in the dark blue eyes. 'Why?' he finally asked.

She laughed softly, keeping the despair firmly at bay. 'Why do people usually get married?' she derided.

'Because they love each other,' he dismissed. 'Now, tell me, why are you and Lucas getting married?'

'Really, David——'

'Christi,' he put his hand on her arm, squeezing lightly, 'it's too sudden to just be a coincidence so soon after I told you about Marsha remarrying.'

Her head went back proudly. 'I happen to love Lucas very much.'

He nodded. 'And it's obvious from the way he was behaving the other night that he feels he has a proprietorial claim on you, too, but that isn't reason enough for him to marry you.'

Christi drew in a ragged breath. 'We're getting married because it's what we want to do.' She *couldn't* lie and say that Lucas returned her love.

'And you're saying Marsha's plans to remarry have nothing to do with it, hmm?' David frowned.

'I'm saying——' She breathed heavily. 'I'm saying that this is really none of your business, David,' she told him regretfully.

He nodded without rancour. 'I suppose not. I just—— Are you sure this is what you really want to do, Christi?' he prompted gently.

She gave a choked groan. 'I——'

'Kendrick.' Lucas's hard drawl cut in on the conversation as he moved to stand at Christi's side. 'I didn't see you here earlier.' His eyes were narrowed on David as he handed Christi her drink.

'I only arrived a few minutes ago,' David dismissed lightly. 'I hear congratulations are in order?' He held out his hand.

Christi watched as the two men warily shook hands, eyeing each other critically, almost as if they were sizing each other up for a fight.

Lucas touched her for the first time since driving to the restaurant earlier this evening, his arm lightly about her waist. 'To me, certainly,' he rasped. 'To Christi, I'm not so sure,' he shrugged.

'Hm.' David eyed him mockingly. 'You certainly aren't my type, but I believe women find you fascinating,' he derided.

Christi gave him a grateful smile for lightening the conversation, looking up at Lucas with loving eyes. 'I'm certainly happy with my choice.' She put her hand possessively on his chest.

'And that's the important thing,' David said lightly, before Lucas could make any comment. 'And now, if the two of you will excuse me, I've ignored my date long enough.' He smiled wolfishly at the beautiful blonde woman watching him across the room. 'Are your beautiful fiancée and I still allowed to have lunch together tomorrow as we'd arranged?' he paused to ask Lucas, as if in afterthought.

But Christi knew that it wasn't an afterthought at all, that David was determined to talk to her again about her plans to marry Lucas. And it wasn't too difficult to guess why! In truth, she had forgotten all about her agreement to have lunch with David tomorrow, but after tonight she had no doubt what their main topic of conversation was going to be!

Lucas was standing stiffly at her side. 'Christi is perfectly at liberty to spend time with whom she chooses,' he grated abruptly.

David quirked a mocking eyebrow. 'You didn't give that impression the other evening,' he mocked. 'Still,' he added lightly as Lucas's expression darkened ominously. 'I'm glad if my intrusion on the situation made you realise you're in love with Christi, after all. See you tomorrow, Christi,' he added firmly before strolling across the room to join the beautiful blonde.

Christi chanced a glance at Lucas, instantly wishing she hadn't; his face looked as if it were carved from granite, his eyes narrowed to silver slits.

'If you would rather I didn't have lunch with David——'

'I told you both, you can spend time with whom you want to,' Lucas interrupted harshly. 'Our marriage isn't going to be a prison, Christi,' he said firmly. 'I don't expect you to give up your friends just because you're married to me.'

As he wouldn't give up his 'friends'? She couldn't survive a marriage like that! 'Friends, no,' she conceded lightly. 'But surely anything else?' she tried to tease, although the subject was much too important to her to take lightly. But wouldn't Lucas, a man who had become used to the freedom of bachelorhood, and the relationships that went along with that freedom, find it difficult to suddenly find himself with just one woman in his life again?

He looked at her steadily. 'I thought you said nothing like that happened between you and Kendrick?' he rasped.

Her cheeks coloured warmly. 'You know that it didn't. I meant—well, I meant *you*.' She frowned.

Lucas's expression darkened even more. 'Just what the hell are you implying?'

Christi glanced about them awkwardly, very conscious of the party going on around them. 'Perhaps it would be better if we left now,' she suggested awkwardly. 'It's late, and I start work on the commercials tomorrow.'

'We'll leave, Christi,' he nodded tersely. 'But this conversation is far from over,' he warned grimly.

She was conscious of David's concerned gaze on her as she stood at Lucas's side making their farewells to their host and hostess. She deliberately refused to meet that gaze, aware that things were tense enough between Lucas and herself without him finding her and David relaying silent messages to each other across the room!

Christi sat tensely at Lucas's side on the drive home, wondering just when he was going to resume that 'conversation' that had so angered him. But could she be blamed for having her doubts? He had never once said he loved her, and his manner hadn't exactly been loverlike towards her today!

'This is ridiculous, Lucas,' she attacked impatiently once they reached her apartment.

'I couldn't agree more,' he said harshly, very dark and forbidding. And, when he had been one of her best friends until yesterday, it was a little difficult to take! 'I realise marriage to me is a big step for you to take, but after Marsha ended *our* marriage because she decided it was too restrictive, do you honestly think I would do the same thing to someone else?'

One of those statements stood out more than the others: marriage to him was a big step for her to take. Because they both knew he was using that marriage in order to try and get his children into his custody, and that once he had them back with him she would be expected to become their stepmother.

'I *like* being married, Christi,' he added gruffly. 'I like sharing breakfast with the same woman every morning, rather than some woman I can hardly remember the name of, I like coming home to that same woman in the evenings, having dinner with her, sleeping with her. I even like the arguments, because making up makes it all worth while,' he said ruefully. 'When I asked you to marry me, I wanted all of those things with you.' His voice hardened. 'Maybe you had better take the time to think about whether those are the things you want, too.'

Her already stricken gaze widened. 'Oh, but——'

'While you're thinking about it, I don't think there should be any repeats of last night,' he told her abruptly. 'You have to be sure about this marriage, Christi——'

'I am sure,' she cried, her arms about his waist as she rested her head against his chest. 'I want to marry you, Lucas. I want that more than anything else in the world.'

'I hope so.' His arms moved slowly about her. 'I really hope so, Christi,' his arms tightened convulsively, 'because I don't think I could survive another divorce.'

She trembled at the thought of anything so ugly happening between them, at the bitterness and hate that was usually all that was left of such a relationship. They had always *liked* each other, surely that would never change.

'Our marriage will last for ever, Lucas, I promise.' She held him fiercely.

His mouth twisted wryly. 'I wonder how many other couples have made the same promise, and a couple of years later ended up hating each other across a courtroom? And the fact that I've already been married once makes it so much worse,' he frowned. 'I have two children, two children I love beyond mere words, and they will always be a part in my life, often have to be put first, before other considerations, even a second wife. That isn't going to be easy for any woman to live with.' He shook his head self-disgustedly. 'I had no right to involve you in the mess I've made of my life——'

'I *want* to be involved,' she assured him firmly.

He looked down at her with dark eyes. 'I should never have taken advantage of you——'

'I've been waiting four years for you to do so!' she attempted to tease.

He gave a slight smile, but his eyes remained sad. 'That doesn't change the way I took advantage of the fact that emotions were running high yesterday, that I made love to you when I had no right to do so.'

'I gave you that right.' She smoothed away the frown from between his eyes. 'And you did offer to make an honest woman of me afterwards,' she reminded teasingly.

Lucas shook his head. 'I don't believe I'm doing you any favours by marrying you——'

'That's for me to decide,' she said, putting silencing fingertips over his lips. 'You'll just have to accept that I'm all grown up now, Lucas, that I'm a woman who knows what she wants. And I want you. And your children,' she assured him softly. 'You know I love Daisy and Robin.'

He rested his cheek against the top of her head. 'I wonder what I ever did to deserve you,' he sighed shakily.

'Ate all your vegetables as a child?' she teased.

She could feel him smile against her hair. 'No,' he drawled.

'Did well in your exams at school?'

His smile widened. 'Not particularly.'

'Were kind to little old ladies and cooed at babies in their prams?'

'Yes to the first, no to the second,' he derided.

'Well, one out of four isn't bad, is it?' She looked up at him lovingly. 'Lucas, I've been waiting years for you to notice I'm a woman——'

'Oh, I noticed,' he said drily.

'Accept, then,' she corrected dismissively. 'I'm not about to let you go now,' she warned. 'Besides, if you cancel the wedding, I'll go contrary on you and definitely be pregnant!'

The humour faded from his face, a haunted look in his eyes. 'Children of our own are—something I think should wait for a while, Christi,' he said softly.

She could have hit herself for the way she kept saying the wrong thing. Of course he wouldn't want any children between them until he was sure Daisy and Robin felt secure of their place in his life.

She gave him a bright smile. 'Then you had better not cancel the wedding, had you?' she teased.

He looked down at her searchingly, his expression clearing slightly. 'Maybe I'd better not,' he conceded huskily. 'I'm not sure how long I'll be able to resist you,' he admitted ruefully.

Christi frowned at him. 'You really mean it about not making love to me until after we're married?'

He nodded abruptly. 'I don't think we should cloud the issue.'

'But I want you, Lucas,' she protested, knowing she *needed* that closeness between them.

He tapped her lightly on the nose. 'You look like a spoilt little girl when you pout like that,' he murmured indulgently.

'I *was* a spoilt little girl,' she reminded irritably. God, after only one night in his arms, the thought of abstinence made her ache inside!

'You're a spoilt *big* girl, too,' Lucas teased affectionately. 'But the answer is still no, Christi,' he added seriously. 'Let's give ourselves time to adjust to the idea of marrying each other, hmm?'

She didn't want to give them time, she wanted to be in his arms tonight, and every other night. But she could see by Lucas's determined expression that he had made his decision and he wasn't about to change it. 'If you insist,' she muttered, giving in with a definite lack of grace; she couldn't help it, she had no pride left where this man was concerned.

Lucas smiled at her bad humour. 'I insist,' he drawled.

'Well, you don't have to sound so happy about it,' she muttered complainingly, moving out of his arms.

He gave a rueful smile. 'Is that really how I sound?' he mused, shaking his head. 'I want you, Christi, probably more than you want me,' he insisted at her indignant snort. 'I'm not at all happy with letting you sleep alone for the next week, I just feel it's the right thing to do. Which isn't to say that I intend staying away from you completely,' he murmured throatily before his lips claimed hers.

Christi felt as if she had been waiting for this kiss for ever; she put all her love into it, feeling his instant response as she pressed eagerly against him.

Joy lit her heart as she knew he did want her, that he must be aching as badly as she was right now.

She whimpered softly as he slowly caressed her body, his hands trembling slightly, their mouths seeking, searching, learning all there was to know about each other.

Lucas was breathing heavily when he moved away slightly to rest his forehead on hers.

'I can't tempt you?' she encouraged huskily.

His mouth twisted. 'Oh, you can tempt me all too easily,' he admitted ruefully. 'But I'm not going to let you,' he added firmly, putting her away from him. 'Shall we have breakfast together?' he encouraged softly.

She nodded wordlessly, her disappointment reflected in her eyes.

Long after Lucas had gone to his own apartment, Christi sat alone in the lounge, wanting him, *loving* him . . .

CHAPTER EIGHT

'I COULDN'T have chosen better for you myself,' Dizzy murmured appreciatively at her side, her green eyes gleaming with mischief.

Christi dragged her own bedazzled gaze away from Lucas as he stood confidently across the room from them, talking to Zach. Tiny Laura was nestled comfortably in her father's arms, quite content to listen to the rich tones of the two men. 'You didn't, did you?' she said ruefully, knowing Dizzy well enough to realise that if ensuring that she dated Dick, Barry and David hadn't worked to bring herself and Lucas together then Dizzy would have gone right on matchmaking until *something* did!

Her friend turned to hug her. 'I can't tell you how much I've longed for your wedding day,' she glowed.

Her wedding day! She was now Mrs Lucas Kingsley—the second. Ordinarily, it wouldn't have bothered her that Lucas had been married before, but waiting for him to mention custody of Robin and Daisy was starting to fray her nerves.

She knew he had seen the children during the last week, to explain to them that he intended marrying 'Aunty Christi', but he hadn't mentioned to Christi his plans for them at all.

It had been a full and busy week, made all the more so by her work on the advertisements, but somehow they had managed to arrive at today with all the arrangements going smoothly. As Lucas had done most of the organising, they probably dared not do anything else!

Only close relatives had been at the actual service, this lavish reception being given for their other friends at one of London's leading hotels.

'I've longed for it, too.' Christi returned her friend's hug. 'Although I'd almost given up hope of it ever happening,' she admitted softly. Lucas was her husband, *her* husband!

Dizzy grinned. 'Zach was most impressed when Lucas turned up at the castle to ask for your hand in marriage.' Her loving gaze rested indulgently on her handsome husband.

Lucas had kept to his original plan to drive up to the Lake District to talk to Zach personally, spending the night there with Dizzy and Zach, and driving back the next day to assure Christi everything was agreed.

She gave a rueful smile. 'Zach's a pushover for the old traditions.'

Dizzy gave her a coy look from beneath lowered lashes. 'He's a pushover for new ones, too,' she murmured throatily.

It never ceased to amaze her how Dizzy had changed since her marriage to Zach; men certainly hadn't been a part of her life until she had fallen in love with him. Now Dizzy was completely sure of her own femininity, secure in her husband's love.

Christi felt a wistful ache in her chest, wishing she were secure of Lucas's love. But he had still made no mention of the emotion, despite the fact that their goodnights had become longer and longer during the last week, each of them reluctant to go to their lonely beds. She would have forgotten Lucas's decision concerning that in a moment if he would have let her, but Lucas seemed determined to play the gentleman now that their wedding was being planned.

'Uh-oh,' Dizzy said indulgently as Laura began to squirm restlessly in her father's arms, giving out a little choked cry at the same time. 'My daughter feels it's time she had something to eat,' she excused absently, her attention all on the tiny bundle who had brought so much more happiness to her and Zach's lives.

Christi watched enviously as Zach's autocratic face filled with unashamed love as he turned to his wife, handing her the baby, excusing both of them as he accompanied Dizzy to the room where she could nurse Laura.

'You look as if you've lost a pound and found a penny,' David murmured softly at her side.

She turned to him with a bright smile, the smile fading a little as she saw his own pain behind the words. She squeezed his arm emotionally. 'There is another door open out there somewhere, David,' she assured him huskily.

He shook off his despondent mood with effort. 'Hey, this is a wedding, remember?' he teased. 'And all us lucky male guests get to kiss the bride!' He suited his actions to his words, gathering her into his arms to kiss her soundly on the mouth. 'Hm,' he still held her as he looked down at her warmly, '*Lucas* is the lucky man.'

She gave a pained frown, pulling out of David's arms to shoot an uncomfortable glance across the room to where Lucas was now talking to one of his friends. He didn't appear to have noticed the exchange between David and herself, and she turned away gratefully. Having lunch with another man was one thing, letting him kiss her was something else, even at her own wedding!

David was watching her shrewdly. 'Although maybe he still doesn't appreciate that yet,' he said thoughtfully, blue eyes questioning.

Christi gave a bright smile. 'He turned up for the wedding, didn't he?' she teased.

David looked at Lucas with narrowed eyes. 'Someone that looks like him did,' he nodded slowly.

Her cheeks were flushed. 'What do you mean?'

He shrugged. 'I want you to be happy with Lucas, Christi—— '

'I will be,' she assured him quickly.

'I hope so.' He still frowned. 'It doesn't seem too good a start to the marriage when the *first* wife is in attendance, though,' he added drily.

Christi felt her cheeks burn again, but tried to remain composed as she saw Marsha and the children join Lucas across the room. 'Lucas naturally wanted his children at our wedding,' she defended stiffly.

David raised dark brows. 'And Marsha just came along to keep them company?'

She had to admit, to herself at least, that she had been surprised when Marsha had been the one to bring the children, instead of the nanny she had been expecting. But what could she have said or done that would have changed anything? Marsha's presence here was already a fact, she had no choice but to accept it gracefully. And that was what she had done, Lucas at her side when they had greeted the other woman at the start of the reception. His own initial displeasure had turned to impatient acceptance as Marsha greeted them warmly, to all intents and purposes delighted with the remarriage of her ex-husband. How could they possibly object to her behaviour after that?

But Christi had to admit she found the situation more than a little awkward, although she realised there was nothing Lucas could do about it, either, without causing an unnecessary scene. And the children's enthusiastic pleasure in the marriage more than made up for Marsha's presence. She couldn't help but feel grateful for the fact that Marsha hadn't tried to poison the children's minds to the idea of her marrying their father. Considering how the other woman had clung on to Lucas all these years, the likelihood of that happening had been a distinct possibility.

'That's right,' she dismissed lightly, not willing to let David, no matter how good a friend he had become, know just how much of a mar on her wedding day having Marsha there had been.

'Well, at least you'll have the same pleasure in attending her wedding next month,' David derided with satisfaction.

And by that time she and Lucas would have been married for three weeks, her position as his wife more than clear. 'I'm looking forward to it,' she murmured softly.

David chuckled at her determined expression. 'Retribution is sweet, hmm?' he mused appreciatively.

'Lucas is *my* husband, that's all the ammunition I need,' she shrugged dismissively. 'And now, if you'll excuse me, I think I'll join them.'

'Let me accompany you,' David offered politely, taking a firm hold of her elbow. 'With a woman like Marsha, you might have need of back-up troops,' he muttered ruefully.

To an outsider, they must look like a happy family gathering, but Christi was more than aware of the tension in the air as she and David joined the other four.

'Now we have two mummies!' Daisy turned to hug her enthusiastically.

Christi returned the hug, shooting Marsha an uncomfortable glance, turning away again quickly as she saw the other woman's mouth tighten angrily.

'Don't be silly, Daisy,' her brother told her with all the authority his extra year afforded. 'You can only have one mummy.'

Daisy looked rebellious. 'But——'

'I'll be your aunt still, Daisy,' Christi explained gently. 'Just like Uncle Julian will still be just your uncle when he marries your mummy soon.' The last was added challengingly, although she didn't dare risk a glance at Marsha, the person the challenge had been meant for.

'But if——'

'Hey, you two,' David lightly cut in on Daisy's puzzled question. 'Have you tried the ice-cream yet?' he encouraged. 'There's a half a dozen flavours, so I think it must be in your honour,' he tempted as two pairs of grey eyes turned to him curiously.

Daisy looked up at her father. 'Really?'

His expression softened indulgently as Daisy still lisped slightly from where her front teeth were still growing back. 'I think I did just happen to mention there would be a couple of children here today who love ice-cream,' he smiled.

'Strawberry?' Daisy licked her lips.

'I shouldn't be surprised,' he drawled softly.

'And chocolate?' Robin put in hopefully.

'I believe so.' Lucas lightly caressed his son's cheek.

'My favourites, too,' David enthused, taking a child by each hand. 'Have you ever tried them both together?' he was questioning as he led them away towards the buffet. 'Stirring them into the same bowl and——'

'Ugh!' Marsha grimaced delicately as David's graphic description of the awful sounding concoction could no longer be heard.

Christi straightened awkwardly, not quite sure what to do now, although she was grateful to David

for removing the children from what was, at best,
a difficult situation to deal with. From the looks
on the children's faces as they scooped up the ice-
cream mixture, they hadn't at all minded being
diverted!

She jumped a little nervously as Lucas's hand on
her waist brought her back against his side, flashing
him an apologetic frown as she sensed his puzzlement at her reaction. She wished they could just
leave to go on the two-day honeymoon which was
all her immediate work schedule would allow, for
she desperately wanted to be alone with him. David
had been right when he had said she looked as if
she had lost a pound and found a penny; she had
lost her friendship with Lucas, and at the moment
she wasn't sure what she had gained in its place!

'You make a beautiful bride.'

She blinked her surprise at the other woman's
comment, looking at her frowningly. 'Thank you,'
she accepted warily.

Marsha gave a soft laugh. 'I believe your little
bride is suspicious of my motives,' she taunted to
Lucas.

Lucas looked warmly at Christi. 'You do make
a lovely bride,' he told her huskily.

She felt warm all over, and wished they were on
their own, so that Lucas could sweep her up into
his arms and make love to her. It was the only time
she had felt secure in their relationship.

'Lucas and I were just discussing the plans for
when I go away on my honeymoon,' Marsha put
in abruptly.

Christi turned to her sharply, the intimacy between Lucas and herself broken. Why on earth should Marsha discuss her honeymoon with Lucas?

'Such a pity the two of you don't have the time for a honeymoon,' Marsha drawled, now that she had their full attention.

'Oh, but——'

'Christi has a contract to fulfil.' Lucas spoke smoothly over Christi's protest.

Marsha nodded. 'It's a pity you didn't have more consideration for *my* career when we were married,' she bit out waspishly.

His mouth tightened. 'I made a lot of mistakes during our marriage that I don't intend to repeat with Christi,' he rasped.

Hazel eyes blazed with anger, the anger fading to a rueful grimace as Marsha saw Christi was watching them with frowning puzzlement. 'Poor Christi doesn't have any idea what we're talking about,' she mused. 'I used to be the fashion editor for a top magazine,' she explained ruefully. 'At the time Lucas didn't approve of his wife working,' she added harshly. 'And, like the fool I was, because I wanted to please him, I gave up my job. The beginning of the end.' She shook her head. 'I was no longer the woman he had married, and I resented him for denying me my career. And having children, believing they will hold the marriage together, is the worst thing you can do,' she sighed. 'All that does is introduce innocents into the mess you've already made of your life.'

Christi had never heard any of this before, had had no idea Marsha had ever had such a demanding career, let alone realised the problems it had caused to the marriage. And what Marsha had just said about Robin and Daisy gave her a whole new insight into their births.

But she had no doubt that, whatever beliefs Lucas used to have about women working and having a career, he no longer felt the same way, for he had always encouraged her career, and he had been the one to insist that their honeymoon should be delayed until after her work was finished on the advertisements.

His arms tightened about her waist as he answered Marsha. 'I told you, I've learnt from my mistakes,' he ground out.

Marsha forced one of her beautiful smiles, shaking off the memories with effort. 'Of course you have,' she dismissed lightly. 'We've both made new starts. Which brings us right back to the arrangements we were making for when Julian and I are away. Having two young children suddenly thrust upon you for a month isn't going to be easy, but——'

'Marsha,' Lucas cut in warningly.

'—Robin and Daisy like you already, Christi, and that's half the battle——'

'Marsha,' Lucas cut in again. 'I haven't had a chance yet to discuss having the children with Christi.' His mouth was a taut line.

Hazel eyes widened. 'You haven't? My God, Lucas,' Marsha said disgustedly. 'I'm sorry,

Christi,' she frowned uncomfortably, 'I felt sure Lucas would have—I wouldn't have—oh, hell!' She glared at Lucas. 'Perhaps you'll let me know when you *have* discussed it with Christi!' She flounced off, crossing the room in search of her two children.

Complete silence enfolded the two of them once Marsha had gone, Christi speechless, Lucas seeming lost in angry thought.

They were to have Robin and Daisy while their mother was away on honeymoon? Lucas was the obvious and natural choice to have the children during that time, although she couldn't help wondering if his motives weren't a little deeper than that. Maybe he would use that month as a trial run for when he applied to have the children with him all the time. She had learnt a new respect for Marsha today, and couldn't help thinking it was an underhand thing to do to take advantage of the situation. But why else would Lucas have waited so long to discuss the children coming to them while Marsha was away, if it weren't because he intended their stay to be a much longer one than that?

Hadn't he realised yet that she would do anything for him, would take half a dozen of his children into their home if it would make him happy?

If this was the way he wanted to do things, she wasn't about to argue. She had known from the first how desperate he was to have Robin and Daisy back with him.

She forced a bright smile. 'I'm sure Robin and Daisy are excited about the prospect of coming to you for a month.'

Lucas sighed. 'I intended waiting until after our honeymoon before mentioning it to you. I felt I owed you that time, at least.' He shook his head irritably.

Two days of happiness before he intended disillusioning her about his real motives for the marriage! She didn't want him to think he 'owed' her anything; the last thing she wanted from him was pity for the decision she had made with her eyes completely open.

'Well, I know now,' she dismissed lightly. 'So we can start making plans for their stay, things we can do, places we can go——'

'All that can wait, Christi,' he told her softly, his eyes gentle. 'We may only have two days, but it is our honeymoon, and I fully intend to make up for the last week of sleeping alone.'

Her heart skipped a beat at the sudden intimacy in his tone, and she looked up at him with widely hopeful eyes. 'We can leave now, if you would like to,' she suggested breathlessly.

'I'd like to.' He gazed around ruefully at their guests. 'But do you think they'll let us go yet?' he derided.

Her mouth quirked. 'I would say they're wondering why we took this long!'

Lucas chuckled softly. 'Then let's get out of here!'

They left amid laughter and good wishes.
Marsha, of all people, was the one to catch her
bouquet of yellow roses, her pleasure in the act so
genuine that, after the initial awkward silence, the
good wishes and laughter became even louder.

They had booked into a lovely hotel by the
Thames, away from London itself, having decided
they didn't want to spend what little time they did
have driving to their destination.

Two hours later, having shared a delicious dinner
with Lucas in the restaurant downstairs, Christi was
glad of the decision. She hurried through her bath,
aware of having longed for the moment of being
Lucas's wife for as long as she could remember.

Dizzy and Zach had come down a couple of days
before the wedding so that Dizzy could help her
with the choice of her dress. The white silk dress
had been a complete success, Lucas's eyes full of
admiration when he'd first gazed at her. But besides the wedding dress Dizzy had insisted that all
brides should have 'a nightgown', and Christi had
quickly learnt what her friend meant by that. The
floaty white creation had narrow ribbon shoulder-
straps, lace cups over her pert breasts, satin falling
silkily to her feet. It was definitely 'a nightgown',
and as Christi gazed at her own starry-eyed reflection in the full-length mirror, she knew that
Dizzy had been right to insist that she buy the
nightgown; she felt beautiful and desirable, as any
new bride should do.

And yet she felt a little nervous about seeing
Lucas now. It was one thing to make love with

spontaneous abandon, the way it had happened the one and only night they *had* made love, it was something else completely to know that tonight she truly belonged to Lucas, in every sense of the word. It almost felt as if she were married to a stranger, and not her dear familiar Lucas at all.

As she hesitated in the bedroom, the door softly opened, and Lucas watched her from the doorway with caressing eyes. Christi turned slowly to face him, seeing the dark leap of desire in his eyes, and suddenly all her nervousness fled, and there was just Lucas and herself left, her emotions revealed unashamedly as she gazed at the man she loved.

'You are so beautiful, you take my breath away,' he finally murmured gruffly.

He was still wearing the suit he had worn to the wedding, minus the jacket, and he probably wished for a leisurely shower or bath himself; yet, as they gazed at each other, they were both filled with a sudden urgency to be one again, to know each other in a way that would leave no doubts in their minds as to how much they needed each other.

Lucas kissed her long and lingeringly, finally raising his head, his lips only inches from hers. 'Give me a few minutes,' he urged softly. 'Better yet, come and keep me company,' he encouraged huskily.

Christi loved every muscle and sinew of his body, and watched with unabashed pleasure as he stood beneath the shower's spray, muscle and bronzed skin rippling as he soaped his whole body.

And when he finally stepped out of the shower cubicle Christi stood up to meet him, knowing neither of them could wait a moment longer, their gazes locked as they moved slowly into the adjoining bedroom.

It was as beautiful as a ballet, as erotic as a dance, each caress, every movement pure poetry and rhyme as they fitted together in perfect unison, the final crescendo more beautiful than anything Christi had ever imagined before.

As she lay nestled in Lucas's arms throughout the night, awakening to passion often as they constantly sought each other out, Christi knew that she was home, that she would always find her home in this man's arms.

CHAPTER NINE

'BUT when can we come back again?' Daisy demanded petulantly, throwing things into the case that Christi was meticulously trying to pack.

Christi sat down with a sigh, taking the little girl into her arms. 'I don't know, poppet.' She smoothed the silky black hair away from the angrily flushed face. 'You'll have to ask Daddy,' she told Daisy ruefully.

She wanted to do the same thing! The children's month of staying with them was up, for Marsha and Julian would be back from their honeymoon this afternoon, and yet during the last seven weeks of their marriage Lucas hadn't mentioned a thing to her about having the children with them all the time. Surely he had to realise that it would affect her as much as it did him—more so, because she had even less experience of bringing up children than Lucas did, and yet with Lucas out at work all day she was sure to spend more time with them than he did. Not that she minded that; the last month of caring for Daisy and Robin had been very enjoyable. They had enjoyed themselves too, hence Daisy's reluctance to return to her mother. But, if Lucas did intend fighting for custody of them, he was going to have to tell them that himself.

Daisy pouted. 'We could at least have stayed until tomorrow. Mummy and Uncle Julian don't get back until this afternoon.'

'Mummy has missed you so much, she can't wait until tomorrow,' Christi told her reprovingly. 'You know she's telephoned almost every day.' And, considering the newly-weds had honeymooned in the Bahamas, she hated to think what Julian's telephone bill had been like at the end of their stay! But it was unthinkable that he would deny Marsha those conversations with her two children, for he was obviously very much in love with his new bride.

'I wish we could have gone with her,' Robin chimed in from the other side of the room, where he was managing to pack his own suitcase, albeit rather haphazardly. 'She says she's been swimming almost every day,' he added enviously.

Christi knew that Robin's wish bore no reflection on the time he had spent with her and Lucas, it was just that swimming was his passion at the moment, worth any other sacrifice, even that of spending time with his beloved father.

'Now you're being silly,' Daisy told him in a prim voice. 'Children don't go on honey—honeymoon, with their mummy and daddy. Do they, Christi?' she prompted knowledgeably.

She held back her smile with effort. 'Not usually, no,' she admitted.

'That doesn't mean they can't,' Robin challenged his sister, more than a little of the usual sibling rivalry between these two.

It had been a little strange to suddenly find herself a surrogate mother when Daisy and Robin had first come to stay with them. Delicately, she had tried to sort out their squabbles without causing resentment towards her, but, as the days had passed and they had all become more used to each other, she had found she was enjoying caring for the two children, although it was hard work, it was also very rewarding.

Which was perhaps as well, if what she suspected turned out to be true!

Lucas had made it clear from the beginning that he didn't want any more children yet, if ever, and so she had taken the necessary precautions. Unfortunately, something seemed to have gone wrong, and she now had a feeling she had become pregnant as early as their honeymoon—those two nights and days when they hadn't ventured from their hotel room except to eat, and sometimes not even then.

She hadn't dared to even mention the possibility to Lucas, hadn't even gone to her doctor yet to have her suspicion confirmed or denied, longing for it to be true, and yet uncertain of Lucas's reaction to it if she should turn out to be pregnant.

He had so much enjoyed having Daisy and Robin here the last month, and spent as much time with them all as he could. As Christi's work on the advertisements was now over, and the children's school closed for the summer, they had been able to go out for several days.

Christi felt for Lucas now, knew he hadn't felt able to come and help with the packing because he didn't really want to take the children back to Marsha just yet, either. But, until he did something definite about taking the children, none of them had any choice.

She stood up decisively, steadying Daisy in front of her. 'Let's get this packing done so that we can all have lunch,' she suggested, deliberately appealing to the fact that they both loved to eat.

Miraculously, the cases were packed within seconds, and she smiled at the two children indulgently as she went to prepare their lunch. Because she had moved into Lucas's apartment, giving up the lease on her own, and because the apartment only had two bedrooms, she had advised Marsha to give the children's nanny the last month off, preferring to look after them herself for that short time. At least that way, if she made any mistakes— and she had made many!—they didn't have to be witnessed by an expert.

Lucas was already in the kitchen, cooking the hamburgers he had promised the children they could have as their last meal of their stay, turning to smile at Christi as she joined him. The children raced into the dining-room, squabbling over who should be laying the table.

As usual, Christi's heart contracted with love as she gazed at Lucas. Moving easily into his arms, she rested her head against his shoulder. She drew in a quivering breath as his arms tightened about her convulsively. 'We're going to miss them, aren't we?' She spoke sadly.

She could feel him smile against her hair. 'It's certainly going to be a lot quieter around here,' he derided as the argument in the other room became louder.

Once again he had passed up an opportunity she had given him to tell her he wanted the children to come and live with them, and she moved away disappointedly, taking over the cooking of the hamburgers. 'I think you had better go and stop World War Three in there,' she advised dully, her face averted as she sensed him watching her with puzzled eyes.

'Christi?' he prompted softly.

Oh God, why couldn't he talk to her, confide in her? The nights they shared were perfect, couldn't have been more giving, and yet when they were together like this Christi always sensed that Lucas was holding something back from her, that there was a large part of himself he wasn't prepared to give.

'I'm just a little tired,' she dismissed shruggingly, still unable to meet his gaze.

'Taking care of Robin and Daisy has been hard work for you.' He was instantly apologetic. 'How about if we try and sort out some time for our own honeymoon?' He took her in his arms, moulding her body to his.

She made a face. 'I start rehearsals for the new play next week,' she reminded, having finally found work in the theatre again. It was another small part, but an improvement on the last one, where she had only had one line of dialogue!

'So you do.' He released her reluctantly as the sound of breaking glass came from the next room. 'Most of the time, they're very well behaved,' he muttered as he turned to enter the dining-room. 'But when they have a bad day everyone knows about it!'

The smile Christi had shared with him faded as soon as the door closed behind him. She had known being married to a man as complex as Lucas wasn't going to be easy, but waiting for him to confide in her didn't make it any easier. Why couldn't he come right out and say, 'Christi, I want Daisy and Robin to come and live with us'? He had to know she wouldn't say no, that she had never been able to deny him anything. It was the waiting that was upsetting her.

And the fact that she was probably pregnant and feared Lucas's reaction to *that*!

'I think you've actually grown,' Marsha told her son indulgently after hugging him. Daisy cuddled up on her mother's knee, her earlier reluctance to return home completely forgotten in the excitement of seeing her mother again.

Christi and Lucas had driven the children home soon after lunch, finding Marsha and Julian very tanned from their holiday, Marsha more beautiful than ever with her sparkling hazel-coloured eyes and her golden skin.

The newly married couple seemed very relaxed and happy together, and for the children's sake, as much as anything, Christi was glad the relationship so far seemed to have worked out. Although she realised not many marriages failed during the honeymoon!

'We have some gifts for the two of you in the bedroom,' Marsha told the two children affectionately, laughing softly as the children let out excited yells.

'We should be going,' Lucas murmured softly.

Christi was just about to agree when Marsha answered him instead.

'Why don't you and Julian get the children's things from the car?' she suggested lightly. 'Christi and I will go and give this excited pair,' she ruffled two silky heads teasingly, 'their gifts.' And we'll all be civilised about this, her tone seemed to add.

Lucas gave Christi a questioning look, to which she gave a rueful shrug, following the other woman from the room. She stood by while Daisy and Robin admired their gifts, an expensive doll for Daisy, a full American-football outfit for Robin, over which he went into whoops of admiration.

'Julian thought he would like that,' Marsha murmured softly as Robin immediately began to pull the outfit on. She turned to give Christi a rueful smile. 'I don't think I had realised just how much I'd missed a man's opinion about things until this last month.'

Christi gave a tight smile, uncomfortable with the confidence. After all, until a few weeks ago, this woman had seemed to consider her part of the enemy!

'I'm glad you're happy,' she returned stiffly.

Marsha raised mocking brows. 'Are you?' she derided. 'Sorry,' she grimaced apologetically, giving a deep sigh. 'You and I haven't been the best of friends up to now, but I hope that will all change now,' she smiled encouragingly.

Friends? How could the two of them possibly be friends, when Lucas intended using any way he could to take Marsha's children from her?

Over the last few weeks she had come to realise that Daisy and Robin *were* Marsha's children, too. Ever since she had realised *she* could be carrying a child. Even though it was only a possibility she was pregnant, even though she had never held a child of her own, loved it, she knew her heart would break if anyone should ever try to take that child away from her. And she didn't doubt Marsha's love for Daisy and Robin, just as Lucas never had.

She was being torn apart in her loyalties, for she knew that, as the children's father, Lucas had a right to want the children with him, but, as it became more certain with each passing day that she carried a child of her own, she could sympathise with another mother's love for her children, a love that was unique and irreplaceable.

Marsha was so happy at the moment, content in her marriage, reunited with her children. But Lucas was so unhappy, wanting the children to stay with him. What an impossible situation this was!

'I hope so, too,' she answered Marsha with a nod. Although she very much doubted it, not once Lucas had started the battle for the children!

Marsha squeezed her arm reassuringly. 'I really am happy for you and Lucas, you know,' she said softly, Daisy and Robin busy on the floor with their new gifts. 'I know I was a bitch to you before, but—well—I am pleased for you now,' she repeated firmly. 'Julian is absolutely marvellous.' She laughed softly, indulgently. 'Oh, I know he's no-where near as handsome as Lucas, that everyone probably believes I married him because I fancy myself as a diplomat's wife. You see!' she acknowledged without rancour, as Christi's cheeks blushed guiltily at the echoing of the comment David had made when he'd first told her of Marsha's intended marriage to Julian Holland.

'Julian seems very nice,' Christi told her uncomfortably.

'Oh, he is,' the other woman nodded with certainty. 'But he's so much more than that,' she added lovingly, leaving Christi in no doubt as to her feelings for her new husband. 'He's a man that *needs* me,' she explained with satisfaction.

She gave a gasp. 'Lucas——'

'Never needed me,' Marsha said without rancour. 'Lucas is a man who is sufficient unto himself. Surely you must have realised that by now?' She frowned. 'He's a man who can do anything, be anything he wants to be, and he doesn't need any-one's help or encouragement to do it. My God, he made millions just because he believed he could, and he certainly didn't ask for any help from me.'

'The fact that you were supportive——'

'Didn't mean a damn thing to him,' Marsha dismissed softly. 'He could have gone right ahead and made a success of his life without me. Haven't the last five years proved that?' she derided.

Christi was frowning. 'But you were the one who decided to end the marriage,' she reminded, keeping her voice low so that the children shouldn't hear their conversation.

'Because I was empty inside. Lucas didn't need me, and the love that had been there in the beginning had slowly died through being ignored. All I had left were my children, and I didn't see why they should be caught in the middle of a loveless marriage that was making me bitter and Lucas distant and withdrawn. I did the only thing I could in those circumstances, and put an end to everyone's unhappiness. The children are well adjusted, and Lucas and I were free to find our own happiness as best we could. My only worry over the years,' a shadow darkened the glow of her eyes, 'was that Lucas would one day try to take the children from me.' She shrugged. 'It made me very defensive, but I don't think anyone can appreciate how desolate such a possibility can seem to a mother, how the fear can just eat you up.' She shuddered at the memory. 'Thank God all that's over!'

But it wasn't, it wasn't! Obviously Marsha considered her marriage to Julian secured the children staying with her indefinitely; she didn't seem to have realised that Lucas's own marriage gave him the same advantage. And Christi was no longer sure

Lucas taking the children was the right thing to do. The children *were* well adjusted, for the most part they accepted their lives as they were, and to uproot them now would be to do them more harm than good. In the past, she had thought only of Lucas's happiness, but her own pregnancy changed her whole way of thinking. Marsha's life would be devastated if Lucas should take Daisy and Robin from her, whereas Lucas, for all that he missed the children, had made a separate life for himself.

'Yes,' she agreed dully, forcing a tight smile.

Marsha gave her a searching look. 'Are you feeling all right?' she frowned. 'You look a little pale, and—Christi, are you pregnant?' she said wonderingly.

She raised stricken eyes, swallowing with difficulty. 'I—I——'

'You are,' Marsha murmured softly. 'Lucas must be over the moon . . . You haven't told him yet,' she said self-reprovingly as Christi paled even more. 'Don't worry, I won't say anything to spoil your surprise.' She patted Christi's hand reassuringly. 'You two were made for each other,' she said a little wistfully. 'To us, the children were just what held us together, to you and Lucas they will just be an added bonus.'

If only that were true, but Lucas had already made his feelings more than plain when it came to having more children. He didn't want any at all just yet, if he ever did!

'I'm not quite certain about the pregnancy yet,' she began hesitantly.

Marsha gave her a teasing look. 'What you mean is that you haven't had it confirmed yet,' she mocked lightly. 'Most women are certain before they even get as far as seeing a doctor.'

She *had* been certain for weeks now, had just been putting off the moment it was made official. Because then she would have no choice but to tell Lucas.

'Don't wait too long to tell Lucas,' Marsha laughed softly. 'I can't wait to see his face when he finds out he's to be a father again!' It was said completely without vindictiveness.

There were several other things she had to tell Lucas before she even mentioned the possibility that she might be pregnant and, close as they had become since their marriage, she didn't relish the idea of telling him she no longer believed he should try to take Daisy and Robin away from their mother!

CHAPTER TEN

'WHEN are you going to tell Marsha you intend trying to take the children from her?' Christi asked Lucas steadily, tired of the polite conversation they had been having since leaving the other couple, about how happy they seemed together. It seemed hypocritical when Lucas was poised to shatter that happiness!

She was unprepared for the sudden swerving of the car, accompanied by Lucas's startled exclamation, and was flung forcefully against the door, bruising her side. She watched with wide eyes as Lucas pulled the car over to the side of the road after gesturing his apology to the driver in the car behind for his erratic driving.

An ominous silence filled the car once he had switched off the engine, despite the fact that they were in a built-up area of London. Christi gazed at Lucas apprehensively. The silence became oppressive as Lucas seemed incapable of speech, until finally Christi couldn't stand it any longer.

'Lucas——'

'What on earth are you talking about?' He turned to her fiercely, her own speech seeming to have triggered his own, his eyes glowing silver. 'Christi, answer me, damn it!' he demanded as she hesitated.

She frowned at his anger. 'I know you haven't chosen to discuss it with me yet, but we both know you want Daisy and Robin to come and live with us.'

Lucas became suddenly still, watching her steadily. 'We do?'

'Yes,' Christi confirmed impatiently, turning in her seat. 'You made love to me, married me, so that you could apply for custody of them.'

He drew in a harsh breath. 'I did?'

She sighed heavily. 'Lucas, *talk* to me, don't keep shutting me out!'

His mouth thinned, his nostrils flaring angrily. 'Talk to you? Yes, maybe I should *talk* to you,' he rasped. 'But, you know, right now I'm so angry I don't think I can talk in a rational way that would make sense to either of us! I will say this,' he grated. 'I married you because I love you, have always loved you, even though I told myself for years that I didn't have the right to draw you into the mess I had already made of my life. One other thing,' he pushed his car door open forcefully, 'I never, at any time,' he spoke precisely, cuttingly, 'considered taking Daisy and Robin from their mother.'

'But—where are you going?' She looked at him desperately as he swung out of the car on to the road.

He bent down to look at her, his eyes bleak. 'I'm going to try and walk the bad taste out of my mouth,' he told her harshly.

'But——'

'Drive yourself home, Christi,' he added dully. 'I'm not sure that I've ever really known you.' He shook his head. 'It's certain you've never really known me.' He slammed the car door, walking away.

It took her only seconds to open her own car door and climb out on to the pavement. 'Lucas,' she called to him as he began to disappear among the people milling about on the pavement. 'Lucas!' she cried again as he kept right on walking, the tears starting to fall hotly down her cheeks.

He had gone, disappeared completely among the people who were now starting to gaze at her curiously, obviously wondering what a crying woman was doing standing beside a car parked in a 'No Parking' area.

It was the latter fact that galvanised her into action. Lucas was gone, swallowed up by the crowd; she couldn't just stand here hoping he would come back—especially when she knew he wasn't going to do that! The approaching policeman made her movements all the quicker, for she didn't relish the idea of explaining her predicament to a complete stranger.

How she made the drive back to the apartment she didn't know; she must have been on 'automatic pilot', because when she found herself unlocking the apartment door she couldn't remember any of the drive back there.

Even with the pets milling around for affection, the apartment felt so empty; Lucas's presence was everywhere—and nowhere. This was *his* apartment;

even after weeks of sharing it with him, it still didn't have her mark upon it, and she suddenly felt like an intruder.

Lucas loved her. Had always loved her, he said. She had known the affection was there, but *love*? He had never *told* her he loved her; he had made love to her, then married her, all without the mention of the word love!

Would he ever come back? Would he ever give them a chance to have that 'talk' they so desperately needed to have?

Would she ever have the chance to tell him she was expecting his child?

She had been sitting alone in the apartment for some time, only the steady tick of the clock and the purring of the cats to break the silence, when she heard the key in the door. She sat up with a jolt, startling Gladys off her lap where she had been taking a nap.

She stood up nervously, facing Lucas apprehensively. He looked haggard, his face pale, as if he hadn't managed to rid himself of the 'bad taste' in his mouth.

Then he looked up at her, and there was a light shining in his eyes that Christi had never seen before, and as he opened his arms to her she ran into them gladly, nestling against his chest with a choked sob.

'I hadn't gone far,' he spoke huskily, 'when I realised that I'd never told you how I felt about you, how I've felt since the moment you came crashing into my arms that day so long ago...' His hands cradled each side of her face as he raised it to look at him. 'I love you, Christi,' he said gruffly. 'I've loved you for so long that you've become a part of me I can't live without.'

'I love you, too,' she cried unashamedly, the tears hot on her cheeks. 'I love you so much!'

He nodded jerkily. 'I know, that's why I have the power to hurt you so much. I never wanted to hurt you, Christi, I was just so busy protecting myself, I couldn't do anything else.' He shook his head disgustedly. 'I left myself vulnerable once before, my darling, and I almost had the heart ripped out of me.'

'By Marsha,' she nodded.

'Indirectly.' He frowned, resting his forehead on hers. 'By the time we separated, we both knew it had to be or we would end up hating each other instead of just not loving each other any more,' he explained with a heavy sigh. 'But only one of us could have the children and, although I hated letting them go, I knew Marsha should be the one to take them, that I could stand their loss much better than she ever could. You heard what she said about her career, about how I denied her that,' he reminded huskily. 'Well, it was true. And, because she didn't have her career any more, the children became her whole life. If I had tried to take them away from her, I would have destroyed her completely.'

'But now,' Christi shook her head, 'now she has Julian, and——'

'And I assured her weeks ago, once and for all, that I would never take our children away from her,' he interrupted firmly. 'I doubt that legally I ever could have done, anyway.'

'But——'

'Oh, I'll admit I was devastated by the news that another man was going to have a hand in bringing up my children.' His mouth twisted wryly. 'So devastated that I gave into the weakness of allowing myself to kiss you for the first time.'

The night she had been out to dinner with Dick Crosby! 'I couldn't understand what Marsha was doing there with you that night,' she groaned. 'But I realise now why you looked so grim when you stepped out of the lift.'

Lucas shook his head. 'That had nothing to do with Marsha; she hadn't even told me she intended marrying then.' He gave a rueful smile. 'I was upset at seeing you with Dick Crosby, a man not much younger than me.'

Oh, Dizzy, your plan worked completely! Christi silently congratulated her friend.

'For years I'd told myself I was too old for you, that I had to let you have your own life, your career, friends your own age—and there you were with a man only a few years younger than I am!' he concluded disgustedly. 'By the time you got to Kendrick in the list of three men your friend Dizzy picked out as "suitable" for you, I had decided that if you wanted an "older" man in your life it had to be me!'

'Oh, Lucas!' She looked up at him lovingly.

He shook his head. 'I hadn't meant to kiss you that night you went out with Crosby, but you seemed to be asking me to, and I had held off for so long! Afterwards, I could have kicked myself, I was sure I had ruined the friendship between us.'

She smoothed the anxious frown from between his eyes.

'And I thought you were disgusted by my wanton response,' she murmured ruefully.

'Disgusted!' he snorted. 'I wanted to take you then and there. If you hadn't got out of my apartment when you did, I probably would have done,' he admitted shakily. 'I told myself the best thing to do was forget it, continue as if nothing had happened—and then maybe I could learn to live with the ache that never seemed to leave me! But the night you went out with Barry Robbins I sat in here in a rage of jealousy all night, imagining what the two of you were doing together. I lost control when you actually told me what he did to you!' Even now he was slightly white about the lips.

Christi sighed. 'I was searching for a reaction from you,' she admitted shakily. 'Any reaction!'

'Well, you certainly got one,' he muttered self-derisively.

'And I loved every moment of it,' she told him huskily.

He laughed down at her indulgently, smoothing her cheek with his thumb-tip. 'You're such a baby still,' he murmured regretfully. 'I should never have married you——'

'I would never have married anyone else,' she cut in firmly. 'Oh, I think—even though I didn't at the time!—that you were right to give me those years to grow up, to let me spread my wings, find my own friends, be free to enjoy my career. I'm sure I would be a different type of person if I hadn't had those years to grow,' she acknowledged softly. 'But I've always known who I wanted to spend the rest of my life with.'

Lucas's arms tightened about her. 'I never felt I had the right to you,' he said gruffly. 'Even once I'd asked you to marry me and you had accepted me, I had my doubts, tried to keep my distance, to give you time to back out if you wanted to.'

'I thought you had only asked me to marry you that night because we'd just spent the day with the children and you had realised how much you were going to hate them having a stepfather——'

'Of course I was feeling it that day, and it's going to take me a long time to get used to it. But none of that had anything to do with my asking you to marry me.' He gave a rueful smile. 'Once I began making love to you, that was something I could no longer fight.'

'And children of our own?' she voiced tentatively. 'Is it because you already have Daisy and Robin, because you've been separated from them, that you don't want us to have any of our own?'

'You're only twenty-two, Christi,' Lucas groaned. 'You still have years to give birth in relative safety if you choose to. For now, you have a career that you still haven't conquered as I know you would like to. Children of our own can wait,' he decided firmly.

It wasn't that he didn't want children, he just wanted to give her even more time to just be herself, allow her the freedom he knew had broken up his marriage to Marsha, when he had been so unreasonable in not giving her the same freedom!

Christi stepped slightly back from him, taking hold of his hand to press it gently against her stomach. 'Not this one, I'm afraid,' she told him softly, her face radiant with love when he glanced up at her sharply, only to look down again dazedly to the place where his hand lay.

'When?' he finally managed to breathe.

'I'm not sure, but I think it was the first night of our honeymoon——'

Lucas gave a laugh that was half choked emotion, half indulgent love. 'I meant, when is it due?' he gently corrected. 'But I suppose now I can work that out for myself.' He shook his head in silent bewilderment. 'I'm going to be a father again in just over seven months.'

'If you think Daisy and Robin will be upset because——'

'Daisy and Robin will be delighted,' he assured her drily. 'In fact, they can't understand why we don't already have other children now that we're married,' he said ruefully.

'And you?' She still looked at him anxiously. 'How do you feel about it?'

Lucas looked down at her silently for several minutes, and then a blaze of love unlike anything

Christi had ever seen before lit up his face. 'I feel proud, tender, protective, but most of all I feel love.' He kissed her gently on the lips.

And that was, after all, all that was important.

'Quick, grab her, before she has the whole lot over!' Christi warned desperately as her nine-month-old daughter attempted to reach the branches of the Christmas tree that lit up the corner of the room.

Robin bent down and gently moved his youngest sister out of harm's way, getting down on the floor with her to tickle her tummy. Daisy soon joined in the game, too.

Lucas chuckled indulgently as he watched the three children together from across the room, then glanced up to meet Christi's gaze, love flowing between them like an electric current.

The last sixteen months had been filled with such love, the birth of Shelley nine months ago only increasing their happiness together. Robin and Daisy openly adored their new sister, and came to stay with them all as often as they could. Which was quite often: Marsha, secure of their custody now, was able to let them go because she knew they would always come back. Last Christmas, the two children had spent the holiday with their mother and Uncle Julian, but this year Marsha had offered to let them come to Lucas. In fact, the other couple were coming to lunch on Christmas Day! Things could still be a little strained between Lucas and Marsha at times, but Marsha's happiness with Julian had enabled her to be more forgiving of the mistakes she and Lucas had both made in the past.

Lucas crossed the room to join her now, putting his arm about her shoulders. 'Maybe we should have put the tree on a table, out of the way,' he murmured ruefully as Shelley once again crawled towards the illuminated fir tree.

Christi bent to scoop her daughter up out of harm's way. 'Now that she can stand up and move about the furniture, even that isn't guaranteed to keep her out of mischief.' She smiled down at the dark-haired, grey-eyed imp. 'I wish everyone could be as happy as we are, Lucas,' she added with impulsive happiness.

'You're thinking of David, aren't you?' His arms tightened about her shoulders.

The two men had become good friends during the last sixteen months and, like Christi, Lucas felt for the other man's loneliness.

She nodded. 'He said he was going to see his family for Christmas.' She shook her head. 'He's never mentioned them before; I'm not sure he was telling the truth.'

'Wherever he is, I'm sure he's all right,' Lucas assured her softly. 'Now, don't you think we should get these children up to bed?' His voice lightened indulgently. 'Father Christmas is going to be here soon,' he added, just loud enough to throw Robin and Daisy into a frenzy of excitement, their cries of wanting to go to bed completely expected—if virtually unheard of before!

'Father Christmas' carried all three children up to bed, Robin on his father's back, a daughter held in each arm.

Christi followed close behind them. Robin and Daisy might live with their mother most of the time, but they were hers and Lucas's, too. They were a complete family, loving and giving. Most of all, loving.

THE LOVING GIFT

For
Matthew and Joshua

CHAPTER ONE

'YO HO HO! Yo ho ho! Merry Christmas! *Merry* Christmas!' boomed the tall, rounded figure in the unmistakable red suit as he ambled into the room, the obligatory sack of toys thrown over one broad shoulder. 'Have you all been good boys and girls this year?'

The loud cries of 'Yes!' from the hundred and fifty children who filled the room, that instantly followed the teasing question, almost drowned out the gasp of stunned surprise made by the woman standing at Jade's side but, completely attuned herself to any minor or major disaster that might befall any of the pupils at what had so far been a very successful preparatory school Christmas party, Jade was instantly alerted by Penny's sudden tension.

Jade anxiously surveyed the room, seeing only the excited faces of the children as they eagerly awaited the calling of their name to go up and collect their present from Father Christmas, most of them lingering to tell him what they would like on Christmas night.

She turned back to Penny with puzzled eyes, her concern deepening when she saw how ashen-faced the other woman had become. And Penny's attention seemed to be focused on the jolly Father.

Christmas as he happily distributed the carefully chosen presents to each child. Which was all the more surprising, considering that the man behind the flowing white beard and artificially glowing red cheeks was, in fact, Penny's own husband!

The only reason Jade could even imagine for Penny's behaviour was if the Father Christmas disguise had come astray and revealed to the totally enrapt audience that only a mere man lay beneath it, and that man was their own headmaster. But the wig and false beard were firmly in place, the rouge unsmudged on the padded cheeks, and the pillow beneath the red coat and wide black belt hadn't slipped an inch since Simon had got himself ready half an hour earlier.

Then what was bothering Penny? Because something certainly was as she took over the task of organising each child going up to collect their gift, her dazed gaze more often than not fixed on 'Father Christmas' as he enthusiastically distributed the gaily wrapped parcels.

Jade didn't find an opportunity to talk to the other woman for some time. 'Penny——'

'And who is this last little girl we have over here?' boomed that overly jocular voice of 'Father Christmas' with lilting emphasis.

'Penny, what——' The sudden silence that had fallen over the room, quickly followed by childish giggles, halted Jade in mid-flow, and she slowly turned her attention back into the spacious hall that had housed the Christmas party.

One hundred and fifty—one hundred and fifty-*one*, pairs of eyes were riveted on her, one hundred and fifty of them with laughing expectation, the hundred and fifty-first pair glinting with mocking blue humour.

'What would you like me to bring *you* on Christmas night?' Father Christmas/Simon prompted huskily.

'Oh, God,' Penny muttered weakly at Jade's side.

Oh, God, indeed. Simon had to have been at the sherry he always kept locked away in his office, for visiting parents, to be acting in this outrageous manner. Maybe Simon's role as Father Christmas *was* the reason Penny was looking so stricken. Jade had never seen Simon partake of more than one polite glass of sherry at one time, with no effect on him whatsoever, but Penny was obviously deeply concerned by his behaviour now—and with good reason.

'What's your name, little girl?' he prompted persistently, and the titters from the watching children increased.

Jade's mouth pursed disapprovingly. Penny and Simon had been very kind to her since she had begun working for them on a temporary basis at the beginning of the winter term, but Simon's drawing attention to her, and himself, in this way, was totally uncalled for. Maybe Simon was one of those worst of things, an unpleasant drunk. Although at the moment his eyes merely glittered with devilish humour.

'Come and sit on Santa's knee and tell me your
deepest desire—for Christmas,' that teasingly provocative voice encouraged again.

Jade felt really uncomfortable now, her cheeks
fiery red as she knew she was what she seemed to
be: the centre of attention, the other members of
staff deeply amused by this unexpected turn of
events, the children fascinated by the show. And if
there was one thing Jade hated it was to be the
cynosure of all eyes.

She plastered a polite smile on suddenly stiff lips,
green eyes flashing warningly. Not that Father
Christmas—Simon—seemed to be at all deterred
by her ferocity, his grin widening wickedly. Good
grief, how much of the sherry had he had?

'Come on, little girl,' he provoked. 'Don't you
realise how busy I am at this time of year?'

Not too busy that he couldn't spare a few minutes
to guzzle down what appeared to be a bottle of
sherry! 'I appreciate that—Father Christmas,' she
spoke softly, huskily, her natural tone, a voice that
her young pupils listened to with eagerness, and
which few other people took note of. Although at
the moment that certainly wasn't the case! 'Which
is why we really mustn't keep you any longer,' she
dismissed with bright lightness.

'Oh, I have more than enough time to listen to
what you would like to be waiting for you at the
foot of your bed on Christmas morning,' he
drawled mockingly.

Jade didn't know how to cope with this situation
any longer, turning desperately to Penny, dismayed

to see that the other woman was still completely speechless. If it wasn't for the fact that approximately one hundred and fifty children were watching the exchange, the incident would have been relatively easy to deal with—but one just didn't go around punching Father Christmas on the chin in front of so many starry eyes! Instead she had to settle for what she hoped would be a verbal dressing-down.

'The space at the foot of my bed is already firmly occupied,' she bit out quietly, green eyes flashing with unaccustomed irritation. She absolutely hated having this attention drawn to her! 'So I think I'll give any gifts you might have in mind for me a miss this year, thank you.'

The Father Christmas was shaking his head even as she spoke. 'Father Christmas has to bring you *something*—doesn't he, children?' he boomingly encouraged their involvement in the conversation.

The excited cries of 'Yes!' filled the room once more.

His persistence was unnerving, and Jade once again turned to Penny, only to find that the other woman had now gone a ghostly white. Which wasn't surprising!

Penny's young sister Cathy had been a friend of Jade's since college, and when she had told Jade about the temporary post at this private preparatory school it had been convenient for all of them that Jade was able to fill in until the usual teacher of the reception class returned from maternity leave at Easter.

The last three months had been rewarding both professionally and personally for Jade, and until this moment she hadn't had reason to regret her move from her London home to a rented cottage in Devon. Now she was beginning to wonder if it might not have been better for all of them if Cathy had never mentioned the vacancy to her—it was a sure fact that there would be repercussions from this incident, if only personally.

Jade gave a tight smile. 'I'll make you up a list when I have more time,' she dismissed curtly. 'Right now we have to prepare the children for going home,' she added briskly. 'We——'

'Oh, surely you can spare just a few minutes to whisper a little something in my ear?' 'Father Christmas' moved agilely across the room to her side—much more agilely than the true bulk could possibly have allowed!—his arm moving strongly about her waist as he pulled her firmly up against him, the twinkle in the blue eyes definitely lecherous now. 'Come on now, sweetheart.' He bent down to her much shorter height. 'Tell me what you would like me to bring you.'

No Father Christmas—and especially a married one!—had any right to be talking to her in this flirtatious way!

Jade gave a furious sigh as she moved closer to the wig-covered ear nearest to her. 'I'd like to take away the key to your drinks cabinet and throw it in the village pond,' she muttered, all the time smiling brightly for their audience, although she could see her colleagues—the braver ones, at least!—were having trouble controlling their mirth now. Ordinarily Jade would have been one of the first to laugh at herself, but not when she was being made a spectacle of.

Blue eyes gleamed wickedly as he moved back slightly to look down at her. 'Really?' he drawled mockingly. 'That wouldn't do you too much good at the moment—the village pond is frozen over!'

She glared. 'Perhaps a little icy air might do *you* some good just now!'

'Oh, I doubt it,' he taunted. 'Father Christmas isn't too bothered about the cold.'

'Only by too much alcohol, obviously,' she returned tartly in a fierce whisper.

He feigned hurt surprise. 'I haven't touched a drop since——'

'At the most half an hour ago,' Jade scorned, feeling deeply for Penny during this embarrassing display. How uncomfortable the other woman must feel at the exchange. And, even allowing for 'Christmas spirit', it was going to be difficult for them all to work together after this; it had gone far beyond the realms of a practical joke.

'Father Christmas' shrugged. 'I may have had a little nip of brandy to keep out the cold——'

'I thought you said Father Christmas wasn't affected by the cold,' she reminded tartly.

'I'm not,' he grinned. 'Not once I've had my nip of brandy!'

She frowned. 'Simon——'

'My, that's quite a list you have there once you got going,' he said loudly enough for their audience to hear, smiling jovially at them all. 'Anything else?' he encouraged brightly.

Considering that she was normally a non-violent person, Jade had an unaccountable urge to hit him! 'I want you to stop this right now,' she grated between clenched teeth.

'Why?' he taunted unconcernedly. 'I'm thoroughly enjoying myself.'

'I'm glad one of us is!' She tried to move away from his arm about her waist and suddenly discovered he was much stronger than he looked in the loose-fitting tweed jacket and plain trousers that were his everyday garb. 'You're going to regret this in the morning,' she warned with impatient rebuke.

'What's that saying?' he grinned. ' "Tomorrow never comes"?'

She chanced a glance at Penny's ashen face. 'Oh, I think it might do for you,' she muttered.

He turned to give the other woman a considering look. 'Hm, Penny does look a little green around the edges,' he mused. 'Maybe I should ask her what she would like on her bed Christmas morning?'

'A sober husband, I should think,' Jade bit out angrily, having found it was impossible to escape that confining arm about her waist—and goodness knew, without being too obvious, she had tried!

Blue eyes gleamed wickedly once again. 'Maybe you would be interested in listening to what I'd like in my bed on Christmas——'

'I don't think so,' she interrupted quickly, unnerved by this streak of flirtation with danger that she had never guessed existed inside a man who,

while full of good humour, never failed to be
thoughtfully kind.

'Perhaps not,' he lightly accepted her rebuke. 'We
wouldn't want to be overheard.'

'*We* have already made enough of a spectacle of
ourselves,' she cut in abruptly, grateful to see that
Penny at least seemed to be coming out of her daze,
some of the colour back in her cheeks as she began
to organise the children's home-going, at the same
time providing an adequate diversion from what
had been proving to be very entertaining for their
avid audience; some of their colleagues even looked
slightly disappointed that they were obviously going
to miss Simon's imminent dressing-down, Penny
obviously intending to wait until they were alone
before tackling him.

'Talking of spectacles, are yours really
necessary?' he took advantage of the noisy organ-
isation around them to whisper seductively in her
ear. 'Or are they just a deterrent against interested
males?'

'If they are, they aren't working!' she snapped,
her eyes flashing darkly, annoyed that he should
have guessed that she really only needed the glasses
for reading but chose to wear them constantly.

'And your hair.' He looked at her consideringly.
'I bet it looks very sexy when it's left free about
your shoulders.'

She drew in an impatient sigh. 'My hair happens
to be a frizzy mess when not kept in this style,' she
claimed defensively, irritated that he should find
anything wrong with the neat coil she always wore

about the crown of her head. She had always worn her hair like this when she was working, although she had to admit it had perhaps become a little more severe lately...

He continued to look at her questioningly. 'I refuse to believe those silken-looking tresses could ever be a frizzy mop,' he finally decided.

'Believe what you want.' Her cheeks still burnt from the lie. 'But for goodness' sake pull yourself together and start acting like the headmaster you are.' She looked about them again uncomfortably, feeling guilty for not joining in the preparations for home-time, but if she should leave Simon to his own devices now, heaven knew what he would do next!

'I am?' He frowned vaguely. 'Oh, yes,' he grinned. 'For a moment there I almost thought I *was* Father Christmas. I know there are several things I would like to give you that——'

'Oh, for goodness' sake!' Jade rolled her eyes heavenwards. 'I hope Penny gives you hell for this,' she muttered.

He turned to smile indulgently at Penny as she helped some of the younger children put on their coats. 'She probably will,' he acknowledged philosophically.

Jade wasn't feeling quite so hot now that they were no longer the centre of attention, although there was still the problem of how they were to face each other again after the holidays. Or how she was going to face Penny! The poor woman must feel devastated by Simon's behaviour.

'You should be ashamed of yourself,' Jade told the man at her side emotionally.

'I probably will be later,' he shrugged unconcernedly. 'Right now I'm enjoying myself too much to feel anything else.'

Who would have believed that the gentle giant of a man whom all the children loved and respected so much could possibly behave in this outrageous fashion?

'Well, you'll have to go on enjoying yourself without me.' Jade felt no compunction about putting him down now that there was activity and noise about them. 'I have work to do,' she dismissed firmly.

'And you think I haven't?' he returned in a pained voice. 'What about all those toys I have to finish by next week? The reindeer to feed and water? The——'

'Simon, for heaven's sake,' she sighed her impatience. 'Why don't you just take yourself off to your office and sober up? We can cope with anything that comes up here.'

Laughter gleamed mockingly in his eyes. 'I'm sure you can; you, especially, seem more than capable. But don't you think I should wave goodbye to all the children as they leave?'

The children would probably love it, but would *he* behave long enough to complete the task without mishap?

'I promise I will,' he chuckled softly at her side, causing Jade to turn to him sharply.

'If you can read my mind that well, you know what I'm thinking right now,' she flashed.

'I do indeed,' he drawled. 'But you're asking the impossible.'

Her eyes widened. 'I am?'

'Hm,' he nodded. 'A thousand miles between us couldn't possibly change the way I react to that clear green of your eyes, how I want to release your hair and run my fingers——'

'Please!' Jade snapped agitatedly, moving abruptly away from him. She was well aware of the fact that an excess of alcohol was supposed to loosen the tongue, but this was ridiculous! Surely Simon hadn't always felt this way about her? It certainly hadn't been apparent from his almost fatherly concern for her to date.

'You're right,' he said briskly, drawing himself up to his full padded height of over six feet. 'The children must come first. We can continue this interesting conversation once they've gone.'

If Jade had her way she would be long gone from here before Simon found her again. And, once on her own, she would have to give serious thought as to what was going to happen next term. She couldn't just walk out on her job, she refused to let people down in that way, also knowing it would be confusing for the children in her class to have yet another change of teacher. Damn Simon for indulging in his secret vice when he should have been preparing for his role as Father Christmas!

She looked on a little dazedly as, walking away from her, he fell easily into playing his seasonal role, his booming voice calling out good wishes to the children as he was surrounded by them as they went outside.

Jade's legs felt weak, and instead of joining in the revelry outside she sank weakly down into a nearby chair.

She *liked* working at the Kendrick Preparatory School, and after only one term of being here she was disappointed that it wasn't to be a permanent position. She even liked living in this small Devonshire village, where she was on a first-name basis with all her delivery men. And after living in town all of her life, the last four years of that in London in an apartment on her own, where she had to go out to the shops to buy all her needs, she hadn't expected to adapt so readily to country life. She willingly admitted that it had been the warm hospitality she had received from Penny and Simon that had helped ease her into this totally different way of life.

Penny, loving Simon as she undoubtedly did, couldn't be blamed for thinking Jade must have encouraged Simon's behaviour of a few minutes ago in some way. She couldn't possibly be expected to believe—as Jade herself found it difficult to!—that her mild-mannered husband could behave so recklessly without encouragement of some sort, even with the artificial confidence of alcohol.

It all had such repercussive consequences, also endangering Jade's long-standing friendship with Cathy, the other woman having no choice but to side with her sister. And she had even tentatively been looking forward to Christmas among her new friends. She had been invited to several functions at Penny and Simon's over the holiday period, their two children home for the holidays to complete the family unit. Cathy would also be trying to come down for a few days later on. Now all of that looked very precarious, although at this moment a long and lonely festive season seemed the least of her worries; her job was in jeopardy, a job that meant more to her than any of the people here could realise.

'Would you like to start clearing up the mess?'

Jade gave a guilty start as she looked up at Penny, feeling ill at how pale and exhausted the other woman looked. 'Penny, about what happened earlier——' she began awkwardly.

'Yes. I—I'm sorry about that,' Penny answered vaguely, not at all her usual authoritative self—and who could blame her? 'I—could you and the others tidy up here?' She looked uncertainly at the debris in the room from the end-of-term party. 'I have to go and look for Simon,' she added agitatedly.

Jade gave a pained frown. 'I just want to try and explain—— '

'Could we talk later?' Penny's voice was sharp; a small, pretty, blonde woman, slightly overweight, and looking all the more attractive because of that, she possessed the sort of organising mind that more or less kept the school running on a day-to-day basis. 'I really do need to find Simon,' she frowned.

That shouldn't be too difficult: she just had to follow the sound of the booming 'Yo ho hos'!

'I quite understand.' Jade nodded heavily. 'But I do need to talk to you afterwards,' she added firmly.

'Of course.' The other woman nodded, her mind obviously elsewhere. 'I'll just go and find Simon,' she repeated distantly before disappearing out of the room in search of her husband.

Jade felt even more deflated than she had before; despite her reluctance to discuss it now, Penny was obviously deeply disturbed by Simon's behaviour. But weren't they all? At least none of the children had guessed that 'Father Christmas' was more than a little inebriated. But it would only need one of the pupils to mention to their parents Father Christmas's more than seasonal familiarity with one of the teachers for more than Simon's relationship with Penny to be in jeopardy; most of those parents were well aware of the fact that Simon annually took the part of Father Christmas!

The Kendrick school was one of the best of its kind in the country, and Jade had instantly felt comfortable and at ease working in such a happy and contented atmosphere. It wouldn't remain that way for long if people were to learn that Simon took the occasional secret tipple. He risked so much for what appeared to be no more than a craving for something that completely changed his personality—and not for the better!

But Jade put a brave face on the incident when the others returned from outside—Penny and 'Father Christmas' conspicuous in their absence—as she helped to organise the clearing-up process, relieved when the only thing left to do was clear away the carol books in a cupboard. She smiled as she thought of the angelic faces of the children as they had all gathered around the piano to sing Christmas carols beside the flamboyantly decorated tree, each child having made at least one decoration to adorn it. There was something so magical about the innocence of children at this time of year, and it was virtually impossible not to feel drawn into the fantasy.

'Dare I hope that at least part of that smile is for me?'

Jade spun around with a start, disconcerted to suddenly find herself face to face with 'Father Christmas' once more. And he didn't look in the least repentant!

'Penny was looking for you,' she told him sharply, watching him warily.

He nodded, taking up most of the doorway to the store-cupboard. 'She found me,' he drawled.

Her frown turned to puzzlement; if Penny had managed to locate him, what on earth was he doing wandering around loose again in his condition? 'You haven't upset Penny again, have you?' she asked suspiciously.

He shrugged. 'She was crying her eyes out when I left her just now.'

Green eyes widened incredulously. 'And you just *left* her?'

'Well—not exactly. But I needed to see you again before you went home,' he excused himself.

'Penny—was—crying—her—eyes—out—and—you—just——!' Jade's incredulity turned to disgust as she stared at him in disbelief.

'I told you, I needed to see you before you left,' he insisted.

'To apologise?' Her eyes flashed warningly at his utter selfishness.

He did manage to look a little shame-faced. 'I suppose I did go a little over the top a short while ago, but I was only——'

'Over the top?' Jade repeated with soft anger. 'You were utterly outrageous!'

He grinned. 'I don't normally act in that impetuous way, it's just that——'

'I'm well aware of the way you *normally* act,' she snapped, wishing she could have the usual Simon back again, instead of this virtual stranger.

'—I was attracted to you the moment I entered the room,' he concluded as if she hadn't interrupted so vehemently.

'That you were——! My God, Simon!' Jade choked emotionally. 'You've really gone too far now. That scene you created a little while ago I could maybe excuse because of the amount of alcohol you've apparently consumed, but to come here to me now, when Penny is obviously brokenhearted, is inexcusable.'

'I was only——'

'Don't you dare touch me!' she warned harshly as he would have reached out for her.

'But I——'

'Don't say I didn't warn you!' she choked at the same time as her hand made contact with the side of his face in a resounding slap.

Jade stared at him in horror after the uncharacteristic violence—and then she swayed dizzily as he began to laugh, a loudly triumphant laugh that convinced her he wasn't drunk, after all, but bordering on the insane! The strain of owning and running the school must have become too much for him. No one in their right mind *laughed* when they had been slapped the way he just had!

And then her own horror turned to a pained groan as Penny suddenly appeared in the doorway. She was terrified that the other woman would actually think she had been encouraging Simon in this madness. 'Penny, I'm so sorry about all this, but I——'

'You have no reason to be sorry about anything,' the other woman dismissed easily, gazing affectionately at the man in the Father Christmas suit as he still grinned idiotically, the only sign of her recent tears a slight puffiness about her eyes. 'He always did have a warped sense of humour,' she excused him indulgently.

Jade had never noticed it before! 'I still wouldn't want you to think that I encouraged him,' she insisted pleadingly.

Penny smiled. 'I'm sure he didn't need encouraging.' She shook her head.

It was wonderful that Penny could take her husband's errant behaviour in her stride—Jade wished she could come to terms with it as easily!

'You really are incorrigible.' Penny shook her head with rueful disapproval at the grinning 'Father Christmas'. 'If you have——'

'Darling, surely there has to be a better place for this conversation than a store-cupboard?' Simon chided lightly as he appeared in the doorway behind his wife—wearing his usual school attire of tweed jacket and tailored trousers.

Jade froze as she stared at him, turning slowly to face the man in the Father Christmas suit. If it wasn't Simon—and she knew now without a doubt that it wasn't!—then who *was* he?

CHAPTER TWO

'I'M TELLING you, Wellington, *he* almost met his Waterloo after that stupid stunt,' Jade muttered as she poured the cream from the top of her milk into a saucer, giving a snort of disgust as the cat merely looked up at her with pitying eyes before turning his attention to the treat she had put down in front of him.

Jade watched the avid lapping of that delicate pink tongue for several seconds; Wellington certainly had the right idea, concentrating on his drink to the exclusion of all else certainly beat working yourself up into a temper because of the stupidity of some totally insensitive man!

Wellington had appeared on the doorstep of her rented cottage only her second day here, immediately earning his name, completely snowy white except for the four totally black feet that gave him the appearance of wearing wellington boots.

In the beginning Jade had assumed the friendly cat had wandered over from one of the cottages close by, but after several days of returning home to find him sitting on the doorstep waiting for her she had found out from a neighbour that the cat belonged to no one, that the old lady who had once owned him had died some time ago and the cat hadn't let anyone near him since then, living wild.

Two strays together, Jade had thought ruefully. Whether he had sensed some need in her that matched his own, or whether he had just decided she looked soft-hearted enough to feed him without demanding too much in return, she didn't know. But, whatever the reason, he had made the cottage his home the last few months, and when the time came for Jade to leave she didn't know what she was going to do about him. Wellington had become her constant companion, her confidant, someone she could talk to without fear of judgement or rebuttal, and she believed that in his own feline way he had come to care for her too, curling up to sleep on the foot of her bed every night, like a sentinel on guard. But at the same time she knew she couldn't take him back to be cooped up in her rented apartment in London, and there was no way she could afford to buy a house of her own out of town.

But there could be no doubt that Wellington had attached himself to her, and she to him.

His drink finished to his satisfaction, he now strolled across to stretch himself out in front of the fire Jade had lit when she came in, proceeding to wash himself with leisurely strokes of his tongue, pausing in the task to look up at her enquiringly as he sensed her gaze upon him.

She quirked mocking brows. 'So, you're finally ready to listen now, are you?' she derided, putting the milk bottle away in the fridge before joining the cat in front of the fire, taking with her the cup of tea she had just poured for herself, knowing she had been right about his readiness to listen to her now as he contentedly began to wash again. 'You're very definite about your priorities, aren't you, boy?' she teased, absently stroking that silky fur, receiving a rasp of the pink tongue over her hand for her trouble.

She leant back against a chair, giving a pained sigh. 'I have had the most awful afternoon, Wellington.' She shook her head, thinking back to what had transpired after Simon had interrupted that conversation in the store-cupboard.

She had stared at 'Father Christmas' with wide, horrified eyes, noticing as she did so that her slap to the side of his face had knocked the flowing white beard slightly askew, some of it having parted with his cheek completely, revealing a face that, although very similar to Simon's in features, was obviously younger than the other man's, something that was unmistakable now that his face was more fully revealed.

Before she could say a word, 'Father Christmas' had burst into speech. 'She slapped my face, Pen!' he told the other woman excitedly before once again giving that triumphant laugh. And he didn't seem able to stop.

Jade looked from Penny to Simon, wondering why one of them didn't step forward and slap 'Father Christmas's' face again—this time for hysteria. But the couple just looked on bemusedly, and so it was left to Jade to take the initiative before the whole thing turned into more of a farce than it already was.

Because her victim was more of a moving target this time, her aim wasn't quite so good, and instead of making contact with the man's cheek she caught the side of his eye. To her horror, this only seemed to fuel his excitement!

'My God, I'll probably have a black eye from that one,' he cried excitedly. 'Penny, Simon, do you realise what this means?'

Jade had more than a good idea; the man behind the Father Christmas suit was ever so slightly insane. No one in their right mind could possibly be *pleased* at having their face slapped, not once but twice! This man's disturbed state of mind might also explain Penny's ashen face when she had realised it wasn't her husband beneath the disguise, for it was obvious now that that was the reason Penny had looked so distressed when 'Father Christmas' came into the room. Simon, she could see at a glance, was as sober as he always was.

'I was attracted to her on sight,' 'Father Christmas' was rambling on. 'But now I know I'm going to marry her!'

Marry her? The man was definitely certifiable!

Penny was the first one to recover her voice. 'David, can't you see you're distressing her?' she soothed. 'Jade isn't used to—no woman is, I'm sure——' she added with brisk dismissal '—to six foot two Father Christmases proposing marriage to her at their first meeting!'

David. At least she could put a name to the man now, and from the similarity between him and Simon she would say his surname was Kendrick.

David Kendrick. No wonder Simon had never spoken of having a brother; David was definitely the 'black sheep' of the family!

And, if anything, Penny was understating her re-action to David's claim that he was going to marry her; she was more convinced than ever that the man in the Father Christmas suit was in need of medical help!

'But, Penny, can't you see it's like a sign?' he was insisting now. 'And she didn't just slap me once, but twice!'

Penny eyed Jade uncertainly, obviously alarmed by the pallor of her cheeks. 'David, I don't think you should persist in this just now.'

Jade had had enough, couldn't take any more today. 'I think I should be going now, Penny——'

'You can't go!' David pounced, grabbing both her hands in his, holding her captive. 'I've only just found you—do you have any idea how long I've been waiting for you to come into my life?' he prompted eagerly, continuing to talk before she could even attempt an answer to his question. 'Do you think I'm going to let you walk away from me now, when all I know about you is that your name is Jade and you're great with kids?'

And that he intended marrying her. Incredible, absolutely incredible. And the day had progressed so normally until his advent into her life, too!

'David, I really think it might be better to leave this just now,' Penny intervened again, shooting Jade nervous glances.

'But I can't,' he insistently refused, keeping a firm grip on Jade's hands. 'It's like a sign, Penny,' he repeated firmly. 'A blessing——'

'If I read all the signs correctly just now, Jade is getting ready to shout "escaped lunatic"!' Penny stepped forward to pointedly release Jade from the steely grasp. 'David, there has to be a better place and time for this,' she told him firmly.

'The poor girl will come to no other conclusion than that you have a few screws loose if you continue to talk in this way,' Simon put in softly.

If he continued . . . ? Jade was already *convinced* the man had a serious problem!

David looked perplexed. 'But you both know the significance——'

'Yes, yes,' Penny quickly silenced him, shooting Jade an embarrassed smile. 'Why don't we all discuss this later over dinner? You are staying to dinner, aren't you, David?' The normally practically assured woman looked less than certain for once.

David's expression gentled as he gazed at the other woman. 'Longer than that, if I'm welcome?' He looked a little shame-faced.

'Of course you are.' Penny blushed her pleasure. 'The kids will be overjoyed to see you.'

'I've missed them.' David's voice was husky with emotion now.

Jade was a little puzzled by the hesitant pleasure in Penny's face, at Simon's emotional smile as he looked on—but she was even more concerned about the thought of dinner tonight, not least because she had completely forgotten that she was supposed to be dining at the Kendricks' this evening! The first week she had arrived here Penny and Simon had invited her over to dinner on a Friday night, a practice that had continued, and as today was a Friday... She had no intention of meeting David Kendrick ever again, and certainly not over a cosy family dinner tonight!

'Maybe I should give dinner a miss for tonight?' she hastened to excuse herself. 'You all sound as if you have quite a lot of catching up to do, and so——'

'My dear, most of the talk will be about you, if I read my little brother correctly,' Simon drawled in an amused voice, blue eyes twinkling teasingly. 'So you might as well come along as arranged and avoid all that unnecessary ear-burning!'

It was her face that burnt now. Penny and Simon really were the nicest couple—she could believe that again now she knew Simon hadn't turned into a drunken lecher!—and she had greatly appreciated those weekly dinners with them in the past, but she really would rather not spend any more time in David Kendrick's company than she had to.

He seemed to sense her impending refusal, giving a wry smile. 'I really haven't "escaped" from any-where—although I understand if at the moment you think perhaps I ought to have done!' he acknowl-edged ruefully. 'But if anyone opts out of dinner tonight it really should be me; I'm the unexpected guest.'

And, as he very well knew, a very welcome one!

Jade frowned her irritation at his deliberate manipulation of the circumstances; she would look very petty now if she still insisted on refusing the invitation.

'I'll be around at eight o'clock as usual,' she finally answered Simon, completely ignoring David Kendrick, hoping that the way that she swept from the tiny room was regal and didn't show how she really felt—like a frightened rabbit!

David Kendrick had had a very determined glint in his eye as she turned to leave, and *she* seemed to be the purpose he was determined on.

'And now I have to spend the whole evening in his company,' she wailed to Wellington as they still sat in front of the glowing fireplace, only to look down and find he had gone to sleep somewhere in the middle of her tale. 'A lot of help you are!' she muttered, getting up to leave the cosily warm lounge with long strides to enter her much cooler bedroom; the radiators that heated the tiny cottage were warmed by the coal fire, and as that had only been alight a short time...

It was only one of the things she had found strange to adjust to when she moved into the cottage, being what she had always considered a 'townie', with all the modern conveniences that conveyed; central heating had been taken for granted back in her flat in London. Having coal delivered, lighting the fire each day, *keeping* it alight, were all alien to her. She usually found that the cottage had just reached an acceptable temperature when it was time to go to bed, but then the fire would go out during the night and she would get up to a freezing cold bedroom! Still, the cottage did have its advantages, the major one being that the cottage was so pretty that you quickly forgot about the lack of heating and the dozen or so other little quirks it had. A thatched cottage, with all of its original beams still intact, was still the sort of home 'townies' dreamt about.

And, despite what she had heard about villages, the neighbours were all so friendly; unobtrusive, but helpful if they should be needed.

Not that Jade 'needed' them very often, preferring, apart from her inevitable involvement with school mothers, to keep herself to herself. The locals seemed to accept that being from London made her prefer it that way. Although she wasn't actually from London originally, what was left of her family—and that wasn't a great deal—still lived in the Yorkshire town she had grown up in. But she rarely returned there now.

Usually she looked forward to these Friday evening dinners as her only social outing of the week, a time when the three of them had mutually agreed not to discuss work but to simply enjoy each other's company. But tonight that was marred by the presence of *that* man.

David Kendrick. What was he really like under all that make-up and disguise? Simon's brown hair, which was thinning a little on top, was cut more for practicality than style; would his brother's be the same? Their eyes, she knew, were the same deep blue, just as their voices were very similar, but the rest of David Kendrick was an enigma. For all she knew, there might not have been any padding under the Father Christmas costume! Even as the slightly ridiculous idea came to mind, she knew, by the slenderness of his hands and the cotton pads in his mouth to make his cheeks look fatter, that David Kendrick had probably needed more padding than his brother to play the role.

He was probably handsome as the devil, and with a charm to match—and he had claimed he intended to marry her!

Marriage wasn't something she contemplated with anyone, let alone when suggested to her by a complete stranger who had made her seriously doubt his sanity by his strange behaviour!

Maybe he wouldn't be handsome, after all; maybe he had a permanent squint, or acne? There had to be something wrong with him—besides his tendency towards insanity—for him to still be single in the early to mid-thirties he must be to be Simon's 'younger' brother. Insanity certainly wouldn't exclude a reasonably eligible man of that age from the marriage market, not if some of the married couples she had observed were anything to go by!

Oh, well, she didn't have the time to speculate about him any more, had to get ready if she wasn't to be late for dinner. And within a few minutes of her arrival at the Kendricks' all her questions would be answered anyway. Hopefully David Kendrick would also have either sobered up or become sane again by then!

It was as she went to pull the curtains over her tiny bedroom window that she noticed the falling snow for the first time; no wonder Wellington had opted for a comfortable night in front of the fire instead of his usual round of girlfriends.

The snow couldn't have been falling very long, but already there was a white covering of it on her pathway, although only a light dusting of it on the garden itself. But the flakes were quite large, and if it continued to fall at this rate...

She only needed the lightest of excuses not to go to dinner tonight, and surely falling snow could be classed as a little more than that?

But, even as a sense of relief at being spared the ordeal washed over her, she saw the headlights of an approaching vehicle coming towards her driveway. Almost instantly she recognised the vehicle as the silver-coloured Range Rover Simon occasionally used to transport the children to and from school during bad weather; the Kendricks certainly weren't going to take any chances of her opting out of this evening's plans! Or maybe Simon had made the two-mile trip from his house to her cottage at his brother's request; from what she remembered of David Kendrick, she had a feeling he could just be persistent enough to do that.

'It's all right for you,' she muttered to Wellington as she passed him on her way to answer the knock on the door. 'You're assured of a nice, comfortable evening.' As she had expected, the cat just ignored her grumblings, too sleepy and warm to even twitch an ear at the sound of her voice.

Jade gave an impatient sigh, wrenching open the cottage door.

Outside, the snow falling on hair so dark it was almost black, was the most lethally attractive man she had ever seen...

The dark hair lightly brushed the collar of the black leather jacket that was zipped half-way up the powerful chest, a chest that tapered down to a narrow waist and muscular thighs beneath tailored black trousers. There could be no doubt about it, David Kendrick had needed plenty of padding beneath the Father Christmas costume, for the rounded waistline at least, although his shoulders looked wide enough to fill the suit without any help.

She knew it was him by his eyes, navy blue eyes that looked at her as if he were eating her up. And there wasn't a squint in sight!

Just as there wasn't a single mark on the devastatingly handsome face, the nose long and straight, high cheekbones, fuller lower lip that hinted at a passionate nature. As if she needed any hints after his behaviour earlier today! If Penny hadn't walked in on them in the store-cupboard when she had, she might have received conclusive proof of just how passionate he was.

But the sensuality was there in the pleased slant of his mouth, in the blue gaze that didn't leave her face for a moment, and the hard muscles of his body were full of male challenge.

His smile widened, revealing evenly white teeth; God, didn't this man have a single defect? Of course he did, she remembered with some relief, he was more than a little strange!

'Hello, I'm——'

'David Kendrick,' she finished abruptly, nodding. 'I know.'

'I wasn't sure you would recognise me without my disguise,' he drawled, his voice pleasantly deep without the cotton wool pads he had had stuffed into his cheeks earlier.

Oh, she had recognised him, all right, probably would have done so even without the help of his arrival in the Range Rover; she was never likely to forget the deep blue of his eyes, the only part of him that had really been recognisable beneath the Father Christmas disguise.

'Penny and Simon sent me over to get you in case the snow put you off coming,' he offered by way of explanation when she made no effort to continue the conversation.

Green eyes flared with resentment. She was pretty confident that the idea to come and collect her had been mainly David Kendrick's.

'All right,' he murmured indulgently, that enticing half-smile on his lips. '*I* had no intention of letting you cry off dinner tonight.'

Jade had to admire his honesty—even if it was what she had already known!

There were a lot of things about this man she could have admired if things had been different. But they weren't, and so she viewed him with the same wariness she did all strangers—more so, because he was even *stranger* than most!

Her gaze met his coolly. 'I would have telephoned if I hadn't intended coming,' she dismissed.

He grinned confidently. 'Now there's no reason for you to have to do so. And don't worry about being able to get back later tonight; the Range Rover can easily get through any English snowfall.'

Giving the impression that this man had been in places where the vehicle wouldn't have stood a chance of doing that. Jade looked at him speculatively. Yes, he looked like a well-travelled and intelligent man, someone she would normally have found fascinating to talk to. Normally. Unfortunately, the situation wasn't normal; how could it be, when the man was so outrageous?

Her mouth tightened. 'Would you care to wait in the living-room while I go and change?' Her tone was distinctly distant.

He smiled, unperturbed by her offhand manner. 'I thought you would never ask,' he murmured as he strolled past her into the tiny room behind, pausing to look around him appreciatively at the antique furniture and décor she had deliberately chosen to complement the olde worlde character of the cottage.

'Hello, boy.' He went down on his haunches to tickle Wellington on his silkily soft tummy. 'At least you have the right idea,' he continued ruefully, still hunched down beside the cat.

Jade mentally acknowledged that a quiet evening spent in front of the glowing fire certainly held more appeal for her than one spent in this man's company. As for Wellington, he was behaving like a complete traitor; usually he ran away to hide when confronted by someone he wasn't familiar with, which was virtually everyone, but with David Kendrick he looked to be in ecstasies, an uncharacteristic look of total stupidity on his face as he still lay on his back, having his tummy stroked.

'I'll go and change,' she repeated stiltedly, turning abruptly to leave the room.

When David Kendrick stood up to turn towards her he was holding Wellington in his arms, still tickling him under the chin—and if Jade hadn't known better she would have sworn the silly feline was actually smiling. Damn it, he *was* smiling!

'Mind he doesn't scratch you,' she warned sharply. 'He has been known to do that without warning.'

Dark brows rose over mocking blue eyes. 'It's always the ones that look the friendliest that do that,' he said softly.

Jade felt the colour warm her cheeks at his obvious double meaning. 'It's a question of watching the eyes,' she snapped.

His mouth quirked. 'I'll try and remember that.'

'Do,' she bit out, trying not to hurry from the room but knowing she hadn't really succeeded; something about David Kendrick made her very nervous. Which was ridiculous. She was a teacher, for goodness' sake, a responsible adult in charge of seventeen pupils on a day-to-day basis—and heaven knew, children could be complex enough to deal with on occasion. And yet David Kendrick completely disconcerted her. Maybe it was the fact that he seemed to have come so close so quickly; usually she didn't allow the type of familiarity he had taken for granted from the first. Whatever the reason, and despite the dinner they would be sharing this evening in the company of Penny and Simon, she had no intention of allowing him to come any closer.

It seemed petty, not to mention childish, to choose her most unattractive outfit to wear for the evening ahead, but she really didn't have that big a selection in her wardrobe. Her only social occasions were spent at the Kendricks', and they didn't bother about 'dressing' for the evening. Unless tonight was going to be different because of the presence of David Kendrick... But no, while David's clothes had obviously been fashionable and of good quality, they had been casual clothes, not in the least formal. She would feel almost dowdy against him in her serviceable navy blue skirt and practical cream blouse. Men really shouldn't be allowed to be so perfect to look at that they were almost beautiful!

Remembering the remark he had made earlier about her hair, she pulled the auburn tresses back in so tight a bun that it made her eyes smart! The pressure eased as she loosened it a little, and with a rueful shrug she realised that now she *was* behaving childishly. She only removed her glasses briefly, so that she could apply a little blue shadow to her lids, before firmly placing the shield back on the bridge of her nose. They acted as a barrier against people like David Kendrick, and she had no intention of going anywhere without them, despite the accuracy of his mocking comment earlier today about them being unnecessary. Or *in spite* of it!

As she surveyed the final result of her ten-minute change of clothes she knew that she didn't look so very different from when she had started, but she felt comfortable like this, and certainly had no intention of trying to impress David Kendrick.

Her expression was one of challenge as he turned to look at her from contemplating the falling snow out of the window. 'Is it still snowing as heavily?' Her tone was defensively sharp as she waited for some critical comment about her relatively unchanged appearance.

'No,' he dismissed. 'You look beautiful,' he told her huskily.

Her cheeks coloured warmly at the unexpected compliment. 'We should leave now if we don't want to be late,' she bit out.

His mouth quirked. 'Something else I'll have to remember; you don't like compliments,' he explained self-derisively.

Jade pulled on her coat without asking his assistance, the expression in her eyes enough to warn him against offering.

'You're right about the eyes,' he murmured softly, laughter glinting in his own dark blue depths.

She shot him a reproving glare. 'If you've quite finished amusing yourself...?' She stood pointedly beside the front door.

David strode across the small living-room with soft footsteps, pausing just in front of Jade. 'I'm not laughing *at* you, Jade,' he murmured softly, perfectly serious now. 'It's just been years since I felt this damned happy, and I can't seem to stop myself smiling!'

She shot him a puzzled glance as he stood at her side while she locked the cottage door behind them, reminded once again that Penny and Simon had never mentioned he had a younger brother; there was obviously some mystery there, and now she couldn't help wondering if it weren't connected with David Kendrick's past unhappiness.

But who was she to question or speculate about another person's past? Anyone probing into her own past was likely to receive a very cutting reply.

She was deep in thought as they began the drive to Penny and Simon's house, aware of the questioning looks David Kendrick kept shooting in her direction, but doing her best not to acknowledge them.

She would get through tonight because she had already accepted Penny and Simon's invitation long before David Kendrick's arrival, but after that she was determined to stay away from the Kendrick family for the duration of David's visit.

'You remind me of someone, you know,' he suddenly said into the darkness, startling Jade out of the hypnotic dream she had fallen into as she watched the snow gently falling against the windscreen.

It was perhaps as well that he couldn't see how pale she had become in the darkness. No one had recognised her since she had come to this quiet little village, her role as a local teacher deflecting questions about her personal life to a certain degree. And now this man, a man who had done nothing but disturb and upset her from the first, claimed to know her.

'She gave me a black eye at our first meeting, too,' he continued musingly.

Jade had guiltily noticed that slight discoloration about his eye on his arrival, but had been too embarrassed—and angry!—about the whole incident to bring attention to it.

She gave an irritated frown now, still disturbed by his claim of recognising her. 'Who did?' she asked distractedly.

She didn't *want* to move on from this job until she had to; she loved the school and the pupils. And yet David Kendrick could leave her with no choice.

He gave her an indulgent smile before his attention returned to the road in front of them, that brief glance not seeming to have revealed the paleness of her cheeks to him. 'The lovely lady you remind me of,' he answered shruggingly.

Jade's frown deepened, and then her expression cleared with some relief as the significance of his words struck her. 'You have someone specific in mind?' she realised slowly.

'Oh, yes.' He grinned his satisfaction at having her undivided attention now. 'As I said, she slapped my face at our first meeting, too.' He shot her a triumphant smile. 'And a week later I married her!'

CHAPTER THREE

JADE gaped at him, couldn't do anything else in the circumstances. If he had married this other woman, then what—— God, he *was* deranged, and once this other woman had realised that she had obviously opted out of the situation. And who could blame her?

'All that proves,' she snapped waspishly, 'is that you're a consistently annoying man!'

He chuckled softly. 'Sara often thought so. But she always forgave me.' He quirked his brows questioningly. 'Are you going to do the same?'

She looked at him uncertainly.

He gave a rueful smile. 'You were right about my behaviour earlier—it was outrageous, and I am ashamed of myself.'

Jade sighed. 'That's something, at least,' she said tartly.

He nodded. 'Of course, it doesn't change the fact that I *do* want to marry you,' he told her lightly.

'Wouldn't Sara have something to say about that?' Her sarcasm was unmistakable.

'Sara's dead,' he explained softly. 'She has been for a number of years. And please don't apologise,' he drawled. 'It really was years ago.'

Jade's cheeks still burnt from the gaffe, burning anew at his mocking acknowledgement of it. How could she have even guessed that his wife had died, especially as she must have been relatively young? Oh, hell, she should have at least *thought* of the possibility. Now she really did feel as if she should apologise, which was exactly the disadvantage David Kendrick wanted to put her at, she felt sure. Not that his regret over his wife's death wasn't genuine, she felt certain it was; he was just mischievous enough to enjoy her discomfort, whatever the reason.

'That's how I knew the slap was a sign,' David Kendrick continued with satisfaction. 'Especially when the second one resulted in this.' He ran triumphant fingertips over the slight bruising at his eye.

Jade frowned, wishing the journey over so that at least Penny and Simon could act as a buffer between her and this strange man. 'A sign?' she repeated warily.

'That Sara knew and approved of the instantaneous attraction I felt towards you,' he nodded. 'That she understood the time had come for that "other door to open" in my life, that she even accepted you.'

Understood and accepted——? Dead women didn't give their husbands 'signs' like that! Besides, she didn't like the idea of possibly being instrumental in that 'sign'—it made her feel uncomfortable, to say the least. The very least!

'There's only one problem with that notion,' she bit out sharply. 'I have no wish to *be* in your life.'

He grimaced. 'After the stunt I pulled earlier by not instantly correcting you over the mistaken identity, I'm not surprised, but—'

'What *were* you doing playing Father Christmas instead of Simon?' Curiosity got the better of her.

'Surprising Penny,' he explained ruefully.

Remembering how pale the other woman had gone when she had instantly realised the man behind the Father Christmas suit wasn't her husband but his younger brother, she would say he had succeeded very well in achieving that!

He sighed, undeterred by Jade's silence. 'You see, we haven't seen each other for—a number of years. My fault, I'm afraid,' he admitted heavily. 'But when the two people you love most in the world remind you too painfully of the one person you ever loved more than them, the easiest—and probably the hardest, too!—thing to do is put them out of your life at the same time as you block out the pain of losing that special someone you loved.'

Jade felt as if she were being privileged with an insight into this man very few people were ever honoured with. And she, of all people, didn't want it, drew back from the intimacy of the confidence.

'That's understandable,' she dismissed stiffly, once again wishing the journey over.

David's mouth twisted. 'Fortunately Penny and Simon feel the same way about it that you do— otherwise my surprise could have ruined more than one Christmas.'

And instead only her own plans for the festive season seemed to have been affected. The

Kendricks had invited her to spend several pre-Christmas celebrations with them during the next few days, but with David Kendrick obviously now in on those invitations too... She would rather go back to her original plan of spending a quiet few weeks with Wellington than deliberately thrusting herself into this man's company.

'We all used to spend so much time together,' David murmured absently, obviously deeply lost in thought. 'Penny and Simon, Sara and me.' He gave a wistful sigh. 'Penny and Sara were more like sisters.'

'I was at college with Penny's younger sister,' Jade blurted out as a change of subject, knowing she hadn't quite succeeded when David smiled his satisfaction.

'Penny somehow seems to have a natural affinity with the women I'm going to marry,' he said with satisfaction.

'How many of us were there at the last count?' she felt stung into retorting.

David gave her a reproving look. 'Do I look like the sort of man who's had a string of wives?'

He *looked* like the sort of man who had never given marriage a thought, the perennial bachelor, in fact. But that could be because, by his own admission, his marriage to Sara had been so long ago.

Jade sighed. 'You look like the sort of man who has had a string of *women* in his life,' she taunted challengingly.

His expression became completely serious, those deep blue eyes looking almost black in the darkness.

'A few,' he admitted thoughtfully. 'Although not necessarily in the way you mean.' He smiled, as if he couldn't help himself. 'Ask me to introduce you to Dizzy and Christi some time. They are the only two women who have been in my life for some time.'

Dizzy and Christi? They didn't sound like the sort of women she would like to meet at all—or who would like to meet her either, for that matter!

'I don't think so, thank you,' she declined frostily.

'I just know you're all going to get along well together,' he said with certainty.

He was expecting a lot, thinking she wanted to be introduced to his harem. Although maybe she was supposed to feel herself privileged; after all, he had offered *her* marriage!

'I doubt the opportunity will ever arise for us to "get along" or otherwise,' she told him drily.

'They're both good friends of mine,' he frowned.

'Exactly,' she said with saccharine sweetness.

God, was that really her sounding so condescending? She wasn't usually bitchy like this, but the fact that David Kendrick just wouldn't accept her lack of interest in him—or his friends!—seemed to have turned her into a shrew.

'What work do you do, Mr Kendrick?' she quickly changed the subject.

'David,' he instantly insisted, as Jade had known that he would. After all, they could hardly go on calling each other 'Mr Kendrick' and 'Miss Mellors' all evening. Penny and Simon might be decidedly uncomfortable about that, to say the least!

'Jade,' she returned distantly.

'I heard that earlier,' he said warmly. 'Looking at your eyes, it isn't difficult to understand why.'

'The colour of my eyes is purely coincidental,' she dismissed flatly. 'They were the usual blue when I was born, and didn't start to turn green until I was about three months old. The reason I was called Jade was because my father collected it. And I suppose at the time I was born he considered me as precious as his collection. But we were discussing you,' she reminded him sharply, regretting her lapse in revealing even that much about herself. Had any of the bitterness she felt at no longer being thought worthy of that place by her father shown in her voice or manner? David didn't seem unduly interested in the comment—thank God!

'The clear colour of your eyes is definitely the most beautiful thing I've ever seen,' David firmly corrected her first statement. 'It isn't in the least coincidental,' he chided her on the use of the term.

'You were going to tell me what work you do,' she prompted distantly, making no effort to hide her displeasure at the compliment. Even if it did sound completely genuine. *Especially* as it sounded completely genuine!

David shrugged, as if he considered the subject of his occupation well down his list of priorities. It was also obvious what—or rather, who—was at the top of it. 'I publish books,' he dismissed uninterestedly.

Her brows rose with mocking censure. 'Really?' she drawled derisively.

'Not those sort of books,' David chuckled with emphasis as he correctly read the thought that was going through her mind. 'Ever heard of Empire Publishing?' He quirked mocking brows, as if her condescension greatly amused him.

As well it might! Good lord, it was like asking an Englishman if he had ever heard of cricket, the Dutch tulips, the Americans hamburgers, the Germans—— Empire Publishing company was constantly on the top of the best-seller list with its numerous popular authors. And its entrepreneur owner was reputedly responsible for personally recognising the majority of those talents. How could she have possibly known Simon's younger brother was *that* David Kendrick?

'Claudia Laurence is one of my favourite authors,' she admitted in an uncomfortable voice, aware that once again she was at a disadvantage.

Her admission only made David chuckle even more. 'Remind me to introduce her to you some time.' He made an effort to contain his humour, only partially succeeding as he still grinned widely.

Jade wondered disgruntledly what was so funny about having admitted she admired his most talented author. 'I thought Miss Laurence liked her privacy.' Her tone was sharp. Really, his habit of finding her a source of amusement was beginning to rankle! No one had ever found her *this* funny before, that she knew of.

'She does,' David nodded, that devilish gleam of laughter still in his eyes. 'But I think she might make the exception for a close friend of mine,' he added with certainty.

'Something which I most definitely am not,' Jade snapped, noticing with relief that their slow journey was almost over, the lights of the Kendrick house coming into sight.

'You're going to be,' he told her confidently as he turned the vehicle into the driveway.

She had learnt a distaste of arrogant men, had found that arrogance was usually accompanied by selfishness, and maybe if David Kendrick had sounded in the least arrogant as he made the statement her wariness of him would have been well justified, but instead he just sounded totally convinced he was right, which wasn't the same thing at all!

Jade had her door open and had stepped down from the Range Rover before David had a chance to get around to her, once again finding herself on the receiving end of his amused glance as he easily guessed the reason for her haste.

'I always feel sorry for those chaps this time of year.' He motioned in the direction of a passing police car as he took a firm hold of her arm, walking towards the house. 'It must be hell keeping an eye open for all those after-work-party drunks that suddenly take to the roads.' He shook his head. 'I think they must have thought I was one for a while; they were on my tail almost as soon as we left your cottage.'

Jade's alarmed gaze followed the departure of the police car as it slowly cruised along out of sight,

given no real chance to question the incident as
Penny opened the door to greet them before taking
them into the warm comfort that was the
Kendricks' home.

Situated in the school grounds, the house had
once been the original cottage hospital that existed
on the site, and Penny had worked wonders trans-
forming what could have been a barn of a place
into a warmly welcoming refuge for all the family
and their friends. Lavishly festooned with
Christmas decorations, most made for them by the
pupils, at the moment it had extra appeal, everywhere bright and glittery, but most of all, warm.

'I hope this clown has apologised for his behaviour earlier,' Penny lightly scolded as she took
their damp coats—although it was obvious by her
open affection as she gazed at David that she would
forgive this man anything—and probably had
during the last few hours.

'Profusely,' he grinned, more handsome than
ever in the intimacy of the hallway.

'He has—explained the situation,' Jade acknowledged more formally, inwardly wishing she
didn't sound so stiff and prim. But this man put
her on the defensive, damn him.

'Although she doesn't accept that the slap—and
this,' he indicated the discoloration at his eye, 'was
a sign, either.' He shook his head sadly.

'Let's not start *that* again.' Penny very firmly
pushed him towards the living-room. 'Go and help
Simon pour out the drinks,' she instructed firmly,

her usual air of authority obviously firmly back in place.

'Women's talk?' David teased softly.

'An attempt on my part to convince Jade you really don't need locking away!' Penny retorted. 'You see,' she pounced as Jade gave a rueful smile. 'She's obviously deeply sceptical that I can convince her of any such thing!' she told him disgustedly.

'It doesn't make any difference whether Jade thinks I'm insane or not,' David announced confidently. 'I still intend to marry her.'

'You would need my consent for that,' Jade snapped, her tone telling him that was something he would never get—unless *she* was insane!

'I'm not going to take no for an——'

'Will you go away, before Jade runs screaming into the night?' Penny told him exasperatedly. 'We don't see you for more years than I care to mention, and the first thing you do when we do see you is try to scare off one of our best teachers!'

'She is wonderful with children,' David acknowledged warmly, as if the fact pleased him enormously.

'Oh, God, don't tell me you have half a dozen of them that need a mother,' Jade groaned.

'Not yet,' he drawled. 'But we'll start work on it as soon as we're married.'

Jade felt completely drained as, having made yet another outrageous statement, he finally took Penny's advice and disappeared into the living-room in search of his brother.

'I know,' Penny said with a sigh as she met Jade's pained glance. 'He exhausts me as badly. I was always grateful that it was Simon I fell in love with and not David; who needs a whirlwind constantly upsetting their life?'

Who indeed? Certainly not Jade. She liked her life to be quiet, peaceful, and most of all without problems, either in fact or looming on the horizon.

Which reminded her very forcefully of the police car David had said followed them from her cottage. Had the police really been following them because they suspected David might have been one of those people who over-indulged in Christmas cheer, or had it been for another reason entirely?

She chided herself for being over-imaginative. David Kendrick's behaviour had upset her more than she realised; there could be no other reason than a routine observation for the policemen's interest in them.

'If the way David is acting is really bothering you, I can always try having another private word with him.' Penny was frowningly watching the fleeting expressions that crossed Jade's face, half right in her surmise that David *was* bothering her.

Jade shook off her distracted thoughts with effort. 'Would it do any good?' she smiled, the other woman's earlier effort having obviously failed.

Penny grimaced. 'I doubt it, the mood David is in, but I could try.'

'Don't bother.' She shook her head. 'I'm sure I can cope with the situation.'

'I'm sure you can,' Penny chuckled. 'Which is why I told Simon we should stay out of it. And if you don't manage to handle it—well, I think it might be rather nice to have you for a sister-in-law!' She softly laughed her enjoyment of the stunned expression on Jade's face before sweeping into the living-room ahead of her, having successfully made her point that David Kendrick could be like an express train if he chose—just as unstoppable.

Jade felt herself the sole attraction for a pair of dark blue eyes as she followed Penny into the room at a more leisurely pace, feeling her confidence slip a couple of notches at the determined glint in those dark depths. She had no plans to marry—ever— and she certainly wasn't going to be bullied into it!

'You braved it, after all,' Simon drawled from his standing position across the room, a blazing fire just to the left of him, chuckling softly as Jade's startled gaze was turned towards him. 'I meant the weather,' he softly explained.

Her cheeks burnt at the assumption she had made, and then she saw the devilish gleam in Simon's eyes that exactly matched that of his brother. He was finding all of this very amusing! And why shouldn't he? He wasn't on the receiving end of the lunacy.

'Do leave her alone, Simon,' Penny chided. 'It's enough that she has one idiot making her life miserable.'

'Hm,' he acknowledged, giving Jade an apologetic look. 'Just let me know if David gets too much for you,' he advised. 'I always could beat him in a fair fight.'

Dark brows rose over confident blue eyes. 'Who says I intend to fight fair this time? You know the saying...'

The affection between the two men was tangible, and Jade had a feeling that if it really came down to it Simon was perfectly capable of aiding his brother in his claim to marrying her! Two Kendrick men on the same side would probably defeat anyone.

Which was why she took the earliest opportunity—while she and Penny were washing up after the meal and the two men were indulging in a friendly game of billiards—to make her excuses to Penny for the arrangements they had made for her to spend time with them during the holiday period.

Penny looked deeply disappointed, a frown over her dark brown eyes. 'I'd been looking forward to your company,' she sighed.

Jade instantly felt ungrateful, and more than a little selfish; after all, the Kendricks had opened their hearts and their home to her.

'And Cathy has promised to try and get down for a day or two because you're here,' Penny chided.

That wasn't strictly true, although she knew Cathy was making a special effort to try and get time off from her exacting job as personal assistant to a man who didn't seem to acknowledge that holidays existed. And if she did manage to get away for a couple of days it would have been nice to see her friend...

But David Kendrick was here, too.

And that said it all . . .

'Besides,' Penny pressed at her continued silence, 'all my plans have been made with a certain number in mind.'

'David's here now,' Jade pointed out drily.

'That just means I have to come up with another woman for the dinner parties, not lose one of the ones I've already got!' Penny reminded exasperatedly.

Jade gave a sigh. It seemed there was no way she could get out of the plans already made without insulting the couple who had been so kind to her. Penny was probably wondering what she was doing running scared just because David was chasing her so hard; after all, there couldn't be that many women who would actually want to run! David Kendrick was everything that was eligible: handsome, fun, charming, rich. Even that tendency he had to be rather intense wouldn't diminish some women's interest, and now that she knew about his first wife she could better understand the conclusions he had drawn about the slaps she had given him. Although that certainly didn't mean she believed in that nonsense! She had slapped him because he'd been acting so strangely, not because she had been inspired to do so by a dead woman. Although she couldn't help but feel curious as to why Sara had administered *her* slap all those years ago . . .

No doubt Penny knew, and would probably enjoy telling her, but she didn't want to seem in the least interested in David Kendrick or his past.

'If it's going to upset things for you...' she reluctantly gave in.

'It is,' the other woman instantly accepted, her expression brightening. 'And if Cathy does turn up, maybe I won't have to find a partner for David for long.'

Jade had no doubts that David could find his own partner, all too easily; she was also certain he would do no such thing when he was so intent on capturing her.

'That's all settled, then,' Penny said briskly as she tidied away the washed and dried crockery. 'I have to admit, I thought I was going to have more trouble convincing you than that,' she confided cheekily.

She gave the other woman a reproving look, mentally berating herself for being so gullible.

'Hey, Simon and I really aren't going to abandon you to his clutches,' Penny chided at her frowning expression.

As David insisted on being the one to drive her back home a short time later, Jade knew the other couple weren't going to be given much choice. Beneath the charm and fun was a will of iron, apparently!

'Cheer up,' he advised lightly as he did up his seat-belt beside her. 'I'm not about to ravish you as soon as we reach your cottage.'

Jade gave him a dismissive glance, considering the remark not even worthy of a reply. Of course he wasn't about to ravish her, he was a man in his mid-thirties, hardly still in the juvenile stage!

'Which isn't to say,' he added softly as he manoeuvred the Range Rover out on to the road, 'that I'm not going to try to steal a kiss or two.' His eyes gleamed with intent.

She felt her cheeks pale, her lips suddenly stiff. 'No one takes anything from me that I don't wish to give,' she bit out harshly. Not any more, no one did that to her any more!

David shot her a questioning glance. 'That was said with rather a lot of feeling?'

'And shouldn't it have been?' she returned defensively. 'What right do you have to try to take something I don't want to give?' Her eyes flashed deeply green.

'I don't take, Jade,' he told her gently, the hand nearest to her reaching out to clasp hers as it rested against her thigh, his hand tightening fractionally as he felt her stiffen, before slowly releasing her. 'Sara didn't slap me because she was physically afraid of me,' he explained softly.

'Sara?' Jade gave him a sharp look. 'What does your wife have to do with this?' Surely that was the last subject they should be discussing in the circumstances?

'I thought maybe you had imagined I had tried to "ravish" her on our first meeting, and that was the reason for your wariness... Obviously I was wrong,' he murmured thoughtfully. 'Would you like to hear why Sara *did* slap me?' he enquired lightly, just as if the last few moments of tension hadn't happened.

Jade was disconcerted, realising that perhaps she was supposed to be, but too relieved by the change of subject to question it. 'I'd love to know what Sara could possibly have found so irritating about you that she resorted to physical violence on your first meeting.' Her tone implied she couldn't imagine a man who had deserved the slap more.

David chuckled softly. 'She thought I was having an affair with her mother.'

Jade gasped; she couldn't help it. Whatever she had been expecting, it certainly hadn't been that!

'It wasn't true, of course,' he added drily.

She raised auburn brows, more in control again now. 'It wasn't?' she mocked.

He gave a rueful smile. 'I know you would love to think it was, but unfortunately it wasn't. Judy was, and is, a lovely woman,' he derided at her questioning look, chuckling as she looked suitably taken aback. 'She was also one of the first authors I signed for Empire: Judy Maxwell.'

Jade knew the author well, another of her favourites, specialising in those big blockbuster sagas that were always so popular.

'We had been having a series of meetings about a manuscript she had submitted to me, and because Judy wanted to surprise her family with her "success", she hadn't told any of them she had sent the manuscript off to a publisher, let alone that we actually wanted to talk to her about it. The first I knew that Sara had found out about the meetings and drawn the wrong conclusion was when this black-haired vixen came into my office and accused

me of seducing her mother, just as she punched me
in the eye. She was nineteen at the time, full of
idealism, and seducing her mother, even though
Judy had been a widow for over five years, just
wasn't on,' he remembered fondly.

The affection and love he had felt for his wife
was all there in his voice, and once again Jade had
the feeling of intruding on something that was intensely private.

'But the two of you did marry a week later,' she
prompted abruptly, the snow having stopped falling
some time during the course of the evening, the
heavy vehicle finding the journey easily manageable. Thank goodness!

He nodded. 'With me still sporting the black eye
she had given me,' he smiled. 'Once Judy and I had
calmed Sara down enough to listen, we explained
the true situation to her. And once she had calmed
down I realised she was even more beautiful then
than she had been when she was angry; I lost no
time in inviting her out to dinner. Within a few days
we were inseparable, and when we decided to marry
there was no doubt in either of our minds that we
were making the right decision.'

But Sara had died, and from the sound of it that
emotional side of this man's life had died along
with her. Until now. She should feel honoured that
David considered *her* worthy enough to take his beloved Sara's place, but she only felt panic.

'Judy was a terrific mother-in-law,' David recalled fondly. 'We're still very good friends. And
we always get together on the anniversary of Sara's

death.' There was naked pain in his voice as he spoke of it.

'She must have been very young,' Jade's voice was gruff.

'Only twenty,' he nodded grimly. 'We had only been married a year. She had leukaemia, we found out soon after our wedding. Nineteen years old and already condemned to die,' he said harshly. 'We put a lifetime of loving into that year, fulfilled all her dreams. Except one. A child,' he explained softly as he sensed Jade's questioning look, staring ahead into the darkness. 'She would have been a wonderful mother; she loved children as much as you do.'

Jade felt a familiar jolt as she realised that she was now the object of this man's emotions. And it sounded as if, when he loved, he loved long and deeply. God, she didn't want to see him hurt again after what he had just told her, but he had to be made to see that he had misplaced his affection, that she was totally unsuitable.

'I love teaching children,' she corrected. 'I've never envisaged having any of my own,' she lied, knowing that that particular dream had been buried some time ago, along with several others she had cherished.

'I won't push for that if it's something you feel strongly about,' David shrugged. 'It might have been nice to have a little girl with your auburn hair and jade-coloured eyes,' he added wistfully. 'But it isn't something I'm going to insist upon.'

He made her feel so helpless, with his certainty that there was a future for them, with or without children! How could you get through to a man who simply wouldn't listen?

He drew the Range Rover to a halt in her small driveway, turning in his seat to look at her after turning on the overhead light. 'I'll pick you up about eleven o'clock in the morning, shall I? Or do you prefer to sleep later than that?' He quirked dark brows.

'I would *prefer* not to be disturbed at all in the morning,' she told him frostily.

'OK,' he shrugged without rancour. 'I'll come over in the afternoon.'

'David——'

'I noticed you didn't have a tree at the cottage,' he cut in softly. 'I thought we could go and choose one together.'

The fact that he had noticed the lack of decorations at the cottage shouldn't have come as a surprise to her; he seemed to take note of everything about him, with little effort. The fact that he felt he had some right to rectify matters rankled.

He gave a pained grimace. 'I can see I've stepped on your toes again.'

Jade's cheeks became warm. 'It isn't that, I just wasn't going to bother with a tree this year. I shall be there so little, you see.' She was babbling, making excuses and explaining herself over something that was really none of this man's business. 'I thought I might spend more time picking it up after Wellington decided to play on it than I would looking at it,' she announced defensively.

'The cat?' he guessed correctly. 'He looked as if his interests lie in quite another direction,' he derided.

'The pine needles might damage his pads,' she insisted stubbornly.

'Then we'll buy one of those plastic ones that are supposed to be so realistic,' he suggested, undeterred.

Christmas trees with pine needles that her mother good-naturedly complained shed all over her carpet and constantly needed vacuuming up reminded her too vividly of Christmases spent at home with her family, of the warmth and happiness that had existed there. All of those things denied to her now.

'If I had wanted a tree, I would have bought one,' she snapped coldly, pushing open the door at her side. 'Thank you for bringing me home, Mr Kendrick. No doubt I will be seeing you again shortly.' She stood outside in the snow now.

'I'll walk you to the door.' David made a move to get out of the Range Rover.

'No need,' Jade told him shortly. 'There's no reason for both of us to get cold.'

He relaxed back in his seat. 'You can't keep running for ever, Jade,' he warned her softly.

'Running?' she echoed in a strangulated voice. 'What on earth do you mean?' Her hands were clenched at her sides.

'Running from me,' he said slowly, giving her a considering look. 'At least, that's what I *think* I meant,' he added with deep puzzlement, intrigued by her reaction.

Jade's eyes blazed. 'I'm not running from anyone or anything,' she grated harshly. 'Once again, thank you for the lift home.' She slammed the door behind her, not looking back as she trudged over to the cottage door, turning the key in the lock to close the door firmly behind her just as she heard the Range Rover engine leap back into life at the switch of the key.

She leant back against the closed cottage door, visibly shaken. For a moment, a very brief moment, she had imagined that somehow David Kendrick had guessed that the only man she had ever fallen in love with had stolen more than her heart, that he had taken so much more from her than that . . .

CHAPTER FOUR

THE thudding noise was soft, but irritating. Jade moved protestingly beneath the soft down of her quilt, the light behind her closed lids telling her it was morning, but the lethargy of her body also telling her it wasn't far enough into the morning for her to have to get out of bed yet. Besides, it was a Saturday.

The soft thudding continued, gently, but persistently.

'Go away, Wellington.' She dragged an arm from beneath the warmth, braving the chill air she knew would meet her outside of it, waving the cat away from whatever he was doing that was so annoying.

The soft thudding continued, gently, but persistently.

'If you want breakfast this morning, cat, I would advise you to stop that now,' she growled frustratedly.

The soft thudding noise came again—just about the same time she realised that the extra warmth on her feet was the still sleeping body of the innocent cat.

Jade gave a weary sigh, so tired she didn't *want* to wake up yet. It had been a restless night, memories she would rather not have relived flooding her mind until she had no choice but to face them. Sleep had been a long time coming after that.

And now that thudding, that out-of-tune-with-her-usual-morning-sounds noise persisted in disturbing her when she would rather have turned over and gone back to sleep for several hours.

But she knew she couldn't do that, that she would have to get up and investigate the sound, especially as they had had the first snowfall last night since she moved in here. One of the roofs could be leaking, or—— Suddenly sleep was the farthest thing from her mind; throwing back the duvet, her body immediately chilled as she quiveringly pulled on the thick robe she had found so helpful in recent weeks.

As she sat on the side of the bed she realised that the thudding noise was coming from the curtained window. The snow was melting already? There would be a lot of disappointed children this morning if that were the case.

She winced as she slightly parted the curtains and the white light from the blanket of snow that covered the ground instantly hit her.

It took her a few seconds to focus in the bright light of this winter morning, but when she did it was to realise there was a large mound of snow sliding down the window. Just as she realised that, a missile struck the window in front of her, causing her to pull back in alarm. And then she recognised it was only a snowball. But the snowball had to have been thrown by someone...

She instantly ruled out one of the village children, knowing even before she tentatively looked down into her tiny front garden who the culprit was.

David Kendrick grinned up at her cheekily, looking disgustingly healthy and robust in the early morning light, the cold air having added a glow to his hard cheeks.

Jade dropped the curtains back into place as if they had burnt her, anger ripping through her as she turned back into the bedroom.

'I should have known,' she muttered as she threw open her wardrobe door to pull out a pair of denims and a thick green jumper. 'I don't know what possessed me to blame you, Wellington,' she furiously apologised as she dragged the clothes on. 'You're the only male I *can* rely on not to let me down or annoy me!' She slammed the wardrobe door on her way out of the room, her feet in the knee-length boots making a clattering noise on the stairs as she ran down them.

David had just gathered up enough snow to make another missile as she threw the door open, his eyes full of devilment as he spied her in the doorway.

'Don't you dare,' she fumed warningly.

The glove-covered hand that held the snow slowly lowered, the black leather jacket worn over a dark blue jumper and denims today, his hair lightly ruffled by the gentle breeze, adding to his rakish attraction.

The last thing Jade wanted at this moment was to be reminded of his devilish charm!

He dusted the snow from his hands. 'No wonder the children listen when you talk,' he said ruefully.

'Well, if you will persist in acting like a child...' she returned waspishly. 'Do you realise what time of morning it is?' A quick glance at the clock on her mantel on her way to the front door had told her it was only just after eight o'clock.

'The best time of day for a snowball fight,' he told her disarmingly.

Jade was taken aback by the endearingly made statement. A snowball fight...!

'OK.' David held his hands up defensively, looking more boyish than ever. 'The truth of the matter is I've hardly slept all night for thinking of you, and I couldn't wait any longer to see if you really did exist or if I could possibly have dreamt you. You can't imagine the relief I felt when you pulled back the curtains a few minutes ago. And don't worry, I forgive you for deceiving me.'

Jade was totally disconcerted by his candid admissions, although she stiffened warily at the last. 'Deceiving you?' she echoed softly.

He nodded, that grin back in place. 'Your hair is gloriously silky when it's loose about your shoulders like that, and you certainly don't need your glasses.'

Her cheeks felt hot as she realised she had been in such a hurry to get down here and give him a verbal dressing-down that she hadn't even brushed her hair this morning, let alone confined it in its usual style, and her glasses still sat on the bedside cabinet...

Bending, she scooped up a handful of the icy snow. 'You're right about the latter,' she accepted at the same moment she drew back her arm and took aim with the snowball. It landed smack in the middle of his chest. 'I can certainly see well enough to hit large objects!' She faced him challengingly.

'Large objects——!' he repeated with a low whistle between his teeth. 'That's fighting talk, Miss Mellors,' he warned silkily as he bent to retaliate.

It was ridiculous—eight o'clock in the morning and she was having a snowball fight with a man who yesterday had given every impression of being disturbed. In fact he hadn't done a single thing to change that impression; waking her up in this way certainly didn't qualify!

After several minutes of exuberant snowball-throwing, the majority of them reaching their mark, they were both glowingly warm—on the inside, at least. On the outside it was a different story, their clothes damp and uncomfortable, Jade's hair no longer 'gloriously silky' but hanging in wet tendrils about her face, and as for her hands—— She hadn't even had the benefit of gloves.

'Time to go inside and get warm, I think,' David recognised as he saw her involuntary shiver.

'No.' She shook her head ruefully.

He frowned. 'That wasn't an improper suggestion.' His frown deepened. 'Why is it I find myself sounding like some Victorian suitor whenever I'm around you?' he said self-derisively.

'I have no idea,' she snapped, not even looking at him as she brushed the snow from her clothing.

'And the reason I said no was because it won't be much warmer inside; I haven't had a chance to light the fire yet,' she explained drily. 'It had nothing to do with keeping you out of my home.'

'In that case, I'll light the fire while you cook breakfast.'

Breakfast? She had no intention of cooking breakfast for him, this morning or any other morning. But she was already too late to stop him going into the cottage, she realised as he disappeared inside.

By the time she entered he was already shovelling out the dead ashes, laying the fire once he had completed that task. And doing it very professionally, too.

'That isn't the first time you've done that,' she admired grudgingly.

He glanced across the room at her, that grin once again in evidence. 'I don't live in an apartment in town, Jade,' he told her softly. 'I live in a house in Berkshire which can only be called rustic, and I enjoy lighting a fire for myself when I come in from work on long winter evenings. And no, Sara didn't live there with me,' he added gently, even as the vision of the couple sitting together in front of the glowing fire sprang into Jade's mind.

She frowned her consternation. 'I wish you would stop doing that,' she bit out resentfully.

'Reading your mind?' he sat back on his haunches. 'I think it's a measure of our instant rapport,' he shrugged.

'We don't have——'

'I bet you have eggs and bacon in your fridge just waiting to be cooked for breakfast,' he lightly interrupted her protest.

'That isn't so unusual,' she scoffed.

'Mushrooms, too?' he mocked.

Her cheeks burnt fiery red. 'What on earth makes you think that?' she said defensively.

'You had a second helping of them at dinner last night,' he shrugged.

'So did you,' she instantly accused him.

'Exactly,' he drawled, his brows raised.

Jade drew in a deep breath, letting it out again in a deep sigh. 'OK, so we both like mushrooms,' she admitted defeatedly.

'And we can have some with our bacon and eggs?' he requested wistfully.

A grown man, especially one as devastatingly attractive as this one, shouldn't also have the power to have the appeal of a little boy; it wasn't fair to the female population! And it was galling to think that even she, someone who had been totally disillusioned about men, should be affected by that appeal.

'The food was for my lunch,' she told him waspishly. 'I don't usually eat breakfast.'

'Indulge me,' he encouraged huskily.

She sighed again. 'I have the feeling people have been indulging you since you were in your cradle,' she said disgustedly, already knowing she was going to be another one who did exactly that—as far as the breakfast went, anyway! She defended her actions by telling herself she was hungry and might as well feed him as she was going to cook anyway.

She didn't wait for David's reply, turning to go into the kitchen, leaving him to earn his meal by lighting the fire.

It wasn't until she had the bacon and mushrooms sizzling under the grill and the eggs cooking on the stove that she questioned what her neighbours were going to think about the Range Rover parked in her driveway when they got out of their beds. It would look as if the vehicle had been there all night! After months of living quietly, slowly melding into the community, of remaining completely apart from any gossip that might be circulating, she was probably going to give them the tastiest titbit they had had for months.

'Why so pensive?'

She hadn't realised David had entered the tiny kitchen, but she turned at the sound of his voice, grimacing her distress. 'The locals are going to be full of speculation about the Range Rover being outside the cottage,' she sighed heavily.

'I won't ask if that bothers you,' David said gently. 'Because it obviously does. But with the aid of our much-respected headmaster's wife I'm sure we can come up with a perfectly feasible excuse for my being here this time of the morning.'

'You must think I'm being ridiculous——'

'Nothing of the sort,' he cut in with brisk assurance. 'I should be one of the first to realise how these misunderstandings are made,' he added ruefully.

Of course, he had met his beloved Sara through just such a misunderstanding!

'Don't look on this as another of those "signs",' Jade warned hastily. 'This is just me being overly cautious.' And with good reason; the last thing she needed was speculative gossip about her.

'Let's eat before the food gets cold,' he suggested gently, his gaze warm.

She still looked hesitant. 'As long as you don't think that I——'

'I *think* that Penny can inform everyone—before they ask—that she was the one that was concerned about your welfare out here on your own, after the snowfall last night, and sent me over to check up on you. Early,' he added with emphasis.

'*Very* early,' she grimaced as they sat side by side at the breakfast bar, which was all the seating arrangement for eating the tiny cottage allowed.

'Right,' he nodded, liberally buttering his toast. 'And while I'm on the subject of your living "out here",' he frowned, 'aren't you a little too much out on your own for safety?'

The fact that the cottage was situated on its own was one of the things she had found hardest to adapt to when she had first moved here, but now she liked the relative solitude its location provided. 'The nearest neighbour is only a couple of hundred yards away,' she answered chidingly.

'What if you should fall down and hurt yourself?' David's frown deepened as if the thought greatly disturbed him.

'I'm sure I could manage to crawl to the telephone somehow and call for help,' she drawled mockingly.

He gave her a censorious look. 'But what if you got trapped somewhere——'

'Like the coal cellar?' she taunted, at his melodrama.

'Exactly,' he pounced, very agitated now as his imagination worked overtime.

Jade shook her head, calmly forking up some bacon and a mushroom. 'I don't have one,' she informed him lightly before popping the food into her mouth, having worked up quite an appetite during their snowball fight.

David didn't look convinced. 'You could accidentally lock yourself in somewhere——'

'The loo, for example,' she nodded.

'Yes. You——'

'I don't have a lock on the loo door,' she sighed, the conversation beginning to irritate her now. 'Besides, there's a window,' she added firmly, determinedly taking another mouthful of her breakfast.

Dark brows rose. 'Big enough for you to climb out of?'

'Just about,' she nodded after some consideration. 'But not for you to climb in!' she warned.

He gave her a reproachful look. 'Do I look the cat-burglar type?'

'Wellington wouldn't let you steal him even if you were,' she returned pertly, trying to introduce levity into the conversation, something he seemed determined she wouldn't do!

'Very funny!' he grimaced, acknowledging her mockery.

'Talking of Wellington...' she mused as the cat strolled into the kitchen for his breakfast now that he had decided he had had enough sleep for the night. Jade got up to mix his food. 'He's all the protection I need; I'm sure he would run for help if I needed it,' she drawled before once again sitting down at the breakfast bar beside David.

'I'm glad you find it amusing——'

'That's the whole point. I don't,' she cut in with irritable impatience. 'I don't need anyone fussing around me.'

'I'm not——'

'Your food's getting cold,' she snapped with finality, no longer enjoying the meal herself. She had spent the last year distancing herself from people, and didn't intend being trapped into a relationship now, even if David Kendrick was one of the nicest men she had ever met.

Nice. Not the dull, uninteresting sort of nice that became boring after a while; he was too unpredictable ever to be that! But he was a truly nice man who cared about others, was concerned for and about them. Cared and was concerned about *her*.

Which was all the more reason for her not to become involved with him, in any way.

'Something else for me to remember about you,' he drawled as he finally picked up his own knife and fork in preparation for eating. 'You don't like to feel protected.'

She gave him a frosty look. 'Protection is one thing; it's when it curtails your personal freedom that it becomes intrusive.' She was being too harsh, and she knew it, feeling almost guilty as he gave a disappointed shrug before starting to eat his breakfast.

Jade's own appetite had deserted her. God, how she wished she dare allow herself the luxury of feeling protected, cosseted and loved. But to do that she would have to allow her defences to drop, and it had been a long and painful process building them up in the first place! Even the slight lapse she had made a few moments ago as she'd tried to banter him out of his concern for her had been a lowering of her defences she dared not repeat. David might begin to think she actually liked him. And that would never do.

She silently dismissed his compliments and thanks for the meal with a shrug of her shoulders, hurriedly clearing away, anxious now to cut his visit short.

David watched her with unruffled amusement, leaning back against one of the kitchen units as she tidied away the crockery he had just finished wiping. Jade's movements became more and more agitated under his steadily watchful gaze.

'Finished?' he enquired casually when Jade could find nothing else to put away.

'In here,' she accepted stiffly. 'But I usually go into town to do my shopping on a Saturday.'

He straightened, taking the keys to the Range Rover out of his denims pocket. 'Then what are we waiting for?'

Her brows rose at his intention of accompanying her. 'That wasn't an invitation.'

'Mine was,' he returned easily. 'How else are you going to get into town?'

'In my car, of——' She broke off with a pained groan. Faithful as Cleo was—she had had the Mini six years now without any serious problems with it—she very much doubted the little car would be able to travel in the couple of inches of snow that still covered the roads in this area. If only she had remembered that damned snow before she had mentioned going shopping! 'I can always leave the shopping until another day now that school has finished for the Christmas holidays,' she dismissed with bravado.

'No need,' David said pleasantly, a determined glint in his eyes. 'Not when I'm conveniently here to take you. Besides,' he added before she could protest again, 'who's to say the snow will clear in time for you to go "another day"?'

He was right, of course, and she couldn't go indefinitely without stocking up on food, the lack of storage space at the cottage meaning she never had too much in at one time. And, reliable as Cleo was, she couldn't expect the tiny car to contend with the roads in this weather. 'Then I accept your kind invitation,' she told him stiltedly—both of them knowing she didn't really have a choice. 'I'll just go upstairs and get my coat.'

Damn, damn, *damn*! Going out to do her weekly shopping had seemed like the ideal way to escape any more of David's company today without having to be rude and actually ask him to go. Now she had unwittingly put herself in the position of being with him for a couple of hours more at least.

It wasn't until she got into her bedroom and accidentally caught sight of her reflection in the small dressing-table mirror that she realised her hair was still a silkily loose auburn cloud about her shoulders and her glasses were still conspicuously absent from the bridge of her nose.

Futile as it seemed, she went through the daily ritual of securing her hair and putting on the shield of her dark-rimmed glasses. She would have felt more businesslike in one of her plain skirts and blouses, but the thought of how cold it was outside was enough to keep her in the denims and jumper. She had already spent the last two hours in David's company dressed like this; it was a little late in the day to be worrying about the way both articles of clothing hugged the slenderness of her figure, clearly outlining the gentle curve of her hips and breasts.

David said nothing about the alteration to her hair or the addition of the glasses as she joined him in the tiny lounge a few minutes later, although she knew by the way his dark blue gaze flickered over her that he had noticed the changes in her appearance. Her cheeks instantly warmed.

'I've put enough coal on the fire to last until we get back,' he told her lightly as he opened the front door for her.

She had noticed the thoughtful action as soon as she came down the stairs. Another one of those 'nice' things about David Kendrick that were too dangerous for her peace of mind. And her need for privacy.

But, as if he were well aware now of how even so small an act could make her wary and suspicious, David seemed to deliberately leave her to her own thoughts on the drive into town, putting on an unintrusive cassette to alleviate the silence so that it shouldn't become too uncomfortable, perfectly relaxed himself as he sat capably behind the wheel of the Range Rover.

This man was worse than dangerous, he was lethal, and it was something she must never forget, despite his seemingly easygoing nature; he was a man determined to have his own way where she was concerned, with honey if he could manage it, but if not, by some other means. He hadn't become, and remained, successful in a cut-throat world like publishing was today, without learning how to be a survivor!

He remained just as unobtrusively in the background as Jade wandered around the supermarket, pushing the trolley along for her after insisting he could at least do that.

It was worth losing that particular battle just for the pleasure of seeing the head of Empire Publishing trying to control an errant shopping

trolley up and down the shop's aisles—*that* seemed
one battle he was doomed to fail at as he constantly
crashed into either the laden shelves or other poor
shoppers.

Jade, walking a short distance ahead of him as
she perused the shelves, had difficulty containing
her mirth as David let out yet another expletive
before impatiently righting the trolley on to a
straight path—for about two seconds! To give credit
where it was due, David was being wonderfully
patient, but that didn't make the whole scene any
less funny.

She paused at a stand where a specialised
saleslady was trying to market a new cheese spread,
giving David time to partially win his battle and
catch up with her. The cheese spread didn't taste
as nice as others she had tried in the past, and,
smiling a polite refusal at the other woman as she
tried to sell her a jar, she turned to continue her
shopping.

'Perhaps your husband would care to try some?'
the woman prompted hastily as she realised she
wasn't about to make a sale after all, despite her
avid sales talk.

'I don't——'

'I'd love to,' David answered the other woman
warmly.

Jade turned slowly, just in time to see David pop
one of the small crackers smeared with the cheese
spread into his mouth.

He chewed it around thoughtfully. 'Very nice,'
he nodded, turning to Jade, pure devilment in his

eyes. 'Try it again, darling, and see what you think,' he encouraged softly.

Irritation darkened her eyes; David had no right to deceive the poor saleswoman into thinking they were actually going to buy some of the awful spread, and he certainly had no right to let her go on thinking they were husband and wife! 'But we aren't——'

'Into cheese, I know,' David completed smoothly—and completely incorrectly; he knew damn well she had been about to vehemently deny they were husband and wife. 'But I think you'll agree,' he bestowed a heart-stopping smile on the middle-aged saleslady, 'that these are delicious.' He indicated the crackers on the display table.

They were no such thing, and they *all* knew it, even the other woman looking a little surprised by his enthusiasm. She was obviously only employed on a temporary basis until the product had been introduced to the general public, probably having to try and sell a different product—just as awful as this one!—every week. All the more reason not to lead the poor woman on now.

Jade's mouth twisted. 'I don't think this is one of those occasions, David, when there's a hidden camera all prepared to get you on film and put you on television next week!'

He grinned, unabashed. 'Try it again, sweetheart. For me,' he encouraged throatily.

She would 'sweetheart' him right around his— No, she abhorred physical violence, remember, and David's discoloured eye still showed the signs of her last lapse; she wondered what the saleslady thought of that! Besides, her last lapse had ended up with David announcing he was going to marry her!

She strolled back over to David's side, giving him a vengeful smile. 'I just wanted to explain that you aren't my husband,' she drawled calmly.

'I'm so sorry,' the flustered saleswoman apologised for her mistake. 'I didn't—I just thought——'

'I'm sure you aren't really interested in our living arrangements,' David cut in lightly. 'Which reminds me, darling,' he turned back to Jade, his expression innocent, 'we ran out of washing-up liquid this morning.'

Her mouth tightened as he neatly turned the tables on her once more. Why was she even bothering to challenge him in this way? It was a foregone conclusion that she would lose.

To give David his due, he did actually purchase a jar of the cheese spread before they left, leaving behind them one satisfied saleslady—even if the jar was likely to go straight in the bin once they got back to the cottage!

David began to chuckle as they loaded the shopping into the back of the Range Rover. 'It was worth the eighty pence to watch you squirm for a change,' he explained at her questioning look.

'Sorry?' she frowned at him.

'You looked as if you were about to explode with laughter in there a couple of times,' he nodded in the direction of the supermarket. 'While I played

ten-pin-bowling with the other shoppers!' He gave
a rueful grin.

She smiled in spite of herself. 'Some trolleys do
seem to have a will of their own.'

'This one certainly did,' he pushed it into one of
the appropriate lanes in the car park with obvious
relief. 'Changed your mind about the Christmas
tree?' he prompted gently as he rejoined her.

It unsettled her slightly that he didn't arrogantly
insist she had to have a tree; if he had she would
have lost no time in telling him 'no'! But, although
he was the type of man who liked things done, she
had also learnt that he wasn't the type who walked
all over other people's wishes. And she could see
that if she said she was still set on not having a tree
then he wouldn't press the issue. Which instantly
made her feel churlish for refusing in the first place.
Besides, she couldn't run away from memories for
the rest of her life.

'Why not?' she accepted lightly. 'But it will have
to be a small one,' she added hastily, not willing
to give in completely.

David nodded consideringly, laughter in the navy
blue eyes. 'I think it might get a little draughty in
the cottage if you had a ten-foot one sticking up
through the roof!'

Jade gave him a narrow-eyed glare, not deigning
to answer as she walked off.

Despite her earlier comments about the imprac-
ticality of real Christmas trees, she opted for one
of those rather than one of the plastic ones. There
were some really lovely artificial ones on sale in the

shops, but that was the trouble really, they *were* artificial, and, painful as the memories were, she had been used to the real pine-shedding type all her life, and couldn't break with that tradition.

After much deliberation they settled on a really bushy tree, about four feet high, which easily fitted into the back of the Range Rover. And then, of course, they had to go back to another big store to get the decorations for it.

It was while David was extolling the virtues of a rather large metallic red ball that could be hung from the ceiling that Jade spotted the mother of one of her pupils watching them a short distance away with open curiosity.

That was all Jade needed, although perhaps it was inevitable she should be recognised by someone in town; most of the people from the surrounding area shopped in town on Saturdays, and it was probably only the fact that the bad weather had kept some of them away that had saved her from a confrontation like this earlier in the morning.

'Mrs Shepherd,' she made a point of greeting the other woman before smiling down at the little girl at her side. 'Hello, Tracy. Are you busy getting things for your tree, too?'

'Miss Mellors,' Tracy's mother greeted while Tracy herself shyly held up the pretty silver tinsel she had been busy choosing. 'Awful weather, isn't it?' Heather Shepherd added conversationally.

Jade smiled in acknowledgement, at the same time realising that David had noticed her transfer of interest and was watching them politely. 'Mrs

Shepherd, this is our headmaster's younger brother, David,' she introduced distantly. 'He's staying with the Kendricks for the holidays,' she supplied economically, her mouth twisting with rueful acceptance as she saw the avid interest in the other woman's face now that she knew David's identity. 'He very kindly offered to bring me into town today because of the bad weather,' she felt compelled to add.

'Actually, it's more a case of Penny wanting me out of the way because I was getting under her feet,' David confided charmingly as he shook the other woman's hand firmly.

Mrs Shepherd gave a wry smile. 'I know the feeling; it's so hectic this time of the year.'

'But worth it,' David said gently as he smiled down at Tracy, whose huge blue eyes dominated her pretty little face, and whose hair, a mass of jet-black curls, cascaded down her back.

Much like the little girl he and Sara might have had together, if only Sara had lived to give him a child...

It was so easy, with his lazily teasing nature, to forget that David had already known so much tragedy in his life. It was to his credit that he hadn't grown bitter from the blow life had dealt him so early in his life.

'Well, we must get on,' the little girl's mother excused. 'Tracy wants to go and see Father Christmas before we go home,' she confided indulgently.

'But I thought you saw him yesterday?' David teased as he went down on his haunches so that he should no longer tower over the shy little girl. Tracy held up one slender wrist, showing off the brightly coloured bracelet she had obviously received as her present from 'Father Christmas' the day before. 'It's beautiful,' he dutifully admired the piece of jewellery she obviously cherished. 'I know why you have to see him again.' He smiled at her mischievously. 'You left something off that enormous list you gave him yesterday!'

Tracy gave a coy giggle, waving shyly as her mother prepared to leave.

'If the list gets much bigger, the attic will collapse under the weight,' Mrs Shepherd told them in a whisper before moving off.

'I remember.' David straightened with a companionable grin Jade couldn't resist sharing. 'I envy you, you know,' he sighed wistfully. 'You must get a tremendous satisfaction working with children as lovely as that one all day,' he explained at her questioning look, still watching Tracy, the little girl sending him another shy wave every now and then as she made her way to the cash-till with her mother.

'I do love my work,' Jade nodded. 'But the children all have their moments!'

He turned with an understanding laugh. 'In other words, they can be little devils when they choose. Even Tracy.' He resumed choosing the decorations.

'Even Tracy,' she agreed lightly. 'Although I have to admit, she's usually good.'

David decided to have the large red ball after all, placing it in the basket with the other things they had already chosen. 'I guess my Father Christmas yesterday wasn't enough to satisfy them until the big night,' he grimaced. 'Although at least now I know who—and what—takes up that space at the end of your bed,' he said self-mockingly.

'Wellington,' she acknowledged drily.

He nodded. 'I plagued poor Penny for hours yesterday to tell me if there was a special man in your life.' He frowned as a closed look came over her face. 'Don't look like that; Penny was the soul of discretion if there was anything to tell, told me to ask *you* any personal questions like that. Although she would admit there had been no one that she knew of during the few months since you've been here,' he murmured thoughtfully. 'Does that mean there's someone in London?'

Jade had stiffened as soon as he mentioned the possibility of there being a man in her life, the easy camaraderie that had developed during the morning rapidly fading as her barriers moved firmly back into place.

David gave a pained grimace at her tight-lipped expression. 'Penny was right, that question was obviously too personal even to ask you.' He took the shopping basket out of her unresisting fingers. 'I think we have enough decorations here now.'

She nodded abruptly. 'It's only a small cottage.' Her voice was strained.

He went to move away, stopped, turning back with a sigh. 'I'm sorry if I've upset you with my questions.' He shook his head in regret. 'I was really enjoying spending this day with you.'

So had she been, until that timely reminder. She had briefly forgotten the reason she chose to distance herself from people, the reason she dared not let anyone close to her, even a man like David who she knew without a doubt was good and kind. But she had remembered all too well now her reasons for remaining apart from such friendships, would have to take care she didn't forget again.

For to forget again, to allow herself the indulgence of this man's warmth, was a danger to her, and to everything she had so painstakingly built up for herself in the last year and a half.

The tragedy in David's past had been tremendous, but her own loss had been almost as great, although luckily no one had died. But she had lost. And she had sacrificed. At the time it had all been more than she had thought she could humanly bear.

She dared not leave herself open to that type of pain again.

She couldn't have guessed then, as her spine stiffened with resolve, how soon the fragile world she had managed to build for herself was to be completely shattered . . .

CHAPTER FIVE

IT WAS difficult to remain distant and unmoved in the face of David's boyish enthusiasm for putting up the decorations and the tree.

But she tried very hard to do just that as the homely cottage was transformed into a glittering world of Christmas fantasy, everywhere she looked a dazzling reminder of the festive season soon to come. Achingly haunting memories surfaced just at the sight of them, causing a painful lump in her throat.

'What do you think, Wellington?' David stepped back from the tree he had just brought inside, firmly established in a bucket of earth, the cat having sat on the hearthrug watching him in fascinated curiosity during the whole procedure of putting up the other decorations. 'Is it straight in the bucket?' He glanced down at the cat, Wellington staring back at him with unblinking green eyes, his head tilted questioningly to one side. 'No, I didn't think it was, either,' David sighed, moving to adjust the trunk of the tree in the bucket of earth.

Jade had been standing in the kitchen doorway listening all the time this one-sided conversation had been taking place, shaking her head ruefully at David's idiocy. 'A little more to the right,' she advised softly as he stared at the tree frustratedly.

He instantly turned to the cat in feigned wonderment. 'You talked,' he pounced. 'My God, Wellington, you could make a fortune going around showing you're the only talking cat ever known to mankind. Of course, we'll have to break it to Jade gently that she's been wrong about your sex all this time, but——'

'Very funny,' Jade drawled drily as she strolled fully into the room.

'Oh, it was you all the time,' he said with mock surprise. 'You've been so quiet since we got back that I felt sure your voice must have gone.'

She ignored the gently questioning gibe, knowing that, although he would understand her feelings of desolation this time of year if she cared to explain, she wouldn't do so. Eighteen months ago she wouldn't have believed herself capable of such distant withdrawal from human closeness; it had just been a lesson she had learnt the hard way.

But the silence between David and herself was companionable now as they adorned the tree, David handing her the angel to put on the top as the final decoration. Jade felt a lump in her throat as David flicked the electricity switch and the gaily coloured lights trailed around the tree were illuminated.

'Thank you,' was all she could say huskily, but she could see by the warmth in navy blue eyes that David understood her emotion.

'Now, how about a late lunch before driving over to see Penny and Simon?' he suggested briskly. 'I told them when I telephoned earlier that I hoped to spend the day with you, and Penny invited us over for tea with them and the children if we cared to go.'

Jade stiffened. 'And you accepted for me?'

'No,' he gently calmed her. 'I told her we would let her know.'

She relaxed slowly. 'I'm sorry.' She felt churlish for jumping to conclusions, wishing he would stop being so damned nice so that she might at least start distrusting him again. Because that mistrust had taken a serious blow today.

David stepped forward, standing just in front of her, long slender hands coming up to cradle either side of her face. 'Whoa,' he gentled softly as she would have jerked away. 'I only wanted to thank you for our time together today,' he explained huskily.

She became still, blinking up at him, her eyes deeply puzzled.

'It's the best time I've had in years,' he told her gruffly, the warmth of his gaze caressing her. 'I really felt as if I "belonged" here with you today. It's the feeling I've missed the most.'

She knew exactly what he meant by the term— the feeling of being a couple, of sharing. It was something she too had known once, something she too had missed, even though she had tried to block it from her mind, something she too had felt briefly between them today. Dangerous, dangerous, *dangerous* . . .

That danger came even closer as David lowered his head towards her, navy blue depths holding her captive before his head had lowered enough for his lips to touch and know hers.

Electrified satin. It was a contradiction in terms, but it was the only way Jade could think of to describe what it was like to be kissed by this man. The feeling washed over her so completely that she couldn't help but be captivated by the contrasting touch. David's lips against hers were like satin, but tiny shivers of tingling pleasure made Jade's mouth throb, almost like tiny electric shocks.

Electrified satin . . .

Jade swayed dizzily towards him, clasping his forearms to stop herself from moulding her body against his. She couldn't, she just couldn't!

David instantly released her as he felt that slight resistance. 'I'll build up the fire while you go up and get your change of clothes for this evening,' he told her huskily. 'You haven't forgotten Penny and Simon are throwing a party tonight?' he prompted lightly at her lack of response, acting for all the world as if that kiss had never happened.

But Jade had forgotten everything in the midst of that kiss, even her name very briefly! What *was* her name?

'Jade?' he prompted again, his expression indulgent at her dazed reaction.

Oh, yes—Jade. Dear God, David wasn't the one that was insane, *she* was. She had enjoyed his lips against hers, found pleasure in the protection they seemed to give her, had actually wanted the kiss to continue, had had to force herself to make it stop.

'Your change of clothes,' he reminded her lightly before turning towards the fire.

Jade continued to watch the broadness of his back for several seconds as he put coal on the fire as professionally as he had this morning, shaking herself to clear the fog from her numbed brain before quickly hurrying from the room. She sat down shakily on her bed.

Madness, utter madness. And the greatest madness of all was that she knew the cottage was going to seem very lonely now that it had known David's presence ...

None of her distress at that knowledge was obvious when she came down the stairs a short time later, having changed the denims for black tailored trousers but left on the dark green jumper. She carried the clothes she intended wearing that evening in a bag.

She coolly met David's gaze as he turned from stroking Wellington to look at her. 'I'll feed him before we go, and then go and check on Cleo,' she told him distantly.

His brows rose. 'Another pet?'

Jade turned back at his puzzled query, a half-smile on her lips. 'My car,' she corrected drily.

'Oh,' he straightened, with a rueful grimace for the mistake he had made.

She nodded briskly. 'I just want to run the engine for a while.'

'It's a good idea to charge up the battery in such severe weather,' he nodded.

She could see that although he approved of that idea he found the idea of a car named Cleo a little on the strange side!

'Personally,' he continued, straight-faced, 'I call mine George!' He grinned.

She gave a relaxed laugh, any moments of tension that might have existed completely gone. She went into the kitchen with a rueful shake of her head.

David went to put her things in the back of the Range Rover while she opened the garage doors to turn the engine over on the car.

He came in to lean on the open window a short time later. 'It looks in good condition,' he admired, smoothing a hand over the perfect paintwork.

'*She* is,' Jade corrected pointedly, revving up the engine. 'I've had her six years now and she's never let me down yet. Her previous owner—and he was the original—said she had never let him down either. She's getting a bit old,' she realised affectionately. 'But I'll keep her until she falls apart now. What's George?' It felt good to be on such a safe topic as their respective vehicles after what had happened earlier!

'A Jag,' he admitted softly. 'Sports model.'

'Don't apologise for it,' she teased his near reluctance to own up to such a powerful and expensive car. 'I just happen to be rather attached to my Mini.'

'A cat and a car,' he remarked thoughtfully. 'There must be room in there for me somewhere!' he added with self-mockery.

The revving of the engine came to an abrupt halt as she took her foot off the accelerator to switch off the ignition, climbing out of the car to put an abrupt end to the conversation too. 'Shall we go?' she prompted stiltedly, her expression remote.

In truth, although she did like to check on Cleo in severe weather like this, most of the reason for her delay was a reluctance to see Penny and Simon after having spent the day with David in spite of her previous hostility towards him.

She could feel her tension mounting as they approached the house, David having accepted her earlier rebuff with good grace, music playing softly on the radio to alleviate the pointed silence.

The presence of 'George' parked in the driveway beside Penny's estate car momentarily diverted her attention away from her own dilemma, a sleek, dark grey car whose lines cried out its distinctive make.

'George,' she admired mockingly as she stepped out on to the driveway.

David ran a hand lovingly down the sleek bonnet. 'The one and only. I can't claim to have had him as long as you've had Cleo, but *I'm* very attached to him.'

Once again their conversation about their ridiculously personally named cars helped to ease the tension between them. 'A family who loves you, a beautiful car—what more could you possibly want?' Jade teased lightly, instantly wishing she hadn't as his expression became wistful. 'I didn't mean——'

'I know you didn't.' He squeezed her arm reassuringly. 'But don't worry, I've found what it is
I "want".'

'David——'

'Now don't get yourself in a panic,' he calmed
her. 'I'm not in any hurry.'

She shook her head. 'But I can't——'

'You don't have to do anything, Jade,' he soothed
gently. 'I have to admit that my first instinct was
to take you away somewhere, lock you up until
you—Jade?' His bantering tone turned to one of
concern as she paled. 'God, what did I say?' he
frowned worriedly. 'Jade, tell me what I——'

'I'm all right.' She waved away his concern as
the front door of the house was swung open, two
children bounding impatiently down the steps to
greet them.

Jade had met the two Kendrick boys before, had
always thought them to be eleven- and twelve-year-
old versions of their father, but as they launched
themselves excitedly at their uncle she could see it
was David they most resembled, their eyes as dark
a blue as his, the boys themselves so much alike,
with their tall, gangling bodies and untidy mops of
dark hair, that they could almost be mistaken for
twins.

David was obviously pleased to see his young
nephews again too, returning their exuberant hugs,
although his worried gaze searched Jade's face
before she turned pointedly away.

Jade was glad of the diversion of the Kendrick
children during the next half an hour. Neither of

the boys were satisfied until they had shown their uncle their bedrooms and then taken him out to the garage to show him the bicycles they had received for their birthdays earlier in the year; Jade had received a jolt she needed time to recover from.

'Was it that bad?' Penny prompted gently at her side after all the male members of the family had been persuaded to disappear outside to the garage. She shook her head reprovingly: 'I thought David was rushing things a little when he rang earlier to say he hoped to be with you all day. The trouble with David is he never learnt any patience,' she added crossly. 'I would have felt like hitting him if he had dared to wake me up at seven o'clock in the morning for a snowball fight.' Her mouth quirked with amusement as she could visibly see Jade's tension begin to relax into a rueful smile. 'Hugging him a little, too, I think,' she admitted affectionately. 'He can be the most infuriating man!'

Yes, he could. But he could also be kind. And thoughtful. And dangerous to her peace of mind. And it was the latter she had to remember.

By the time the other members of the family returned, and she and Penny were dragged into a boisterous game of Monopoly, she had almost forgotten that moment of sheer panic she had experienced when she and David had first arrived here. Almost...

'Penny hasn't lost her ability to throw a successful party,' David drawled on the drive back to her cottage several hours later.

It had been a pleasant evening, most of the people there familiar to Jade. What had made it slightly uncomfortable for her was the interest all of Penny and Simon's friends had taken in Simon's brother. As David's obvious partner for the evening—no matter how much she might have wished it didn't appear that way!—she had come in for considerable interest herself. No doubt a lot of those people had believed her to have moved very fast to capture David's interest in that way! To his credit, David had made very sure everyone knew he more than returned any interest she might feel.

'I can't get over how much the boys have grown.' He gave a rueful shake of his head. 'They were only seven and eight the last time I spent any time with them,' he admitted heavily. 'I've missed them both so much,' he added gruffly.

The boys had obviously missed their uncle too, even though four years must have seemed a very long time in their young lives.

But at least now Jade had some idea of how long David's wife had been dead. And the four years had seemed even longer to him than it had to the boys, because he had had nothing left in his life.

'I should have known not to play Monopoly against you,' Jade derided, lightly changing the subject. 'I had forgotten that I once read about you that you're considered the "entrepreneur with the Midas touch"; a little game like Monopoly was child's play to you!'

He grinned in the half-light, several small street-lamps illuminating the small village. 'Simon and I always used to win when we played as children.' He gave her a teasing look. 'Simon was better at it than me, if anything; in fact, he would have been a more successful businessman than me if he had chosen to go into that profession instead of teaching.'

'He's an excellent headmaster,' Jade told him quietly.

'Even better than he would have been a businessman,' David nodded. 'I'm sure he gets a lot more satisfaction out of it, too,' he frowned.

She gave him a curious look. 'You sound almost—disillusioned?'

'Not really,' he shrugged with a sigh. 'I just—— Sometimes I wish I could have done something that made me feel—more fulfilled. Useful, I suppose I mean.'

'But the books you publish fulfil a lot of people's lives,' Jade protested.

'So why not mine?' he accepted. 'I've been searching——' He glanced at her. 'But I really think that time is over for me now,' he said with satisfaction.

She swallowed hard. 'David——'

'They're really on their toes around here,' he murmured, his attention briefly on the driving mirror to the side of his normal vision. 'You're either a very dangerous lot or they have a serious drink-driving problem in this area,' he teased.

She blinked at him, disconcerted by the sudden change of subject. 'Sorry?'

'We have another police car behind us.' He nodded in the direction of the blazing lights visible in his mirror. 'They joined us a few minutes ago.'

Jade turned in her seat to look at the car, quickly swinging back again to lean weakly against the head-rest behind her. Twice in as many days—*could* it be a coincidence still? And if not, what could they want with her after all this time?

'Uh-oh,' David groaned, and Jade tensed anew. 'They just turned off to follow another car; I hope the driver hasn't even looked at alcohol!'

Thank God they had gone! This was ridiculous, she hadn't felt this hounded in a very long time. And she wished she didn't have to feel that way now.

And yet the incident had thrown her again; what had been quite a pleasant evening was now shrouded in uncertainty, leaving her restless and ill at ease.

Wellington got up from his place in front of the fading fire to leave the room with a disgusted flick of his tail as soon as they entered the cottage.

'He's annoyed because I've been out two evenings in a row and left him all alone,' Jade murmured ruefully as the cat walked unhurriedly up the stairs.

David smiled. 'I would be pretty annoyed myself in the same circumstances.'

'Coffee?' she prompted brittly; after all, it was what he had come in for!

'Please,' he nodded, not in the least perturbed by her sudden frost, already moving to build up the fire.

He had made himself quite considerably 'at home' in the cottage the last couple of days, Jade recognised moodily as she prepared the coffee, and it wasn't a feeling she was comfortable with. In fact, she had been uncomfortable about one thing or another ever since she had first met David Kendrick!

She was even more disconcerted when she went back into the sitting-room to find the only illumination in the now cosily warm room was the glowing fire and the small coloured lights on the Christmas tree. And with the tray of coffee taking up both her hands, there wasn't a thing she could immediately do to remedy the intimacy!

David seated himself beside her on the sofa, his smile so innocent it couldn't possibly be sincere. 'All right.' He sat back defeatedly as she continued to look at him, her brows raised. 'It's not very subtle. But then, I didn't think you were in the mood to appreciate subtlety.' He grimaced. 'I can see now that you aren't in the mood to appreciate the "bang on the head" approach either!'

He was so bluntly honest, had been from the beginning, and he looked so much like a little boy caught with his hand inside the 'cookie jar', that Jade couldn't help but smile, the smile turning to a chuckle as he gave a cross-eyed look of self-derision.

They shared a warm smile as Jade poured out the coffee, their silence companionable as they sat drinking the hot brew in the quiet of the room, gazing at the beauty of the glittering Christmas tree.

'You'll have to help me a little and tell me what *will* induce you to come into my arms,' David suddenly groaned. 'Because I'm not sure how much longer I can wait to hold you!'

Jade turned to him sharply, frowning at the expression of pained longing in his eyes, feeling a sudden light-headedness as she swayed towards him.

It was the sign he had been waiting for, all the encouragement he needed; his arms were firm and warm about her, not imprisoning, but not about to release her either unless she demanded he do so. Which she didn't.

Electrified satin... It hadn't been her imagination this afternoon, nor indeed been blown out of proportion in her distress.

Electrified satin...

There could be no doubt about it, nor the fact that her reaction to his touch was just as volatile as it had been earlier. And just as insane. But this time she was unable to stop his kisses and caresses. Unable to deny David—or herself...

He felt so good to touch, the softness of the material of his shirt doing nothing to hide the hardness of his body beneath, her fingertips moving tentatively up his chest to his shoulders, clinging there as the smoothness of his lips moved to the fluttering column of her throat, his tongue probing moistly.

Oh, God, the sensation, the raw, burning sensation, unlike anything she had ever known before. Her throat arched as his lips moved in a downward path, pushing aside the high collar of her dress to probe the sensitive hollows beneath with moist pleasure.

Briefly, so very briefly, she tried to resist the questing hand that trailed lightly across the soft curve of her breasts, but it was only briefly and she groaned low in her throat as gentle fingers slowly parted the top three buttons of her dress.

That same hand burnt her flesh as his fingers rested above the soft curve of her breasts, not moving, just burning her with its warmth.

Their mouths fused, clinging damply together, moving together in erotic rhythm, Jade whimpering longingly with a need to know the full touch of that hand that still lay so hotly against her.

'David,' she gasped when their mouths parted. 'Please!' she voiced her need, moving impatiently against him. 'Why don't you—what are you waiting for?' she groaned in half-pain as he still made no effort to touch her more intimately, her body throbbing with a need to know that touch.

He closed lids over darkened blue eyes, wincing as he opened them again. 'Your cat to get his claws out of my thigh!' he told her calmly.

Jade blinked up at him dazedly for several seconds, the full impact of what he had just said not hitting her. And even when it did she still looked up at him disbelievingly, glancing down at his legs to see that Wellington did indeed have his claws stuck in David's flesh—and he didn't look as if he intended removing them in the near future, either!

'Good God!' she gasped as she struggled to sit up. 'Don't move,' she advised worriedly as she began the delicate operation of removing Wellington.

David's mouth quirked in spite of the pain he was in. 'I don't intend to.'

As fast as Jade removed Wellington's claws from David's leg he put them back in again, seeming determined to maim the poor man.

'And I thought earlier that he had taken to me!' David winced as the claws dug into his flesh with renewed vigour. 'He certainly knows how to put a dampener on the mood.' He massaged his punctured flesh as Jade at last managed to release him and shoo the cat out of the room. 'I suppose Wellington was just trying to tell me that he'll let me so close and no further.'

A little as she had since the first moment they met! 'I'm sorry.' She shrugged uncomfortably, not knowing what else to say.

'I'm not.' David stood up to move away from her. 'I told you earlier, I'm in no hurry, and that includes trying to seduce you in front of glowing fires—romantic as the idea seems,' he added ruefully. 'We have time, Jade,' he told her seriously. 'And I don't intend rushing you one step of the way.'

When Jade found the footprints around the house and garage the next day in the fresh fall of snow, she wasn't sure she was going to be able to stay in the area, to be hurried or not!

The snow had fallen during the night while she'd slept so restlessly, and when she got up at seven o'clock the next morning no one had called at the cottage, it was still too early even for the milkman to come, and yet a brief walk outside to clear the cobwebs from her tired brain had revealed those footprints in the pure carpet of snow that covered the ground.

The coincidence of the police car following them two nights in a row instantly came to mind, her panic renewed even though they had made no effort to approach her either time. They didn't need to approach her, just to let her know they were there, and if she made a complaint no doubt they would have a ready excuse for being there; David's belief that they were looking for Christmas revellers who had over-indulged would no doubt be as good as any. But she knew that wasn't really the reason, just as well as the police did. Why had they started hounding her again after all this time; what more could they want from her that hadn't already been taken?

As she heard the seven-thirty news on the radio, she finally knew the answer to that . . .

CHAPTER SIX

'IT HAS now been disclosed by the police that three prisoners escaped while being transferred from one prison to another two days ago. Two of the men have since been recaptured, but a third man is still being hunted by police. No further details are available at this time.'

The announcement, slotted in so casually among other general news, was the sort of information most people would listen to and then dismiss, forget even, paying no further attention to such a trivial matter. What did it matter to the general public that one prisoner had managed to escape, a prisoner they didn't even feel it necessary to be called by name?

But Jade wasn't just any member of the general public, she knew the man's name, was sure beyond a shadow of a doubt that it was Peter. And the police were watching her because they believed either that she would know where he was or that he might actually come here.

She wouldn't take a single step to help him, she despised him with all the loathing that she was capable of! As for him searching her out, she had every reason to know he wouldn't do that, either.

But the police had never believed her version of what had happened, had tried for weeks to get her to admit to something she had no knowledge of. Peter's own testimony that she hadn't been involved had done little to convince them, either. Not that she had wanted or welcomed his help anyway, she'd been so disgusted with him by then, hating him for using her to hurt others.

As he continued to hurt her. God, she had begun to actually hope last night, to imagine she might finally be able to put the past behind her, to make a new life for herself, possibly with David. But, even if that third prisoner didn't turn out to be Peter, the incident had served as a reminder that the past was all she could ever have, that there could be no real future for her, with David or any other man.

Before David had left the evening before they had chuckled together about Wellington's jealous behaviour, Jade accepting his invitation to spend the day with the family without hesitation. She had even been anticipating the day she would spend with him!

He was such a good man, made her feel so special because that was what he was and he seemed to care about her. Why, oh, why couldn't she have even had just a few days' happiness with him? It might have been enough——

No, it wouldn't, because she had it inside her to care very deeply for David Kendrick, already did care more than she should.

And it was over now, over before it had ever really begun.

She listened to the news bulletin on the radio every half-hour after that until ten o'clock, but nothing was added to that particular news item, and as she saw the Range Rover turn into the driveway she switched the radio off, no longer willing to listen so anxiously, certainly not for David to see that anxiety.

Sadness darkened her eyes as she caught sight of the Christmas tree glittering in the corner of the room on her way to open the door to him. The tree no longer glowed magically as it had yesterday, no longer represented putting the past behind her. That romantic glow had been ripped from her eyes to leave only stark reality; now it just looked like a slightly misshapen tree covered in lots of gaudy ornaments and over-bright lights.

'Good morning, good morning,' David greeted cheerfully, cupping her face in his hands to kiss her lightly on the lips. 'Ten-fifteen on the dot,' he announced with satisfaction as he strode forcefully inside the cottage. 'I've been up and wanting to come over and see you since six o'clock, but resisted the impulse.' He gave a self-derisive laugh. 'The people that know me in London probably wouldn't believe my self-control; I'm not known for my reserve there.'

She could imagine he wasn't. He was a forceful, dynamic man who had forged an empire for himself by sheer self-will and determination. Probably those women, Christi and Dizzy, would have trouble believing his forbearance last night, too!

She couldn't help the jealousy that shot through her at the thought of the role the other two women had in his life.

'Dizzy and Christi would probably be amazed,' she said brittly.

He chuckled. 'I'm sure they would,' he acknowledged, without apology for talking of the other two women in his life, his grin one of pure devilment. 'They're going to be even more surprised when I tell them I intend marrying you as soon as I can persuade you to have me!'

She could imagine surprise wasn't all the other two women would feel if he were ever to make such an announcement!

Not that he ever would, of course; she would make very certain that he knew she never would 'have him' before he returned to London. His life had been in ruins once already, and she wouldn't allow it to happen to him a second time because of something in her past.

It was already too late to prevent herself being hurt; she knew now that she had started to love him!

How could she help it? David was everything any woman could possibly want. Everything. But there was one thing she was determined he would never be, and that was hurt by what had happened eighteen months ago. She wouldn't allow that to touch him.

'I'm not going with you today.' Her voice was gruffly abrupt as she forced the words out. 'I—I don't feel too well after yesterday,' she hastily in-

vented as disappointment clouded his face. 'I think
I must have caught a chill when we were out in the
snow.'

Concern instantly darkened his ruggedly
handsome face. 'God, I never thought—you
shouldn't be out of bed if you feel ill,' he frowned,
already taking a firm hold of her arm and marching
her towards the stairs. 'I thought when I arrived
that you looked a little pale, but I put that down
to——'

'What do you think you're doing?' Jade gasped
as they reached the top of the stairs and he gently
pushed her towards her open bedroom door.

David gave her a mockingly chiding look, sitting
her on the bed and going down on his haunches in
front of her to take off her shoes. 'Helping you,
nothing else,' he derided her alarm.

'But——'

'God, your feet are like blocks of ice!' he scolded,
rubbing them between the warmth of his hands.

She had got her feet wet trudging out in the snow
this morning, and they hadn't felt warm since,
although she had felt little inclination to go and put
dry socks on.

There was something very erotic about having
David massage her feet in this way, and she pulled
sharply away from him.

'Steady,' he reproved, not releasing her.

'There's no need for this,' her voice was harsh.
'I just have a chill——'

'I can feel that.' He wasn't in the least deterred
by her dismissive attitude. 'I'm not surprised; it's

freezing up here.' He looked about the tiny room censoriously.

'The heat from the fire downstairs hasn't quite reached this far yet——'

'I think the best thing to do is get you into bed and then I'll go down and check on the heating,' David murmured to himself, almost as if she hadn't spoken—which she might just as well not have done, for all the notice he was taking of her. 'I'm not sure you should stay on here anyway if you aren't feeling well.' He shook his head.

Her eyes widened. 'Of course I'm staying here——'

'The heating is unpredictable at best,' he continued as if she still hadn't voiced a protest. 'And you can't possibly keep the fire going if you're ill up here in bed. I think it would be best if I took you back with me to the house——'

Jade gasped. 'I have no intention——'

'Unless, of course, you'll agree to the idea of my moving in here for a few days to take care of you?' He looked at her with mocking eyes. 'Just until you get over the worst of it.'

'It's only a slight chill, David,' she cut in firmly. 'Not enough to incapacitate me, just enough to make me feel slightly unsociable.' God, she wished she had never started the deception of the chill now; it was bringing more problems than it was solving! 'I'll be perfectly all right here on my own, in fact I would prefer it.' How she would prefer it! The idea was to get him out of her life, to keep him out, not to have him actually move in here with her!

The look David gave her told her he was perfectly well aware of her preference for being alone.

'I couldn't possibly leave you here alone when you aren't well,' he dismissed briskly. 'No matter what you would prefer,' he added as she seemed about to protest again.

She wanted to tell him she didn't care what *he* couldn't possibly do, but she knew from experience that David was perfectly capable of ignoring her, that he was already doing so, turning back the duvet and plumping up the pillows ready for her to get into bed.

'David...' Her voiced trailed off lamely as his brows rose silencingly. 'But I don't want to go to bed,' she sighed her impatience.

'The story of my life,' he drawled mockingly.

'Very funny,' she grimaced her irritation with his humour. 'I'll be perfectly all right if I just spend the day sitting quietly in front of the fire. There's no need to spoil everyone's day,' she told him determinedly.

'My day isn't being spoilt,' he dismissed easily. 'And Penny would never forgive me if I didn't take proper care of you.'

'I'll forgive you——'

'Besides,' David added teasingly, 'what would all your neighbours think of my concern for your welfare yesterday if today I calmly drive off and leave you when I know you're ill?'

'None of my neighbours know that I feel ill,' she protested exasperatedly.

'*I* know,' he mocked chidingly. 'Now get into this bed and stop being argumentative.'

Maybe if she just got into bed and pretended to be asleep he would go away and leave her alone! She could definitely add stubborn to that description of nice, and the two together were an unstoppable combination.

'Do you usually go to bed fully clothed?' he drawled as she lay down on the smooth sheet.

'When there's a man in my bedroom, yes!' She very firmly pulled up the duvet, glaring at him over the top of it.

David grinned down at her, his arms folded across the width of his chest. 'How often have you gone to bed in your clothes?'

Her mouth pursed. 'In other words, how often have I had a man in my bedroom?'

He raised innocent brows. 'I wouldn't presume to ask such a question.'

'That's good, because I have no intention of answering it, either!' Jade muttered, settling herself more comfortably beneath the warmth, not looking at him again as she pointedly closed her eyes.

She could sense his mocking gaze on her for several more minutes before he quietly left the room. She listened intently for the sound of the door closing as he left the cottage, the start of the Range Rover's engine. What she did hear was the tiny ting of the telephone as he picked up the receiver to make a call, followed by the soft murmur of his voice, and then silence. Absolute silence.

Damn it, he had really meant it about not leaving. She should have known that he wouldn't be affected by her feigning sleep—it had probably made him all the more determined to stay on!

She moved over on her back to stare up at the ceiling in silent frustration.

She had wanted to be alone today, to wait for—whatever. There would eventually be news of that third prisoner, there had to be, and whether it was Peter or not, she really needed to be alone when that happened.

If the police didn't come here first. That was always a possibility. They had kept away so far, simply keeping a silent watch on her and the cottage, but that couldn't continue if the prisoner really was Peter, as she believed it was.

The trembling she had known this morning, when she'd first heard the news, returned. She had thought this fear, at least, had gone from her life. Maybe it would never really be over for her, she would certainly never be able to forget that dark shadow that dogged her life. This incident, no matter what the outcome, had shown her that.

'You're supposed to be sleeping,' David chided as he put his head around the side of the door and saw her lying there on the bed wide-eyed, entering the room fully to look down at her reprovingly. 'You—my God, you're shivering,' he realised with concern, moving to sit on the side of the bed, taking hold of her hands in his.

Her hands did feel chilled, but she certainly wasn't shivering with cold; David had seen her trembling, and to correct him in his assumption would be to arouse his curiosity about that trembling, and the reason behind it.

At the moment he was preoccupied with her condition, 'Maybe I should call the doctor——'

'Don't be silly,' Jade dismissed impatiently, her pulse-rate giving a lurch at the suggestion; a doctor would soon spot her symptoms for what they were; fear, not the 'flu. 'If you called a doctor out every time you had a chill, the poor man would never be in his surgery. And there isn't a lot he can do for the condition.'

'Maybe not,' David conceded with a frown. 'Maybe a hot drink would help,' he murmured, half to himself. 'It certainly couldn't do any harm,' he said scowlingly, obviously worried about her as he went over to the doorway. 'Don't move,' he warned sternly.

She had no intention of going anywhere, was too comfortable, the warmth beneath the duvet finally reaching her, and she wriggled more fully beneath the covering with a weary sigh of satisfaction.

Maybe she didn't really have a chill, but the shock of that news item on the radio had certainly shaken her up. Added to the tiredness she felt after her restless night, it wasn't surprising she felt so exhausted.

So exhausted she didn't hear David return with the hot drink because she had fallen into a deep sleep...

*   *   *

The eyes. All staring. Accusing. Everywhere she looked those eyes stared back at her. Disgust. Accusation. All of them hostile.

Except one pair. Navy blue eyes caressed her warmly, loved her, wanted her, embraced her. She ran towards those eyes, towards the warmth they offered, towards the arms that now reached out to her.

But as she reached those arms they began to disappear, to dissolve, and the warmth to fade with them, leaving only the cold loneliness.

'Don't go,' she sobbed pleadingly. 'Oh, please, don't go.' Her arms reached out in desperate need. 'David!' she cried his name, knowing he was the source of that warmth.

'Jade...' Those warm arms enfolded her now, gathering her close. 'Jade, I'm here.'

She clung to him, sighing her shaky relief when he didn't disappear beneath her touch, resting against him as she slowly relaxed, knowing she was safe now, that David wouldn't hurt her, ever.

She had had the strangest dream—frightening, oppressive. She had wanted to escape, to get out of the fear, but she hadn't been able to break free, had had to live through the nightmare.

And then the warmth had come, an engulfing warmth that still comforted her and held her. She settled more comfortably against that warmth, her nose twitching as the softness of wool tickled her.

Jade pushed the irritant away, feeling the hardness beneath her hand as she did so, puzzled by it but reluctant to relinquish the last hold she had on sleep and the lingering feelings of warmth she had so briefly known. Feelings so long denied her she was afraid to give them up now in case she never had them again, her eyes closed against the intruding outside world.

But the puzzle of that hardness beneath wool still troubled her, and even at the risk of losing the protective warmth she knew she had to open her eyes and solve that puzzle.

The warmth didn't fade as she raised her lids, but she was instantly lost in the navy blue depths above her, at last knowing what the woollen hardness was—a man's muscular chest!

'David...' she breathed wonderingly.

He nodded. 'I came to check on you because I could hear you moving about restlessly, and you asked me not to go,' he explained his presence apologetically, his face in shadow where he had pulled the curtains earlier against the daylight.

Jade remembered the dream, *David's* eyes welcoming her, wanting her, felt again the warmth his arms had offered, her fear that they would leave her. And they hadn't left her, *David* hadn't left her, was still holding her protectively against him, where the rest of the world couldn't touch her.

She smiled up at him tremulously. 'I'm glad I did.' Her eyes glowed with inner emotion.

Uncertainty flickered across the strength of his face. 'You aren't awake properly yet——'

'Because I'm not pushing you away?' she said self-derisively. 'Oh, I'm awake, David, completely awake. And I know exactly what I'm doing,' she added huskily as she slowly put her arms up about his neck and pulled him down to her.

He frowned down at her still. 'I'm not sure that you do——'

'David,' she rebuked firmly. 'Unless you don't want to kiss me?' she challenged, auburn brows arched questioningly over dark green eyes.

'Don't provoke me, Jade,' he sighed his impatience with her levity at a time when they should be so deadly serious.

Her expression softened, knowing he was hesitating for her sake, the hardness of his own body, the dark passion in his eyes, telling of his own need. And he had no need to hold back because of her; she knew that this was right between them. 'I just want you to make love to me,' she told him with simple honesty, her jade-green gaze unwavering.

His breath was sharply indrawn, and he shook his head. 'Don't think that just because we find ourselves in this—position,' he indicated the closeness of their bodies in the bed, 'it has to—lead—to anything.'

She smoothed the ruggedness of his cheek with gentle fingertips. 'If I didn't realise that your concern is for me, I could be quite hurt by your seeming reluctance to make love to me,' she teased.

'You know damn well that I——'

'I *do* know,' she soothed his explosive outburst. 'And I'm equally sure that this is what I want for myself,' she told him steadily.

He swallowed audibly. 'You are?'

'Yes.' She smiled with quiet confidence in her decision. 'And David,' she added softly, their lips only a fraction of an inch apart now, 'I've *never* gone to bed in my clothes before.'

His eyes glowed fiercely possessive at the admission she had made, his mouth moving to claim her sweetly before passion exploded between them and the sweetness turned to fiery need.

David was the lover she had been waiting for all her life, a man of strength and gentleness, rather than power and weakness, and she knew only pride in his gaze as he slowly removed the clothes that now seemed so unimportant to either of them, knowing what he would see, her high-breasted, narrow-waisted body a gift she had saved especially for him, although it had taken her until now to admit that even to herself.

But now she knew, her breasts fitting perfectly into his hands as his lips and tongue loved first one fiery tip and then the other before claiming them with heated moisture.

He was like a child against her, and yet the heat that engulfed her body could only come from this man, an aching need joining that heat to totally enslave and claim her.

She moved up on her knees on the bed beside him in a need to know the warmth of that hard body she had only touched through wool and denim, glorying in the male perfection of him as he helped her to remove his clothing, knowing the strength of their need for each other as his body trembled uncontrollably at her touch, the satin hardness pulsating with that need.

'You're so beautiful.' He caressed her with hands that trembled slightly.

'So are you,' she told him tremulously, no embarrassment or awkwardness between them, only beauty and emotion.

'I don't want to hurt you,' David breathed shakily as his mouth moved caressingly against her throat.

'You could never hurt me.' In that moment she had never been so sure of anything.

'I may not be able to prevent it,' he told her with husky regret.

'If there is pain, it will only be the kind that will bring pleasure,' she assured him softly. 'The pleasure of joining my body to yours.'

He drew in his breath raggedly. 'It's difficult to remain sane when you say things like that.'

'I don't want us to remain sane.' Jade gazed at him longingly.

'And lord knows I don't,' he muttered self-derisively.

'Then let's go quietly insane together.' She knelt proudly before him, her body beckoning.

They melded together perfectly as David came up beside her on the bed to heatedly claim her lips once more, the disparity in their heights when they were standing not apparent in that moment, breasts against a hard chest, their thighs cupped together perfectly, both of them aware only of the need they had to be just one flesh moving together in perfect harmony.

The pain, if it could be called that, lasted only briefly, unimportant, as that throbbing passion made their movements as beautiful as any ballet, a slow and tender building of pleasure until it was too late for tenderness and only throbbing need and burning desire remained, their movements frenzied now, desperate, climaxed by tiny cries of mutual pleasure found and received, their movements relaxing slowly before they fell damply together against the bedclothes.

Beautiful surrender, not just for her, but for David too. He had surrendered his heart as well as his body, and it was a moment Jade would cherish for the rest of her life. Because she had surrendered her heart, too.

How could any woman this man chose to love help but feel the same way?

And how long before she saw that light of love ripped from his eyes to be replaced by—what? Contempt? Disgust? Hate?

Dear God, she didn't think she could bear to see any of those emotions in eyes that had been misty with love!

As she saw Peter's photograph flash on the television screen as the third prisoner, the one the police were still searching for, later that evening, she knew she might not have any choice, that she was going to have to suffer through the nightmare again, and

that this time there would be no David's arms to
protect her warmly from those accusingly hostile
eyes; once he knew the truth about her, his would
probably be among them!

CHAPTER SEVEN

DAVID insisted on preparing her a light snack and serving it to her in bed, feeding her each mouthful of the fluffy golden eggs and toast, his arm supportive about her shoulders as she sipped the hot, sweet coffee, before he would even contemplate eating his own food.

And then he removed the tray from the bed between them and they made love again.

It was just as beautiful as before, made even more poignantly so for Jade because she had the inner knowledge that this would probably be her last time in his arms, her last chance to know the warmth he gave her.

That knowledge made it doubly difficult for her to be parted from him later that evening, and yet she knew she couldn't allow him to stay the night as he wanted to do; it was only a matter of time before the police no longer only watched from a distance. David accepted that they had her reputation to think of with the village people and also with Penny and Simon. It was no longer those things that worried Jade, but it was easier to let David go on believing it was.

'I don't want any clouds to mar our future happiness together.' He kissed her lingeringly on the lips as they stood close together in the living-room as he prepared to leave.

Pain darkened her eyes; after the encouragement she had given him today he no doubt felt he had more than a passing right to assume she was more open to his suggestion that they should get married. The truth of it was, she was even less open to that idea than ever before; at least before today she had been able to look on it as fanciful foolishness on his part; now she just knew the idea was totally impossible.

'No clouds.' David smoothed the frown from between her eyes. 'And no more doubts, either. You couldn't have made love to me the way you did if you didn't love me.'

It was true, all of it. She had made love to him, and she did love him.

He smiled gently down at her silence. 'I know, it's still too new to take in. But we have the rest of Christmas to get used to the idea, and in the New Year we can——'

'How you do love to make plans,' she teased huskily, her fingertips light against his hard cheek.

His smile became rueful. 'And how you do love to avoid them,' he chided.

Jade shrugged, moving slightly away from him, holding her robe wrapped tightly about her. 'I'm just not as impetuous as you are...'

He gave a soft chuckle. 'That's something else I'm not known for in the business world. You make me throw caution to the wind—but I suppose I can stop being so damned impatient now,' he announced cheerfully. 'We belong together, and we both know it.'

She swallowed hard. 'It's getting late,' she urged him, anxious to be alone now.

'At least Wellington has decided he likes me again now.' David moved down on his haunches to stroke the purring cat as he lay in front of the fire.

She didn't doubt that was because Wellington could see how happy David made her; the cat wasn't really in the least possessive, he just wanted a happy and contented mistress to feed him. Jade didn't walk around in a daze when she was happy. And she didn't forget to feed him then, either. And he even got titbits from her plate to eat when this man was about. Yes, Wellington had decided he liked him again.

She had never stopped liking him—that was the problem!

David straightened, moving to kiss her lightly on the lips. 'I wish I could stay... But I know I can't,' he accepted ruefully. 'So I'll be on my way.'

'Could I have—could I be alone tomorrow?' She looked at him with widely pleading eyes, knowing that if he insisted on seeing her she wouldn't be able to say no to him.

He looked down at her searchingly, his expression softening with love. 'Of course,' he readily agreed. 'But don't forget Penny is throwing one of her famous parties in the evening.'

She had forgotten, but it didn't matter. Almost twenty-four hours on her own should be enough to shore up her sadly depleted defences. Not that they

would ever be quite that strong again, her love for
David weakening her in a way she had hoped never
to be weak again.

'I won't forget,' she nodded abruptly.

'Now I really had better go and let you get some
rest.' He seemed to feel her distant behaviour was
due to tiredness. 'A fine nurse I've made today,'
he said ruefully. 'I've succeeded in tiring the
patient out rather than letting her rest.'

Warm colour darkened her cheeks at the mischievous glitter in his eyes. 'All the more reason for
me to have tomorrow on my own to recuperate,'
she bit out tartly.

David held up his hands defensively. 'I've
already conceded tomorrow,' he reminded her
gently, his expression slightly reproachful.

She knew that; she just needed to assert some
control, to re-establish that distance she needed to
put herself back on that course of self-survival. If
she could survive loving a man as wonderful as
David and having to let him go...

'Get some sleep now.' He lightly grasped her arms
to kiss her firmly on the lips. 'I'll call you
tomorrow. Just to check how you are,' he defended
ruefully at her frowning look, pulling on his jacket
to tug the collar up about his neck and face against
the driving snow that had begun to fall a short time
ago.

Jade stood at the doorway and watched him go,
anxious for these last glimpses of him, because by
tomorrow—— Oh, God, she didn't want to think
about tomorrow.

David turned back after he had gone only a few steps. 'Go back inside before you catch pneumonia,' he shouted against the wind that whistled about him in the icy darkness.

Flakes of snow were clinging to her hair and clothes, melting on the warmth of her face and hands, but she made no effort to move, watching until he had climbed into the Range Rover and driven off with a wave of his hand before turning back inside.

She closed the door slowly behind her, lost in her own thoughts, miserable thoughts of the loneliness she had to return to. She glanced down as she felt Wellington rub against her calf. 'Except for you, boy,' she choked as she bent to pick him up. 'No offence to you, darling,' she told him gruffly. 'But I don't think you're going to be enough any more.' Tears cascaded down her cheeks and into the snowy white fur as she hugged him to her, her face buried against his purring body. 'I love him, Wellington. I love him so much!' she sobbed brokenly, her control slipping completely.

How could she have come to love him so quickly, so deeply? How could she have allowed it to happen, for both their sakes? But she had needed— oh, God, how she had *needed*——

She gave a shaky sigh as Wellington seemed to look up at her reprovingly. 'I know, I was being selfish. I *am* selfish,' she groaned self-disgustedly, dropping down on to the sofa, her wind-tousled head thrown back against its softness, closing her eyes as the tears silently continued to fall.

The silence instantly closed in about her, with only the howling of the wind outside to alleviate the oppressive stillness that suddenly surrounded her.

She couldn't stand it, not when she had been surrounded by so much love and happiness since the moment she woke in David's arms, and she leaned forward abruptly to switch on the television set.

But that was little comfort either, the picture just flashing in front of her eyes, meaningless people who couldn't even begin to fill the sudden void in her life.

She had been staring at the photograph displayed on the screen behind the newsreader for some seconds before she realised that it was Peter. She scrambled forward on to the carpet to turn the sound up to an audible level, on her knees in front of the set as she heard confirmation of what she had already known within her heart.

'—it is hoped that, now the escaped man's name and photograph have been distributed by police, his capture will be forthcoming. And now we turn to the North of England, where——'

Jade no longer listened to what the attractive newscaster was saying, having heard all she needed to. She sat back on her heels with a sigh that was almost as heavy as the weight she now carried on her shoulders. The weight of guilt. Not for anything that had happened in the past—although goodness knew she had enough to blame herself for about that!—but for taking David's love so selfishly today.

She buried her face in her hands and wept.

David hadn't asked about past men in her life, although he had to know there had been some. But even if he had asked she couldn't have told him about Peter, a man she had loved with such joy that when she had learnt the shattering truth about him it had made it so much harder to bear.

David loved her with that same joy now, she was sure of it, even though the words had never been spoken. How much deeper he was going to be hurt when *this* all shattered about the two of them.

It was so easy to *say* she shouldn't have allowed him into her heart; it was another thing completely to keep him out. And because of the nature of the man he was, she knew that getting over him was going to be an impossibility.

She gave a guilty start as a knock sounded on the door, staring at it like a startled doe.

It had to be David, he had to have come back for some reason, she realised in dismay, brushing hurriedly at the tears that still dampened her cheeks. She couldn't allow him to see her like that, wasn't up to answering the questions that would engender.

The two men standing outside in the driving snow didn't need blue uniforms to proclaim their profession, the casual clothes and heavy winter coats doing nothing to disguise the fact that they were policemen.

Jade recoiled as if she had been struck, caught completely unawares. And then she admonished herself for showing such a reaction; she had been expecting them for some time, after all. In fact, she was surprised they had taken this long to come and talk to her.

She faced them with calm dignity now that she had herself under control again. 'Please come in, gentlemen,' she invited stiffly.

'Miss Roberts, we're——'

'I know who you are,' she calmly interrupted the older of the two men as he seemed determined they should introduce themselves in their official capacity. Who else but policemen would know her real name in this vicinity?

'Detective-Inspector Shelton, and Detective-Sergeant James,' the man continued as if she hadn't spoken, although the younger man looked a little uncomfortable about the intrusion, a fact he quickly disguised as he saw she was looking at him.

'I hope we haven't interrupted anything.' He looked pointedly at the television set as it still continued to play, the sound not too intrusive, although it was noticeable.

Detective-Inspector Shelton made a point of looking at the watch on his wrist. 'Been watching the news, have you, Miss Roberts?' Grey-blue eyes pinned her to the spot. 'It *is* Miss Roberts, isn't it?'

He was good, Jade realised abstractedly, knowing he meant to unnerve her. But she was used to experts, had learnt to distance herself from the pressure they could exert while seeming to be polite. 'Why don't you just get to the point of your visit?' She moved impatiently to switch off the television set.

'Unless you would prefer us to use the name Mellors——'

'I'm sure none of us has any time to waste,' she prompted waspishly, wishing she had on something more substantial than her robe for this confrontation, all the more defensive because she felt at such a disadvantage dressed like this.

Grey brows rose over those hard grey-blue eyes, iron-grey hair brushed rigidly back from his face, deep lines grooved beside his pale features, as if the life he lived had totally disillusioned him more than once. And in the profession he had chosen to pursue, maybe that wasn't so surprising. 'I'm sure none of us has, Miss Roberts,' he drawled. 'But we didn't like to announce our presence before this.'

Jade looked at him blankly for several seconds, and then, as his meaning became clear, humiliated colour darkened her cheeks, pain clouding her eyes. They had been watching from a distance all the time David was here, had—had—— Oh, God!

'We thought it might make things less awkward for you if we waited until after your—guest had left,' the younger man explained quietly.

She sat down heavily in an armchair, all pretence of self-confidence gone. And not even the fact that these two men had probably desired just this result made any difference to the way she now felt; David had seemed like a beauty completely separate from this part of her life, and now even that time with him had been made to seem as ugly as the rest of it.

'You will have realised that Peter Gifford has escaped from prison?' Detective-Inspector Shelton prompted with husky intent.

That was right, hit her when she was already down. But then, wasn't that just the way they were trained to carry out these sort of investigations? Jade acknowledged with dull pain.

'Has Gifford been in touch with you, Miss Roberts?' Once again the younger man was gentle with her, but Jade distrusted even that, knowing it was another part of the routine, one man tough, the other seeming more approachable and sympathetic.

'Been in touch with me?' she repeated incredulously. 'Been in touch with me?' she said again, more shrilly this time. 'I've spent the majority of the last eighteen months trying to forget I ever knew the man; why should he be in touch with *me*?'

The older man held up his hands defensively. 'Miss Roberts, we're just making enquiries——'

She stood up forcefully, her eyes blazing, her hands twisted painfully together. 'I was subjected to the same sort of "enquiries" eighteen months ago,' she snapped tautly. 'And unless you have some charges you wish to make against me, I suggest you——'

'Miss Roberts, please believe me when I say we have no intention——'

'If some of our colleagues were a little—heavy-handed, in the past then I apologise,' the older man cut in with slow emphasis. 'But these investigations are completely separate from those, and we——'

'Do you, or do you not, have any charges you wish to make against me?' she insisted through clenched teeth, so tense she felt as if she might snap with the strain of it.

'Of course we have no charges to make,' Detective-Inspector Shelton said impatiently. 'We're just making routine enquiries, and as you were once involved with Gifford we naturally——'

'Naturally,' she cut in sarcastically. 'But I have no intention of "helping the police with their enquiries",' she bit out harshly. 'Now, if you have nothing further to say,' she wrenched the door open, standing rigidly beside it as the snow blew inside in gusts, 'I would like you to leave.'

The younger man looked at her sympathetically. 'We understand this is difficult for you, Miss Roberts, but we have a job to do——'

'I doubt you understand the first thing about how I feel,' she choked scornfully. How could these two men possibly understand?

Detective-Inspector Shelton gave a heavy sigh. 'We're sorry to have bothered you, Miss Roberts.'

The blaze in her eyes told him exactly what he could do with his perfunctory apology.

'We realise you're upset, Miss Roberts, but if you should happen to hear from Gifford——' He broke off uncomfortably as the blaze in her eyes became a fierce fire.

'I won't!' Jade rasped as the two men reached the door, daring him to dispute the claim with the proud lift of her chin.

The older man shook his head. 'I wish you would realise that we're only trying to help——'

'The best way you can help *me* is to leave!' she grated forcefully.

He sighed. 'You have our names if you should change your mind——'

'I won't change my mind because I won't hear from Peter.' She was shaking with her anger, staring rigidly at the wall opposite as first one policeman left and then the other, the latter, Detective-Sergeant James, giving a regretful shake of his head as he passed.

Jade closed the door with controlled movements behind them, the gusting wind outside muffling the sound of their departing vehicle, but she did hear them leave, and relaxed with shaky relief.

Not only had those men brought the past back into sharp focus, but they had also managed, in the last few minutes, to degrade something that had been so beautiful to her. Not with what they had said particularly, but with what they *hadn't* said.

The nightmare of having once loved Peter Gifford just went on and on and on...

CHAPTER EIGHT

THERE was no soft thud of snow on the window-pane to wake her up this morning, no gentle laughter with David in the snow, with them both soaking wet, but happy and relaxed together. There wasn't even a gentle awakening, with Wellington stretching lazily at her side as he started his day; the hammering below on the door had caused him to leap off the bed with an indignant yowl, digging his claws into Jade's thigh as he leapt across her.

Which was why she had awoken with such a sickening start of surprise.

The clock beside the bed told her it was almost nine o'clock, late by her standards, but she had had such a restless night's sleep that her lids felt like sandpaper rasping across her eyes as she moved them up and down to clear her vision.

And she didn't want to go downstairs and face whoever it was on the other side of that door.

She didn't want to face anyone ever again. In fact, if she could have done, she would have left last night without having to see David again, but the falling snow had made her departure impossible. And now it seemed she wasn't to make her escape today without at least one confrontation.

The pounding on the door grew louder, more insistent, and she knew the culprit wasn't about to be fobbed off by the lack of response so far to that determined knocking.

Wellington was glaring fiercely at the front door when Jade got down the stairs a few seconds later; if it was David—and she couldn't think of anyone else that persistent!—then he was definitely going to be out of favour with the cat again!

The banging came to an abrupt halt as soon as Jade threw back the bolt at the bottom of the door in preparation of turning the key in the lock, and she felt her tension rise as she hesitated about doing the latter, a sick feeling in the pit of her stomach as she just stood there. What if David had realised who she was after all the renewed publicity in the media about Peter? What if——

'Jade, open this door,' she was told firmly, the voice definitely female.

Jade dazedly did as she was told, her fingers fumbling slightly with the key.

'Jade, thank God!' The woman outside threw herself gratefully into her arms.

Jade was still so stunned that she couldn't think straight, and then the relief at the identity of her visitor washed over her, filled with a choking exhilaration. 'Cathy!' She tightly returned the other woman's hug. 'Oh, God, Cathy!' The tears began to fall; she was hardly able to believe that her best friend was really here. She had felt so alone until now, so devastatingly alone——

'I know, love. I know.' It wasn't until Cathy answered her that Jade realised she had spoken out loud, Cathy still holding her as she looked down at her compassionately. 'But you aren't alone any more,' she assured her with quiet confidence.

Jade pulled her friend fully inside, closing the door to shut out the icy cold, although the act didn't do anything to dispel the chill inside the cottage. Not that that was important at this moment; she could see by Cathy's expression that the heating— or lack of it—was the last thing on Cathy's mind at the moment too.

Cathy Gilbert was the exact opposite of herself to look at: tall and blonde, with a natural grace and sophistication that even the denims and thick jumper over a blouse couldn't disguise. She looked as if she should be an actress or a fashion model with her beauty, instead of the personal assistant— to one of the most difficult men to work for in the City—that she was in reality.

Jade gave a heavy sigh, pushing back her own untidy locks. 'You heard about Peter?'

'On the news late last night.' Cathy nodded acknowledgment, even her voice sexily attractive. The way that she looked often fooled people into ignoring the fact that she was also a very intelligent woman. At twenty-six she had managed to fend off even the most persistent of male advances, and Jade had a feeling that was because she had more than an inkling of affection for her infuriatingly demanding boss, Dominic Reynolds. 'I came as soon as I heard.'

She gave a rueful smile. 'And Dominic meekly allowed you to do that?'

Grey eyes flashed. 'I didn't ask him, I *told* him I was coming!'

Jade's brows rose; she knew Cathy wasn't in the habit of 'jumping' when Dominic Reynolds said 'jump', but she also knew Cathy didn't openly challenge him either. Usually. 'I haven't caused friction between the two of you, have I?' she winced regretfully.

'No more than there usually is,' her friend dismissed carelessly. 'It won't do Dominic any harm at all to realise that helping one of my friends is more important to me than being his damned personal assistant!'

Jade sensed a hidden story behind the remarks, but she could also tell from the reckless glint in Cathy's eyes that she wasn't yet ready to talk about it. 'He would never be stupid enough to really upset you,' she drawled. 'You're too good at your job.'

'And always too damned available,' Cathy snapped a little bitterly. 'At least, he *assumes* that I am. Damn him.'

There *was* something new, an undercurrent, in Cathy's relationship with Dominic Reynolds that hadn't been there before, and at any other time Jade might have tried to persuade her friend to tell her about it, but she knew by the stubborn set to Cathy's jaw that she wouldn't be successful today, that for the moment Cathy would only discuss Jade's own problem.

And, lord knew, that was bad enough!

'What on earth did Peter have to escape from prison for?' Cathy said crossly.

Jade shrugged. 'He still has quite a lot of his sentence to finish——'

'I didn't mean that quite as literally as it sounded,' her friend said ruefully. 'I just meant, why on earth did he have to *do* something like that?' She scowled, her beauty in no way marred.

Jade had never been able to understand why Dominic Reynolds didn't see and appreciate that beauty, but he seemed to be a man who was completely engrossed in his career, a man who didn't see women as women at all, except as an unnecessary diversion to what was really important to him: his business empire.

'He probably heard that you were finally putting your life back together and wanted to ruin that for you, too!' her friend continued scathingly.

There had never been any love lost between Cathy and Peter, but since Peter's behaviour eighteen months ago Cathy had been openly antagonistic. As Jade had herself!

But she doubted Cathy realised just how much she had been 'putting her life back together', just how much Peter had robbed her of this time. Unless she had already been to the Kendrick house? Spoken to David himself?

She looked at her friend warily. For all that she and Cathy had been friends for years, she had realised from talking to Penny the last few days that Cathy was more than a little fond of David, in a brotherly fashion, of course, Penny had hastily assured her. Cathy might not feel too happy about the possibility of her having hurt him, unintentional though it might be.

But Cathy didn't seem angry, not with her, at least.

'He succeeded,' Jade answered dully.

Cathy looked at her sharply. 'You aren't thinking of doing anything silly?'

'Such as?' she prompted flatly.

'Such as leaving here,' her friend said impatiently. 'You told me you love it here,' she reminded Jade of what she had written in her letters to her since coming to Devon.

'I do——'

'Then you have no reason to leave now,' Cathy told her firmly.

'Peter is on the loose out there somewhere, and he's already been the cause of two policemen paying me a not-too-friendly visit, and you claim I have no reason to want to leave!' She shook her head in nervous agitation.

'Penny and Simon are well aware of your involvement with Peter in the past——'

'But my pupils' parents, unfortunately, aren't,' Jade reminded her with self-derision.

'But——'

'They would probably form a lynch-mob if they did know,' she added bitterly.

Cathy gave an impatient sigh. 'You were never charged with anything——'

'That doesn't alter the fact that I was involved in the thing right up to my neck!' Tears glistened on her lashes. 'No, I'm finished here, Cathy.' She shook her head, knowing she was finished in more ways than one. 'I'm very grateful to Penny and Simon for giving me this chance, but I intend leaving for London as soon as I can make my excuses to them.' She dared not even think about saying goodbye to David. 'I'm sure they will understand in the circumstances.'

'You're running away,' her friend accused.

Her eyes flashed. '*Yes*, I'm running away! As fast as the weather will allow.' She frowned out of the window at the blanket of snow on the ground, for the first time noticing the Audi Quattro in the driveway. 'Yours?' She turned to Cathy.

'Dominic's,' her friend grimaced. 'Once he realised I was serious about coming here he was only too happy to provide my transport.'

At the risk of losing the best personal assistant he had ever had if he didn't, Jade wouldn't be surprised!

'It really is good to see you,' she told Cathy emotionally.

Her friend's expression softened. 'You, too. Although I had thought it would be under different circumstances.' Cathy frowned. 'You can't let him chase you away from here, Jade,' she added pleadingly. 'They will have recaptured him within a few days, and a couple of days after that he will have been forgotten again.' She shook her head. 'He simply isn't worth completely upsetting your life for a second time.'

'I wish I had realised that the *first* time.' Jade gave a derisive laugh that completely lacked amusement. 'But I—oh, no,' she gave a pained groan as an all-too-familiar, silver-coloured Range Rover pulled into the driveway behind the Audi.

She didn't for one moment believe Penny and Simon had broken their confidence to her by talking to David about Peter, and David *had* promised he wouldn't come here today, so what other reason could he have for turning up now? Unless—oh, God, she couldn't bear it if somehow the media had already picked up on her part in Peter's past and had dragged the whole sordid business up once again!

She gave a shudder of distaste as she remembered the horror she had known eighteen months ago when she had seen her own photograph next to Peter's on the front page of the daily newspapers. Of course, she had looked a little different then—about forty pounds heavier in weight, for one thing!—but perhaps she was still recognisable from those photographs to someone who knew her well. And David had come to know her very well in the last few days, intimately so.

'What is it?' Cathy had come to stand at her side, looking out of the window too. 'David!' she cried excitedly, turning to run and open the door to him as he came down the pathway.

'Cath——' But she was too late to stop the other woman running out into the snow to launch herself into David's arms, laughing and talking at the same time as she did so.

David looked initially stunned at being assaulted by a blonde-haired woman he didn't at first recognise, a heavy scowl crossing his features. But, as he realised who his assailant was, his smile was one of open pleasure, his arms closing about Cathy as he swung her around in the snow, much to her obvious delight.

Jade watched them enviously. Oh, not because of the affection that was so apparent between them, she could see that was that of a brother and sister. No, she just wished she felt free enough to show her own pleasure so completely without restraint at seeing him. As it was, she wasn't quite sure what sort of reception she was going to get from David, didn't know yet what he was doing here.

The other couple were walking towards the cottage now, their arms about each other's waists as Cathy chattered excitedly, and David smiled down at her indulgently as he listened.

Jade tensed as they entered the cottage, looking searchingly at David. His enigmatic expression didn't tell her anything at all about his thoughts or feelings, although he did look slightly grim around the eyes.

'David's here,' Cathy announced unnecessarily, unable to take her glowing eyes off him. 'I can't believe it!' She shook her head, obviously overjoyed to see him once again. 'Just as I don't believe there isn't a story behind that black eye,' she added teasingly. 'Although he insists there isn't!'

The fact that she *was* seeing David again after all this time, that he was apparently back among the family, seemed to have blinded Cathy to the most obvious fact of all: David was *here*, at Jade's cottage, and definitely without the knowledge that Cathy would be here. But it was a lack of vision on Cathy's part that Jade was grateful for at this moment. Cathy wouldn't give her any peace at all once she realised she and David had become more than friends since his arrival here, and she hoped to have left the area herself before that happened.

Navy blue eyes looked at Jade compellingly, and she met that gaze guardedly, still uncertain as to the reason David had altered their arrangements and come to see her this morning, after all. Although she was grateful to him for not giving Cathy the details about that black eye.

'Your telephone line is down,' he explained softly as he was easily able to guess her thoughts.

She looked surprised, turning to frown at the offending instrument as it sat so innocently on the table; as if frowning at it was going to do any good! 'I had no idea,' she said weakly, wishing she had at least known that fact so that she could have been half prepared for his arrival, when he hadn't managed to reach her by telephone as he had said he would this morning, instead of being caught completely unawares.

'Unfortunately, so are a lot of others,' he shrugged, very attractive in a dark green jumper and faded denims beneath his leather jacket, 'so I don't think you'll be treated as a priority.'

'It doesn't matter,' she dismissed abruptly. 'Although it was very nice of you to come out and check up on me,' she added awkwardly, more for Cathy's benefit than anything else.

'I thought you had—company—when I first drove up,' he told her, his eyes narrowed.

'And aren't I company?' Cathy pretended indignation, her eyes twinkling mischievously.

'Not the sort I meant,' David drawled.

He had believed, when he saw the Audi outside, that she had had the ulterior motive of another man for not wanting to see him today. And that was the reason he had been scowling when he arrived. It was a relief to know that the past hadn't all blown up in her face. At least, not yet.

Cathy pouted prettily. 'I do think Penny and Simon could have telephoned me to let me know you were here.' She shook her head reprovingly. 'I would have come down here all the sooner if I had known.'

David gave Jade a piercing look before turning his attention to the other woman. 'Maybe they didn't think Dominic could stand the competition,' he teased.

It didn't surprise Jade at all that David should speak of the other man with familiarity; the two men moved in the same business circles.

'There would have been no competition,' Cathy dismissed scathingly. 'As soon as I had heard you were here I would have come down. It's been too long, David,' she added softly, her face full of emotional affection.

'Yes,' he acknowledged gruffly. 'But don't you think you should let Penny and Simon know you are here? Penny was so sure you weren't going to make it again this year either.' He shook his head ruefully. 'The names she's been calling Dominic...! I think I should have a word with him, you know; he's obviously working you much too hard if he can't even give you Christmas off!'

'As bosses go, he's pretty awful,' Cathy conceded.

'But?' David arched dark brows.

She looked at him slightly defensively. 'Is there a but?'

He returned her gaze speculatively. 'I would say so—but that is obviously another story,' he dismissed shruggingly at Cathy's warning glare that he was trespassing on a very touchy subject. 'From the look of Jade, we've both caught her at an inconvenient time.' He lightly drew attention to the fact that she was still wearing her dressing-gown when they were both fully clothed. He turned back to Cathy with a puzzled frown. 'You must have driven most of the night to get here this early; there's nothing wrong, is there?'

'Not at all,' she dismissed breezily, her gaze unwavering in her lie. 'The opportunity came to leave and so I took it!'

'Before Dominic changed his mind,' David drawled understandingly.

'Exactly.' Cathy gave him a companionable grin.

He nodded before turning back to Jade. 'How are you feeling this morning?'

That bogus chill came back to haunt her once again! She wished she had never invented the damned thing.

'I feel fine, thank you,' she answered abruptly. 'Although a nice long soak in a hot bath wouldn't come amiss,' she added pointedly. After all, these two could go off somewhere and reminisce without her. She badly needed the time to do her packing.

'Have you been ill?' Cathy instantly frowned her concern. 'You should have told me——'

'It was only a chill.' Her dismissal was made irritably this time, annoyed that David had drawn attention to yesterday's indisposition—or rather, the lack of it!

'Nevertheless——'

'I have a feeling Jade would rather we changed the subject,' David drawled as her eyes flashed at Cathy's continued concern.

'But—oh, where did you come from?' Cathy enthused as Wellington walked haughtily into the room to see what all the noise was about, going down on her haunches to call to him, gently stroking his silky fur as he deigned to stand in front of her. 'What's your name?' she cooed at the disdainful cat.

'Wellington—for obvious reasons,' David supplied drily at Jade's lack of response.

She had got to the stage where she just wanted them both to leave, something neither of them seemed inclined to do!

'You're beautiful,' Cathy told Wellington admiringly. 'You never mentioned in your letters that you have a cat now,' she lightly scolded Jade, still stroking the silky cat, who now seemed to consider that anyone entering Jade's home had to pass his approval, too! Cathy obviously did.

'He's a stray.' Jade shrugged frowningly, as if that explained her lack of explanation earlier.

'He doesn't look like a stray to me,' her friend admonished teasingly. 'You surely don't intend to leave him behind when you go?' She sounded scandalised at the idea.

'Of course Wellington will go with me, *when* I go,' she muttered the last warningly.

'Well, I should think so.' Cathy took absolutely no notice of the warning, her attention back on the cat as he twirled in and out of her hands for extra cuddles. 'It would never do to leave this beautiful creature behind.'

'No,' Jade grated, frowning darkly, keeping her eyes averted as she sensed David's searching gaze on her.

'All this talk of your leaving,' he spoke slowly. 'Is that imminent?'

Well, Cathy was certainly doing nothing to give the impression it wasn't!

Really, much as she loved Wellington herself, and had no intention of leaving without him, she wished her friend would pay a little less attention to him and a little more to the conversation.

'Cathy was talking about when the permanent teacher returns at the end of the next term,' she explained lightly. Although until yesterday she had half hoped the other woman would decide not to return to work, after all, so she could remain in her place. That was now an impossibility for her.

'Of course,' David nodded, but he looked far from convinced. 'Talking about leaving——' He looked pointedly at Cathy.

'Hm, I suppose we should be on our way.' She straightened, innocently assuming he would be leaving with her now that he had satisfied himself as to Jade's health and safety. 'Actually, it's a lot worse here than it was in London, so I'll be glad of the back-up to Penny and Simon's.' She grimaced. 'Not that I'll ever admit to Dominic how bad the weather has been; he thought I was slightly insane coming down last night in the first place!'

'Only slightly?' David derided drily.

Cathy gave him an affectionate punch on the arm. 'It may be years since I last saw you, but you're still a dreadful tease!'

'And you're still as impulsive as ever,' he mocked. 'You must have wanted to join Penny and Simon very much to have driven down in that storm last night.' There was a question in his tone, his gaze piercing.

'Or else I wanted to get *away* very badly,' Cathy lightly avoided, not committing herself either way. 'Now we had better go so that at least Jade can get dressed in peace and quiet.'

'Hm,' David accepted reluctantly, obviously not satisfied with the arrangement at all. But what else could he do in the circumstances? Jade, by her own behaviour, had made it obvious she had no intention of telling Cathy about their relationship, and he simply wasn't the type of man to openly claim that relationship without the woman's permission;

especially when in the past Jade had made it so apparent that she would rather there *wasn't* a relationship. And her attitude towards him today had given him little encouragement to believe there *was* a relationship between them!

''Bye, love.' Cathy came over to hug her. 'I'll see you soon. And don't you dare leave!' The last was added in a fierce whisper. 'We still have so much catching up to do,' she added loudly as she stepped back.

Jade searched her friend's face for any hidden meaning behind those words, wondering if Cathy had picked up on that tangible 'something' that there was between David and herself, after all. But Cathy just looked very stern, daring her to go before they had spoken again.

'I'll call for you at about eight this evening,' David told her quietly but firmly.

'The party may be cancelled if the weather doesn't improve,' she dismissed.

He shook his head. 'Even if it's only the five of us there, plus the children, Penny will want to throw a party for the arrival of her little sister.'

'Not so little,' Cathy grinned.

'I can see that,' he teased, receiving another punch on the arm for his trouble.

Jade sighed, more or less sure in her own mind that she wouldn't be here by this evening. But she nodded non-committally. 'I'll give Penny and Simon a ring as soon as my telephone has been reconnected.'

She stood at the door as the other couple left, coming back inside as the icy cold wind pierced her brief clothing. But mainly she just didn't want to watch David drive away from her, probably out of her life completely.

She turned around sharply as the cottage door opened quietly behind her, unable to stop her cry of joy as she saw it was David returned. Just as she was unable to stop herself running into his waiting arms...

'I know you didn't want to see me today,' he spoke warmly into the thickness of her hair. 'But when I discovered your telephone was out of action I was worried about you. Don't be angry with me for being concerned, Jade,' he groaned.

How could she be angry with him? She loved him, knew it beyond a single doubt.

'Jade?' He looked down at her pleadingly, his eyes dark with the same emotion as was in her heart.

'I'm not angry with you.' She shook her head, gazing up at him. 'Kiss me. And then you'll have to go, before Cathy becomes curious about your delay and decides to investigate.'

His mouth twisted. 'I told her I'd forgotten to relate some message from Penny. God, I missed being with you last night!' he added raggedly. 'Jade—oh God, Jade, I——'

Her fingertips over his lips stopped further talk; she couldn't bear to actually hear his emotions put into words. Because they too closely resembled her own. And there was no future for them together.

Only now. This moment. And she put all of the depth of her feelings into the kiss they shared, clinging to him unashamedly as their lips parted and they just held each other, neither needing anything else but that closeness for the moment.

'If only Cathy weren't outside,' David shakily murmured his longing.

'But she is,' Jade smiled gently. 'Drive back carefully.' My darling, she didn't add, but wished she dared. For he was. Her darling. In a matter of days he had become the most important part of her life. In a matter of days? More like a matter of minutes! For that was all the time it had taken, she felt sure, for David to find his way into her heart.

He looked down at her darkly. 'Let me stay with you when I bring you back tonight?'

Tonight...

'Yes,' she agreed breathlessly, knowing it was a promise she would never keep. Because by tonight she would have gone.

The apartment looked more unwelcoming than usual, just four walls that succeeded in assuring her privacy, with no fire burning warmly in the hearth, because there wasn't a fireplace. Oh, the flat was comfortable enough, with its central heating, but it lacked any real warmth.

Wellington definitely wasn't impressed with it, just as he wasn't impressed with the fact that he couldn't go outside to investigate his surroundings, totally disgusted with the cat-tray she had managed to provide for him.

'It won't be for long, boy,' Jade assured him distractedly. 'Just until I can find somewhere more comfortable.'

His expression of disgust didn't change, and Jade knew she was going to have more than a little trouble with him in the near future.

Not that any of today had been easy, least of all finding a hire-car company that could provide her with a four-wheel-drive vehicle at such short notice. She had only managed to do so in the end because the company had received a cancellation from someone who had considered the road conditions too unsafe to drive on even in such a heavy vehicle. She had had to leave poor Cleo at a local garage, promising to collect her when the weather cleared if they would service her for her. Not that the car needed servicing, but it had given her a legitimate excuse to ask them to hold on to it for her.

So here she was, back in London, in a flat that seemed more lonely than it usually did, and even this was only a temporary stop, any further escape limited because of Wellington's presence. But, as Cathy had pointed out, she couldn't even think about not bringing the cat with her. As soon as she could find somewhere else, out of London preferably, for them to stay, they would be moving on.

When the knock first sounded on the door she thought there had to be some sort of mistake; she had been away from the flat for months, so who on earth could be calling on her tonight of all nights? She knew very few people in London

anyway, certainly no one who could know she was
back here——

'Open this door, Jade, I know damn well you're
in there,' Cathy suddenly called angrily through the
door.

Cathy. She should have known her friend
wouldn't let the situation rest with her departure.
What did she do now? If she refused to acknowledge her, she didn't doubt for a moment that
Cathy would persist until she did. But she simply
wasn't sure she was up to the verbal chastisement
if she did open the door.

'Wellington's pleased to hear me, even if you
aren't,' Cathy pointed out drily.

The silly cat was meowing at the door as if he
had found a long-lost friend! And maybe he
thought he had; Cathy had certainly been present
when he was in that other, more comfortable world,
at the cottage. A life he obviously wanted to return
to.

Cathy marched straight by her into the flat once
Jade had unlocked the door for her, her grey eyes
blazing. 'How could you?' she attacked furiously.
'How could you just up and leave like that? Poor
David is devastated. And don't try to deny that the
poor man's in love with you, because we both know
that he is. God, I must have been so blind not to
have seen that this morning,' she said self-
disgustedly. 'But little old innocent me accepted
completely that he had driven over because Pen and
Simon were worried about you—until David fell
apart when he got to the cottage and found you

had packed up and left! That was cruel, Jade, so damned cruel.' She shook her head disappointedly.

'*That* was cruel?' she echoed shakily, knowing how devastated she had been by *having* to pack up and leave, feeling that wrenching pain again as she heard about David's heartache. 'How much crueller would it have been to have stayed and involved him in the mess I've made of my life?'

'You didn't make it——'

'Does it really matter who made it so?' Jade said wearily. 'The facts are that it is.'

'You could try telling David the truth,' Cathy challenged. 'He would have understood, I'm sure of it. Penny says he's in love with you—if I needed any additional proof after he got back from the cottage,' she said raggedly.

Yes, she knew David was in love with her now, as she was in love with him, but how long would that love survive, how long after he was told the truth would he begin to have doubts and believe what the police, her family, and almost everyone else in the country had believed so easily eighteen months ago—that she had been involved with Peter in the Marshall kidnapping, in the abduction of a defenceless five-year-old girl for the money they would receive in exchange for her release...?

CHAPTER NINE

IT HADN'T been true, of course, none of it. But, despite the fact that she had never been officially charged with the crime, she had always felt guilty. The evidence against her had been so great...

She was Selina Marshall's form teacher, one of the five teachers in charge of the pupils that day they went to the beach on a trip, she was engaged to marry the man who had eventually been proven to have planned the crime, had even, unwittingly though it may have been, provided Peter with all the details of their movements that day, having believed he was taking an interest for her sake.

She had been a fool ever to believe Peter's interest in her was genuine, had often wondered at her luck in attracting such a handsome man when she was so obviously overweight, wore heavy-rimmed glasses, and had hair such a deep shade of red that she tried to keep it hidden as much as possible by pulling it back in a bun at her nape. It had even been summer when they'd met, and she had been covered in freckles! But Peter had assured her he found everything about her delightful, even the freckles.

She still cringed at how gullible she had been: an overripe plum ripe for the picking—or in this case, fooling!

With hindsight, she was able to see that even that very first meeting between them had been engineered by Peter when he 'accidentally' gave Cleo a gentle knock on the bumper which necessitated an exchange of addresses. Even then Peter hadn't rushed things, simply making sure the minor damage to Cleo was repaired. Then they had met in town one day, another 'accident', Jade had thought, as they fell easily into conversation, shyly accepting when he had offered to buy her a cup of coffee. That had been the beginning of the relationship that had shattered her life.

She had been a fool, and that was the only crime she had really been guilty of, and Peter, with his handsome, blond-haired, blue-eyed good looks, had known exactly how to flatter her and convince her that he found her utterly irresistible.

How could she have guessed that he had an ulterior motive for becoming close to her, that it was imperative to his plans that he gain the confidence of Selina Marshall's teacher? God, she could have been a sixty-year-old spinster, and his plans would still have been the same!

As it was, Jade had been flattered by Peter's interest, had accepted when the coffee together led to a dinner invitation.

It had been the first of many dates they had had, and for over two months Jade had lived in a euphoria of believing her love was returned. They had even become engaged, her ring of tiny diamonds surrounding an emerald that Peter claimed matched the colour of her eyes.

How could she have known, how could she have even guessed, that it was all because Peter was looking for a chink in the security that always surrounded all of the Marshall family, but their only child in particular?

And she had unknowingly provided him with that chink, had blithely told him of the visit of the lower three classes at the school to the beach for the day, giving him the opening he had so patiently waited for.

Even once Peter and his associates had Selina he hadn't left Jade's life, had even been the one to comfort her during the next two days while the kidnappers made their demands and waited for them to be met. He wasn't taking any chances on not being completely informed, and he knew, because of her love for him, that Jade had every reason to confide in him!

The only thing she could say to his credit was that Selina had been returned to her parents once the ransom money had been paid over, physically unharmed, at least. Mentally it was another matter, the little girl suffering with nightmares, giving every reason to suppose that she would suffer the mental torment of what had happened to her for the rest of her life.

And still Peter had stayed on. To do anything else would have looked too suspicious. His idea had been to break their engagement and disappear from her life after a decent interval had elapsed since the kidnapping.

So he had stayed on, helping Jade through the trauma of what had happened to one of her pupils, discussing wedding plans with her just as if he actually intended to go through with the spring wedding.

She had received the shock of her life when the police began to requestion her before moving on to Peter. They had claimed it was 'routine', but they kept coming back again and again, until finally Peter had cracked under the strain and tried to get away from the country with the ransom money.

In the midst of the pained shock of realising the man she loved had committed such a heinous crime, Jade had had to stand by while he told her—and the rest of the world!—that she had merely been a means to an end, a gullible convenience he hadn't hesitated in exploiting.

In the eyes of the law his testimony had cleared her of any guilt, but in the eyes of the general public it had been something else entirely. The fact that Peter had stood in a court of law and denounced her for the simple fool she had been didn't mean anything to them, and Jade had had to face their stares and speculation. No one had asked for her resignation, but she had tendered it just the same, knowing she had become an embarrassment to all concerned.

Her family had stood by her through it all, and she had turned to them as her salvation once she didn't even have a job, moving back home with her parents. Until she realised that her parents had stopped going out to see friends, and that no one came to see them at the house either. When her father had his heart attack she had known she had to leave, that she was as responsible for that as much as she was for Peter's success in kidnapping Selina. And so she had left her parents' house, and she hadn't told them where she was going, either, sure they would be able to put their lives back together if they no longer had her for a daughter. Maybe it was self-pity that made her do such a thing, but she just hadn't known what else to do.

For over a year she had lived alone in London, surviving off the money she had managed to save in the years before she left her job, Cathy her only visitor; she had not even bothered to look for other employment, even though there was nothing except her own guilty feelings to stop her from doing so. She felt too sickened with herself, with her stupidity, to face the outside world again.

It had been Cathy who had finally pushed her out to face that world, arranging for the temporary job at Simon and Penny's school, the other couple also of the opinion that she didn't have to suffer for the rest of her life when she was completely innocent of doing anything wrong except for falling in love with the wrong man.

And now she was in love with the right man, a gentle, beautiful man, who she wouldn't drag back down with her. Because she *was* about to go down again, would never be free of Peter and the guilt he had brought into her life.

'Yes, perhaps you're right and he would understand,' she answered Cathy bitterly. 'But he's already known so much unhappiness in his life; I have no intention of adding to it.'

'You make him happy,' her friend protested. 'Penny told me all about the way you first met, about his claim that he's going to marry you——'

'None of that matters now, Cathy.' She shook her head, doing all that she could to block the memories from her mind. 'David loves children, would make a wonderful father himself; how could he ever accept the pain I unwittingly caused an innocent child?'

'The key word in that statement is "unwittingly",' Cathy pointed out firmly. 'You had no idea what was going on. Anyone who really knows you would realise that.'

Her parents had 'really known her', and yet, before she left, before her father had his heart attack, she had sensed them watching her whenever they thought she wasn't aware of it, had felt their doubts. And they had known and loved her all her life, so what chance did David have of coming through what had happened in her past with his feelings unscathed? She couldn't bear to see that disillusionment in his eyes.

'Possibly,' she answered non-committally. 'But the doubt would always be there, festering, growing, until it utterly destroyed the love.' She knew; hadn't she watched it happen with her own parents? They loved her, she had never doubted that, but even they couldn't help the doubt that had crept in un- wanted... 'How happy would I make him then, Cathy?' she said harshly, knowing she had to be strong now for both David's and her own sake. She just had to!

'You're underestimating him, Jade——'

'No, I'm trying to protect him!' she defended fiercely, her eyes dark.

'Oh, Jade.' Cathy's face was full of compassion. 'You love him so much, too.'

'I——' She broke off, shaking her head against the denial she had been about to make. 'Yes, I love him,' she admitted in a controlled voice. 'And no one can take that away from me.'

'Oh, love.' Cathy's arms came about her to hug her tightly.

Jade's control shattered, the tight hold she had maintained over her emotions since leaving Devon this morning completely gone as she sobbed out her utter despair.

'What a pair we are,' Cathy finally choked self-derisively, her own cheeks wet as she stepped back slightly. 'Oh, Jade——' she shook her head '—what are we going to do with you?'

'Is this a private cry-in, or can anyone join in?' an all-too-familiar voice murmured.

Both women spun around, Cathy in surprise, Jade guiltily. She couldn't really claim to be surprised to see David again, hadn't for a moment believed he would accept her departure and telephone call to Penny and Simon as final to their relationship. She just hadn't expected to see him again as soon as this, that was all!

That he didn't look well was her first thought as she drank in the sight of him. That sparkle of the

pure enjoyment of life that had been in his eyes
since the moment they met had gone, and in its
place was an aching pain, his face haggard and
drawn. Of course his strained appearance could just
have been due to the fact that he had been driving
for several hours in bad conditions—and yet Jade
knew that it wasn't. She was the one that had done
this to him, had given love back into his life only
to rip it away again.

'I did knock, but no one answered,' he explained
gruffly, a defeated hunch to his shoulders in the
thick sheepskin jacket.

Cathy looked awkwardly between the two of
them. 'I think I'll go and make us all a nice cup of
tea,' she hastily excused herself.

The silence crackled with tension once Cathy had
made her hurried exit to the kitchen.

Jade felt herself shrinking back at the pained re-
crimination in David's eyes, swallowing with difficulty, moistening her lips nervously, waiting for
his words of reproach, bracing herself for them.

'Do you mind if I take my coat off?'

She gave a visible start; it had been the last thing
she expected him to say, despite the heat in the flat.

His mouth twisted. 'It's only my jacket, Jade,'
he taunted softly.

Colour warmed her cheeks. 'Please,' she invited
abruptly, inwardly wondering if he was going to be
here long enough to merit removing the jacket.

He shrugged out of the thick garment, laying it
across the back of one of the armchairs with
measured movements.

Jade's tension grew. Why didn't he just come right out with it and demand to know what she thought she was doing leaving Devon so abruptly? Why was he standing there so calmly, looking for all the world as if he had just casually dropped in for a visit?

It was certainly obvious to Jade, from the lack of noise coming from the kitchen, that Cathy had no intention of making them some tea, that she intended leaving them to it, would stay out of the way in the kitchen for as long as it took them to have their conversation.

'Nice flat.' David nodded appreciatively.

It was an awful flat, just four walls that had no character to them. 'David——'

'Have you lived here long?' he continued politely, just as if she hadn't spoken in that aching voice.

'About a year,' she dismissed impatiently. 'David, please—— '

'You kept it on even after your move to Devon?' He sounded surprised.

'The job at the school was only a temporary one.' Which was the only reason she had allowed Cathy to persuade her to do it in the first place! 'And flats in London aren't that easy to come by.' She shrugged, frowning deeply. 'David, I'm sure you didn't come here to discuss the merits of my flat.'

'Why not?' he shrugged. 'It's strange really, on the drive up here my mind was whirling with the things I was going to say to you, but now that I'm here none of those things seem to apply.' He gave a deep sigh. 'Why did you leave? What difference does it really make, when you did leave,' he answered his own question. 'You had your reasons for going, and from the wary expression in your eyes—eyes I obviously forgot to "watch",' he added self-derisively, 'you don't feel any more disposed to discussing those reasons with me now than you did this morning!'

'No,' she admitted dully, blinking back the fresh tears that clouded her vision.

He gave a regretful grimace. 'Sure?'

Of course she wasn't sure. She would give anything to be able to tell him the truth and have him tell her everything was going to be all right. But it wasn't, and it wouldn't be, and she wasn't about to hurt him any more than she already had by involving him any further.

'Very,' she told him firmly.

David sighed. 'There doesn't seem a lot more to say, does there?'

Not when your heart was breaking. And hers was shattered, fragmented. 'I wish you hadn't come here, David,' she said huskily.

He gave a harsh laugh, moving an agitated hand through his already tousled dark hair. 'It would be so easy to say I wish I hadn't, too—but it wouldn't be true. You may have decided you don't want me after all, but I'm glad I had this chance to see you again. I'm just sorry I hounded you so much that you felt you had to leave.' He shook his head. 'As soon as Cathy told us where she was going, and why, I realised I had forced you into leaving. I know

now that it wouldn't have mattered how much time I had given you, that time alone doesn't produce love. You tried to tell me, but I didn't want to listen,' he said sadly. 'I came here to tell you that you have no reason not to return to Devon. I don't intend going back myself.'

'Oh, but that's ridiculous,' she protested heatedly. 'You have no reason to leave, and Penny and Simon were so thrilled to see you again.' She frowned. 'I— what if I were to tell you that—you didn't really have anything to do with my leaving?' For the main part that was true; it was Peter's escape that had meant she had to move on. And if it weren't for Peter she could have allowed the beauty of David's love into her life.

David drew in a shuddering breath. 'I would say that if you were hoping to make me feel better you didn't succeed; I feel as if someone just punched me in the stomach while I was standing under a cold shower!'

'I'm sorry,' Jade choked.

He made a rueful face. 'You can't force love.'

'No woman in her right mind could help but love you!' she said intensely.

His mouth twisted. 'You happen to be talking about the woman I want to marry.'

'I wish I could—oh, David,' she quivered emotionally, 'what are we going to do?' Her hands twisted together in her deep agitation.

'*We* aren't going to do anything,' he told her gently, lightly clasping the tops of her arms before tilting her chin up so that she had to look at him.

'*You're* going to return to Devon, to your work at the school, and forget you ever met a delinquent Father Christmas!'

Forget she had met him, when he was the most wonderful thing that had ever happened to her? She would never forget him; it was impossible to forget the man she loved.

Just as she must *never* forget the man she had thought she loved, the man who had fooled her into believing he loved her in return when all he wanted to do was use her for his own ends. It was that misplaced love in her past that had forged her future; a long, lonely existence.

'I never stood a chance of making you forget him, did I, Jade?' David sighed defeatedly.

'Him?' she repeated sharply, her expression one of alarm.

He nodded abruptly. 'The man in your past, the one you can't forget.'

She swallowed hard, her stomach churning. 'What do you know about him?' Her voice was a pained squeak, her throat suddenly dry.

'That he existed,' David said self-derisively. 'It seems to be enough that he did.'

Jade frowned. 'I'm not sure I understand...?'

He shrugged, sighing heavily. 'I loved Sara, I'll never forget her or the love we shared because it meant too much to me to ever do that, but I've learnt to let go. You haven't let go,' he explained simply.

'Because I can't. I can't!' She shook her head in desperate denial. 'You're the one who doesn't understand,' she groaned, tears glistening in her eyes.

'Because I can't,' he said dully. 'I—hello, boy,' he greeted Wellington lightly as he came into the room, going down on his haunches as the snowy white head rubbed against him. 'Not what you're used to, is it, boy?' he sympathised with the cat's obvious distaste for his new surroundings.

'We won't be staying here,' Jade told him defensively, standing tensely across the room from him and the purring cat now.

David looked up at her piercingly. 'No, I don't suppose you will,' he accepted heavily, straightening to shrug his shoulders back into his coat. 'Be happy, wherever you go. I'd better go now.' He sighed his reluctance with that idea.

'I—will you go back to Devon?' she asked unhappily.

He shrugged. 'There's no reason for me not to now, is there?'

She knew he meant her own decision not to go back. 'No,' she answered flatly.

Dark blue eyes roamed hungrily over her face. 'I do want you to be happy, Jade,' he said finally. 'And if you ever do think of that delinquent Father Christmas who wanted more than anything else to be the gift in your bed on Christmas morning—— Forget it,' he dismissed wearily. 'Why should you think of me?' he said wryly. 'Take care, my darling,' he told her softly.

'David——'

'I'll just go and say goodbye to Cathy.' He turned away abruptly.

Jade ached, ached with needing him, with resisting that need.

The closing of the apartment door behind him a few seconds later was like a shot being fired—into her heart!

But she had no time to reflect on her pain as Cathy rushed out of the kitchen, her anger obvious from the fury on her face, her hands clenched fiercely at her sides.

'How could you?' her friend accused heatedly. 'How could you?'

Jade was completely taken aback by the attack. 'I don't——'

'You let David go away from here with the impression that you're still in love with Peter,' Cathy stormed.

'I did no such thing,' she gasped.

'Of course you did,' Cathy disputed disgustedly. 'What else do you think he was talking about when he said you can't forget Peter? And don't tell me I shouldn't have been listening to your conversation,' she warned fiercely. 'The walls are made of papier-mâché, and I was only in the kitchen!'

She hadn't been about to rebuke the other woman, was too disturbed by the other things she had said. Had she let David think she was still in love with Peter, the man in her past? Perhaps, but she couldn't tell him the truth about that time, so it was better that he think she was in love with someone else. 'What difference does it make if he did think that?' she said dismissively. 'Whatever he thinks, there's no future for us.'

'Because you've decided there isn't,' Cathy told her impatiently. 'You're my best friend, Jade, but I have to tell you now that this self-pity can't go on——'

'It isn't self-pity——'

'Of course it is,' her friend dismissed scathingly. 'OK, so Peter played a dirty trick on you, and a lot of people suffered because of it, but no one expects you to keep on suffering for ever. David loves you, and I'm more convinced than ever that you love him; the two of you should be together.'

'It isn't as simple as that——'

'Nothing in life ever is,' Cathy scorned. 'A fact I intend pointing out to Dominic when I give him my resignation.'

'Cathy?' she gasped. 'What——'

'Let's not get sidetracked,' she was told fiercely. 'David loves you, and you love him; you should be able to work out the rest of it. Even Peter,' she put in firmly as Jade would have protested again. 'Tell David the truth and let him decide for himself what was or wasn't true, but for God's sake don't give in without even giving him that chance,' she said disgustedly.

'I'm afraid...' Jade trembled at the thought of being so totally vulnerable.

'Do you think I don't know that?' Cathy groaned sympathetically. 'Of course you're afraid, but that's part of being alive. You've merely been existing this last year, Jade. Do you really want to live in the shadows all your life, or are you willing to take the risk of loving and being loved? It's either that or returning to what it's been like the last year; is that what you want?'

To go back to the emptiness. The loneliness. The nothingness.

Was that really what she wanted?

CHAPTER TEN

THANK God the snow had stopped falling now, although even without that the going was tough.

To Devon.

To David...

Cathy was right, she knew that, knew that however much she feared David's rejection when he knew the truth about her, she had to at least try to come out of the shadows. Just those few hours at her apartment had shown her how lonely her life was going to be again, and even though she had only known David a few days, with him she was alive, truly alive. And those shadows would still be there waiting for her if David didn't want her.

And so she was going back to Devon. Wellington was totally confused at again being bundled into the travelling basket she had so hastily purchased this morning, and the hire company she had got the vehicle from found it a little strange that she wanted to return it to their local office in Devon, after all.

But none of that mattered when David would be waiting at the other end of her journey. Even if it was only briefly, he had to know she loved him in return, probably had since the first moment his dark blue eyes had looked at her so mischievously.

Nevertheless, her body ached with the tension of the drive, and her eyes felt sore from the intense concentration when she at last drove back into the village later that evening. It had been dark for several hours, making driving doubly difficult on the icy, unfamiliar roads, and she just wanted to find David, say her piece, and then know either the ecstasy of his love or the return to those grey shadows that had been her life for the last year.

Penny opened the door to her ring on the doorbell, a Penny whose eyes widened incredulously at the sight of her, her black cocktail dress indicating that she had been expecting quite another sort of guest. 'What——? We thought you were in London,' she gasped, her statement so obviously incorrect as Jade now stood before her.

Jade's mouth twisted. 'I needed to talk to David rather urgently.' She gave a rueful shrug.

The other woman looked puzzled. 'Oh, but— come inside,' she instructed distractedly, opening the door wider to usher Jade into the hallway, opening the door to the dining-room. 'I'm just taking Jade into the sitting-room,' she informed Simon. 'Yes, I said Jade,' she answered his surprised exclamation. 'If anyone arrives for the party just bring them in here and tell them I've been delayed. Or something,' she dismissed impatiently.

'Penny, there's really no need,' Jade protested as the other woman turned in the direction of the sitting-room; in truth she had forgotten all about the party Penny and Simon were having this evening. 'If I could just quickly talk to David——'

'He isn't here,' Penny told her quietly.

Jade's face fell. 'Oh,' she sighed heavily. 'But he said he was coming back here,' she frowned, a sudden pain behind her eyes.

'Perhaps he is,' the other woman shrugged, closing the door behind them. 'But we haven't heard from him since he telephoned to let us know he had arrived safely in London.'

Jade sat down defeatedly in an armchair. 'He said he was coming back here,' she repeated dully, hardly able to believe she had made that horrendous journey only to learn David wasn't here after all.

'Then he probably will,' Penny assured her gently, bending down in front of her. 'Is it going to be all right between you two?' she probed softly.

Jade drew in a shuddering breath, her disappointment extreme at not finding David here when she had so desperately needed to talk to him. If she wasn't able to talk to him now she might never have the nerve or courage to try again.

'Jade?' Penny prompted.

She shook her head. 'I don't know. I thought— I hoped that if I could just talk to him, tell him about——' She broke off, swallowing hard.

'Peter,' the other woman finished with feeling. 'He's been recaptured, you know,' she added softly.

She had heard the announcement on the radio news, but it had meant little to her when his escape had totally disrupted her life a second time! The fact that he was now back behind lock and key where he belonged left her cold, his recapture making little difference to her life, except the relief of knowing he was once again being punished for his crime.

Jade frowned as the doorbell rang. 'I really mustn't keep you from your guests...'

Penny straightened. 'Maybe it's David.' But they both knew it wasn't as Simon could be heard talking jovially before closing the dining-room door behind himself and the new arrival. 'Join the party as originally planned,' Penny invited softly. 'Then if David—then stay the night, at least,' she insisted as Jade fiercely shook her head at her other suggestion. 'It's too late at night to go back to your cold cottage.'

She had to admit the prospect didn't seem very inviting. 'There's Wellington, too,' she grimaced.

The other woman smiled. 'I don't mind, if he doesn't!'

On the few occasions Penny had called at the cottage in the past Wellington had lost no time in letting her know it was his home, and he was to be treated with respect! Jade had no doubt in her mind that Wellington wouldn't distinguish between the two establishments; he had lost no time earlier in letting her know who was boss at her apartment.

'If you're sure you wouldn't mind...?' She frowned. 'I'm really not in the mood for a party.'

'Of course you aren't,' Penny dismissed briskly. 'I'll take you upstairs and see you settled into a room, and then when David returns——'

'*If* he returns,' she corrected heavily; his not being here when she arrived was something she hadn't even considered.

'He told you he was coming back, and so he will,' Penny told her firmly, leading the way up the wide staircase. 'David is a man of his word.'

The last was said a little defensively, Penny obviously wondering how she dared question David's loyalty and trustworthiness. Not that Jade could blame her for feeling a little indignant; there was no comparison between the two men.

It was a lovely, sunny-looking room, decorated in gold and creams, that Penny showed her into, explaining that she would have to share the bathroom with the two boys, their bedrooms just across the hallway. 'They'll be coming up to bed shortly,' Penny dismissed. 'They only stayed up to say hello to everyone. They're getting so excited about Christmas now,' she added affectionately.

Jade had forgotten all about it! The day after tomorrow would be Christmas Day, and she wasn't prepared for it at all. By that time she would either have everything, or nothing, to celebrate....

She was right about Wellington's reaction to his new surroundings: he wasn't at all impressed, although he curled up and went to sleep on the foot of the bed quite amiably once he realised they were staying put for the night.

Jade lay awake in the darkness; she could hear the muted sounds of the party below, heard Penny putting the two boys to bed a little later, and then she was aware of nothing else, the exhaustion of the day taking its toll on her.

She was dreaming of the eyes again, everywhere she looked, accusing eyes. And this time, hard as she searched, she couldn't find that warmly caressing navy blue pair. She looked and looked, but as those navy blue depths remained elusive her panic began to grow.

'Where are you?' she muttered. 'You have to be there. You have to be!' she groaned. 'Oh, David, David, where are you?' she cried, still searching, searching.

'I'm here. I *am* here,' that comforting voice assured firmly as she continued to thrash about wildly.

But she still couldn't find him in that sea of eyes, moving restlessly, whimpering softly.

'Jade! Darling, wake up,' that voice prompted tensely. 'Jade, you have to open your eyes.'

She struggled through the layers of sleep, searching for that voice, but the accusing eyes wanted to hold her back, keep her down in the shadows with them. And she wasn't going to stay, was determined to leave that behind, wanted to be out in the light. With David. And he was waiting for her out there, she knew he was.

'Darling.' She was shaken gently. 'Open your eyes and look at me.'

She trusted him, had faith in him, opening her eyes as he told her to. And there he was, so beautiful in the golden glow of the bedside lamp, the concerned frown leaving his brow as her face lit up with happiness at the sight of him, and she launched herself against him, her arms about his neck as she clung to him.

'I don't know how you come to be here,' he spoke joyously into her hair, holding her just as tightly as she held him. 'But I do know I never want to let you go. Oh, God, Jade, I love you. I love you so much!'

She had known that, known it from the first. The words had never been spoken, but then they hadn't needed to be—every glance, every touch, every gesture had been full of love.

The kiss they shared was a rapturous delight, and Jade never wanted it to end. But of course it did, though not the warmth; that remained like a sunny day, bright and beautiful.

'I love you,' Jade told him ecstatically.

Light blazed in his eyes. 'I hoped as much when I walked into the room and found you waiting in my bed.'

She blinked. '*Your* bed?' she gasped. 'But— Penny.' She smiled tremulously at the other woman's machinations.

'Decided to give me an early Christmas present, did she?' David lovingly smoothed her hair back from her face, touching her cheek gently. 'I must remember to thank her,' he mused.

'We both must.' Jade gazed up at him glowingly.

'And to think I almost didn't come back here at all tonight,' he breathed softly. 'As it was, I left it until after midnight to arrive; I didn't feel in the mood for a party.'

'Neither did I,' she grimaced. 'But Penny made very sure that the only people we would see tonight was each other.'

David nodded. 'This was the room she gave me for the duration of my stay. If you had looked in the wardrobe and drawers you would have seen that I had left some of my clothes in them.'

She wished she had looked; at least knowing his things were there would have made her feel closer to him. 'Who would have guessed Penny is a romantic?' she teased.

David smiled. 'I'm just glad that she is.' He spoke huskily.

They kissed again, lingeringly, desire rising heatedly, neither able to stop touching the other in the wonder of their love.

'What made you change your mind and come back?'

Jade knew they had to talk, resting her head against David's shoulder as she drew in a ragged breath. 'Shadows,' she explained dully. 'David, there are some things about me that you don't know—— No, don't let me go just yet.' She clung to him as he would have moved back slightly so that he could look at her. 'After we've talked, you may not want to hold me again,' she told him tremulously.

'That won't happen,' he assured her softly, firmly. 'Not ever.'

She swallowed hard. 'Don't be so sure.' She quivered. 'I—the man who escaped from prison a couple of days ago—— That man, Peter Gifford, he——'

'Darling,' David cut in determinedly, 'I can't bear to see you putting yourself through this. Jade, I know who Peter Gifford is, and what he once was to you.'

'You can't!' she gasped, shaking her head in fierce denial.

'I do,' David insisted gently. 'Darling, I'm in publishing, and I take an active interest in all parts of it. Some of my best friends are newspaper magnates. But last of all,' he added softly, 'I know the Marshalls quite well.'

'Oh, God,' Jade choked, her face buried in her hands.

'Love, I realised who you were after you reacted so strangely to a couple of what I thought were harmless comments, began to question myself as to why that could be after you became really panicked the couple of times we saw police cars, and finally came up with the answer.'

'Then why did you continue to love me?' she cried in distress. 'How *could* you?'

'Jade, you only have to be seen in the company of children for it to be obvious you couldn't have been involved in hurting one the way Selina was,' he told her firmly. 'But I couldn't tell you that I knew the truth, I was frightened that would drive you away from me altogether.'

Jade looked up at him slowly, afraid to believe, and yet so desperately wanting to. The love she had always seen in his eyes for her hadn't diminished in the slightest, still darkening his eyes to navy blue, clear and strong, unreserved.

'I didn't know Peter intended—I had no idea he—I never would have——'

'Darling, I know that, whatever happened, you weren't involved in it,' David interrupted forcefully. 'Just as I'm sure the police do; they just have to cover all their options, unfortunately. Darling, I'll understand if you don't want to talk about any of it,' he reassured her gruffly. 'But if you do want to tell me I'll gladly listen—for your sake, not mine,' he added firmly. 'I don't need any more reassurances.'

And so Jade told him, every revealing, heart-rending, foolish detail.

'My poor darling,' he rasped once she had finished, his arms tight about her. 'Left with no one to turn to——'

'Don't pity me.' She shook her head. 'Selina was the one who was hurt.'

'Yes, she was.' David nodded, not even trying to dispute or gloss over that fact. 'But the scarring you have is just as deep, if of a different kind. And to think I believed you must still be in love with the bastard, that you had returned to London in the belief that he would contact you and the two of you could go away together!'

Jade gasped at that. 'I hate him, blame myself for ever being taken in by him!'

'Love can make fools of us all.' David sighed heavily. 'If I hadn't been hurting so much at your rejection of me I might have realised that, far from looking forward to seeing Gifford again, you were actually frightened. Jade,' he framed her face with gentle hands, 'will you marry me, live with me, be my beautiful, beloved wife?'

'But your friends? The Marshalls——'

'My friends will all love you. And I'm sure the Marshalls never believed you were involved in Selina's kidnapping. I remember them saying what a favourite you were with her, how she turned to you even more once she came back to school.'

Yes, Selina had clung to her quite considerably once she had been returned to her parents and had come back to school a few weeks later, but that had only made Jade's feelings of guilt all the deeper once she'd learnt the truth.

She didn't want David to suffer socially because he had married her.

'Darling, don't cross bridges before you come to them.' He smoothed the frown from between her eyes. 'And we're going to pay your parents a visit and tell them of our engagement. Don't be too hasty to judge them either, Jade,' he told her firmly as she would have interrupted. 'I think you were just too sensitive at the time, may have misjudged their reaction to what had happened. There could have been any number of reasons for their sudden lack of a social life, but the one that springs to mind the most is the fact that they may have wanted to devote all their time and love to you, to protecting you. The fact that they watched you only shows that they were concerned. Whatever, Jade, we will go and see them, there's nothing to be lost by doing that. And if they care about you, as I believe they do, then they're probably worried out of their minds about you.'

Whether he was right or not, she knew she could face what had to come. With David at her side she could face anything.

'In the meantime,' he drawled softly, 'at least I don't have to wonder any more what will be in my bed Christmas morning; it will be you, and every other morning of our lives, too!'

It sounded wonderful. Heaven.

But just before she sank into his arms, another thought popped into her mind. 'You still haven't explained completely about Christi and Dizzy,' she frowned.

His soft chuckle, before his mouth claimed hers, was full of wickedly mischievous humour...

'Gently,' David said sharply. 'Careful of her head,' he advised softly, for all the world as if Jade's mother had never held a baby in her arms before.

Jade shared a humorous smile at David's expense with two of the women who had stood as godmothers to Lia Sara, Christi and Dizzy returning the smile as they all watched the indulgent father as he fussed over his three-month-old daughter.

Lia Sara had been born exactly nine months to the day after Christmas Day, a tiny, red-haired, and now green-eyed, bundle of mischief, who her father had claimed was his last Christmas gift to Jade!

Christmas Eve one year later had seemed an ideal day for their daughter's christening, with Lia having four godmothers: Christi, Dizzy, Cathy and Penny, and four godfathers too: Lucas and Zach, Dominic and Simon.

David had lost no time after their wonderful Christmas together the year before in introducing her to his friends Christi and Dizzy. That was when Jade had learnt that when he had called them friends that was exactly what he had meant, the other two women both the proud mothers of young babies, their husbands, Lucas and Zach, two of the most attractive men—David excluded, of course!— Jade had ever met.

Lucas could seem a little daunting at first, un-approachable, until you saw the unashamed love in his eyes for his young wife, and then he became as humanly vulnerable and likeable as the rest of them.

The other couple, Dizzy and Zach, on the surface, were the most ill-matched pair imaginable, Dizzy so bubbly and flamboyant, Zach a staid professor of history, obligatory pipe, tweed jacket and all! But beneath Dizzy's outgoing nature was a sensitivity and vulnerability that her husband was completely attuned to. And the myth about Zach himself was completely shattered when David introduced him as Claudia Laurence, the author of all those passionate historical novels! No wonder David had been so amused when he promised to introduce Jade to 'her'!

In a very short time the other couples had become Jade's close friends too, until Jade wondered how she could ever have doubted she would fit into David's world.

Guests of honour today at Lia's christening were Jade's own parents, to whom, through David's help and understanding, she was now closer than ever. And the other guest of honour was Judy Maxwell. Sara's mother had become an honorary 'grandmother' to little Lia, she and Jade having formed a warm understanding that they had both felt from their first introduction. Maybe Sara really did approve of the love Jade and David shared...

Thank you, Sara, Jade offered up a silent prayer to the other woman on this day when all was so very right with her own world, knowing Sara wouldn't begrudge her that happiness; rather, she would rejoice in it.

Jade smiled tremulously as her gaze met David's across the room, their love passing between them like an electric shock.

Electrified satin, his eyes promised for later.

And Jade knew, beyond a shadow of a doubt, that she would always have David's love. As he would always have hers. And that love would always keep the shadows at bay.

FREE READER OFFER

3 FREE BOOKS

Plus a FREE Surprise gift!

Here's an opportunity to receive 3 "Best of the Best" novels from Mira® Books at NO COST and NO OBLIGATION! And, we'll be so pleased if you accept this offer, that we will even give you a FREE surprise gift! So, to take advantage of this great offer, just fill in the coupon and return it to us at the address below!

REPLY TODAY - NO STAMP NEEDED!

YES! Please send me 3 FREE "Best of the Best" novels and a FREE surprise gift. If after I receive my free books, I do not wish to receive any more books I will let you know and be under no further obligation. Otherwise, each month I will receive 3 "Best of the Best" novels for only £3.99 each—saving me 20% off the combined cover prices! Even postage and packing is free! I may cancel at any time, but the free books and gift remain mine to keep in any case. (I am over 18 years of age).

B8GE

Ms/Mrs/Miss/Mr ....Initials.................................
BLOCK CAPITALS PLEASE

Surname...

Address ....

....Postcode..................

Send coupons to:
THE BEST OF THE BEST, FREEPOST, CROYDON, CR9 3WZ
EIRE: PO Box 4546, Dublin 24 (stamp required)

Offer not valid to current "Best of the Best" subscribers. We reserve the right to refuse an application and applicants must be aged 18 years or over. Only one application per household. Terms and prices subject to change without notice. Offer expires 31st January 1999. You may be mailed with offers from other reputable companies as a result of this application. If you would prefer not to receive such offers, please tick box. ☐

MIRA® is a registered trademark, used under license.

THE BRIGHTEST STARS IN WOMEN'S FICTION

MIRA

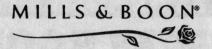

Presenting
A Special Selection of
"The Best of the Best™"

MIRA®

If you have enjoyed these *Carole Mortimer* stories, below is a further selection of best-selling titles from MIRA® Books for you to try. If you wish to place an order, simply tick the titles you require, complete the coupon and send it with a cheque or postal order made payable to *The Reader Service*, to **MIRA Books Casual Sales Dept., P.O. Box 236, Croydon, CR9 3RU.**

Please do not send cash.

Ref.	Title	Author	Price
❑ B30	Gypsy	Carole Mortimer	£4.99
❑ B7	Merlyn's Magic	Carole Mortimer	£3.99
❑ B1004	A Day in April	Mary Lynn Baxter	£5.99
❑ B37	Glory Seekers	Rebecca Brandewyne	£4.99
❑ B1035	Love Child	Patricia Coughlin	£4.99
❑ B1048	Sweet Memories	LaVyrle Spencer	£4.99

Non Reader Service subscribers in the UK, please add £1.00 P&P for the first book ordered,
50p for the second and 25p thereafter. Overseas and Eire please add £1.50 P&P
for the first book ordered and 50p thereafter.

If you are a UK Reader Service subscriber, please quote membership number to benefit from free P&P and speed up the processing of your order.

Information on subscriptions is available from our Customer Care Team on (0181) 288 2888.

B8GCB4

Ms/Mrs/Miss/Mr: ....Initial: ....Surname:..................................
                                                                  BLOCK CAPS PLEASE
Address:..

....

....Postcode:..

I enclose a cheque/postal order for: £ ....Date..................

Offer expires January 31, 1999 and is only valid to applicants of 18 years or older. Prices and availability are subject to change without notice. You may be mailed with offers from other reputable companies as a result of this application. If you would prefer not to receive such offers, please tick box. ❑

MIRA® is used under license by Harlequin Mills & Boon Limited

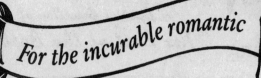
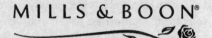

Reader Service™

The best romantic fiction direct to your door

Our guarantee to you...

The Reader Service involves you in no obligation to purchase, and is truly a service to you!

Your books are delivered hot off the press, at least one month before they are available in the shops.

Your books are sent on 14 days no obligation home approval.

We offer free postage and packing for subscribers in the UK–we guarantee you won't find any hidden extras.

Plus, we have a dedicated Customer Care team on hand to answer all your queries on
(UK) 0181 288 2888
(Ireland) 01 278 2062.
There is also a 24 hour message facility on this number.

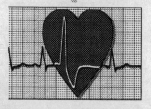

SINGLE LETTER SWITCH

Here's a fun puzzle for you to try!

There are two five letter words provided in the grid. The first one being STOCK, the other PLATE. All you have to do is write down the words that are missing by changing just one letter at a time to form a new word and eventually change the word STOCK into PLATE. You only have eight chances but we have supplied you with clues as to what each one is. Good Luck!

When you have found all six missing words, check your answers at the bottom of the page.

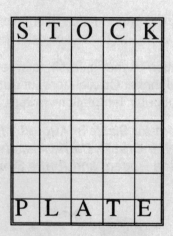

S	T	O	C	K
P	L	A	T	E

Clues:

A   To pile up
B   To ease off or a reduction
C   A dark colour
D   Empty or missing
E   A piece of wood
F   Common abbreviation for an aircraft